THE LAST RHINEMAIDEN

LEE MCAULAY

First published 2012
This edition published 2012
Copyright © 2012 Lee McAulay
The moral right of this author has been asserted.
This work is protected by copyright. All rights reserved. No part of this publication may be reproduced in any form or by any means – graphic, electronic or mechanical, including photocopying, recording, taping, information storage and retrieval systems – without the prior permission of the copyright owner. The moral right of Lee McAulay to be identified as the author of this work has been asserted in accordance with the Copyright, Designs and Patents Act of 1988. All the characters in this work are fictitious, and any resemblance to actual persons living or dead is purely coincidental.

ISBN 978-1475158366

Cover image by Lee McAulay
Images courtesy of Wikimedia:
Gustav Klimt, *Danaë*; 1907
Claude Monet, *The Houses of Parliament, sunset*, 1903
Font: Birmingham Titling by P J Lloyd © 1995

TO TDG, WITH LOVE

HWAET!

CHAPTER 1 — First Kiss

London, 1888.

Sunrise touched the eastern horizon over the city, a chill breeze from the North Sea pushing upriver and skimming the mist which lay across the surface of the Thames. High tide, and the docks busy. Tall-masted ships pulled away from the wharves and settled on the water, withdrawing into deep channels that led to the open sea.

A million chimneys puffed smoke into the city, coal and coke and timber, brown and black and white all turned to shadow in the darkness. The air shivered. Hoar-frost coated the grass of all the little parks and open spaces, lay white upon the scaffolding of the new bridge foundations down by the Tower and the glass canopies of the Railway Termini, made clouds of the steam that poured from breweries and laundries and turned those clouds to ice upon the tip of Cleopatra's Needle.

The bridges hung dark across the Thames. At Westminster where the clock-tower of Big Ben guarded the crossing between Waterloo and Victoria, at the barracks on Birdcage Walk, in the parish of Hanover Square where the wealthy slept; even there, the frost took hold, froze the lake in Palace Gardens and the broad streets all the way down to the Chelsea Hospital.

The first of the milk trains from Surrey began to arrive at Victoria Station. Crossing the river at Battersea, between the waterworks and the cricket ground, each one waited on the tracks by the Grosvenor Canal until a platform was available, then crept under the station roof to disgorge its produce.

Porters rushed to unload the early trains up from Clapham and Ealing, the milk still warm in its steel churns and a pleasure to handle on such a freezing March morning. Less popular were the loads from further out in the country, two hours or more on the train and as cold as the open wagons.

Alf Winchester stepped out of the third-class carriage of the first train from Windsor and breathed deep the station air, pleased to be clear of the sweat-and-tobacco odour of his compartment. He straightened the cuffs and collar of his shirt, itching where his country jacket scratched his neck, and his shoes pinching in unfamiliar places. When he glanced down he saw with dismay that they were caked with mud from his trip to the station that morning, four miles in the dark on the open road from his school. He blasted his fellow scholars for advising him that such an adventure was worth it.

He closed the carriage door behind him and pulled the flaps of his jacket closed, tugging his hat down low over the tops of his ears. *Should have brought an overcoat,* he thought. *And gloves.*

He shoved his hands into his trouser pockets like an office-clerk and strolled along the platform towards the exit. The station porters unloading the train paused while he passed by, then continued to haul milk churns onto the flagstones, all clanging steel and sloshing. Alf's stomach rumbled in response. Another train from the countryside pulled in to the buffers, its wheels creaking against the rails as it braked.

He sauntered out towards the ticket-hall, self-conscious in his city suit, glancing up at the station clock. *I have three hours to waste*, he thought with a frown, *until my tailor opens shop*. He vowed to have words with those of his classmates who'd suggested he take the earliest train. In addition to the discomfort of an unheated third-class carriage, the early start meant he'd missed breakfast in the school hall and a good two hours' sleep.

A boy of about ten approached him with an armful of newspapers. "'Times' or 'Telegraph', sir?"

"The 'Times', please," said Alf, secretly pleased at age seventeen to be called 'sir', and paid the boy a half-penny for a copy of the early issue. He glanced at the headlines – *Riots in Holborn, Irish Blamed; Kaiser Unwell;* – and folded the paper under his arm. With no particular aim in mind, he strolled off across the marble floor towards the station buffet. He tried the door and pursed his lips when he found it locked.

"Too early, squire," said a passing porter pushing an empty trolley. "Don't open until six."

Alf nodded acknowledgement of this news, frowning. He looked around at the near-empty railway terminus and saw that his only companions were station staff, porters, and the newspaper vendors, none of whom showed the slightest interest in him. He sighed and wandered into the ticket-hall, only to find it almost entirely deserted. There was a shoe-shine bench but no attendant. He headed out of the terminus onto Wilton Road.

Outside, the city was caught in a half-life between night and day, the bleakest point of transition, its boundaries blurred by the mist laid flat on the rooftops. Street-lanterns, still whispering through gas mantles in this part of town, shone brighter than the first hints of dawn in the sky above the buildings on the opposite side of the street. Alf glanced up at the clouds that lay in strips across the darkness beyond, their undersides pale with oncoming sunrise, and shivered.

Wilton Road itself was crowded with empty dairy carts awaiting the milk delivery brought by suburban trains like the one on which he'd travelled up from Berkshire, horses hooded with nosebags full of oats and the carters stood around smoking cigarettes, each man wrapped up against the chill of the night with cap and overcoat and muffler. A group of them huddled round a brazier, jagged lumps of wood poking out of the top amongst the flames, and as he passed they drew closer round the heat, cheap tin mugs filled with what smelled like tea gripped for warmth.

Alf meandered onto Victoria Street, keen to find a breakfast somewhere that would pass the time and warm him up. He crossed the street to look into the window of a steamed-up café, then sidestepped the men who jostled out of the door with a laugh, carters or station staff or cab-drivers, sharing out a handful of rough cigarettes between them.

A hansom cab trotted past and disappeared around the corner into Palace Street, its wheels clattering on the cobbles in time with the horse's hoofbeats, and Alf slipped his hand into his trouser pocket to check his change. The coins he had brought with him would pay for a better meal than the cabbies' bread and tea. *Not in this part of town*, he thought.

Unfurling the newspaper, Alf continued down the empty pavement towards the Houses of Parliament in the distance, glancing up briefly to check the time on the face of Big Ben, then dropping his pace to a crawl as he flicked through the paper. He finished the Colonial News and turned to the correspondence page, then burst out laughing as he read the first letter to the editor.

"What nonsense," he said out loud, glancing around him although there was no-one nearby. "The first cuckoo of Spring! Why do they always print this rot?" He shook his head and laughed again, turning the page.

At the junction of Victoria Street and Buckingham Gate he heard running footsteps approaching and paused to listen, suspicious of the big city and the rumours of his urbane schoolmates, tales of footpads and pickpockets like the urchins of "Oliver Twist" ready to pounce on the unwary. He turned his head to check if he was being followed, but the pavement behind him was empty. He turned his attention back to the Times.

The owner of the running footsteps hurtled around the corner and barrelled into him. The newspaper flew up into his face as he fell backwards onto the pavement with the force of the impact. "Hey, watch out!" he snapped, wriggling under the unknown assailant who struggled over him. He grabbed a wrist and then the shoulder of the other person and shook the newspaper off.

It was a woman. He felt the warmth of her body even through her rough woollen dress, and when he glanced up into her eyes he was startled to find himself staring at a girl no older than he.

Her cheeks were flushed and her eyes were fierce. She said something to him and wriggled to try to escape from his grasp, but he was cautious, and would not let her go.

"Why don't you look where you're going?" he asked, still gripping her wrist as he helped both of them to their feet. Flustered, he felt angry and sheepish at the same time, unaccustomed to dealing with girls and worried that he'd been rude.

She spoke again. Her accent was unfamiliar, and the language sounded like German.

He shook his head. "I don't understand." With his free hand he patted his pockets to make sure she hadn't rifled through them while they'd been on the ground, and when he found everything in the correct place, he relaxed, although he did not let her go. His hand encircled her wrist with ease and he felt ashamed to have grasped her with such force.

She was a tiny woman with a neat figure and bare feet. Her hair was an indistinct shade of brown or red under the light of the gas-lamps, bound up in a simple way that framed her face and spilled down her back, stray wisps around her brow like filaments of silk. She was breathing heavily as if she had been running for some time and her shoulders heaved with the effort.

He felt her tremble, as if she were exhausted, and it occurred to him that maybe she was shivering with cold.

She looked up at him with an expression that softened beyond succour and raised her free hand to his face, cupping his cheek in her palm, her skin warm and scented with flowers and pine-pollen.

He gazed at her, noting the delicate hairs of her brow, a faint line of freckles across the bridge of her nose and her curved lips smiling. His heart thudded as she drew nearer to him. He was entranced.

"You should be more careful," he said in a quiet voice, unsure of how to behave in such a situation.

She reached up on tiptoe and kissed him, briefly, and he stepped back in surprise.

Again she spoke to him, and this time he almost understood what she said. Then she glanced beyond him and a look of fear flashed across her face. She broke free of his grip and backed away, muttering and shaking her head, her eyes filled with alarm.

"Hey," he said, reaching out towards her. "I'm sorry."

She shook her head sharply, turned, and pelted off down Victoria Street in the direction of Westminster Abbey.

Alf stood transfixed, watching her go, puzzled and confused. His newspaper lay crumpled on the pavement and when he bent to pick it up he found a heavy leather purse underneath it. It was still warm. *This must be hers*, he thought, and waved at her receding figure. "Hey!" he yelled again. "Wait!" With a shrug he abandoned the newspaper and began to sprint after her.

She made good speed and Alf found himself running faster than he would have expected, just to keep up. Between them they hurtled past side streets with no thought for the traffic, avoiding the scant few pedestrians with ease, past Broadway and Tothill Street until Storey's Gate, where the girl faltered and looked around before dashing across the street towards Westminster Abbey. Alf gasped as she narrowly avoided a single-horse cab, then crossed the street himself.

At Parliament Square she turned again and paused, glancing to either side, and he made up a few yards of the distance between them before she sprinted off again across the grass.

Alf followed her and dodged around a cream-coloured coach that barely missed him as he crossed St Margaret's Street. Above them the chimes of Big Ben began tolling the half-hour. On its eastern face the first rays of the sun illuminated the clock against an incoherent sky.

She rounded the corner of the Houses of Parliament and turned onto Bridge Street without a pause. The traffic leading up to Westminster Bridge was heavier here than in the side streets and Alf was concerned in case she came to harm.

"Wait!" he yelled. The leather soles of his shoes slithered on the damp cobbles as he skidded across the street and caught his balance with the aid of a standard lamp. "Hey, wait!" He clutched at his side, a stitch tugging beneath his ribs. The leather purse was heavy in his hand.

Please stop, he thought in breathless despair. *I can't keep this up much longer.*

The young woman glanced over her shoulder, eyes wide in panic. She turned away again and it seemed as if she quickened her pace.

Alf cursed under his breath and set off in pursuit once more.

She ran on, barefoot in the pale morning, and sprinted onto Westminster Bridge without looking ahead or to the side.

Alf followed her, unable to keep up, his pride dented. He was gasping for breath when he reached the lamp-stand over the first arch and was relieved to see her slow down. She glanced over her shoulder and he tried his best to smile.

She slowed to a walking pace and reached out one hand to the parapet as if to steady herself, and when she reached the middle of the bridge she halted. Out there above the river the chill wind blowing upstream from the North Sea whipped at her hair, freeing it from whatever tied it back from her face, and she glanced towards Alf with a look of panic.

"I was just –" he panted, and slowed to walking pace. "I was only –" He reached out with his left hand, offering the purse she had dropped before this chase had begun.

Her face softened but did not smile. As he walked towards her, his breath bursting out of his lungs, she spoke to him, and it sounded like an apology.

"Pardon?"

The focus of her eyes shifted to something beyond him and the fear returned. She shook her head and began to gather up her skirts, raising them higher than decorum allowed.

"I don't –" he began and raised his free hand to shield his gaze at the first glimpse of pale thigh. He felt himself blushing, felt blood tingling in his extremities, flooding and thumping in his ears. When he glanced back she'd climbed onto the parapet.

"Steady on!" he cried and rushed forwards just as she sprung out into the dawn. "No!"

His stomach dropped with her, off the bridge and into the river, and he saw her fall the last few feet to the Thames. She barely made a splash when she hit the oily water and the turbulence swallowed the folds of her plain dress in a second. So swift the river flowed under the bridge, she left no trace upon its surface.

Alf's voice choked in his throat. He gripped the parapet, the stone cold and damp beneath his hands as he leaned out to scan the surface of the river. He felt sick.

Downstream of Westminster Bridge the river was deep and empty until Blackfriars. The high stretch of Victoria Embankment pushed the water fast around the curve on the north bank, the south bank a mass of warehouses with tiny windows and heavy brickwork. Lights on each bridge pier glowed orange on the water beneath.

Alf stared at the bubbles of froth clinging to the stonework, then let his gaze follow the flow. Greasy, the river curled around itself in darkness and threw up a rotten stench even as its little whirlpools sucked and gurgled, the current scouring out new depths as the tide turned and began to withdraw from the city. A dog appeared in the swift flow under the bridge, eyes wide as its pale paws scampered in the water, close to exhaustion and swept away towards the railway bridge at Waterloo.

Alf followed its trail with his eyes, his dismay growing into despair, as it disappeared under the surface of some foulness that drifted over into the main flow of the Thames and downstream, in ripples that broke over the bows of the boats moored at the Whitehall Stairs.

And suddenly he saw something else, a glimmer of more than hope that shocked him, thrilled him, enchanted him. Far out on the surface of the water, halfway between the north and south banks, a pale face appeared. It bobbed like a seal on the choppy waves, golden and sleek in the weak daylight but unmistakably human.

He gasped. Slowly the shape on the river rolled over, gently turned by the current, and a slender white arm rose as if in salutation. It stood out against the flow of the water, unmoving, stiff. Alf let go of the bridge and waved frantically.

His arm faltered in mid-wave as the figure disappeared beneath the surface of the water. Around him London seemed to fall silent and he felt light-headed, his breathing shallow, all sense and mettle departed.

As though the world had shrugged beneath his feet.

The clock of Big Ben chimed the quarter hour. Alf heard footsteps strolling on the pavement to his right. Cart-wheels rumbled across the bridge behind him, horses clodding with sackcloth tied around their hooves to keep from slipping with the frost. From the barges at Whitehall Stairs came the rattle of metal rings, shouts and thumping sounds as the bargemen wrestled with boathooks and prepared to cast off their moorings and slip into the stream. Alf took each sudden noise like a blow.

The smell of the city hit him too. Horse manure. Coal smoke. Tired vegetables, salt on the wind, the stench of bleach from the laundries of St Thomas's Hospital. He almost gagged.

In his hand the soft leather of the woman's purse was warm and supple, and the scent that rose from it had the sweetness of honey and pine resin. Alf's heart raced. He felt like a thief.

"Lost something?"

The voice was close and it startled him. He glanced around and found a police constable stood a few feet away with a wary look on his face.

"Don't do it, son," said the constable as he laid his lantern on the parapet, its beam lost in the faint daylight that made shadows of them all. He spread his hands wide like a man calming a dangerous dog, and stepped closer to Alf.

"Did you see her?" Alf was dismayed to hear his voice tremble.

"What?"

"Did you see the girl?"

The constable shrugged. "If it's a woman you're after, there's plenty more down the docks." He laughed at his own humour, a wet crackle lodged deep in his chest.

"Look," Alf insisted, "A girl just jumped into the Thames. Aren't you going to do something?"

The constable looked at him as if he were requesting something unreasonable. "Now look, sir," he said, "I don't see as how I can do anything." He nodded in the direction of the river sweeping fast downstream beyond the parapet. "Not much point, I tell you that for nothing."

"But I saw her!" Alf cried, unable to stop the shaking that spread from his feet to his stomach to his heart to his hands. "I saw her come up again!" He stopped and dropped his head in shame before he said anything more. *What* did *I see*?

"Dead and gone, they is, once they're in the water," said the policeman. He pursed his lips and glanced over Alf's shoulder, up towards the Houses of Parliament on the north bank. "If the river takes 'em from here, Lord knows where you'll find 'em. Mostly I reckon they gets swept out to sea."

Alf stared, horrified at this news, speechless.

"Good riddance, says I," the PC continued, licking his lips, "They're mostly drabs and drunkards all and needs to be meetin' their maker."

Alf turned to the policeman, making sure he kept the purse hidden in his hand, and scowled. "Don't you care, man? A young woman's just killed herself –" *possibly, maybe,* he thought – "Can't you do something? Won't you help?"

The constable chuckled. "Do yourself a favour, sir, and forget it."

Alf stared at him.

"All right," the policeman went on with a sigh, shaking his head. "She'll maybe wash up at Wapping, or the Shadwell Steps. If they find her on this stretch they'll likely take the body to Limehouse Mortuary. But don't expect to recognise her!" His chuckle split into a mirthless laugh.

Alf turned away from the policeman in disgust, his heart pounding with frustration. The constable passed him by, still chuckling, his hobnail boots scraping the stone pavement as he slouched away towards the north bank.

Alf stared out across the water towards the sunrise, scanning the surface of the river as far as his eyes could see for some sign of his mysterious swimmer. Gulls squealed overhead, fighting over some scrap from the floating debris, and a slim yacht slipped under the arch of the bridge beneath him like a spy's whisper, headed for the sea.

He realised he was gripping the girl's purse so hard his fingers had cramp. Hoping for some sign of the girl's identity, Alf undid the simple fastening and opened it up. A handful, no more, of tiny gold coins gleamed against the soft leather as it unfolded like the petals of a flower. They were heavy for their size. Alf had the feeling they would sound very different to modern coins if he were to drop one on a wooden table.

He picked one up and examined it closely. It was as thick as a brass threepenny piece, not quite circular in shape, and when he flipped it over he was not surprised that the head on the back wasn't Victoria. The inscription could have been

Latin, for all that was left of it, only the lower half of the letters still visible, the rest worn smooth by years of use. On the front was some sort of animal – a horse, or something similar, its legs tangled.

He heard footsteps close by and quickly gathered up the loose folds of the purse, and almost without thinking he slipped the loose coin into his waistcoat pocket. The passer-by went on his way without stopping, but Alf began to feel nervous. *This must be worth a King's ransom*, he thought. *What was she doing with it?*

CHAPTER 2 — Polly On The Spike

In the shadow of the boiler-house of St Thomas's Hospital, on the south bank of the Thames close to Waterloo Station, Polly Parker stood, hating herself. She hated her life, and on this particular morning she also hated the cold mist from the river, hated the fact that she was almost sober, and hated the lack of money that forced her out onto the streets at this early hour. She hated her best friend Annie Cook, shivering beside her in the doorway overlooking Westminster Bridge.

"Come on," she said to the shorter woman. "It's been three hours. If we don't move on the Bill will be onto us again, and I ain't seen hide nor hair of the mark."

Annie squinted up beyond the hospital buildings to the clock face on Big Ben. "We got another ten minutes, Poll."

"You keep watch for that rozzer, then, while I go check the infirmary again."

"Don't leave me, Poll," Annie snivelled. "I don't want to be on my own."

Polly sighed. *Not this again*, she thought. "All right," she muttered. "I reckon we got no chance anyhow."

"What was you looking out for anyway, Poll?"

"Coach and pair, remember?"

Annie shook her head.

"Three weeks ago, right, we was in the Feathers with Molly and Cath. Remember? You was sat between 'em, an' you had a bad head so you wasn't drinking. Fred the Chinaman stood us a round and promised a shilling to the first of us what found him the coach and pair."

"No, Poll, I don't remember."

Polly shook her head and folded her arms across her chest. "That's why we've been out on the Spike every night since, love. The others are over at Smithfield Market, or working the docks. They ain't out on the Spike. We got a better chance of seeing things, out on the streets all night. Fred the Chinaman ain't daft."

Annie squinted up at her again. "He ain't a Chinaman either. Not like any Chinaman I ever seen, anyhow."

Polly grinned without humour. "It's what he gets from China that gets him his nickname."

"What's that then, Poll?"

"Stuff that means he can throw shillings around like Lord Muck, that's what." Polly's lips thinned out against her teeth in a bitter line. *But he hasn't been seen for a fortnight*, she thought, a sick feeling in her stomach, *and maybe I've been played for a mug, again*. Since that night in the pub none of the women had seen anything worth reporting.

"Seems too easy to be worth a shilling, Poll, just to see a coach and pair." Annie stamped her feet on the pavement. "What I wouldn't do with a shilling, Poll, eh?"

"I reckon Fred's going to make far more than a shilling when he passes the information on to whoever's paying him," Polly said in a grim voice. "But a shilling's a shilling, any road up. Good enough for a hot bath and a warm bed for the night."

Annie looked at her with wide eyes, her expression wary.

"Both of us, Annie," said Polly and reached one arm over Annie's shoulders, pulling her into a close embrace that failed to provide any more warmth than when they stood apart. *Maybe*, she thought with a flash of anger.

Annie's head dropped against her chest and Polly watched her eyelids droop. *If I make this shilling off Fred*, Polly thought, *I could set myself up again. On my own, a shilling's enough.* The shorter woman's eyes fluttered and closed. *Poor little Annie. It's all your fault.*

She saw the coach turn off Westminster Bridge into Belvedere Street – cream, bay pair, some kind of heraldic pattern on the door – and prayed it would stop as it turned in the road and headed back towards them. "Come on," Polly growled, "We got a job to do." She nudged Annie and unhooked her arm from their embrace, setting off across the hospital yard at a brisk pace.

The coach slowed its approach and drew up twenty yards in front of the hospital gates, blocking her view of the bridge and the street beyond. *Don't go, dear sweet Jesus don't go*, Polly thought with a desperate thudding in her chest. *I got a shilling in my pocket already, I can almost feel it*. She fixed her bonnet and smoothed down her blouse, rubbing at her cheeks to raise a healthy flush. She strolled out of the hospital gates with one arm crooked against her waist.

"Hello, lover," she called out in a calculated tone. "Are you looking for someone?"

The coach driver peered down his nose at her as she approached, his body hunched over his knees on the high perch of the seat. There was no sign of movement from the darkened interior of the coach. The coach lamps flickered and the horses breathed clouds of steam. One of them tossed its head at some irritation and the other began a sudden forceful urination that splashed onto the cobbles. Polly stepped around it with care, towards the carriage.

"Maybe if you ain't interested, your master might be," she said, craning her neck to catch a glimpse into the curtained interior.

"Be off with yer," the coachman said with a toss of his head. "My master can afford better'n the likes of you."

"Cheek!" screeched Annie, right behind Polly at the gates, and spat at him.

"Piss off!" the coachman snarled. He shook his whip in a threatening gesture, his teeth bared.

At that moment there was a sharp rap from inside the carriage and the coachman gathered the reins, jolting the horses into action, splashing the wheels in the now-cold puddle in the gutter as he pulled the coach out into the early morning traffic.

"Piss off yourself!" Polly yelled to the back of the coach driver's head, her spirits sinking again. *There goes any chance of a sly coin.* She watched the coach roll onto Westminster Bridge at a cautious speed. "What's he up to?" she said out loud.

"Wot?"

"Come on." Polly gathered up her skirts and trotted onto the bridge after the coach, taking care not to get too close. Behind her she heard Annie's chesty wheezing as the shorter woman tried to keep up.

The cream-coloured coach stopped at the crest of Westminster Bridge and Polly rested against the parapet for a moment. She glanced over her shoulder and spotted

Annie closing the distance between them. Turning back to the coach, she waited for it to make a move.

After a minute or so, the driver flicked his whip and the horses pulled the carriage away from the kerb at a slow walking pace. Polly had just set off in pursuit once more when the coach reached the north bank, turned in a half-circle across the sparse traffic and started back towards her. "Oh, Lord," she cursed. Her breath caught in her throat.

"Is he coming back for us, Poll?" asked Annie. Her eyes were wide, but not with fear.

Polly frowned. The coach pulled up on the eastern side of the bridge not thirty feet ahead of them. She watched out of the corner of her eye, avoiding the coach driver's gaze, as a young lad approached the coach from the bridge parapet and engaged in conversation with whoever was inside.

Oho, she thought with a sneer of disgust. "So that's your stinking game."

"Poll?"

"Fred the Chinaman must be snitching to the Bill about toffs who go with boys," she said in a low voice, averting her eyes from the scene opposite. "Hell mend 'em."

Annie yawned. "Can we go to the park now, Poll? I need a kip."

"Me too," Polly said, fatigue showing in her voice. *I've got my shilling.* "Then we get back to the Feathers and see if we can find Fred, or someone who knows where he is." *And have a drink*, she added. *Dear sweet Lord, a drink.*

CHAPTER 3 – The Killer of Mayfair

In Mayfair, Louis Beauregard lay in bed struggling for the last bars of fitful sleep. The sunlight that broke through the gap in the curtains provided no relief, although he was pleased to be granted the opportunity to see it. Around dawn he'd felt a pain like an iron band tighten round his chest until breathlessness forced him upright, gasping. It troubled him, as it always did when Crown Prinz Wilhelm was in London.

It had woken him the night Wilhelm was born, almost thirty years earlier, in 1859. It had crushed him then like heartbreak, a loosening of the Lady's attention, the moment when a man discovers his wife no longer loves him.

The old Kaiser is dead, he thought with nothing more than instinct as proof.

Louis swung his feet out of bed and sat there until his breathing returned to normal, more alert at this time of the morning than he liked. He looked at the clock on the bedside table, counted the time it took for him to recover. Each time it was a little longer, just a few seconds more, and he was more afraid of that entropy than he'd ever been of a violent death.

I wonder where Wilhelm is? he thought, staring at the carpet on the floor between his bare dangling feet. *He always surprises us. How does he manage to slip into London unnoticed?*

He swung his feet back into bed and lay down again, his thoughts abroad, tugging at him. He cast his mind back through more than sixty years of memory, linking events together while his gaze rested on the familiar objects and ornaments of his bedroom. He remembered the constitutional crisis that was narrowly averted when the then Princess Victoria took the throne – her bachelor uncle holding onto office for just long enough after the death of the old King, while the bloodlines of Europe were scoured for a suitable heir.

The Hohenzollerns came close, then, Louis reminded himself. *If Wilhelm I is dead, then Friedrich is now Kaiser* – Friedrich the old Kaiser's brother, a wounded man, his recent treatment for throat cancer leaving him voiceless and breathing through a tracheotomy that would never heal. *Yet another of us old men*, thought Louis, not without compassion. *I hope, for Her sake, I die soon.*

He climbed out of bed this time.

Breakfast was already laid on the small table in his study. His manservant brought a pot of Assam and the earliest edition of the 'Times' before returning to the kitchen, and Louis read the headlines while he poured himself a cup of the tea and waited for it to cool: 'Riots in Holborn, Irish Blamed; Kaiser Unwell'.

Louis turned the page to the full report of the old Kaiser's health, shaking his head. *Poor old soul*, he thought while his mouth set in a grim line. *What have you damned us all into?* He checked the date of the newspaper and turned to the tide times for Greenwich, Tilbury and Mersea Island.

Glanced up at the clock on the mantel, and called his manservant again.

"Is that clock right, Dodman?"

"Yes, sir."

"Ten to seven?"

Dodman nodded.

"Thank you," Louis said, dismissing the man with a brief nod of his head.

He moved rapidly through the announcements like a bird skimming insects off the surface of a stream and turned to the page of letters to the editor. Above the usual heated correspondence about the Irish Situation was an innocuous missive announcing the first sighting of a cuckoo in spring, in the vicinity of Green Park. Louis's mouth went dry. *So the Lady WAS in London last night.*

He read the letter again, nodding in recognition at the eminent name signed against it, a ripple of anticipation igniting his impatience. *So now what?* he thought. In accordance with the Rules, the membership of the Cuckoo Club had been summoned to an emergency meeting. *How many will come? And what do they know? More important, what can they tell?*

Louis checked the time on his pocket-watch. Barely an hour after sunrise. He was puzzled, and not a little concerned. *Where is She?* he wondered. He felt saddened, more so because he hadn't felt Her presence in his city. Like a devoted husband he counted the days since their first meeting, marked the years of their togetherness with each anniversary, never losing sight of all he'd given up to keep faith with Her.

Was this the reason he'd been woken with the pain across his chest? The first time, when Wilhelm was born, he'd been out of the country, carousing his way around the Greek islands in the company of poets and brigands. At the time he'd felt like Byron gripped with fever in Attica while he fought the civil war, and Louis had imagined something similar for himself, not realising how wrong he was. But it shaped his future as much as any of the experiences on that trip.

His thoughts strayed to the men he'd had to kill over the last sixty years. Each one was a blot on his character, a stain on his soul, and he carried them all with him even as he enjoyed the benefits of surviving those encounters. *Will it be this time?* he thought, without fear. One thing he was certain of – he was still Consort. He still had the Cuckoo Club behind him, and that was no small cause.

Not being the type to mope, he rose from his chair and spent little time preparing to leave the house. He wanted answers. And he knew they were his by right.

As Dodman helped him put on his coat in the hallway, the telephone rang. Dodman picked up the two-part apparatus and greeted the caller officiously, then held the contraption out to Louis.

"The French Ambassador, sir," he announced.

Just as I expected, Louis thought. "Thank you," he said to his manservant and took the telephone from him, the stalk in his right hand and the earpiece in his left. He remembered to bring both parts up to his mouth and his ear, shaking his head at the silliness of the thing. "Ambassador?"

"Good morning, Monsieur Beauregard, and I trust it finds you well." There was a pause on the line, then the Frenchman went on, "I read the news in the 'Times' just now."

"Are you in your office?" Louis asked.

"No," said the Ambassador, "I'm still at home. I didn't think this could wait. What's it all about?"

Louis took a deep breath, and stared up at the hall ceiling. "I don't know." *Damned machine*, he thought as he strolled back towards the parlour door, trailing the cloth-wrapped cord of the telephone across the parquet floor. "News travels fast, Bourgoine. Perhaps you have more information than I, at this moment."

"Damned if I have!" the Frenchman spluttered down the line. "There's no news from Paris – not yet. I'll have to call you from the Embassy."

Perhaps, thought Louis, *you could have thought of that before you rang me*. He turned and strolled back to the hall table, taking care to avoid the unravelled telephone cord as he did so. "Please get in touch when you have news," he said in a warm tone. "I have to admit that the Club has been expecting something of the sort for some time – just not so soon."

"Wilhelm has not been a well man, these last few years," Bourgoine admitted. "If he dies now –"

Louis cleared his throat and interrupted the other man. "He may already be dead."

"Really?" The shock in the Frenchman's voice was obvious.

Louis nodded, then smiled at himself in the hall mirror for doing so, remembering that the telephone did not transmit his movements. By the time he opened his mouth to reply, the French Ambassador continued in the silence.

"Then that's terrible news," he said, his voice rich with genuine emotion. "We have no plans in place as yet. You – of all men – know how much is at stake here! I must –" He broke off and his voice became distant, as if he'd turned his head away from the mouthpiece, and he rattled off a stream of orders in French too rapid for Louis to catch all of it. There was a pause, an even fainter response, and another pause, then the Ambassador's voice came on the line again. "Beauregard?"

"Still here, old chap," Louis replied with bonhomie. *Still here*, he added in his mind, *but who knows for how much longer?*

"You're aware of the implications?"

"Of Friedrich becoming Kaiser? Of course."

"I meant Wilhelm."

I know you did, thought Louis, but said nothing. He counted to four before the ambassador filled the empty wire.

"Where is he now?"

"I don't know," Louis said with a pang of regret that such honesty produced. "Gone to ground, I hope."

"Of all the possible heirs!" Bourgoine tutted and snorted, "Why him?"

"Bourgoine," Louis chastened, "Don't get ahead of yourself. Much is yet to be decided. If the old Kaiser is dead –" *of course he is*, he reminded himself – "Then Friedrich inherits the Prussian throne."

"Ah! That old cripple! What use will he be? He can't speak – he can't even breathe properly! – and we already know that the Crown Prinz has a link to the Lady."

"As do Victoria's boys," Louis reminded him. "Although I grant you, we've seen no sign of it so far."

The silence on the line this time was one for Louis to fill. He let it hang while his thoughts raced over the sons of Queen Victoria who had survived childhood – Edward,

Alfred, Arthur, Leopold – and very faintly shook his head. "Of all the possible heirs, can you choose one better?"

"We all know he loves his uniforms and his army too much."

"He also loves his grandmother," Louis reminded the Frenchman, becoming tired of the argument now. *Always the same discussion with this man*, he thought, growing irritable. *Always the same conclusion, too.*

"I still think he needs a stronger influence," Bourgoine stressed. "One that binds him more strongly to our cause."

"He's a man of science, so he says, and you know that he won't hear of it. Besides, what else do we have at our disposal to provide reason in this modern age?" Louis tapped his gloved forefinger on the earpiece and was pleased to hear its dull thud like an extra heartbeat. *Maybe that will distract him*, he thought.

The Ambassador began his next phrase in French then his voice became dim, and Louis pictured him pressing the mouthpiece to his chest while he gave orders to his staff.

"Come to lunch at the Club," Louis said into the silence.

"What?"

"Come to lunch," Louis repeated. "Go to the Embassy and if there's any news, let me know this afternoon. I can't imagine events would move any quicker, can you?"

There was a loud snorting sound down the line and the French Ambassador rung off with a curt agreement.

Louis smiled and listened to the wire disconnect from the far end, then hung the earpiece back on the other part of the telephone. His manservant offered assistance, without a word.

"We managed perfectly well without this infernal contraption for the entirety of history, and now, because we can pass on information in an instant, we all have to react instantly too," said Louis, handing back the telephone apparatus like an empty decanter.

Dodman nodded, still silent, and tidied the machine away.

"If anyone else should call," Louis instructed the man as he put on his hat and gloves, "Tell them I'm at the Club. There's a telephone there, and I can always be reached by telegram or by runner."

"Will you be out all day, sir?"

"I don't know, Dodman." Louis sighed, considering what were the possibilities for the day ahead. "It depends on events, I suppose. Can you handle it if I'm ad-hoc today?"

Dodman nodded again.

"Good man." Louis buttoned his overcoat, stepped out his front door down the short flight of steps to the pavement, and hailed a cab. "Cuckoo Club, Soho," he instructed the cabbie. "And take care." *The Old Consort isn't as well as he might be.*

CHAPTER 4 — The Russian Invitation

Alf was so lost in his own concerns that he barely noticed the coach approaching. It wasn't until the solid thud of the window sliding open broke his concentration that he turned away from the sunrise.

The coach was cream and both the wheel trims and the horses' legs were spattered with chalky mud, as if the coach had driven in from the countryside or Hampstead. The window of the coach stayed open and a gloved hand appeared, cigarette in a slim amber mouthpiece from which a swift tap of the gloved wrist detached the slug of ash. The hand disappeared into the carriage and when it reappeared it was empty, a beckoning finger crooked at Alf.

He took his hands from his pockets, stood up straight and stepped up to the coach door.

"Are you in some kind of trouble, young man?" The voice was smooth, not deep nor unnaturally high, the accent one Alf couldn't place but not English. It had a tone of command, and Alf felt immediately he could trust its owner.

"I'm not sure," he admitted, his eyes sliding to his brown patent brogues.

"Not sure?" the stranger asked. He coughed and again his hand snaked out to tap the ash off his cigarette. "Excuse me," he said, dabbing a handkerchief to his thin lips. "Not sure? Perhaps I may offer my assistance in some manner?"

"Thank you sir," Alf said, felt himself blushing again.

The carriage door clicked and swung open, and a gust of warm air scented with cherry-tobacco swept out. "Please step inside," said the stranger. "I mean you no harm."

Alf accepted the offer without hesitation. The exertions of his sprint had warmed him up but that was wearing off and the chill in the morning air was beginning to bite. Beautiful sunrise or not, it was still early March. He pulled the carriage door shut behind him and the stranger slid the window closed with a firm click.

"Cigarette?"

Alf shook his head. "No thank-you, sir. I promised my late mother that I wouldn't." He mentally berated himself, then felt ashamed. He'd never been ashamed to admit it before, but somehow in the presence of this sophisticate he felt embarrassed. Here he was, a man of 17, still holding onto his mother's apron strings. He cringed inside at betraying the memory too.

"Bravo!" the stranger murmured. "I like a man who keeps his word – keeps faith with his family." The man's dark eyes glittered. "Allow me to introduce myself. I am Sylvester De Winter, Vicomte de Utsire, special adviser to the Russian Ambassador to the Court of St James. Here – " he drew a small silver case from his waistcoat pocket," – is my card." He removed a card from the case and passed it to Alf.

"Pleased to meet you, sir," said Alf, shaking the proffered gloved hand. "I'm Alfred Winchester. I don't have a title yet, nor a position. I'm a scholar, at least until the summer." Alf stopped before he added too much detail to his reply and waited in the short silence that followed. The walls of the carriage were glossy, a resinous colour like honey from some northern pine forest, and Alf realised they were panelled in amber.

"Ah, education," said Sylvester de Winter, exhaling aromatic smoke through his mouth and snorting it into his nostrils. "So there are great things ahead for you, Alfred?"

Alf dropped his head, stared at a blank spot on the plush red carpet of the carriage floor. Sylvester de Winter's woollen coat had a broad Astrakhan collar and a Russian hat of the same material was perched on his head. The turn-ups on the man's pinstripe trousers were immaculately pressed and not a fraction out of fashion, his black leather shoes smooth like riding boots. Alf couldn't think of a suitable reply.

"Come now," said Sylvester de Winter in a forgiving tone, "What brings a young gentleman from Berkshire all the way to London at such an hour? And to such a spot?"

"I'm up to visit my tailor," Alf explained. "I'm to go to Sandhurst in September, and I needed to order some things."

"Sandhurst, eh?" said the Russian. "I would expect a young man of your stature to join the Admiralty. It's the place to be, in my opinion."

"Really?" Alf was unsurprised, but felt he had to be polite. "I was enrolled in the Army by my parents, before they went to India." He stopped short of explaining anything further. "I've never given it much thought."

Sylvester de Winter nodded with an understanding expression on his face, exhaling smoke from his nostrils. "Often," he said, "We are driven by the expectations of others, without our own considerations being accounted for.

I myself –" he broke off with a wave of his hand. "No matter. Tell me more about yourself, Alfred. Is it Alfred? Or something else?"

"Alf, usually, sir."

"Then tell me, Alf, what brings you to this spot at such a *fresh* hour of the day?"

Alf explained his night of troubled sleep and went on to describe the trip up from Windsor on the milk train. He sketched the briefest of details about his initial encounter with the girl – bashful, he omitted the part about her kissing him – and his pursuit of her through the streets of Westminster.

"What a curious thing to do," remarked Sylvester de Winter, one eyebrow arched and a smile playing about his lips.

"I – I was under the impression she was in some sort of trouble," Alf mumbled. "She dropped a purse, too," he added. "I wanted to return it."

"Do you still have it?"

Alf nodded.

"You didn't return it to her, then?"

Alf shook his head. "No," he said, breathless. "She – she jumped off the bridge before I could explain."

"Oh, how unfortunate!" Sylvester de Winter exclaimed with genuine distress. "My dear boy, what a terrible experience for you. Have you reported it?"

"Not yet," said Alf. "I told a policeman, on his beat I suppose, just a few minutes ago, but he didn't want to know. He said I should go to Limehouse."

Sylvester de Winter nodded, deep in thought. "That would make sense," he said almost under his breath. "Shall we go?"

"If it's not too much trouble, sir," Alf acceded, then climbed back into the coach.

Sylvester de Winter took a pinch of snuff and shook his head. "I'm a gentleman of leisure," he explained with a faint smile. "I have no particular agenda, this morning. Besides," he went on, "Your story intrigues me. And we all love a little intrigue, don't we?" He smiled like a music-hall compère, and winked.

He slid the carriage window down and a gust of cold air whirled around the interior of the coach. It brought the smells of the sea, and seemed to promise snow. Sylvester de Winter gave orders to his driver and slid the carriage window up once more.

Alf noticed, for the first time, that the window-pane was a golden colour with tiny flecks and bubbles, much like the amber panels that lined the coach body. He put his hand out to it, surprised to find it almost warm to the touch, with a tiny jolt that tingled in his fingertips.

Sylvester de Winter smiled and lit another cigarette. "It's amber, dear boy," he said. "An indulgence of a rich man, if you like. And it reminds me of – another place, another time, when I was younger and not so troubled." He paused, smiled wistfully, and leaned forwards on his silver-topped cane. "Tell me more about yourself. Actually –" he stopped himself, and put one gloved finger up to his lips – "Do you still have the lady's purse?"

Alf nodded. He patted his jacket pocket and brought it out, amazed by how warm it seemed in his hands.

"Well, let's see what's inside,eh?" said Sylvester de Winter with a keen eye.

Alf balanced the purse on his knees and teased the drawstring open, taking care not to spill the coins, and when it was wide enough he sat the purse on the palm of his hand and held it out towards the Russian.

"Oh, magnificent," gasped Sylvester de Winter, one index finger edging down the rim of the purse. "Those must be worth a fortune, don't you think?"

Alf shrugged and tidied the coins away once more. "I don't know much about coins, sir," he said. "I was going to hand them in to the Lost Property office."

Sylvester de Winter raised his eyebrows in surprise. "Lost Property? Are you sure?"

"Why?"

"Don't you wonder whether the policemen of this city are to be trusted with a treasure trove of gold coins?" The Russian laughed, and shook his head. "Actually, of any city," he went on in a quiet tone. "Even my own."

Alf sat considering this for a moment, but his mind had been made up when he picked the purse off the pavement, and he was not to be swayed. "No, sir," he said, "I would like to report it." *And I don't feel safe wandering around London with a pocket full of gold coins.*

Sylvester de Winter shrugged. "As you wish, dear boy." He slid the window open, removed the cigarette-end from the amber mouthpiece and flicked the stub away into the street. "Ah, there's Blackfriars," he said as he craned his neck against the window at the bridge that passed above them.

Alf suddenly felt queasy. He clutched his stomach and felt his hands tremble. His face broke into a clammy sweat and he glanced towards the Russian in concern, one hand pointing to the window. "Please, sir?"

Sylvester de Winter stopped the carriage while Alf disembarked for a breath of fresh air. The Russian offered him a snifter of what smelled like brandy from a silver hip flask, but Alf declined.

"I don't know what came over me," Alf said as he returned to the carriage when his shaking spasm had passed. He felt safer in the carriage than he did outside, coins in his pocket, crowds on the pavement.

"You've had a nasty shock," Sylvester de Winter said in a soothing voice, his eyebrows angled in concern. "You ought not to be alone, I suggest at least until you feel well once more." He slid the carriage window down and redirected his driver, and they set off once more.

Past Shadwell and out to the Limehouse Basin where the Regent's Canal cut inland from the river, Alf sat in Sylvester de Winter's carriage in a half-daze, barely nodding when, like a tourist, the man pointed out landmarks such as St Paul's Cathedral, the Tower and the Royal Mint. Alf felt nauseous on more than one occasion, but by the time the coach turned off Brook Street towards Commercial Road, he felt more relaxed than he had done all morning. The Russian's gentle conversation coaxed out the details of his life – his childhood in Sussex, father in India and mother drowned while sailing to meet him, the early enrolment at school and his subsequent career – without judgement, with sympathy, and with a nod to his future plans.

"Of course I've never had to consider such things myself," confided Sylvester de Winter. "The course of my life has always been steady. I consider myself highly fortunate in this regard." He smiled, inattentive to the actions of his free hand as it stroked the amber panel of the carriage side, a self-absorbed gesture as if his thoughts were elsewhere.

Alf nodded, unsure of how to reply. At that moment the coach rocked to a halt in the street opposite Limehouse Station, and Sylvester de Winter, distracted, slid down the carriage window in a smooth movement to peer out like a tortoise emerging from its shell.

"Here we are."

Alf climbed out into the cobbled lane. He paused. He could hear children's cries from the nearby riverbank and felt drawn to them for no other reason than they reminded him of happier times. The odour of Sylvester de Winter's tobacco was exotic and overpowering and some of it still seemed to cling to his clothing, even in the slight breeze off the river. Alf felt ill.

De Winter watched him through the open door, calm brown eyes unwavering. "If you should be free later," he said, "Will you honour me by joining me for lunch? At my Club."

"The Russian Occidental, sir?" Alf said in astonishment, and patted his waistcoat pocket where he'd stashed the Baron's visiting card. "Thank you, sir."

"You're welcome," said Sylvester de Winter after a short pause. "I'll be in the Smoking Room at twelve." He rapped the roof of his cab with his cane and the driver shook the reins, the horses slow to react. "See you later," he said and slammed the window up, concealing the interior from view once again.

Alf watched the coach until it disappeared around the corner towards the old Ratcliffe Highway. He turned to face the Police Station, his heart hammering, and stared up at the two-storey building before him, its windows thick with iron bars and an air of menace hovering over its roof like a dark cloud. Policemen on horseback trooped out of the station gates and passed him as they headed off into the city, the noise of them confusing and harsh.

He slipped his hand into his jacket pocket and felt the purse, heavy and soft, with a sudden breath of air that scented of pollen and pine-resin. His confidence, boosted during his journey with Sylvester de Winter, seemed to evaporate into the sunlight as he hesitated on the opposite side of the street, staring up at the station's reinforced door. The thought of his mystery girl being taken here distressed him. Nonetheless he felt a sense of responsibility which overrode his apprehension, even as he paused to ask himself: *How am I to explain all this?*

CHAPTER 5 – Mudlarks in Limehouse

Surrounded by the high walls of the London Docks, the police station in Limehouse was a formidable building which was dwarfed by the warehouses around it. Built on the edge of the West India Import Dock, a site that overlooked the old Wapping gibbet on a clear day, it once functioned as the City of London gaol for overflow prisoners from the Tower of London.

It still handled miscreants in preparation for transportation to the colonies, mainly Irish immigrants whose new life in London had proven more criminal than they had the wits to survive. As Alf stood on the street summoning his courage, he could hear the banter in the cells below ground, a mixture of Irish and English in accents so thick it sounded utterly foreign to him.

Loose straw drifted round the street. A cart full of the stuff was drawn up by the wall of the police station and the carter, red-faced and puffing, wrestled with the horses as he fought to apply the brakes to the vehicle. With a screech and a loud clanking noise that descended into a rattle, the cell hatch opened up in the pavement. Someone down there began to eject filthy straw through the hole onto the street in small forkfuls. The smell was not unusual, but the dust was unpleasant. Alf whipped his kingsman handkerchief from his pocket and clutched it to his nose before scurrying into the station.

In spite of the hour, the place was lively. Alf took a seat in the hall and waited his turn while the desk sergeant discharged the night's inmates. When the last one was gone the desk sergeant came out from behind the screen and propped open the front door. A rush of cold air raised the goosebumps on Alf's hands and wisps of straw, fresh as well as soiled, blew in from the street. He heard the scrape of a shovel on the paving-stones outside.

"That's the last man out," the desk sergeant said cheerily. "Get some fresh air in now. Now – what's up, lad?"

"I think I've come to report a missing person."

"You only 'think' she's missing? Or you only 'think' you've to report it?"

"I'm not sure," Alf said, embarrassment washing over him again. "I saw a girl – woman – no, a girl, I saw a girl jump into the Thames off Westminster Bridge. The beat constable said I should come here."

The desk sergeant gave Alf an appraising look. "A girl?" he asked. "Who was she – one of the household staff? Got herself into a spot of bother, had she?"

"No," Alf began, and faltered. "I – I bumped into her in the street."

"Yes?" said the desk sergeant with a raised eyebrow. "THAT kind of girl."

"No!" said Alf forcefully, then paused. "I really did just bump into her in the street." He replayed the moment in his mind as he spoke. "I came out of Victoria Station and as I rounded a corner, she ran into me and we both ended up on the pavement. She picked herself up before I had a chance to offer her some assistance and then she hared off again without a word."

"I thought you said Westminster Bridge. It's a long way from Victoria Station."

"She dropped her purse."

"So you ran after her, hm?" The desk sergeant looked him up and down.

"Yes," said Alf. He began to feel rather helpless. "I followed her all the way to the Embankment but I couldn't catch her. I tried calling out to her but I didn't know her name, so perhaps she didn't realise."

"You didn't catch her then?" The desk sergeant leaned against the doorpost, watching Alf. "You're a fit healthy young lad. I reckon you've got a bit of a lick on you. But she kept ahead of you?"

"All the way."

The desk sergeant heaved himself away from the doorpost and plodded round to the back of the desk.

"I couldn't stop her," Alf said, lost.

"Couldn't stop her?"

"When she went over the bridge." Alf looked at his hands and realised they were shaking. His mouth was dry.

"Into the river," the desk sergeant said softly.

Alf nodded.

The desk sergeant let out a deep breath. "Why don't I fetch you a cup of tea and you can make a formal report?"

Alf nodded and looked up at him again, feeling desolate. The draught through the door made his fingers ache. He couldn't shake from his mind's eye the view of her bobbing to the surface downstream as if waving, and the flash of silver as she disappeared. He couldn't make sense of it, not in a rational way, and he was ashamed to speak of it.

The desk sergeant disappeared into the back of the station leaving Alf alone in the hall. A couple of young constables, slightly older than Alf and boasting of something lewd, passed out through the hallway on the start of their beat. They glanced at Alf with a look of pity and envy, and he realised that Limehouse probably didn't see many public schoolboys.

The desk sergeant reappeared at the door and beckoned Alf in. "Come into the interview room," he said in a friendly tone. "It's warmer – and more discreet."

Alf took a deep breath when he stood up, hoping to dispel the butterflies in his stomach, then followed the desk sergeant into the depths of the station. Along this first corridor the flaking paint on the walls changed from green to plain white, above a timber dado stained dark with the passage of time and many greasy hands.

The desk sergeant ushered Alf into a tiny room with a small window, barred with a single bar, high up in the far wall. Through it Alf saw a patch of pale blue sky and a slice of the warehouse roof outside.

Another middle-aged PC came into the room and nodded to the desk sergeant as he sat down opposite Alf.

"Constable Brookes will take your story from here," said the desk sergeant, closing the door behind him.

Alf looked around but there was no sign of the promised cuppa. He cupped his hands around themselves instead and looked at the PC expectantly.

Constable Brookes flourished a pencil and notepad and began to question Alf again about all the details he'd given to the desk sergeant.

Alf went through his story patiently, step by step, up to the point where the girl leapt into the water. Somehow that part always seemed so hard to explain. The words caught in his throat, a dry whisper.

Constable Brookes cleared his throat and flipped back through the notepad a couple of pages. "And the purse?" he asked. "Do you still have it?"

Alf reached into his waistcoat pocket where the little drawstring bag tugged its weight against the fabric. The leather was soft and warmed by his body heat, and as he withdrew it from the pocket the tiny room seemed to fill with a rich heady odour, a mixture of pollen and honey and loam that reminded Alf of the water-meadows down by the Thames at Maidenhead.

As Alf put the purse on the table he suddenly felt reluctant to let go of it. His heart beating faster now, he covered it with his hands, the one thing that connected him to her, the girl who had kissed him that morning before dying.

"Anything inside worth it?" Constable Brookes asked, disinterested. With the tip of his pencil he gently forced Alf's hands apart.

Alf pursed his lips, opened the drawstring and tipped the contents into his palm. The tiny gold coins glinted dull in the electric lamp.

Constable Brookes gave an indrawn whistle. "Not just your ordinary working girl, then."

"I have no idea who she was, or what she was, sir," he said, still inclined to protect her honour. "She wasn't old, or ugly."

"Not all of them are, lad."

Although he knew of the existence of prostitutes, mainly from the tales of some of the other boys at school, Alf couldn't imagine the fragile creature he'd chased out onto the bridge being involved in such a trade. He shook his head but felt himself blushing.

Constable Brookes poked the coins with the end of his pencil. "Not British," he said, almost as a question. He proffered them to Alf then snatched them away again. "Heavy, too. I ain't never seen a sovereign, but I reckon it ain't as heavy as this." He picked one of the coins up between finger and thumb and bit down on it. He gave another indrawn whistle. "I reckon these is real gold."

Alf shrugged. "I don't know," he said again, miserably. "Can I have the purse back, please?"

Constable Brookes tutted his teeth and shook his head. "It's not your property, is it?"

"No," Alf admitted, a sense of unease growing in the pit of his stomach. *I just want the purse,* he thought, *because it's hers.* "I'm not bothered about the coins."

"We'll have to keep it," said Constable Brookes and sat back in his chair. "Lost property. The owner may come back to claim it."

"But she jumped into the Thames!" Alf cried out. "How is she supposed to come back?"

"Now, sir," said the PC, "Please calm down. It's just procedure. The purse is put into Lost Property. If it isn't claimed in six months, it belongs to the finder. But we have to try to find its rightful owner. The purse may not belong to the person who dropped it."

"You can't say that."

"Not for certain," Constable Brookes admitted. "But you have to admit that it's a bit rum for a London streetwalker to have a purse of solid gold coins."

"I wouldn't know about that!" Alf blustered. He was embarrassed again.

Constable Brookes smiled. "No, sir, I expect you don't. Take my word for it, sir, it's more likely it was stolen."

Alf nodded slowly, mulling the new idea over. "She did seem to be rather frightened," he mused, "Even before I began to follow her."

"Was she being pursued before then, sir?"

Alf remembered the clatter of the rushing mail-carts that seemed to throng the streets around Victoria, then the crisp chill of Parliament Square with its empty silence throwing his own footsteps back at him. He pictured again the wide roadway on Westminster Bridge, empty of traffic except for a couple of open carts and a hansom, a few pedestrians on the pavements like wraiths in the mist. He shook his head.

"You are sure, sir?"

"No," he said clearly. "I think she was alone."

"Thank you, sir. Where exactly did she jump?"

"Westminster Bridge," he began. "At sunrise." As Alf explained the situation for the fourth time that morning he noticed that his hands, although still cold at the fingertips, had stopped shaking.

When he'd finished Constable Brookes thanked him and rose from the table.

"What about the purse?" Alf asked again. "I understand you need to keep the coins, but what about the purse? It's not worth anything."

"I'll bring you a form to complete for our records. You never know, there may be a reward for coins like this." If Constable Brookes was hoping to see a glimmer of avarice in Alf's eyes he was disappointed.

Alf barely blinked. "I'm not interested in the money," he said half-heartedly, his miserable mood returning. *I just want to see her again, to say I'm sorry, to ask her – to tell her –*

His thoughts faltered. He pictured the frightened face glancing over her shoulder at him, then beyond him, before she leapt from the parapet.

Whatever she was afraid of, a cold death in the depth of the Thames had seemed more preferable.

Alf shivered.

"Are you all right, sir?"

Alf nodded. He wasn't certain.

"You're probably still in shock, sir," said Constable Brookes, and patted him on the shoulder as a father might before he left the room.

Out in the fresh air once more, Alf found himself alone in the weak sunshine of late morning. The voices of children still came from over by the river, their cries overshadowed by carts and men as the docks bustled to life. Alf took a deep breath to clear his head, noting the wisps of old straw swirling in the breeze that lifted off the river. The door of the police station behind him slammed shut. He squinted his eyes against the sun and strolled off to the waterside.

Wharves perforated the riverbank where the great dock basins retreated. The mudflats below were reached by a thousand sets of stairs, on north and south banks, from the Isle of Dogs as far upstream as Vauxhall Bridge, each named according to their location or function.

Alf crossed the Shadwell entrance and strolled along Wapping Wall until he came to one of these and descended to the platform below, where he smiled a weak greeting to the occupants and peered out towards the glinting river.

This far east, at low tide the waters receded to a strip of fierce flow in the centre of the main channel. Deep waters extended into the docks, lifelines of commerce upon which the small boats plied their trade, but the tea-clippers sat liminal in still waters, awaiting the tide. Not here the sprawling marshes of Tyburn; the broad mediaeval Thames had been trammelled by modern engineering into a powerful creature of weight and speed.

In the curves, the backwaters, those still places where the water swirls in circles that suck and gurgle, the river threw up whatever rubbish the new sewer system washed into the subterranean rivers. The Effra, the Wandle, the Tyburn, the Peck – all flushed into the Thames. The river still stunk like it did in Byron's day, but the problem appeared off the East End, not Parliament Square. The poor still lived by the filthiest river in Europe.

And where there was filth, there was profit. On the mud revealed by the withdrawing waters of the tidal Thames, as Alf shaded his eyes against the low-risen sun, a group of shadows stalked.

The children's laughter that drew Alf to the riverside belonged to a group of boys between the ages of five and twelve. Barefoot, with threadbare trousers rolled up high, they picked their way along this stretch of the Thames, each footstep knee-high in sucking mud down at the water's edge. They raked through the detritus left behind by the retreating waters, day in, day out, in rain, hail or heatwave. When the bitter sleet blew in from the North Sea in late December, or when August's boiling summer left them working naked but for a cloth around the mouth and nose, the mudlarks worked the river and the wealth that was left behind.

Alf stood and watched them in curiosity. If he hadn't had the morning's experiences, he'd never have known about their existence.

He watched two of the younger ones pelt each other with turds. One of the larger boys growled at them; they giggled and desisted. One brought a crust of bread from a pocket and gnawed on it.

The tallest of the boys spent ages throwing a rope with a stick attached at a bobbing grey lump, which turned out to be the corpse of a small dog when it was dragged ashore. The boy slipped the collar off and into his pocket, bundled the corpse into a sack at the pier side.

Alf realised with mild horror that one of the children was a girl, but only because she had dropped her trousers to squat and urinate.

The wake of a passing boat lapped upon the shore a few times before subsiding and the mudlarks as one threw curses at the distant vessel.

Alf watched for a few minutes longer, fascinated thoughts going over in his mind. He thought of his modest allowance paid out each week by the housemaster at school from the sum his father had endowed. He looked at the mudlarks, filthy, unwashed, probably lousy and generally coarse. What might they do for a shilling?

"Hey!" he shouted, waving to attract attention.

The mudlarks looked up at him then glanced at the tall one. He sucked his feet out of the mud and stepped over to the edge where the gravel underfoot made him stoop. But at least he removed his cap.

Alf found himself momentarily lost for words.

"Wot you want, mister?"

"I'm looking for something," was all Alf could think of.

"I know your sort," said the senior mudlark. "How much?" He eyed Alf. "Boy or a girl? I can get you both."

"No, no," Alf protested. "I – I'm really looking for someone –" He faltered. "I want some information," he said more boldly. "A woman leapt off Westminster Bridge this morning. I need to find her."

"Wot's innit for me?" the senior mudlark asked, a born entrepreneur.

"A sixpence?"

The senior mudlark snorted. "Make it a half crown and you got a deal."

Alf paused. "A shilling." His funds could stretch that far, as long as it wasn't often, and he had just thought of another use for his money.

"What's she look like?"

Alf described her again while he pictured her in his mind, surprised to find the details already blurring.

All the while the senior mudlark observed him with an air of almost pity, squinting his eyes in the sun. The junior mudlarks were moving upstream, their conversation lost details except for the piping and shrieking of thin reedy voices echoed by a flock of seabirds that swooped low over the outflow of Wapping Basin. The senior mudlark waited until Alf had finished his description then glanced after the juniors, scratching his nose as if he wanted to pick it.

"You ever seen a dead body out of the river?" he asked.

Alf shook his head.

The boy snickered. "How do I let you know?"

Alf hadn't considered this.

"Tell you wot," said the senior mudlark, glancing again at his companions, "You come see me tonight down at the Bluebell, I'll see what I've got. All right?"

Alf nodded. He had no idea where the Bluebell was. "It's a public house, is it?"

The boy gave him a look of disbelief. "You're a right one," he said with a sneer that irritated Alf.

"Do you want this reward or not?" he snapped.

At the mention of the word 'reward' the boy's eyes glinted. He looked at Alf with a sly grin as if he couldn't believe his luck, then nodded and turned away without another word.

Alf watched him pick up the sack with the dead dog in it and sling it over his shoulder, tiptoeing between the shoreline debris as the sack dripped down his back in a soggy stream.

He felt nauseous again, not for the first time that morning, as if he'd just made a pact with the devil.

CHAPTER 6 – Readings In The Water-Chamber

Louis arrived at the Cuckoo Club at that time in the morning when it was too late for breakfast, and too early for lunch. He descended the stairs in a flurry of energy. One floor below street level he knocked on the door of the Shooting Gallery, and was greeted by the Club Armourer.

"Morning, sir," said the Armourer with a smile of acknowledgement. "Will you take the readings this morning?"

Louis nodded. "I don't see why not, Cummins. No need to ignore tradition, even for unusual coincidences."

Cummins paused only to collect an iron key and a cloth-bound ledger from a shelf by the door, then led the way down a further flight of steps, Louis close behind.

Three floors underground, beneath the water table, the Cuckoo Club's Armourer unlocked a plain wooden door at the very bottom of the stairs. Before Louis entered the room beyond, he signed an entry in the Armourer's ledger, noting the time with the other man's fob-watch.

"I won't be long, Cummins" he said, and the Armourer nodded. "Just the usual observations today, I think." In his heart, he knew different. This far down in the building, at certain times, the walls seemed to shake to some ancient heartbeat.

"Five minutes, sir, and I'll break the door down," said Cummins with a grin.

Louis shook his head with a grin of his own.

He slipped through the door into the Water Chamber and reeled from the pulse in the stonework. He'd felt the same effect at certain points on the Piccadilly Line where the deepest of the London Underground tracks crossed the boundary between earth and water. Louis caught his breath and leaned against the doorframe. He glanced around the room.

The walls were lined with instruments of measurement, some in cases, others free-standing. Louis strode gently to a wall-mounted barometer and tapped the glass gently. It swung, a tiny amount. He noted the change in a log book. *More than yesterday,* he thought.

In the centre of the room was a great bronze cauldron hung on thick iron chains from a wooden beam in the ceiling – the Water Compass. Louis stepped round it – *always read the Water Compass last*, he reminded himself – and moved around the room as if following a set path.

An instrument like a thermometer was set into the wall opposite the barometer. A glass tube filled with water instead of mercury or alcohol stood in a channel cut into the stonework, pale sandstone blocks on both sides marked with gradations of scale in Egyptian hieroglyphics.

Louis had been to the Nile – and no further – fifty years after Napoleon. Amidst the desert sands, the river had gleamed with a natural beauty far wilder than the Thames, a beastly strength and power born in the African Highlands and rough with centuries of the desert.

In the footsteps of Giovanni Belzoni, in similar disguise, Louis had crept into the depths of the Great Pyramid to wonder at the wealth of a nation built in stone, and realised that perhaps he, alone in all the world, understood the volume of denial in that monstrous monument. Within its dry cool darkness he had felt at peace for the first time since he'd become Consort. At that point he realised he had to return to London, but he took the Nilometer with him. It took him three months to bring it back from its original position beside the Nile at Dendera.

His heartbeat skipped and quickened when he saw the reading – it was way up, almost forcing the top off the glass tube. Louis caught his breath. Only once before had the Nilometer reacted in such a way since he'd set it up here in the basement: on the morning Crown Prinz Wilhelm was born. Louis felt a sense of unease growing in his fingertips.

There was another throb in the walls that Louis knew few others noticed, although the phenomenon was well documented. He never stayed long in the Water Chamber. Even on a normal day he found himself growing dizzy after only a few minutes.

There was an orrery on a map chest at the back of the room and it vibrated slightly on its bronze wires. Louis moved over to it, clicked a button on the base of the contraption and watched the planets move, by clockwork, one day further into the future. He noted the positions of the moon and planets on an open ledger next to the machine, then turned around.

The wall behind the door was marked with a lunar calendar. Updated every year with the data of the following decade, Louis had seen it change from the 1830s to the '40s, and then so on until now, when its markings reached almost into the new century. He sighed. It was a long, long time to be Consort.

He turned to the Water Compass at last.

The bowl of the cauldron was two-thirds full of water from the whirlpool off Skagerrak which had been gathered, at great personal danger, by Edward Forbes in 1833, on his way home from explorations of the east coast of Norway. The Water Compass swung gently in the earth's gravitational field. The water on the inside rose and fell against a series of lines inscribed on the inner curve of the bowl, marking the effect of the moon on the tides. On the floor slabs beneath were inscribed the points of the compass. Salt crusted the edges of the water inside, marking the high points of its movement with the actions of the moon and the sun.

But recently he'd observed the water curled up on the lip of the cauldron against all laws of gravity, and the great hanging bowl did not swing freely on its chains but instead was strung taut out towards the east-north-east. Louis checked the angle with a plumb-bob. It confirmed what he already knew. Even the tidal surge of 1887 had failed to make such an impact.

He made notes of his observations and left the room swiftly, suppressing a shiver. The Armourer signed him out and locked the door behind him.

"I'll be in my office until lunch," Louis said, disappointed to hear his voice lie flat against the stairwell walls. "I've asked for the Raven Master to call me."

"If you need my help," said Cummins, "Just let me know."

Louis nodded, paused, then continued upstairs, leaving the Armourer to return to his office in the Members' Shooting Gallery one level down from the Hall.

Besides, keeping busy helped Louis avoid the deep pit of despair gnawing away at his insides. *If she was in London last night*, he thought often, *Where was she going?*

And a small voice wailed in reply, *Not to me, not to me, not to me.*

In the hallway of the Cuckoo Club Louis was hailed by the concierge waving another telephone apparatus in his direction. Louis lifted the earpiece out of the cradle and answered the call with his usual unhurried politeness. *Soon,* he thought, *we will be waging war on this device, nation informing nation of invasions over distant borders*. The thought filled him part of with a vague, mild disappointment.

"Beauregard speaking," he said after a pause.

The caller responded and after a short moment Louis placed the voice as Robert Napier, 1st Baron Napier of Magdala and the Constable of the Tower of London.

"Can't make it to lunch, Beauregard," was the second thing Napier said, his curt intonation instantly recognisable even over the telephone. "Busy. Sorry."

"What news of the Lady?" Louis asked.

"Apparently, there was a sighting around the West India Docks last night." Napier paused. "According to reports from my contacts in the Admiralty, and a confidential briefing I received this morning from the Dock Master in Shadwell."

"Of course," said Louis in a level tone. *West India Docks*, he thought, *that makes sense. Where was she heading? Not the*

Tower, not this time. No-one there worth the candle. Limehouse? Stepney?

"It wasn't a definite sighting," Napier went on. "No-one actually saw the – "

"No," Louis interrupted hastily. "She's very discreet."

"So we all would be," said Napier, "If we'd been hunted for years like she's been."

As Louis smiled to himself, a shiver ran through him. He couldn't separate the emotions aroused in him, lust and fear combined, desire and worship. And he'd seen the Lady at her most vulnerable, at the point where her spirit became flesh, her bones hardened to amber and her consciousness dimmed from a flame to a smoulder, embers almost dead.

She was older than he could imagine, more powerful than he could believe; yet she was fragile and delicate as a mortal woman beyond the tidal reaches of the Thames. "Where did she go?" he asked.

"North," stated the other man. "No further details, I'm afraid."

Louis paused, counted to four. In a face-to-face conversation the pause was usually longer, but people were generally reluctant to leave an invisible silence hanging in mid-air. It made them uncomfortable. Louis had mastered this part of telephony well. "That would make sense," he said at last.

"Of course," Napier replied. "Anyone who arrives on the north bank intends to head north. Doing so from the south bank would be a pointless waste of effort. Look, Beauregard, I must go now. I have a state function to organise. You WILL keep me informed, won't you? I'm sorry I can't be there. Really sorry."

"I understand," Louis said, and Napier hung up on the other end of the telephone line.

Louis stood in the hallway with his hat and gloves in his hand, mind on other things. *Head north from Shadwell*, he thought, *and that takes you to Whitechapel. Further north through Bethnal Green – and then what?* He reminded himself that the fields and scrubland he remembered from his youth were filled with houses now – *and beyond those, there is no safety.*

He rapped his fingers on the crown of his hat, the pulse of his fingers like a multiple heartbeat, hollow, gentle. *It has to be somewhere in the city, not far from tidal waters. So – up the Fleet? The Walbrook? The Tyburn stream? What other tributary is there along that stretch of the Thames?*

He raised the telephone earpiece again with the plan to contact another of the Club's Members who might have access to that information – perhaps Bazalgette's successor at the City of London Waterworks – but by the time the operator's voice interrupted his thoughts, he'd changed his mind.

"What number, sir?"

"Prussian Embassy," Louis said on a whim. *Perhaps the news from Berlin doesn't reach us as fast as it might.*

The connection was made, the call answered by a secretary, the secretary despatched to fetch the Ambassador. The man snapped a greeting down the line to Louis.

"Tell me," Louis asked in a nonchalant tone, "Where was Wilhelm last night?"

CHAPTER 7 — The Times, Clueless

Alf wandered for an hour along Wapping Street, taking detours each time he found a side street to the river, watching the little band of mudlarks diminish into the distance ahead of him. The back streets took him past all manner of businesses, their various noxious smells pervading the air, invading his nostrils, some of them glutinous odours hard to shift.

He made a nuisance of himself on Parsons Stairs and was threatened with violence by a coster along Lower East Smithfield after he'd stepped into the road without looking.

When he finally lost sight of the mudlarks, for his own amusement he walked all the way around the outside of the Tower of London, then took a cab to Jermyn Street to keep the appointment with his tailor that was the purpose of his trip to the city.

"I'm to join my father," he said as the tailor's mate silently chalked and measured him.

The man looked as if he may be one of the recent immigrants from Eastern Europe, didn't seem to speak or understand English, but he knew his trade and worked efficiently. It took less than an hour for Alf to order new shirts and the uniform for his impending stint in the Indian Army.

It was late morning by the time he found himself, more by fortune than intent, at the offices of the Times. He was surprised to find the newspaper office so quiet, even at that time of the day.

The paper had an early edition, a late one, and a City Edition which came out at six o'clock when the closing results from the Stock Market had been reported. Alf had arrived in the lax period between the early and City editions, when the journalists were next door in the bars, or out gathering news, or at the very least having luncheon with MPs and lawyers and stockbrokers.

A sleepy looking clerk glanced up from the crossword – compiling, not completing – and shambled towards the desk at the front of the room. "Yes?" He drawled rather than spoke, a boy from out of town.

"I'd like to place an advertisement," said Alf, fumbling as he spoke into his waistcoat pocket, glancing away from the clerk just as the lad opened his mouth in a wide yawn.

"What kind?"

Alf glanced up, still fumbling, then tipped the contents of the entire pocket onto the table in front of him. In amongst the pocket fluff there was a pencil stub, a few flecks of loose tobacco, his pocket watch, a small tube of Vestas and the gold coin from the woman's purse. "Lost property," said Alf and realised he'd been holding his breath. "Or rather, found." He picked up the coin and put it in the palm of his left hand and recanted the other detritus back into his pocket.

The clerk rattled off a list of prices – cost per word, box number, number of insertions, regulations – in a flat tone that suggested he'd learned it by rote. He produced a notepad and pencil from somewhere and thrust these towards Alf in his languid way. "Let me know when you've composed your message. Payment up front," he added before sauntering off back to his crossword.

Alf stood weighing the tiny gold coin in his hand, trying out suitable words for his advert. He couldn't quite bring himself to describe the item as 'lost', because he wasn't certain it was. He couldn't say it was 'found' either, because he hadn't really found it. He was also aware of his dwindling funds and reminded himself of the implication by the police constable – *Brookes, was that his name?* – in Limehouse that the coins may not belong to Alf's mystery girl at all.

"How much is it per word, again, please?" he asked and the clerk recited the fees again, box numbers included, without glancing up. Alf scribbled them down on the pad.

The door swung open behind him. A gust of air brought in a tall man in a tweed suit who swept by in a rush of pipe tobacco smoke and the clerk snapped to attention at his greeting.

Alf bent himself over his task once more and after a few minutes came up with a brief. "Antique coin, possibly Roman," – because Alf wasn't certain –"Found with others, Victoria, morning of the 23rd. Box No. ~" and he left this last blank because he hadn't rented one yet.

He straightened up and waited for a pause in the murmured conversation between the two other men before he coughed politely. He fiddled with the pencil between both hands, the coin resting like an exhibit on the paper before him.

The clerk glanced in his direction and after the briefest of glimpses the other man moved into a glass fronted office at the end of the room. "Done?" asked the clerk.

Alf nodded. "I think so."

The clerk came back to the desk, his fingers now inky from the crossword type.

Alf snatched up the coin and held it between finger and thumb, the flat face uppermost with its curious water-horse markings, while the clerk checked his message.

The lad squinted at the paper and wagged his head as he spoke each word noiselessly, counting up the fee which Alf could have told him would amount to fourpence, box number hire included for two insertions.

"Fourpence," the clerk announced. He glanced up from the paper, eyes on the coin, nodded towards it. "That's pretty. Valuable, is it?"

Alf shrugged. He was suddenly ambivalent towards advertising for the owner to come forward. He couldn't shake the image of the girl on the bridge and the expression on her face as she leapt. The thought of it still made him shiver, sent a thrill down his spine, flipped his stomach over.

His fingers curled around the coin, concealing it in his palm. He took a deep breath, thinking only of her and her death in the river, its cold water forcing open the warm lips that she'd pressed against his. His mouth went dry momentarily then he was aware that the clerk had spoken. "Pardon?"

"Fourpence," the clerk repeated in a steady voice. "Box number 437. How can we contact you?"

Alf paused and hadn't realised he had a puzzled expression on his face until the clerk tutted, rolled his eyes skywards impatiently.

"So we can let you know if anyone replies."

"Well, I'm at boarding school –" Alf began, then paused.

The clerk bent over the desk and poised the pencil above Alf's message. "You going back there today?"

Alf hesitated, then opened his mouth to reply.

Obviously the pause was just a little too long for the clerk's liking because he butted in. "Look, you need to give me an address where you can be contacted tomorrow. Now, that doesn't have to be in London," he explained as if he were talking to a child, "But it's quicker."

Alf put the coin back in his pocket, confused and lost, scratching his chin with his free hand while he racked his brains. His hand brushed against Sylvester de Winter's visiting card and he plucked it from his pocket with a gasp of inspiration. "You can contact me at the Russian Occidental Club, care of Baron Sylvester de Winter, until this evening," he said grandly. He stood up straighter, a sense of importance returning with his confidence.

The clerk never batted an eyelid. "And thereafter?"

Alf felt himself shrinking again, his attempt to impress the other lad obviously a failure. He muttered the name of his school to the clerk and fumbled a sixpence out of his trouser pocket, feeling a blush rise hotly to his cheeks. He paid the fee and hurried out of the newspaper offices into the chill sunshine of Fleet Street.

Around the corner in the Inns of Court he threaded his way through a squadron of wigged barristers until he found a discreet space against the walls of the Records Office. He shut his eyes, leaned back against the solid building, breathed deep the reeking air. Carts and carriages clattered by and he found himself yearning for Sylvester de Winter to turn up and rescue him once more.

He'd never been good with the serving classes, found it hard to talk to strangers without stumbling over his words.

There were worlds full of people, he knew, somewhere out there beyond the confines of school, but he had yet to find a way of contacting them. He envied the other boys who confidently handled – and often manhandled – the maids and housemasters, negotiated their way out of tricky situations with charm and charisma. He envied the born leaders amongst his classmates, those team captains and Head Boys and future politicians. At times like this he felt unspeakably alone.

He breathed in sharply and held it there while he opened his eyes.

A cream coloured coach, one of many vehicles on the street in that moment, caught his eye as it turned the corner from Chancery Lane. It rolled past at speed and disappeared to the east while Alf watched it go, open-mouthed, a glimpse of the occupants stuck in his mind's eye, their faces frozen in a moment of glee. He felt those churning butterflies in his stomach again, mouth dry even as he swallowed.

I need advice, he thought.

He needed advice, needed support, and his thoughts turned to the only person who'd aided him recently: Sylvester de Winter. Hadn't the man offered him lunch? The thought of food and a chance to sit down, to talk, perhaps to get the benefit of the older man's experience, was so appealing he would have taken lunch with the Devil himself.

Confused, footsore and feeling a little defeated, he stood up straight, thrust his chest out and strode off towards town and the comforting warmth of a welcome (he hoped) at Sylvester de Winter's club, the Russian Occidental.

CHAPTER 8 – The First Cuckoo Of Spring

Louis arrived at the Cuckoo Club at that time in the morning when it was too late for breakfast, and too early for lunch. He made his way to the Smoking Room and was heartened to find it busy for the time of day. He nodded in greeting to a couple of Club Members at the far end of the room, casting his eye over the empty chairs until he found the man he was looking for.

With a nod, he summoned the editor of the Times and headed upstairs to his office. He had just settled into his chair when the other man slipped into the room and closed the door at his back.

"I lost him." George Buckle behaved like a schoolboy in the headmaster's office. He gripped the chair arm with one hand and expressed his disappointment with the other as he spoke. "He was placing an advertisement and I walked right past him, on my way to the office, and overheard the end of the conversation before I closed the door. By the time I'd got out onto the street, he was gone."

Louis tried to keep his face expressionless, his mind making connections, considering possibilities like a chess Grand Master. "What was the message he left? The one for the advertisement?"

"Something about gold coins. He left a forwarding address," Buckle blustered. "Care of some Russian, at the Occidental – a Sylvester de Winter. Have you ever heard of him?"

"Sylvester de Winter? Maybe the same Sylvester de Winter who was in Paris last year when our man ended up in Pere-Lachaise?" Louis sucked at his teeth. "Not good," he added, "But interesting. Look him up for me, will you? I believe your predecessor lodged a paper on the subject in the Club Library. Might be useful to have it to hand for the Committee Meeting this afternoon."

"Right. D'you think it's the same man?"

"Perhaps. I knew a man who answered to that name, many years ago. I thought his type had disappeared."

"Apparently not."

Louis rubbed his chin, remembering a man with whom he'd disagreed, trying to recall the exact circumstances of the encounter. So he's a Russian nobleman now, is he? Louis laid his hand lightly on the top of the table between the two men. "Tell me more about the boy."

"I didn't see him," said Buckle. "It was the crossword-compiler who dealt with him."

"No matter. Tell me what you know." And Louis's pulse quickened as the other man sketched out a physical description. "How did he seem?" he interrupted. "Agitated? Concerned?"

"Naive."

Oh, dear god, Louis thought, and briefly let his eyes close. "You say the lad had a coin of some kind?"

Buckle nodded.

"And there were others? Left in the care of the police, like a well-brought-up young fellow, no doubt. Or not?"

The editor shook his head, smiled with only his lips. "Limehouse Station. He filed the report of the leaping lady there, and it was telegraphed to us before he arrived in Fleet Street." He felt some small satisfaction at having heard the news before Louis had. "They gave me his school address."

Louis raised his eyebrows in a question.

The editor told him.

"Not one of the greater schools," Louis said softly. "Do we know the family?"

The editor shook his head. "I checked with Burke's Peerage on my way over here. Nothing – not even land in Ireland."

Louis sat back in his chair, the leather crumpling as he moved, and steepled his fingers up to his lips. "On another note," he went on, "Do we know where Crown Prinz Wilhelm was last night?"

"As I understand it, the Crown Prince was in Belgravia," said the editor. "The society column reported as such in the first edition."

Louis pulled a face. "Can we verify that? I mean, within the bounds of propriety."

"Find someone who was with him? I don't see why not. How soon do you want to know?"

Louis looked at the man but said nothing.

"I'll see what I can do," said the editor with a nod. Again he felt like he'd been dragged in front of some legal authority.

"And what do we know of the Kaiser?"

This time it was the turn of the editor to purse his lips. "Is there news?" he asked, irritated that he hadn't heard.

Louis nodded. "Only found out myself this morning," he said, with a degree of good cheer which seemed inappropriate. "Ambassador telephoned me, gave me the news. Friedrich became Kaiser overnight."

"Friedrich? I thought he was dead."

Louis chuckled. "Very nearly. His doctors reckon on six months at most."

The editor racked his brains for details. "Throat cancer," he said, almost a question. "Does this complicate matters?"

Louis nodded, and relaxed until his hands rested on the tabletop, where he picked up a mechanical pencil and began to turn it over in his fingers. He seemed distracted, his gaze off in the distance, when he spoke. "I ought to ask James Frazer for his opinion," he said with a sigh, "But I think I know his reply. You know that the Hohenzollerns have been working towards this for generations?"

The editor of the Times nodded.

"Well," Louis went on, "The bloodline means that Wilhelm is in a prime position to be the next Consort of the Lady. However," he smiled, "He has yet to assassinate the current Consort. Or somehow arrange the assassination." Louis poked a hole in the blotting-pad with the tip of the mechanical pencil, and sighed. "Wilhelm will inherit the throne of Prussia, and all that entails, with its roots in the order of the Teutonic Knights, and the amber fields of the Baltic seaboard. Do you start to see the connection?"

"Not sure I do, Louis."

No, I don't suppose you do, Louis thought. "We have a limited amount of time until Friedrich succumbs to his illness. Until he does so, he remains on the throne of the Hohenzollerns, a king with a wound which will not heal." Louis tapped his throat.

George Buckle snapped his fingers. "A tracheotomy, that's right. Isn't he unable to speak?"

Louis nodded. "Unable to command. Unable to summon, either, on an astral plane, whatever he may say in church."

"Ah. But that's good, isn't it?"

Louis shook his head. "It's virtually astral castration. He's not fit for much else except dying, poor man. There but for the grace of – " He raised one finger to his lips in the universal gesture for silence, and put the mechanical pencil in his jacket pocket. "Wilhelm's inheritance is only a breath away."

The editor said nothing for a while. When he spoke, it was careful and considered. "How can I serve you?"

Louis nodded. "Look for the boy," he said, his manner grave now. "And when you find him – because I believe you will – do not let him out of your sight. I believe he may be the next Consort."

"Doesn't the current Consort have to be assassinated first?"

Louis raised his eyebrows at the other man, who seemed to have asked the question without guile. He broke into a broad grin, and winked. "Damn right."

The editor's jaw dropped. "That's, an... unusual situation to be in."

"Damn right," Louis repeated with vigour. "But where would we be if it were otherwise? I want to *live*, even at my age. I'm not done with all-night cribbage sessions, breakfast at sunrise, beautiful sonatas and sopranos. But I won't last the century out, mark my words, and I certainly won't mark the next one."

"For a man so keen on his own death, you're remarkably positive."

"I don't *want* to *die*," Louis growled, "But I *have* to be killed."

Some time after the editor of the "Times" left his office, Louis placed a call to Scotland Yard. He wanted to know about this purse full of coins, and he had the means at his disposal.

He placed another call to the Tower of London and had just rung off when his ongoing thoughts were interrupted by the appearance of Baron Ferdinand de Rothschild at the door.

"Louis!" the Baron greeted him warmly. "I came as soon as I heard. Is it true?"

"Apparently so," Louis conceded. "I'm glad you're here."

"Wouldn't miss this for the world. It's like the birth of Victoria's latest, isn't it? Have you a drink yet?"

Louis smiled fondly and shook his head. "I'm so busy right now," he apologised.

"Come on, then," said de Rothschild. "I'll stand you one at the bar."

Louis let the Baron lead him down to the Cuckoo Club bar, and accepted with gratitude the large whisky poured for him by the barman.

"To the Lady," said de Rothschild, raising his own glass in a toast.

Louis just nodded, clinked glasses with the Baron, and inhaled the oily fumes from his own tumbler.

De Rothschild drained his drink and beckoned for another. "You seem out of sorts, old man."

"Hm?"

"Out of sorts. Seems like. Got a lot on your mind?"

"As always, my dear fellow," Louis replied. He found the natural bonhomie of the other man to be a blessing at the worst of times, and could not bring himself to spoil it. *How could he understand?* thought Louis. *It's like seeing a ghost – with your own face.*

He shook his head to clear it and put his untouched drink down on the bar. "Were you out in town last night?" he asked, changing tack.

"Of course!" the Baron laughed. "Took my sister to the Opera – Covent Garden. Great performance. You'd have loved the soprano, Louis."

"Hungarian, isn't she?" Louis asked.

De Rothschild nodded. "Beautiful voice. And such poise!"

Louis tapped his pockets as if looking for his pipe, while he framed the next question. "Was Crown Prinz Wilhelm von Hohenzollern there?"

The Baron pursed his lips. "Can't say I noticed, dear chap. Is it important?"

"Might be," mused Louis, then spotted the Assistant Commissioner of the Metropolitan Police in the hallway, just arrived. "Will you excuse me?" he said to the Baron, and left the bar. "Douglas?" he called out.

Lieutenant-Colonel Douglas William Parish Labalmondière turned to face Louis, half-in and half-out of his greatcoat. "Louis," he greeted the older man. "Good. I hoped to meet with you before the Committee meeting this afternoon."

"There's news?"

"Good and bad. Can we talk in private?"

"*Certes*. Come up to my office."

Louis's office on the second floor of the building was a haven of peace. The wide window was open to the street and Louis closed it before he got down to business, waving the Assistant Commissioner into a chair.

"I don't know what you've heard," he began, settling gently into his own chair.

Labalmondière shook his head. "Not much on this subject, I'm afraid. There were disturbances on the south bank all last night – Southwark all the way to Lambeth Palace – and I've spent the morning reviewing the reports. I heard the news, though," he added hurriedly. "It was in the papers, of course."

Louis nodded. "I'm trying to gather evidence myself," he said in a wry tone.

"How can I help?"

"It's a long story, Douglas, but the basic facts are these," Louis began. "A young lad reportedly saw a woman leap off Westminster Bridge at dawn this morning. He's placed a listing in the Times which, amongst other things, refers to a purse of gold coins." Louis held his hand up to stave off the Assistant Commissioner's interruption. "I just need you to find them for me."

Labalmondière let out a long laboured breath. "Louis," he said, "That won't be easy."

"On the contrary," Louis said with a grin, "They're in the custody of one of your police stations. I don't know which one, of course," he went on, "But I'm sure it won't take much to find out." He looked at the Assistant Commissioner keenly, watching him squirm in his chair.

"Louis," Labalmondière protested, "There are rules – laws – concerning lost property."

"For Gods' sake, man," Louis snapped, "The life of the Lady may be at stake. If I'm right, those coins belong to Her – and She won't be back to claim them any time soon." He paused, and as an afterthought he added, "Or else She'll be back damn sharpish."

Labalmondière sighed. "There's something else, isn't there? Why is it so important now?"

Louis leaned forward, still unable to control his unease. "All the signs suggest that the boy will be the next Consort."

Labalmondière seemed genuinely shocked. "Really? Oh, gods, Louis, what will you do? Is it really – time?"

"I don't know. Do any of us, when it's our time?" Louis turned away from the man and stared, his eyes not quite in focus, at the bookcases lining the walls. "So," he went on, "Can you find these coins for me?" He glanced sideways at the Assistant Commissioner.

"Yes."

"I know you feel uncomfortable, Douglas," Louis said, reaching out with one hand in a gesture of sympathy. "We all do. How do you think I feel?"

"I can't put myself in your position," Labalmondière admitted. "I'll see what I can do."

At that moment the telephone on Louis's desk interrupted with a single loud ring tone, and as Louis bent to answer it the Assistant Commissioner rose from his chair and silently made his departure. Louis nodded and waved him through the door as it closed behind him.

"Yes?" he asked down the mouthpiece.

"Ah good, you're there," the voice crackled down the line.

"Who is this?"

"It's Benton," the voice replied. "Numismatics. Russell Square."

What the hell does this man want? Louis thought warily. He let the empty telephone line ask further, knowing how the silence unnerved its users.

"Buckle telephoned me," Benton went on, his words tumbling out in a breathless rush. "George Buckle? From the 'Times'?"

Louis waited while the man paused and then continued.

"I heard you had a bit of trouble with some gold coins."

"Not quite," Louis said, his mind alert now. "How can I help you?"

The numismatist chuckled. "More to the point, I believe I may be in a position to be able to help you."

"Really? How?"

There was another pause at the opposite end of the line to Louis, and then Benton's voice, a little puzzled and unsettled, said, "I'm at the British Museum." The man hesitated. "Numismatics?"

"Yes," said Louis, "You said."

"I catalogue the ancient coins."

My, my, Louis thought in appreciation. *So Buckle can work swiftly when it matters.* He smiled into the emptiness of his office and nodded. "Thank you, Mr Benton." His tone was warmer now than he had used previously with this man. "I'm grateful for your offer. Now," he went on, "As it happens, I may be able to take you up on it. I'll call you later this afternoon, if I may, when I know the details."

"Oh," Benton said on the end of the line, a little disappointment showing in his voice.

"I'm waiting for some information," Louis went on, "From another source, before I can make any plans." He spoke cautiously, still uneasy at the situation.

"Anything to help," gushed the numismatist.

Not until I find out who you really are, Louis thought, *And who you serve.*

He rung off without making further commitments, then rose from his chair and left the office, feeling in his wrist to check his pulse. It was strong, and just a little too fast.

CHAPTER 9 – Luncheon At The Russian Occidental

The clock on the building at the far end of Piccadilly was just striking the hour when Alf turned off Dover Street and came within view of the Russian Occidental Club. The desk clerk ushered him into the Smoking Room, where Sylvester de Winter greeted him warmly.

"Dear boy!" the Russian called across the crowded room, beckoning with his arm.

Alf picked his way through the tables and flustered up to the bar.

"Have a brandy, dear chap!" de Winter said, slapping him on the shoulder while shaking his hand. He turned to the barman and snapped his fingers, pointed to his own glass and ordered another.

"Thank you, sir," stammered Alf, and felt himself blush.

"Think nothing of it," Sylvester de Winter said with a smile. "How are you? Are you well? Everything dealt with in its own way?"

"Yes, sir," said Alf, taking hold of the large glass of liquor which Sylvester de Winter thrust into his hand. "Thank you," he said, for want of anything else. Drinks before lunch were not part of his usual routine. *The boys back at school will die of envy when I tell them*, he thought, but what he really wanted was a glass of water. He sipped at the drink like he wasn't thirsty and hoped there would be water with luncheon.

"Excuse me for one moment," said de Winter, his finger raised in front of his lips, and left Alf at the bar while he greeted another man who had just entered.

Alf glanced around him, holding the brandy glass in both hands like an amulet. The Russian Occidental was a plush place, the furnishings ornate and as exotic as the clientèle. Around him, conversations in Russian were interspersed with French and the sort of English used by his tutors at school. Alf took another tiny sip of the brandy and began to relax.

His social interaction at home was limited. The maiden aunt who looked after him during school holidays never dined – she ate whatever her thin cook prepared, and took it alone in her rooms. Alf did likewise until last summer, when he was old enough to frequent the local taverns, rough houses filled with labourers working on the suburban railways that had begun to snake out through the Surrey countryside past Esher and beyond. He took meals there in private rooms away from the men and women of the tap room. His aunt would not approve had she heard of him mingling with the lower classes.

He found himself with the same degree of awkwardness when visiting friends – once he was old enough to dine with the adults, he felt he lacked the sophistication to endure the port and cigars with the menfolk after the dishes were cleared away. He was always relieved when the time came to rejoin the women, perhaps because he lacked the company of the female elsewhere in his life. He still missed his late mother, was embarrassed to admit it, and found his embarrassment shameful.

There was a deeply hidden level of need, of course, a sense of something to be discovered – the late awakenings of desire that led some men to explore continents or produce masterpieces and others to simply sire dynasties. The sort of men he saw as he glanced around the Smoking Room of the Russian Occidental, their grooming impeccable, their confidence unassailable and daunting.

Alf was more sensitive to soothing words, soft hands, praise or kindness from the fairer sex; mysterious creatures of which he knew so little. And of course he was aware of their baser nature, but he'd never dealt with it – no older sisters to pinch and slap and tease him – but nor were there any comely servant-girls to succumb; not even a fat cook to slip him the occasional pie hot from the oven. His life – or at least the womenfolk therein – seemed, to him, to be a parade of Mr Dickens' more severe characters.

He touched the brandy glass to his lips again, tilted it until the liquid scorched the tip of his tongue, held the sensation in his mouth. It wasn't that he didn't want to experience all the pleasures the world had to offer. The problem was always finding a way to do so, within the bounds of his monthly allowance. He suddenly realised that Sylvester de Winter had spoken to him.

"Pardon, sir?"

"Would you like a cigar?" Sylvester de Winter waved a still-gloved hand towards an open box on the bar, then nodded. "Please forgive me," he continued, "I forgot – you don't indulge, do you?"

Alf shook his head. "No, sir." The smell of the things always made him think of high meat – game that had been hung for too long. He found it hard not to gag at the odour. Even the remnants on someone's clothing – or worse, breath – was enough to wrinkle his nose. Nonetheless he smiled at Sylvester de Winter, noting that the man was smoking yet another of his perfumed Turkish cigarettes. It was almost as if the man couldn't breathe without them.

"So," Sylvester de Winter went on, putting his arm on, rather than around, Alf's shoulders in a paternalistic manner, or at least would have been but for the discrepancy of height between the two men. "Have you tracked down your mystery girl?" The man's eyes twinkled.

Alf shook his head and took a good swig of the brandy. The caramel fumes blazed in his sinuses and he had to pause before he replied. "No," he said, "But I'm working on it."

"Good man!" Sylvester de Winter exclaimed, patting Alf on the shoulder before he dropped his hand and reached for his own tumbler of brandy. With a casual wave of his cigarette hand he asked, "In what way, exactly?"

Alf explained his visit to the "Times" that morning, leaving out the conversation with the mudlarks. "I hope you don't think it forward of me," he went on, and paused as doubt and embarrassment took over.

Sylvester de Winter caught his eye and spoke warmly, in a voice as soft as snowfall. "What is it, dear boy?"

"I – I hope you don't mind, sir," Alf stammered, gripping the brandy glass too hard with both hands, "But I gave them this address as a contact – under your patronage."

Sylvester de Winter's expression was keen, but not harsh, and when he spoke again it was a gentle murmur almost to himself. "Splendid," he breathed. He took a deep draught of his cigarette and shrugged his shoulders back as he exhaled. He seemed then to awake from some kind of torpor – his bearing straightened and his voice became strong. "Splendid! An excellent course of action, dear boy! No better than I could have hoped for myself. And, of course, if you give me your address at Eton I can forward messages on to you. Yes, yes," he muttered, "Simply splendid."

From somewhere deep in the club a hand-bell rang out, and Sylvester de Winter raised his eyes from his glass in its direction. He turned back to Alf with a hungry grin on his face. "Ready for luncheon?"

Alf nodded vigorously and grinned back.

Lunch began with Sylvester de Winter singing the praises of London over the entrées. "It's so much more vibrant than St Petersburg or Vienna with their stuffy procedures, rigid class roles and endless soirées," he explained. "How much better the system in London, where one can meet a man at his club. Leave the tiresome balls and musical evenings to the womenfolk and those nobles hoping to marry off their offspring. Men of commerce, men of state, need another sort of meeting place. In Paris," he snorted, "It's all brothels!" He roared with laughter.

Alf noticed how some of the other diners looked over to their table, and glanced away nervously. He was embarrassed but didn't want to show it, his restricted upbringing like a blot on his character.

"Just think," de Winter went on, chortling, "How difficult it can be when you catch a diplomat with his favourite cocotte, to take him to one side for an intimate chat! Impossible!" He chuckled again, the apples of his cheeks rosy above the rim of the wineglass he raised to his lips.

Alf felt the heat of a blush prickling at his collar again, uncomfortable with the subject of the conversation and with no experience of his own to add. He chewed slowly and felt his ears burning with shame. When he glanced up again, as the pause in the conversation grew longer and the hubbub of the room murmured on in the background, he found Sylvester de Winter's eyes twinkling at him over the empty plates.

The Russian remained silent and sat back in his chair while the waiter replenished their wine glasses and cleared the table. When he resumed the conversation, he changed the subject to commerce.

"Steel, dear boy. It's the way ahead." He wagged a finger in Alf's direction. "Not iron. Steel is the thing. The Bessemer process –" and he was off, an enthusiastic tour of the German's new steel smelting process that brought the promise of cheap steel to the industrialised world. He painted a broad-brush landscape of trade, raw materials from around the Baltic being funnelled into Russia to feed the burgeoning factories of Muscovy and the Volga. "They need iron, the Russians, and steel too," he went on as the main course was served, "They need to build railways to open up the vast peasant lands east of the Urals, to link up with Peking and Shanghai and Vladivostok."

"Just think of the journey, dear boy," de Winter continued, "The Russian ambassador at Kyoto returns home the long way round, a journey unthought of in the times of your Raleigh or Drake. He sails across the Pacific to San Francisco, then rides that magnificent railroad across America to New York and takes a boat to Hamburg. Thence, it's rail all the way to the court of the tsar in St Petersburg. And do you know why?"

Alf shook his head.

"Because it takes less time than the overland route through Siberia." The Russian barely paused for breath. "Have you ever been to Siberia?"

The rhetorical question was not meant for Alf to answer. De Winter barely paused to acknowledge Alf's shaken head denial.

"It's vast, boy," the Russian said, his voice hoarse with reverence. "Vast. So cold, so huge, so unknown. Its ancient forests and rivers, and so few people – just reindeer herders and Ugriks. And the ice," he wheezed, "Ice like we never see in Western Europe. Six feet down in summer and the earth itself is frozen, still solid. Huge cracks in the soil like the entrance to some frozen hell. And the мамонт! They dig mammoths out from the ice, their bellies still full of grass! The meat still so fresh you can eat it, even after so many years!"

Alf toyed with the remaining beef stroganoff on his plate, a faint distaste developing in his mouth. He forked the last of the peas into his mouth and sat back in his chair.

Sylvester de Winter leaned closer across the table. His breath was so still it barely seemed to stir the air between them. "They say there are still living ones out there somewhere," de Winter went on, his eyes distant. "Perhaps roaming the steppe or the tundra, hiding from humans because they can. And if they have mammut – and they do, even if only the frozen ones, what else –" his voice broke – "What else might be there, under the ice? What ancient creatures may still stalk the forest, frightening the peasants like the monsters they are?"

Alf at last felt he could say at least something. His bored scouring of the daily newspapers in the college library was not wasted, although he hadn't anticipated this kind of setting for the conversation. "Are you referring to the Abominable Snowman of Tibet, sir?"

Sylvester de Winter flicked his eyes onto Alf. His voice was soft and spoke of conspiracy, of mystery and adventure. "Similar kinds of creature exist," he breathed, and briefly glanced away, then locked his gaze on Alf again. "No, I'm referring to something much older, much more – elemental, you might say. Creatures like the one you saw this morning."

Alf felt the pit of his stomach drop like a gallows trapdoor. A sweat of panic pricked out on his palms. He wiped his hands on his trouser knees, mouth dry. "What do you mean exactly, sir?" he asked, irritated to hear a tremolo in his voice when he had tried so hard to make it bold. He hadn't spoken a word of this to Sylvester de Winter, of the flash of silver and the waving arm, and he felt open, raw, vulnerable, as if the other man could read thoughts Alf couldn't bid away. He grabbed the wineglass and took a deep gulp to sluice his throat.

At that point a waiter appeared with a message. Sylvester de Winter dabbed his lips with the linen napkin, dropped it on his plate and left the table with a polite nod.

Alf sat staring at his empty plate, bemused and startled. Since this morning his world had become a little less secure. He ran through what he would say when the Russian returned to the table. He resented the implication in Sylvester de Winter's parting words. *I may be seventeen*, Alf thought, *But I'm hardly fanciful, am I?*

His hands begin to tremble again, resting limp in his lap. He took another gulp of wine to rinse the dryness out of his mouth, felt the tannic bite purge him drier. A wave of laughter rolled over the room from a far corner and it made him self-conscious, sat there on his own, out of his depth in a world that wasn't yet his. He grew irritated as well.

He felt like this for some time, even when the plates were cleared away and his wine glass was refilled. He sipped at it again, the cherry blackness warming him, stilling the tremble in his hands, settling the ripples of uncertainty, before Sylvester de Winter returned with a brisk flourish of cigarette smoke and an intaglio of fresh air, chill as if he'd been outside.

"Sorry about that, dear boy," said de Winter, waving the cigarette hand towards the door behind Alf in a dismissive gesture. "Matters of state," he growled in a stage whisper. "Now, where were we?"

"Frozen mammoths, sir," Alf said in a level voice, a weather eye on his host's reaction.

"Ah yes!" The Russian clapped his hands together and rubbed them briskly as if wringing the life out of some small slippery creature. "Mammut. And the rest." He rested his gaze on Alf, the eyes keen and hot.

"You did mention other creatures, my Lord," said Alf, the wine emboldening him beyond his usual manner. "What might they be?"

Sylvester de Winter removed his elbows from the table and leaned back away from Alf, his pearl-white lower teeth flashing as he spoke. "You tell me, boy. You saw her this morning; you were closer than I. What did you see?"

Alf took a deep breath, tired of repeating the same old story, but as he opened his mouth to begin Sylvester de

Winter suddenly leant forward over the table and interrupted him.

"I don't want the story you gave the police. That's commonplace." He waved his cigarette hand again and fixed Alf with a fierce gaze. "What did you see when she hit the water?"

"N-nothing, sir," Alf stammered, shocked that Sylvester de Winter should get so close to the question he'd been asking himself all morning. Maybe it was the wine making him a little fuzzy, or maybe he'd just had enough, but part of him wanted to share what he'd seen even though another part of him was scared to reveal it in case he wasn't believed, in case he was mocked.

Sylvester de Winter didn't let Alf's hesitation ruin the moment. "If not at that point," he hissed, "Then later – not much later, for sure, it wasn't much before sunrise. What was it?" His voice softened, his eyes' fire drew low, he relaxed his hands into a cradle on the table in front of him.

Alf felt an overwhelming urge to unburden himself of the nagging doubt he'd had all day. "I – I don't know how to explain it," he said. His palms itched again, his heartbeat thudding in his ears.

Sylvester de Winter leaned closer, attentive and caring, his voice soft and his breath cool. "Just do your best," he soothed. "I will believe you. You needn't fear me."

Alf's shoulders were tense and he realised he'd been holding his breath again. "She went into the water," he began, and then it came out in a rush that explained in a thousand words the flash of silver, the waving arm, his confusion and the feeling that she was waiting for him.

Sylvester de Winter nodded throughout, a look of caring concern on his face, and when Alf had finished he left a long pause in the conversation, his cigarette hand up close to his lips, the smoke curling up past his half-closed eyes.

Alf noticed how the room around them suddenly seemed empty, and glanced around to see that all the other diners had left or had fallen silent. The waiting staff were moving amongst the tables like wraiths, removing cloths and cutlery, and Alf heard pans clattering in the kitchen somewhere. From across the room came the low murmur of a conversation; behind the oak doors that led to the bar came another outburst of that lusty laughter which had already made him cringe. A clock ticked, loud, slow, and he counted his heartbeat against it.

Sylvester de Winter spoke at last in a gentle voice that barely stirred the cigarette smoke.

"I believe you."

Alf's hands began to shake again, and this time his wine glass was empty. Sylvester de Winter's gentle acceptance of this unnatural event released a flood of his emotions and Alf struggled to maintain a stiff upper lip. *This has been driving me mad all morning*, he thought while his breath trembled, *and the man believes me. How can that be?* He wasn't sure whether he was relieved or even more confused than before.

Sylvester de Winter snapped his fingers and gestured to someone over Alf's shoulder and a few moments later the barman brought over two large glasses of brandy.

Alf swallowed half of his at a gulp and cradled the glass balloon in his unsteady hands. He couldn't look at Sylvester de Winter, just stared at the carpet, his own mud-spattered shoes, the fringed velvet coverlet on the table. The room was so quiet he could hear his own breath whistling in and out of his nostrils and he tried to contain the flutter in his stomach stirred up by the strong spirit.

The older man remained silent.

Noises filtered into the building from outside. Familiar sounds that seemed odd to Alf, out of place with how he felt. He heard – very loudly – the sounds of Sylvester de Winter lighting yet another cigarette: the rustle of fabric on skin and metal as the Russian took the cigarette-case out of his pocket, the snap as it opened, the scratch of the vesta match, the pintuck of his lips on the end.

"What is she – it?" Alf asked in the end.

Sylvester de Winter leaned in and put the used vesta in the ashtray. "She's a goddess."

Alf jerked upright and stared in astonishment. "H – how?"

"Oh, she's very special, dear boy. The last we have in this part of the world." Sylvester de Winter smiled and sat back in his chair, removed the cigarette from his mouth and held it between the second and third fingers of his right hand, close to the knuckle.

And Alf sat carelessly fascinated as Sylvester de Winter described an Ice Age in northern Europe so severe that it froze all the rivers but one.

"A super-river, that flowed out into the Atlantic through the English Channel," explained the Russian, "It combined the waters of the Seine, the Thames and the Rhine all together. Why do you think the English have been at war with the French for so long?," he added, a smirk on his lips. "And the Germans with each other?"

"For her?" Alf asked, incredulous.

De Winter nodded.

"But why?"

De Winter smiled at him. "Wouldn't you want a goddess on your side? Think, boy!" he hissed, leaning forward again, shaking the ash off the cigarette with his violent movement. "You've only seen her in human form – only seen her in peril. Remember your Bible stories! Children found on the banks of some great river who grow up to become leaders of men! Wasn't Moses one? And Gilgamesh?"

Alf nodded. He was growing uneasy again, his stomach churning.

"Not just fairy stories, tales for children!" Sylvester de Winter's eyes gleamed. "Those men were born of creatures like her. Think on that!"

Alf felt the brandy fumes from his half-empty glass fizz in his nose. "So there are more of them?"

"Not here," mused Sylvester de Winter, grave now, waving his cigarette hand in the air. "Yes, in India, in Africa, in the Americas. But not in Europe – north of the Alps."

"Why?"

"The Ice Age, dear boy. Those it didn't kill were warped, made monsters. All our heroes killed them off. Siegfried – he fell in love with her, and slew the others to protect her. Do you recall the story of Beowulf and Grendel's mother?"

Alf shuddered. The story had given him nightmares at the age of ten.

"Her bones are amber. She's as old as the lizards they pick out of rocks." Sylvester de Winter leaned forward. "And she's as much of a monster."

Alf bristled at this. He couldn't bear to hear her described that way, and he shook his head in anger. "I don't believe you."

Sylvester de Winter's voice dropped again, low and sibilant. "Then how do you explain it? The river doesn't treat its guests so well, dear boy. Once they're over the threshold, so to speak, they disappear completely." He paused, sucked at his damp cigarette. "She waved to you, boy. She came up for air and she waved to you."

"No!" Alf cried. "It was a trick of the light! It was far off! I didn't see it properly!"

Sylvester de Winter breathed. "I did."

The statement hung in the air while Alf blustered out all the sensible explanations that had gone through his mind that morning. His hands cut through the layers of cigarette smoke drifting across the table as he grew agitated, and when his arguments dried up he fought to keep his face from twisting in anguish at his own confusion. "What's happening to me?" he whispered.

"I've seen her before, dear boy," de Winter said as the barman approached the table. The Russian ordered another brandy and dismissed the man. "Accept it as fact. She is a creature of the past, a thing of habit. She has taken a shine to you – of that I have no doubt. How can I convince you that you will see her again?"

Alf shook his head, fighting back tears as the alcohol lowered his reserve, hating how the conversation had turned out. "I don't want her to be a goddess," he blurted. *I want her to be an ordinary woman, warm and soft and free of the fear in her eyes.* Somehow, now, he couldn't bring himself to say this out loud.

The barman brought the brandy, set it in front of Alf. He picked it up to keep his hands steady but didn't drink.

After another long silence Sylvester de Winter stubbed out his cigarette and rose form the table. "I must go now, dear boy. There are other matters I must attend to, matters of business, and as they say, time and tide wait for no man."

He straightened the amber cufflinks on his shirt-cuffs and patted his pockets in a routine once-over.

Alf stared at the table, seeing all this out of the corner of his melancholy eye.

"You may continue to enjoy my hospitality, here, for as long as you wish," Sylvester de Winter went on as the cloakroom attendant arrived with his coat, hat and gloves. "Make yourself at ease here. I don't expect I shall be back until much later this evening, but perhaps you would join me for a late supper. Good day." He doffed his hat in Alf's direction, gave him a fatherly pat on the shoulder, and left.

Some short time after this, Alf noticed the brandy glass warm in his hands, still full. He didn't want to drink any more. It seemed to have made him all flushed and queasy. The fumes were stinging his eyes. He set the glass down on the table and stood up, taking care to steady himself on the arms of the chair. His legs felt weak and he breathed in deeply, the odours of the room striking him anew and seeming stale.

I need time to think about this, he thought. *Fresh air, too*. He wasn't due back at school until that evening, had a note from his housemaster to prove it in his jacket pocket. He patted it for comfort and then remembered the coin in his waistcoat.

With a rush of joy that brought a hidden smile to his lips, he slipped his hand into his pocket and felt the curve of the coin as it lay flat and warm against his ribs. *Westminster Bridge*, he thought with a lilt of sadness that tugged at him. He straightened his back and left the bar.

On his way out of the Club he stopped at the front desk. "May I use the telephone?"

CHAPTER 10 — The Cuckoo Club Awakens

Lunch was never going to be the most relaxing event of the day. The Club Dining Room buzzed with rumour. Louis heard the hubbub in his office, even with the door closed. He stood at his window with the sash down and watched a bird building a nest in the cherry tree outside, pulling twigs together into a platform that would defy storms and sunshine, in order to woo a female and secure the future. He felt a lot like the bird.

He waited until lunch was almost over before he left his office. He slipped into the Dining Room and made his way to the table where the Committee Members sat while a hush rippled through the other diners. When he sat down, whispering murmured round the room. He smiled to himself.

"Will you address the whole club?" asked the Chairman. "We've answered the summons, Louis. It seems only fair."

Louis unfolded his napkin. "Why not?" he said, his voice light. "We may need as much help as we can muster, soon."

"Tonight?" asked the Secretary.

"I don't know yet. Perhaps." Louis glanced at the men around the table and nodded in greeting to the Commander of the City of London Police, the Lord Chamberlain and the head of the Royal Naval College at Greenwich. The other

Committee Members held less auspicious positions outside the Club, amongst them James Frazer the linguist, Sir Henry Farnham Burke and the Marquess of Camden.

"Once the Members have been briefed, I'll call a Committee meeting," said the Chairman. "If we need to act, we'll need to make plans."

"Some of us have work to attend to," said the Lord Chamberlain with a grumble. "Those Irish riff-raff protesting outside the House need sorting out. Charles?" he went on, and turned to the Commander with a discussion that took over the table's conversation for some while.

Louis listened without taking an interest and ate without tasting a bite. The instruments in the Water Chamber ticked at him like a metronome, three floors below, as he began to realise the nature of the problem.

"Gentlemen, your attention, please!" The Chairman called the Cuckoo Club to order as the serving-staff cleared away the luncheon dishes. He banged a gavel on the top table and waited until the conversation died down. Coffee and cigars circulated.

The curtains were drawn over the window to the Club's interior courtyard to shut off the weak spring sunshine. Louis nodded to the Porter who locked the door to the bar. When the last of the serving-dishes were cleared away, the serving-staff departed to the kitchens and Louis had the concierge lock that door as well. The room was sealed, and further curtains drawn over the doors for complete privacy.

The Chairman thanked the Club Members for their attendance and handed the floor to Louis.

Louis stood up and glanced around the room. He counted more than a dozen MPs and members of the

Cabinet; Admiral Hood, the First Sea Lord was there, sharing a table with the Duke of Westminster and the novelist Wilkie Collins. Bishops and Law Lords mingled with City bankers from all sizes of bank; merchants and shipbuilders and ironmasters. And all round the room he knew similar questions had been discussed since the letter had appeared in the Times that morning.

"Gentlemen," he began in a grave tone, "We are privileged. Our patron was in London last night."

The Club Members murmured, the tone tinged with excitement and a sense of duty that was not without apprehension.

"Sighted entering the city from the east, via the Shadwell Basin, so I'm told. Then headed north through Whitechapel and out towards Spitalfields. This was before midnight, just as the tide was running in." He paused and looked down at his thumbs resting on the rostrum then glanced up again. "The next sighting was at Victoria, in the hour before sunrise."

"And nothing in between?"

Louis shook his head. "As far as I'm aware, no. If anyone else has any news...?" He left the question hanging over his audience.

They replied with silence.

After a long pause, Louis cleared his throat. "There is a possibility that –" He found his voice faltering, his words muddled for the first time in an age. He coughed into his clenched fist and spoke. "There may have been direct contact."

A gasp ran round the room.

"Who was it?" The question came from the floor.

Louis didn't see who asked. It didn't matter much. He felt his palms grow moist as he drew breath to deliver the answer he dreaded. "Not one of us."

"One of the Princes?" asked a man sat close to the front of the room, a man Louis did not recognise.

Louis shook his head and sat down again, one hand over his mouth while he signalled for another member of the Committee to take over the conversation. His throat was tight, his mouth dry, a concern he had not felt in years gripping him. In his ears the pounding of his heartbeat thudded out all traces of the silence in the room.

The Chairman rescued him. "At the moment, all we have is conjecture. If I might ask my honourable friend, Mr Buckle, to continue?"

George Buckle, the editor of the Times, looked surprised as he rose to his feet and glanced around the room. "A young man reported the disappearance of a woman this morning, at around six o'clock, by suicide." He paused, fumbled with his handkerchief as if addressing the Club was flustering him, and stared at the floor. "Apparently she leapt into the Thames."

"I'd heard that," said Robert, Lord Camden, sat at the Committee's table behind Buckle. "The verger at Westminster told me. Spotted her running across Parliament Square as he was going to work." He shook his head. "Sad business."

The room erupted quietly, the men muttering oaths or expressions of disbelief.

"Thank you," Buckle said to Lord Camden, "I understand the police reports have yet to come in to my newsroom. I'll keep you informed –" he turned to Louis and the Committee – "When I know further details." He resumed his seat in the audience as if he were glad to be obscured again.

Louis sipped at a glass of water to loosen his throat. He was disappointed, as he had been since he awoke that morning, but he was growing angry. *This won't do*, he thought. *There has to be more.*

The Chairman brought order to the meeting once again. "The fact is, our patron may be in some danger."

There was an ashen silence in the room. Louis felt the tension in the air, like a tide rising. The gentlemen of the Cuckoo Club were waiting.

Admiral Hood, the First Sea Lord, broke the spell. "Well, Beauregard," he asked in a measured tone, "What are we to do?"

The Cuckoo Club members, to a man, turned their eyes to Louis. He felt the old thrill course through his blood, the rush of heady adrenaline required for action. He took a sip of water from the glass in front of him before he spoke. "We must be vigilant," he said, his voice firm and even. "There are signs that the Russian Secret Service are on the lookout, and our actions – the letter in the Times this morning – will have alerted them, and many others, to the news that something unusual is afoot."

"And the French?" asked another member of the audience. "Are we working with them, or not, at the moment? I can't keep up."

His offhand comment caused a ripple of laughter in the tight room and dispelled some of the tension, but Louis didn't even break into a smile.

"I think we can assume that we have no allies in this matter," the Chairman said. "There is much at stake. Crown Prinz Wilhelm von Hohenzollern is in London, so I understand, and may be the object of our patron's attention."

Louis interrupted. "Gentlemen," he said, "Your assistance may be required, at some length, in the near future. It's barely a week before the equinox. Unusual tides have been observed for the last few days. I thank our colleagues at the Royal Observatory –" he nodded in the direction of a bespectacled man off to his left, the Astronomer Royal, William Christie – "for this information. London is awash with unruly mobs of hooligans whose only goal is destruction, and they can be bought by any faction for a pittance. Our patron is not aware of such activities, and needs protection. In order to plan for such actions, I need information."

"Why not issue a summons? To here, or somewhere else?" asked the man in the front row.

"I've got room on my estate," said another, farther back in the room.

Louis shook his head with a grim smile. "Impossible, gentlemen, but I thank you for your offers. No," he went on, drawing himself up to his full height with an intake of breath, "It may be too early for such efforts. Without information, we may be simply adding to the agitation already palpable throughout the city. Keep a lookout for anything out of the ordinary, any odd gossip in the courts, any strange transactions in the Stock Exchange. I'd be grateful for any information over the next twenty-four hours – the next tide – if you would be so kind as to notify any of the Committee Members as soon as you are aware."

It may yet be too early, he thought, but gnawing away at him was the notion that it might already be too late.

"That's all?" asked the Astronomer Royal. "Isn't there anything more we can do?"

"That's enough," said Louis in a terse tone, and sat down.

The Chairman rose to his feet to continue. "The Committee will decide what course of action we need to take when the time comes. There's an extraordinary meeting after this lunchtime session closes, gentlemen, and if we make any decisions that require your further assistance, telegrams will be despatched to each of you personally, as per the club Code of Practice."

After a handful of further questions, all of which the Chairman fielded without assistance, Louis signalled the Porter to unlock the doors and was the first to leave the Dining Room. He was relieved to find the air in the hallway much fresher and his footsteps found new vigour as he climbed the stairs to his office.

The window was still open, the cherry tree outside still tight-budded. Louis poured himself a glass of water from the pitcher on his desk and downed it in one draught. He heard the Club Members depart, their footsteps echoing up the stairwell and through the open door of his office, their farewells filled with muddled ideas and bonhomie. He drank another glass of water and waited for the Committee Members to arrive.

"So, gentlemen, do you think the Lady will return to London tonight?" Louis asked the four Committee Members gathered in his office.

Someone coughed. The Club Secretary spoke up. "You're the man to know, Louis, if any of us are. Why?"

Louis fiddled with a bit of food between his teeth with his tongue. "She has left behind something she values, something personal."

"What?" asked the Chairman. "The purse? The coins?"

Louis shook his head, and his next words tore at his heart. "More valuable than me."

"Louis?"

"The past, gentlemen, is past. The future is what matters."

"We have traditions –" said the Treasurer in a cautious manner.

"To build on!" Louis interrupted, "Never to lose, but as a foundation for what is to come!"

"Is there something you're not telling us, Louis?" asked the Marquess of Camden.

Louis swallowed hard. "She's found a new Consort."

There was a general quiet within the room as the Committee Members absorbed this. Louis glanced around him.

"Is that why the Russians are involved?"

Louis nodded, almost to himself. "There is a Russian at the Occidental who has made some sort of contact with the youth who reported the coins in the Lost & Found. George Buckle advised me this morning. I don't know the details."

"Wilhelm's in London," said the Chairman.

Louis frowned. "Yes," he said abruptly. "Somewhere. I think She was trying to find him, last night."

"What makes you say that?" asked Lord Camden.

"Remember," said Louis softly, "The world moves so much slower for her. The advances of the past hundred years, the Renaissance, the Reformation – all these things that form the basis of society today – these are just so much scenery to her, passing like the seasons do to us. And they pass faster with each year, as we grow old. More to do and less time in which to achieve it." He leaned back in his chair and withdrew a small map from a desk drawer. "We can see how She thinks by following Her route from the river last night."

While he unfolded the map across his desk, he explained his reasoning, pointing at the locations he described. "Up from the Shadwell Basin, which lies on the site of the old Roman port, She takes the road north, along the route away from Houndsditch and the Saxon fortress of the City that extends out from Tower Bridge. By the time She's out at Spitalfields, She's at the edge of medieval London."

He leaned forward on the table in front of him, using it like a lectern. "She's trying to skirt round us, and each year we eat further into the countryside. She can only go so far from the river until She weakens. There will come a time when She can't escape the city – when we've built over all the fields even out beyond Islington. Where will She go then? Will London lose Her?"

He let the question hang in the air for a moment as he gathered his argument. "She is in greater danger now, at this moment," he went on. "Who knows what kind of creature this Sylvester de Winter is, and what he intends with Her?

The Committee Members were silent and Louis put his hand up to rub at the bridge of his nose. He was frustrated at the lack of information he had at his disposal, and he realised how precarious his future was. It wasn't a new feeling. It still caught him off guard.

The Treasurer spoke. "Friedrich's as good as dead and we all know it. It can't be long before Wilhelm becomes Kaiser. It's a breath away. That must be why She's here."

"And, perhaps," Louis said with an air of resignation but delight too, "Perhaps She will look for the boy." He drew a sharp intake of breath. "I just don't know."

The world would shake, he thought, *if it knew what secrets are shared by these men. Or the plans we authorise. And what if they knew more? What of our members who explore foreign rivers, distant mountains, ancient cities? If the world knew what desire spurs them on, THEN where would we be?*

"Sylvester de Winter doesn't care if She survives, and perhaps it would fit his purposes better if She were not to." He paused. "I think She will return tonight."

"You think he's hunting Her, here, in London?" The question came from Lord Camden.

Louis smiled but there was no mirth involved, and his voice when it came out was strong and cold, with an edge to it like the wind off the North Sea. "I think so. What's the biggest game you've felled, gentlemen?" His voice rose with emotion until it dominated the small room. "What's the greatest trophy that hangs on your walls? None can match Her!"

"Do you think he'll kill her?"

Louis breathed deep, trying to control his feelings. "Kill or capture," he replied in a softer voice, controlling his feelings. "Either will do, I think."

"How?" asked the Treasurer. "She's –"

Louis silenced the man with a raised hand. "Don't say it, man. You know the rules." He sniffed in a deep breath to fortify himself against the words that came next. "In human form She's vulnerable. She can be captured as easily as an ordinary woman."

"What do the others want with her?"

Louis sighed. "Look it up in the Club History," he said in a weary tone. "Napoleon marched on Moscow *after* the Nile campaign. Moscow was never his objective. He wanted St Petersburg." His voice dwindled to a whisper. "Catherine's Winter Palace."

"Why?"

Louis put his head in his hands. He found it hard to put his thoughts into words, not because the words did not come but because they disgusted him.

"The Amber Room," said the Treasurer. "He wanted the Amber Room."

"It's what they all want," Louis sighed. His stomach twisted with unease.

There was a murmuring of assent, rumbling round the room like a rolling drumbeat.

"Imagine Her trapped in the Amber Room," Louis went on, fighting his own rising distress. "The horror of it for Her, the last survivor of Her kind, so delicate in spite of Her great age. In the Amber Room She can return to Her natural form and still be within his control."

"But what does he want Her for?" asked Lord Camden.

Louis sighed. *What does any of us want her for?* he thought. *What do we want with any of her kind?* Even though it turned his stomach, it had to be said. "He might breed from her."

This time the silence that descended on the room was absolute, and Louis felt revulsion swell in his chest like a tight knot. He felt as though he could read their thoughts, those others gathered before him, a mixture of fury and fascination that turned the air crisp as a November dawn. He counted in shallow breaths how long it took to break this icy silence.

One, and the crispness hardened.

Two, and it thawed.

Three, and then the sudden snap.

"Breed from her? How?"

"The usual way, man. When She's in human form, She's human." Louis looked the Treasurer straight in the eye, daring him to press his questioning beyond the bounds of discretion. *Don't make me share her secrets with you*, he thought angrily.

James Frazer, sitting next to the man, nudged him and whispered something in his ear. The man's eyes widen, then he nodded.

"She controls Wilhelm," came a voice in a cultured accent. "She's hung on his crippled arm since he was born. Whoever controls Her also has a stake in controlling him. Although I don't think Wilhelm realises it."

"No," said Louis, "Not yet. But he's still young and impetuous."

"He's older than you were, Louis."

Louis nodded. "Yes, I know. But I wasn't hers from birth." He closed his eyes and refrained from adding any more.

The Committee meeting dispersed like pack ice breaking up in spring. Louis felt old, tired and defeated. He sat at the desk for a while as the room emptied, feeling the pull of the river on him, the mechanisms of the Water Chamber shadowing his mind. Since his accident – since he'd been with her – he felt the tides roll up the Thames each day, and he knew it was at its apogee, and all afternoon there would be a lull as the waters turned.

She came to him by chance, at a point when his youth was turning him into a man. The youngest member of the crew in the annual boat race, when his boat capsized he'd been swept away. And she rescued him, plain and simple.

It was four days before he surfaced again in Oxford – upstream of Eton by forty miles – and he had never told any living soul about what had happened during that time. His family had given him up for dead; but not the aged members of the Cuckoo Club. The news that a beautiful boy had been lost, drowned, in the Isis had set them running then too. And from the moment he'd reappeared his path was strewn with roses.

He'd known it would happen sooner or later, this new youth for her affections. He tried to put himself in her position, trying to imagine what it was like to see brief beauty wither across the centuries, to lose lovers almost as soon as one had met them. He could see how it made sense, for she seemed not to age, not by human standards. And the boys she chose were always blond, blue-eyed, muscular and shortish – all the way back to Siegfried and who knows who beyond.

He had a wound more personal and unhealing than his mortality: the pain of knowing she could never be his, despite a love undying, unquenched. And no, he'd never married. Somehow all other lights seemed dim in the presence of her lamp, all other bloodlines thin.

CHAPTER 11 – A Bullet On Westminster Bridge

Louis hardly noticed the ringing of the telephone in the hallway of the Cuckoo Club. He was deep in conversation with the Treasurer over an unrelated matter and the other man was holding forth on his own views. Around them the members of the Club mingled as they took their leave in a noisy hubbub. Louis felt old, tired, his energy drained more by circumstance than by the conversation.

It was the Treasurer who directed his attention to the concierge, behind him, and when he turned he found the man holding the telephone receiver out towards him.

Damned contraption, he thought, not for the first time. "Yes, who is this?" he asked into the mouthpiece, and recognised in a word the distinctive voice on the other end of the line.

"He's made contact." It was George Buckle, the editor of the 'Times'.

"Who?" asked Louis. "Our mystery boy?"

"That's the one." Buckle sounded breathless with excitement.

"Did you speak to him?"

There was a pause and Louis imagined the man moving his head in either denial or agreement.

"No," Buckle replied. "He spoke to the clerk. He asked to change his advertisement – he no longer wants the Russian's address on it."

"Well that's a relief," said Louis. "What prompted this, d'you think?"

"How should I know?"

Right, thought Louis, *All right*. He paused, and let the silence be his interrogator.

"Perhaps there's been a falling-out, or maybe some indiscretion." Buckle had a salacious note in his voice.

"Whatever the cause," Louis said, "It's a relief. The further the distance between Sylvester de Winter and the Lady, the more pleased I am."

"There's been a report of mob violence in Limehouse, just come in from one of the local reporters," Buckle went on. "Sounds as if a gang of Poles tried to break into the police station. I thought it might be of interest."

Damn right, thought Louis, but he said nothing.

"So what happens now?"

For gods' sakes, man, how am I meant to know? thought Louis in irritation. "We wait, I guess," he said. "We arm ourselves, and wait. Until the tide turns, there's no point in action. Nothing will move us further towards or away from the Lady. Just do what you would do at this time of day, on a normal day. We can't expect anything before dusk."

"Well, thank goodness for that, eh?" Buckle expressed his relief. "Shall I run the advert?"

Louis rolled his eyes, glad that the other man could not see him, and shook his head in disbelief. "Why not?" he said lightly. "See who it flushes out, eh?"

"Right," said Buckle, although he didn't sound certain, and rung off.

Louis handed the telephone back to the concierge and wiped his fingers on his handkerchief. *What would I do?* he thought, nodding acknowledgment to those remaining Club members departing the hall. *If I knew nothing – or very little – of these things, would I be content to go home, alone, unsatisfied? Or* – and here he couldn't help grinning to himself – *or would I mope around like a lovestruck teenager hoping to catch another glimpse of her?*

He slapped his gloves into his open hands and drew a sharp intake of breath, his grin spreading. He began to head off down the corridor to the bar.

"Louis!"

He glanced round and saw the man who hailed him prepared to leave the Club in the company of a short man in a tweed suit.

"Camden," he greeted the taller man, and turned to the other. "And Viscount Smedley. Back from the country, I see?"

Smedley nodded in a polite way, using words sparingly as was his habit.

"We're returning to the House," Lord Camden continued, forcing his hands into his gloves so vigorously the leather squeaked. "Care for a ride?"

Louis paused for a brief moment, then shook his head. "I'm going home," he said. *The alternative is to sit around here all day,* he thought, *like some fossilised clam.*

"Right," said Lord Camden, smacking his gloved hands together with gusto.

At that moment the telephone rang behind the concierge's desk, and Louis debated whether to wait until it was answered – just in case it was for him – then shook his head in irritation. *Can't be a slave to the damned device*, he thought, and led the other two out of the Club door into the weak afternoon sunshine of Mayfair.

Lord Camden and Viscount Smedley were disembarking from their carriage in Parliament Square when a shot rang out. Smedley flinched and glanced around sharply. Camden barely noticed.

A group of protesters, carrying placards advocating Home Rule for Ireland, blocked the entrance to the Square and were being corralled by a cohort of police on horseback and a phalanx of constables who seemed more intent on conversing with each other than with policing the crowd.

"What was that?" Camden asked.

"Small-bore rifle," Smedley replied in a casual, droll voice.

"In Parliament Square?" Camden asked. He glanced around, nervous, at the surrounding buildings. *Could have come from anywhere.*

The Irish crowd began to move towards them, the voices within it raised in protest, most of them nervous. Not as nervous as the police, however; those on horseback made a half-hearted effort to contain the crowd broadside.

"They won't kick off here, will they?"

"Not this lot," Smedley sneered.

Lord Camden nodded in agreement. "Usual bunch of ruffians, I see. Have a few shouting matches with the police, cheer a few slogans, but in general they don't cause a fuss." He raised his head to gaze over the top of the crowd, a good six inches taller than most of them. "There's more here than normal, mind you."

"Bound to be a few troublemakers, then," Smedley sniped. "Looks like you'll have trouble getting into the House, Camden."

"Not a problem. If we go round the Embankment Gardens, we can use the entrance in Whitehall. It's only a few minutes on foot."

Lord Camden sighed. *Get on*, he told himself. *Exercise does you good.*

As the pair left the square, Camden turned to look back at the crowd. *Something's in the air*, he thought. *Everyone's on edge – including me*. He hurried back to his companion as they turned the corner into the Embankment Gardens, a broad grassy strip bordered with flowerbeds that lay between the Houses of Parliament and the Embankment proper, bounded by iron railings as tall as a guardsman.

"I'll stand you a snifter in the Long Bar for your efforts," said Lord Camden as they strolled vigorously across the grass in defiance of the edict against it.

"Not if they can help it," Smedley said, pointing to a small crowd on the north side of Westminster Bridge. The group, no more than twenty strong, was agitated and while one or two were waving their arms in the direction of Parliament Square, the majority were gathered round the figure of a youth leaning against the parapet of the bridge, his blond hair a golden halo in the sunshine.

Something in Camden's memory twisted. His palms broke out in a sweat and he felt his pulse quicken. "That's our boy," he said quietly under his breath, shaking his head in disbelief, then the youth slipped under the ledge of the parapet beyond sight, the crowd surged forwards to hide him and he repeated it with more force – "That's him!"

"What?"

"Go on," urged Lord Camden, "Get up there post haste. That's our boy!"

Behind him a muffled cheer echoed from Parliament Square, followed by the cacophony of a policeman's rattle, whistles and catcalls rising above the clatter of hoofbeats on the cobbles. He turned to see elements of the crowd – men, a few with black handkerchiefs tied over their faces – running along the street towards the bridge.

Smedley stared at Camden as if he were deranged. Then he tore his cap off his head, pushed Lord Camden aside and took off at a sprint. "Come on!" he cried, breaking into a run as he crossed the street and headed up onto the bridge.

He reached the little crowd ahead of them and the group parted as if in shame to let him through, then bunched around him in a knot. Camden pulled up, a stitch at his side making him gasp for breath. "Go on, man! Quickly!" he said to himself between breaths.

He followed at a slow plodding pace, the stitch pulling at him so fiercely it felt like more than just a muscle strain. He glanced to his right and realised he was out over the water, beyond the first pier of the bridge.

When he finally reached the crowd of bystanders, Smedley was remonstrating with a police constable over the need to tend to the wounded man.

"Wounded?" Camden asked with a sigh of relief.

A man on the edge of the crowd nodded.

So he isn't dead, yet, Camden nodded in acknowledgment. "What this man needs is a doctor," he said to interrupt Smedley and the police constable. "One of you hail a cab please?" he asked of the crowd. "This man needs urgent medical care."

One of the bystanders, a stout fellow in an out-of-town suit, began to do as he asked, as Smedley and the constable began to argue again.

Smedley straightened up from tending the youth on the pavement. "Being on the bridge exposes him – all of us – to the risk of further gunshots," he said in a flat voice. His right hand was smeared with the boy's blood, but his expression was unflustered.

The constable turned with a look on his face that told Camden all he needed to know. The man was young, barely older than the victim, and alarm glowed in his pale eyes. "Call for assistance," the Marquess told him in a tone of calm authority.

The PC hesitated then blew three sharp blasts on his whistle. It silenced the small crowd around them for a moment, then their conversation resumed, voices lowered.

"I'll need to take witness statements, sir," said the PC in a trembling voice as Camden knelt beside the young man.

The Marquess glanced up and nodded. "Of course," he said, running his experienced eye over the shooting victim, noting the bloodstain spreading across the crisp white shirt, the lad's sharp gasps of breath, his unfocused eyes reflecting a state of deep shock. He laid a hand on the boy's head, feeling damp sweat beneath the blond locks, the youth resisting the urge to struggle. "Rest easy, boy," he said in a soft voice, as if he were soothing a favourite hound. He stood up and turned back to the others.

"Smedley?" he asked.

The stocky man nodded in acknowledgment.

"What's your opinion?"

"Definitely a bullet wound," said Smedley. "Like I said, probably a small-bore rifle, if it's connected to the shot we heard earlier."

Camden nodded and gave a non-committal grunt. On the north bank of the river a group of the Irish protesters had broken away from the rest of the crowd, evaded the police on horseback and were tearing up the flowerbeds in the Embankment Gardens while the cries and whistles of the main body of protest drifted over the river, lost in the open air above the water.

A second PC joined the first and the pair spoke to each other in rapid London staccato, one explaining and the other nodding. Camden saw a hansom cab wheel round across the body of the bridge from the opposite side, heard it stop nearby, saw the hooves and wheel rims at the kerb between the parting crowd. Their mood was still curious, but the Marquess knew it would not take much for it to change to outrage. They had to act quickly. He nodded to the others that he was ready to depart.

"Help me here," he said to Smedley and between them they hoisted the whimpering youth to his feet.

"Good lad," said the Marquess as they led him to the kerb. "Let's get you into the cab, shall we?"

"No!" the young man shouted and began to struggle, grimacing with the effort.

"Look, man," said Camden in exasperation, "It wasn't us who shot you, and whoever did it may be taking aim again! We need to get off the bridge! It's too exposed for this kind of nonsense!"

The young man glanced around wild-eyed and then slumped through the open door onto the floor of the cab. Camden caught Smedley's eye. He couldn't be certain but he realised the sportsman may have had a hand in the lad's collapse. Smedley bustled around the youth, folding him into the body of the cab while Lord Camden withdrew a calling-card from his wallet. He gave it to the young constable in front of the other policeman who seemed to be equally taken aback by events.

"I'll take care of this young man for now," said the Marquess. "Please contact me –" he tapped the card with his fingernail "– at either of these addresses."

The PC glanced from the card to Camden and back again as the Marquess tipped his hat and joined the others in the cab, arranging himself with care around the injured youth on the floor.

The cab wheeled round in the street and rocked on its springs, raising a groan from the young man, then began the usual jig-and-clatter as it rumbled over the cobbles, off the bridge onto Embankment, south around Parliament Square. Camden breathed a sigh of relief as the carriage began to thread its way through the back streets of Whitehall towards Mayfair, away from the river. He sat back in the seat and stared at the ceiling, breathing hard.

"Are you sure this is him?" interrupted Smedley, his eyebrows raised in query as he indicated the youth with a cocked thumb.

Lord Camden glanced at the boy, his thoughts elsewhere, into a face he almost recognised. "It's him," he whispered, nodding, as the cab picked up speed along the broader streets beyond Westminster. He forced himself to stare out of the window all the way to Louis Beauregard's home.

Louis felt uneasy. He was struck most of all by how fragile the boy looked. His pale face was covered in a sheen of sweat, his eyes glazed. Louis had seen that look before, on the faces of men and animals, and to see it on this boy alarmed him.

The wait for the doctor seemed to take an age, during which time they managed to strip the young man to the waist, laying him on thick folded towels on the polished parquet floor of the lounge. Dodman stoked up the fire and brought brandy, which Alf refused.

"Had enough of that already," he wheezed. He winced as the butler poured iodine and water onto the wound to clean it.

In spite of the young man's protests, Louis gently lifted the boy's jacket away from his side. The white shirt beneath was saturated with blood. The boy had one hand across his eyes, grimace with pain evident. His other hand gripped his waistcoat pocket tightly, the knuckles white. Louis guessed there must be something in there worth hanging on to.

"Let's move you to the couch, shall we?" Louis suggested, but they barely got the ashen youth to his knees before he passed out. Dodman and Lord Camden finished the manoevre and the Marquess bent over the lad to rearrange him for comfort before examining the wound.

"We must save him," Louis murmured.

"Hm?" Lord Camden glanced up from applying a basic field dressing on the boy's shoulder.

"We have to save his life," Louis said, more force in his voice this time, but already he felt a great gnawing dilemma. *How many men have this opportunity?* he thought. He folded his arms tightly across his chest as if to keep his heart silent. He began to pace the carpet. Each time he turned towards the boy on the sofa, his breath came out in a short gasp.

"Louis?" Lord Camden watched him with a look of reproach. "Are you all right?"

Louis nodded, a purely automatic reaction, before he had time to think of his reply. When it came, it was, "No."

"Are you injured?" Camden rose from the settee, his face full of concern.

"No, no," Louis said with a dismissive wave of one hand. "Just – don't leave me alone with him."

"Louis?"

"Just – don't."

Lord Camden reached out a friendly hand and gripped Louis's shoulder. "My dear old friend," he said calmly, "You're troubled by this."

"Damn right I am," Louis snapped, turning away. His heart was racing. "Where is that doctor?"

"You're sure this lad's the one?"

Louis shook his head. "No doubts about that, I'm afraid." He sighed. "And that makes him a rival."

"Ye gods," said Lord Camden, raising one hand to his mouth as the situation dawned on him. "You won't –"

"I don't yet know what I'd do." Louis glanced at Camden, then at the boy on the settee, then back to his friend. He folded his arms again and paced over to the wide bay window, where he stood staring out into the street, saying nothing as he watched the sparse traffic.

After a short while an ordinary hansom cab drew up at the kerb and Louis watched as two passengers disembarked, one with a black leather bag, the other Smedley who tipped the cabbie and turned towards the steps at the front of the house. "Thank goodness," he said over his shoulder. "Here's the surgeon now."

He stood firm in the bay of the window while behind him he heard Lord Camden move to the door, and the boy's laboured breathing caught at him. *I need time to think.*

The doorbell rang deep within the confines of the house and within the space of a few heartbeats, a handful of footsteps, Louis heard the front door open and Dr Ponsonby greeted his manservant. Dodman's voice, muffled by the closed parlour door, gave what sounded like instructions, and then Louis heard Smedley's boots on the staircase up to the bathroom and knew he had gone to wash the lad's blood off his hands.

Is this my opportunity? he thought, disturbed by uncertainty. *The boy is weak, already injured – easier for me as I am now to kill him.* He raised his head and stared at the sky above the rooftops of the houses opposite. *But I want him to live*, he thought in despair. *For the good of the Club, for the sake of the Lady.*

The doctor came into the room and while Louis heard him discussing the situation with Lord Camden, he made no move to greet Ponsonby further than a brief grunt. Louis was in deep debate with himself, and wished he knew someone to whom he could seek for advice.

"He has to live," he said out loud before he realised it was said. He put one hand up to cover his mouth, unsure if he would speak his thoughts out loud again. Behind him the doctor snapped his bag open and there was a creaking of settee springs as some weight was shifted.

Louis turned and, without glancing at the scene before him, stepped towards the door. He paused before he left the room and said, "Make him well. He's no use to us like this."

Then, with his head down, he strode from the parlour into his study.

It was another hour before the doctor was rinsing his hands off in a basin laid on the study desk, the wound cauterised and stitched and bandaged. The patient was sleeping under anaesthetic.

"I'm no expert," Dr Ponsonby began, "But it looks like a Russian bullet." He had the thing in a tin food dish and rolled it back and forward as he spoke and peered at it. "The pattern of damage it caused is intriguing. I've never seen anything quite like it."

"He was with Sylvester de Winter for lunch, so I'm told," said Louis. "The Russian's visiting card was in his pockets."

"What was he doing with *that* creature?"

"De Winter was chasing the Lady last night, apparently. Almost caught Her, in fact, when this young blood ran into Her by mistake."

The doctor grunted. "He's a difficult character," he said. "I don't trust him one inch."

"You know him?" Louis asked. "Well?"

The doctor shook his head. "I have dealings with him, on occasion. Hospital business." He dried his hands on a thin towel. "I warn you, Louis, the man has the morals of a body snatcher."

I know, thought Louis. "I assumed the name was a false one," he said. "There are too many coincidences – Sylvester is the German for New Year; de Winter is a common pseudonym in France. And as for the Count of Utsire!" He snorted. "What foolishness!"

The doctor picked at the bullet in the bowl with a pair of tweezers, a frown concentrating his face into scrutiny.

"Louis," he said, "I think you're up against someone who is playing an altogether more sinister game."

Louis felt his scalp prickle. "What?"

"Look," the doctor said, holding a fragment of the smashed bullet in the tweezers, turning it against the light on the study desk to illuminate its peculiarities. "This isn't brass. I dug enough of those out of men in the Crimea. This is something else entirely."

Louis shrugged, patience never his strong point. He held out his hand for the object, and Ponsonby laid it in his palm.

A pain he'd felt before coursed up his arm and tightened his chest like the iron bands that had woken him that morning. The air shimmered. He felt the blood drain from his face and a breathlessness crushed his throat. His knees buckled. He clutched the edge of the desk, dropping the bullet, an icy shock flooding his veins. The air in the study smelled dry, crisp, void.

"Dear God, man!" he gasped. "You could have warned me!"

The doctor helped him into a chair and waited until he breathed again. "I'm sorry," he said, shaking his head.

"Did you see where it went?"

The doctor nodded and while he scrabbled around under the desk, Louis rang for his butler to order a glass of water. When the doctor flourished the salvaged bullet, Louis winced. "Keep that away from me," he said, his voice weak.

"I didn't think," the doctor said, as shaken as his patient. He replaced the bullet in the tin dish and examined it further. "It's silver, I'll wager. And it's not solid. There's some gel – or resin – inside."

Louis nodded. Dread grasped his throat. "It was meant to mark him," he croaked. "The silver is only to contain the body of the thing. If there was no outer casing, or if it split when it was fired, the velocity would have melted the core, and that would have failed to penetrate our boy."

"You've seen this before? What is it?"

"It's amber."

"Damn!" The doctor shook his head in disbelief and poked the thing with the tweezers. "Why would someone try to mark him?"

"Goddammit, man! She'd never come near him, not even recognise him – perhaps even cause him harm." Louis struggled to sit up and leaned forwards, his heart hammering but thankfully still his. A chill ran through him as he inspected the bullet. "Have you any idea whether there may be some of it still in him?"

"Impossible to say without further examination. But it's always a possibility."

Louis heard his heart pounding. Maybe the other side didn't mean to kill the new Consort – just mask him, but keep him always in waiting, forever hidden, like a card up the sleeve of a trickster. What would happen then? If Louis should die of old age, would the Lady be weakened? He needed to know. He made a mental note to summon the Club Member within the British Library and set him to research in the club archives.

"Well," said the doctor after a long pause, during which he watched Louis drink the glass of water without distress, "There's nothing more I can do here, for the moment, if you're well."

Louis nodded, and swallowed.

"Your lad should come out of the anaesthetic in a few hours, feel a bit sick but not otherwise be harmed. Give him this if you want him to sleep," he said, lifting a bottle of pills out of his bag. "Two, every six hours. The only drawback is that he has to be awake to take them." Ponsonby snapped the clasp of his bag shut. "Keep him warm and stop him from moving around too much for a couple of days."

Louis nodded again, although he was unsure how he was going to achieve this, and his concentration was elsewhere.

"If there's any deterioration in his condition –"

"Don't worry, I'll call you," Louis said tersely. "I'm not taking any chances with this one."

"Will She return for him tonight?"

Louis paused, his mind still racing ahead of the conversation. "I think so," he said. "How soon until the anaesthetic wears off?"

"A couple of hours, at most," replied the doctor, glancing at his fob watch. "Does it matter if he's awake?"

Louis frowned. "I don't know," he admitted. "I was unconscious when she came to me."

"But you were in the water then, weren't you?"

Louis nodded, remembering that far-off afternoon the day his life changed forever. They'd found a bruise the size of an oyster on the back of his skull where an oar had hit him after he went overboard.

The doctor glanced at his watch again. "I have to go now," he said. "The hospital pays my wages, not the Club."

Yes, thought Louis as he waved the man out of the room, *but the Club summons you, and you come.*

When the doctor left, taking Lord Camden and Smedley with him, Louis got his butler to transfer the bullet to a small ivory box which he slipped into his pocket before he returned to the parlour and sat contemplating the sleeping youth. The contents of Alf's pockets sat on an occasional table beside him and Louis parsed through them with a mechanical pencil, not touching anything, pausing to glance up at the sleeping form beside him.

However he tried, he couldn't suppress a nervous flutter in his abdomen. He itched for action. Itched to get back at the man who'd done this. Itched for the turn of the tide that would bring the Rhinemaiden back to London, to him. He burned with curiosity about Alf, wanting to know more about him, aware that the boy's safety relied on his anonymity.

Aware, also, that the boy had to kill him, somehow, sometime soon, for the natural course of events to occur.

Amongst the lad's possessions on the occasional table was a small gold coin of indeterminate age which sat amongst a handful of loose change and a sovereign. It seemed to warm the room, and Louis reached out with a tentative fingertip to touch its ridged surface. The scent of birch pollen and honey washed over him. He shuddered, joy and not agony; he was still linked to the Lady.

The silence of the house oppressed him. Nothing would happen, nothing would change, while the tide remained full, at its lax period, waiting for the moon to pass round the other side of the planet and begin to pull the river out to sea again. Louis listened to the clocks of the house ticking a fraction of a second apart. The coals in the fire ruffled a flame from a pocket of gas; embers settled in the grate; Alf breathed, deep, measured, regular.

The sudden clarion of the telephone rang out in the hallway. Louis glanced at Alf, who slept on. He heard the butler answer the phone and waited for the man to find him.

"It's the Club, sir," said Dodman. "The Armourer has important news."

Louis left the house without a word. In truth, he'd always preferred action to thinking. And a voice in his heart whispered, sang, chorused: *She loves me, She loves me not.*

CHAPTER 12 — The Hanged Man and The Telegram

Louis ended up at the Cuckoo Club once more. While he was sure no-one there would understand his dilemma, he could at least lock himself in his office until his mind quietened down.

No such luck. The concierge greeted him with a note of two telephone messages and a telegram for his attention. One was marked "Police of The Metropolis" and the other, "The Times, Fleet Street". Louis called the Assistant Commissioner first.

"Louis," Labalmondière greeted him with caution. "I've found the coins."

"Coins?" For a moment, Louis was lost, then his memory returned. "Ah, yes, the coins. Great news. Where are they?"

"Limehouse," said Labalmondière. "I'm about to send one of my men to collect them."

"Hold on," Louis said. "I've a better idea. Give me five minutes, will you?" He rung off without ceremony and placed a call to the British Museum. "Benton, please – Numismatics."

"I'm afraid we don't have a telephone in that department, sir," the telephone clerk informed him. "I'll have to send a message."

"All right," Louis replied. "Please let him know that Louis Beauregard called, and would like to speak to him." He gave the clerk his number at the Club and rang off.

The other phone message was from George Buckle, at the Times. *He can wait*, thought Louis as he unfolded the telegram.

It was an official missive from the Prussian Embassy, and Louis realised as he read it that it had been sent to a number of recipients, by the tone of the announcement. It was brief and to the point:

KAISER WILHELM DEAD COMMA 09 MARCH 1888 STOP KAISER FRIEDRICH INFORMED STOP STATE FUNERAL TO BE ARRANGED STOP ALL SUMMONS HOME STOP

Louis folded up the telegram and put it in the top pocket of his jacket. *Now I really* do *need to sit down*, he thought, and headed upstairs to his office, where he lowered the window and sat with his door open, listening to the sparrows in the treetops outside.

He was not alone for long. The Club Secretary joined him with tea and a gentle line of questioning about paperwork and the Club accounts, which Louis was disinclined to occupy himself with at that point.

Louis took the telegram out of his jacket pocket and tossed it onto the blotting-pad on his desk. "Martens," he addressed the younger man, "You might as well read that."

While the Secretary unfolded the message and skimmed over it, moving his lips while he read, Louis poured himself a cup of team and sat watching him.

"What happens now?" Martens asked, glancing up as if he'd been caught red-handed in some act of sin.

Louis leaned back in his chair and steepled his fingers over his chest. "I don't know," he admitted. "We have to wait. For a start, it's high tide."

"Right now?"

"Yes," Louis said. "For about an hour, nothing moves."

"I meant –"

"I know," Louis interrupted. "And I told you, I don't have an answer. At my age, a man takes each day as he is granted it." He could see that Martens was lost for words. The man's ambition was not a threat to Louis's position as Consort – he had not the courage to challenge anyone, a fact evident from his record. Nonetheless Louis felt the Club Secretary's scrutiny, saw his eyes searching across the lines Louis knew to be mapped on his face. "You young chaps seem to think we old ones are all used up," he provoked.

"No, no–"

"Certainly you do – I know I did when I was your age. But the world has changed since then." *And not always for the better, nor for the worse*, he added to himself. "The past, is past. The future is what matters."

"We have traditions –" the Secretary said with a shake of his head.

"To build on! Never to lose, but onward!" Louis heard something in the man's voice which irritated him and he was losing patience. "Martens, you're a clever man, and a good Secretary," he sighed. "Don't get out of your depth."

For a moment the Club Secretary looked as if he were about to explode, but he stifled whatever his instinctive response was and spoke in a quiet voice that shook with emotion. "How does a man tell? I mean, whether he can handle a situation?" Behind his plain spectacles, his eyes were bright.

Oh, you poor fool, thought Louis. *Your ambition's burning a hole in your common sense.* He sighed. "I don't think we do," he began, then paused. "Trial, perhaps?" The suggestion seemed incomplete. "When I was a young man," he went on in a cautious tone, "I was reckless – with my own safety, and that of others. I survived. I have never seriously asked whether I am personally charmed, or whether I merely seem so in the eyes of other men."

"You can't tell?" There was a hint of fascination in the other's voice, some sickly obsession, a perversion, like a man who'd read too many penny dreadfuls.

"No," Louis shook his head with a wry smile. "Look," he went on, "If a man meets his challengers, and beats them, he becomes greater in the eyes of his fellow men. Now, some chaps see that as a challenge in itself. Do you remember your Julius Caesar? *Commentarii de Bello Gallico?*"

"Caesar's commentaries on the war in Gaul?" said Martens. "Of course."

"Take that example, then. Caesar praised the Gaulish leader, Vercingetorix, as a great warrior at the head of a mighty army – and remember, the Gauls had sacked Rome barely a century earlier. Many men remembered the history, and trembled before the reputation of the Gauls."

"Julius didn't."

Louis shook his head. "Julius beat Vercingetorix and his mighty army, if you recall. In the eyes of the Senate, who then was the greater warrior? And who had the mightier army?"

The Club Secretary nodded vigorously. "I understand, but what good does that do? Is there something you're not telling us?"

"I have been Consort for over sixty years," Louis said. "In all that time, I have had to defend my right to that status by defeating any challengers."

He could see that the younger man was impressed, but again there was that gleam of immorality in the man's eyes.

"I killed them, Martens. All of them. That's why the Club has scholarships at the better schools, and the Widows' Fund, that you are so keen to rationalise into the Club's general investments. Oh, I know about that," Louis went on, waving the man's objections away with one hand as if they were inconsequential. "You'd have to change the Club constitution, by the way, to get your hands on those accounts."

"How many men have you killed?" Martens voice was a greasy whisper.

"More to the point, Martens, how many have I not killed, because they never had the courage to challenge me in the first place?"

Martens stared at him and shook his head, uncomprehending.

"There seemed to come a point where my reputation was unbounded," Louis went on, wistful as he recalled that time of his life. "Perhaps I have survived so long because I am charmed. But perhaps, as I said, I merely seem so in the eyes of other men. And I cannot tell which it is."

The Club Secretary gulped at the cup of tea in his hands, although it had long since cooled.

"Well," Louis went on, feeling his spirits rise, "We may be about to find out."

"Wh – what?" The teacup clattered against the saucer as Martens hurriedly placed it back on the tray on Louis's desk.

"The Lady has chosen a new Consort. The old Consort –" Louis indicated himself with a hand gesture and a shrug – "Is not yet dead. There must be a reckoning, and soon. Kaiser Friedrich –" Louis nodded towards the telegram, still resting on the edge of the blotting-pad where the Secretary had placed it – "Friedrich's interregnum may be short. I must act quickly. Whatever the outcome."

Louis's thoughts went back to the weak boy lying pale on the settee in his parlour in Mayfair, comparing the unknown youth with the man in front of him. The Club Secretary was a bureaucrat who found time to work for the Club almost full-time while holding down a junior position at the Admiralty. There was nothing of note in his record in either employment. *And the boy?* Louis thought. *He's an unknown quantity.*

"I hope he has courage," Louis said absentmindedly.

"Who?"

"My successor as Consort." Louis looked in the other man's eyes and saw a greed there that he recognised from so many others. *Ah, Martens, you don't have it in you.* Louis smiled at the thought. "The Club needs a man with courage, more so than bravery. And he needs to be in tune with the modern age – it's no use replacing me with anyone over the age of thirty."

The Club Secretary's face betrayed his disappointment at this pronouncement, which he recovered well. "And what if the Consort the Lady has chosen is unsuitable?"

Louis watched the man's greed wane and be replaced by politics. "By then, Martens," he said with a cold smile, "I will no longer be in a position to care."

The telephone rang on the desk and Louis let it ring out, knowing that the sound echoed out of the open door and along the hallway to the offices of the other Committee Members. One of them would respond. The Club Secretary grew agitated as each shrill alarum broke the silence.

"Why don't you answer it?" he snapped after the fifth ring.

Louis shrugged. "Why don't you?"

The Club Secretary's nostrils flared and he stood up in one smooth movement to grab the earpiece from the apparatus and knocked it over in his haste. The papers he had placed on Louis's desk went flying, scattered across the floor, and in the time it took him to recover the documents and file them in order, Louis leaned over the table and answered the call.

Benton, from the British Museum, was on the other end of the line. "Mr Beauregard?" he said, breathless. "I got your message. What can I do for you?"

"Meet me at the corner of Russell Square and Montague Place in ten minutes," Louis instructed. "Bring one of those cases you chaps use for carrying bullion."

"It might take me a while to find one," said Benton, the disappointment in his voice undisguised even over the wire.

Louis glanced at his pocket-watch. "Make it half an hour, then," he said into the mouthpiece, and hung up. He pushed himself out of his chair and faced the Club Secretary over the desk. "I have to go," he said, and ushered Martens to the door. "I have a prior engagement."

"More important than these matters?" The Club Secretary brandished the dishevelled documents like a laurel wreath.

Louis nodded. "Yes," he said in a calm voice that held such tones of command the younger man stepped back from him. "Whatever they are, they can wait."

The Club Secretary snorted in exasperation, turned on his heel and strode off down the corridor towards his own office. Louis smiled to himself, satisfied, and locked his office door behind him, shaking his head as he set off down the stairs to the hallway.

Louis knew the tide was on the turn, simply from the feel of the air. *Nothing moves*, he recalled, *nothing flows. Like the Hanged Man in a pack of cards, we rest in limbo between one state and another.*

He descended one flight of stairs from the hallway to the first level of the Club cellar, where the shooting gallery ran the entire width of the building and out under the little garden courtyard at the back. "Cummins?"

"Right here, sir."

"You will, I presume, have heard the news?"

"Yes, Mr Beauregard." The Armourer stood under a single electric light bulb in a kiosk behind the door, a workbench loaded with tools at his side and the bare stone wall at his back. In his hands he held a pistol's mechanical parts and a rag. The pistol's velvet-lined case lay open on the bench, its ornate grips detached for cleaning, its components stacked with care in the case lid.

"Whose are those?" Louis asked with a nod of appreciation towards the firearms.

"These belong to Mr Frazer," said the Armourer. "He asked me to clean them this morning."

"Been used recently?"

Cummins shook his head. "Not for over a year, sir," he replied. "They'll be ready by teatime, though."

Louis paused, sniffing the air. The shooting gallery was used rarely nowadays but the smell of gunpowder still clung to the soft panelling of the walls. "Good," he said, his thoughts elsewhere. The room's trophy cabinet caught his eye and he glanced over the silverware without avarice, noting those where his name was engraved on their little plaques, when he had last been troubled to compete for them.

The Armourer's uniform jacket hung on a hook on the back of the door, its buttons polished, its medal ribbons fresh. His heavy walking-stick – more a crutch than a crook – was propped in a corner.

"Will you be wanting your own pistols tonight, Mr Beauregard?"

"Hm?" Louis, distracted, turned towards the man and shook his head. "No, not tonight, Cummins. I don't think I'll need them."

The Armourer puffed a short breath of air through one of the apertures he had been cleaning with a pipe-cleaner, and peered at the gap before laying the piece down on the workbench. He glanced at Louis, then towards the cabinet behind him where a thick register rested behind glass, a wide ribbon keeping the page. "Would you be wanting to see the log book, then, sir?"

Louis nodded. "Have we enough guns?"

"Well, sir," the Armourer said as he cleared a space on the workbench, "I reckon we could do with another dozen or so pistols or small arms. Although a couple of Maxims wouldn't go amiss."

Louis chuckled. "I know what you'd *like*, Cummins, but I can't just lay my hands on things like that. Plus," he dropped his voice to a throaty whisper, "Some of the members aren't as accurate with a pistol as you – or I – would like. I don't care for the idea of half of them running through London armed to the teeth – even if they *were* with Garibaldi in their youth."

The armourer grinned. "Right you are, Mr Beauregard. I can give you ten, maybe, and I'll leave it to you to choose who handles them."

The Armourer opened a drawer, removed a set of iron keys on a ring that spanned his palm, and fetched the Club Almanac from the trophy cabinet.

"I'll just make a few notes," Louis said and flipped the heavy book open. "If you have any recommendations, I'll be glad to hear them."

The Armourer went back to cleaning the pistols on the workbench, slotting one of the firearms together again with a regular click-click which was loud in Louis' ear, like a stopwatch telling off time, muffled down to an insect's tick in the padded chamber.

"Can you be ready to brief the Committee this evening, Cummins?" Louis asked as he copied the names of the Club's sharpest shooters into his notebook.

"Right you are, sir." The Armourer slid the restored pistol into its place in the velvet-lined case and wiped his hands on the rag before turning to the remaining firearm on the bench. "Which set of maps?"

"The Cromwell," Louis said without looking up.

"With the parishes of the East End? Or without?"

Louis straightened his back, taking care not to strain himself, and sighed as he thought about his response. *She was seen at St Katherine's Dock last night, before Westminster*, he reminded himself. "Might as well," he said. "We have enough manpower to cover them all, don't you think?"

The Armourer pursed his lips. "It's maybe a bit thin on the ground, sir. The Cromwell Maps are larger than the others."

"I know," Louis said. "I never got round to creating my own set. Shame," he said, and took a deep breath. "Never mind. Too late now to worry about that."

The Armourer regarded Louis with a look of concern on his face. "How far up river do you intend to keep watch?"

"Don't worry, Cummins," Louis said with a smile. "I've got the Parliamentary Shooting Club on guard all the way to Lambeth Palace."

The Armourer tutted under his breath with a faint smile. "As you wish," he said, and there was a hint of gentle mockery in his voice.

"Can you contact the Tower for me?"

The Armourer nodded and continued to clean the second of the pair of pistols. "Constable owes me a favour anyway," he said, his smile broadening.

Louis raised his eyebrows, then shook his head. "I won't ask," he said, amused, and folded his notebook closed over the list of names.

"All done, sir?"

"I wish it were, Cummins. I really do."

"Come on, sir," said the Armourer cheerfully. "Whatever happens tonight, make a fight of it. Them bastard Russians are owed one after what they did to our boys at Balaclava."

Louis was surprised. "Were you there?"

Cummins shook his head. "Not me, sir – my brother." His mouth was set in a thin line that showed no emotion, but his eyes shone as if there were a story to tell behind that simple statement, while he continued to clean the pistol with extra attention. "If you need an extra gun, I'm your man."

Louis's guffaw of laughter was smothered flat by the soft-panelled walls of the shooting-gallery. "Come off it, man," he grinned, "You've only got one leg!"

The armourer grinned back. "Yessir, but it ain't my legs I shoot with."

Louis chuckled and slipped his notebook back into his pocket. "I don't know what to expect tonight, Cummins," he said, more sombre now. "It might be nothing, or it might be a bloodbath. I'm hoping for a quiet night."

The Armourer looked him straight in the eye and smiled with eyes of steel. "I'd talk to the Raven Master before you choose, sir."

Benton was waiting for him at the arranged spot and when Louis's hansom crunched to a halt on the cobbles, the numismatist pushed a flat tray with a glass top and a significant padlock device onto the floor of the cab before he climbed in.

"Is that the case?" Louis asked, indicating the object with a tilt of his head.

Benton nodded. "It's just a standard type. Had to remove the coins we had stored in it, though. I wouldn't have been able to obtain permission if it was for any other client."

"You had to gain permission?" Louis raised his eyebrows in surprise.

Benton nodded again, a little sheepishly.

"Benton," Louis said gently, "You're not Head of Numismatics, are you?"

"No," said the young man. "That will be Sir Edwyn Currie. Do you know him?"

This time it was Louis's turn to nod. "Yes, I know him. I was at school with his father."

Benton's mouth dropped open and he stared at Louis before he recovered his manners. "I – I wasn't aware."

"It isn't important," Louis said with a genuine smile. "We need all the young men we can find, in this endeavour." Already he was sizing Benton up, assessing his character with a seasoned eye while he observed the man's bearing and mannerisms. What he had seen so far was promising, and while Louis had little doubt the youth on his parlour settee had been chosen to be the next Consort, he knew from long and bitter experience that such a man needed all the friends he could find.

"Where are we going?"

Louis glanced at Benton's worried expression and caught a glint of excitement underneath. *Good lad*, he thought to himself. "To the Tower," he said, and winked. But his bonhomie was forced.

CHAPTER 13 — Trouble At The Tower

Polly Parker and Annie Cook paid a farthing each to sit in the kitchen of 53 Flower and Dean Street all morning. Annie, being a tiny woman, found a way of slipping in beside the cast-iron range to a warm spot, where she slept quietly with the wall at her back. Polly sat at the kitchen table watching her with a familiar mixture of envy, pity and hatred.

She sat sharing a glass of rum with Bill Hickey, a sailor off the coal boats from Newcastle. He had a bit of a soft spot for her, Lord knew why. And he knew where Fred the Chinaman was.

"He was lifted the other night," he said, pulling on a moist cigarette. "They threw him in the Clink."

"What, in Southwark?" Polly asked, surprised. "It's not like Fred to find himself south of the river."

"Nah," Bill said, reaching for the rum glass with coal-tainted fingers. "It was down the docks, wasn't it? He come off a boat, the Master wouldn't pay 'im for some reason, so he clocked him one. Next thing, the rozzers have 'im on the floor, he's up before the Beak and away for ten days. Ten days!" He laughed in disbelief. "Ten days, just for punchin' one of the Bill. There ain't no justice in this world."

"Nor the next," said Sally Cox from the doorway. She nodded to Polly, who acknowledged her in turn, and the newcomer slid onto the bench at the side of Bill Hickey, her arms snaking round his shoulder. She whispered something in his ear that Polly didn't catch, and he smiled, pecked her on the cheek, and gave her a sip of the rum.

Polly sat fuming. "I paid for that, Bill Hickey," she snapped.

"'s all right, Poll, isn't it?" Sally Cox asked, the glass still in her hand. "Jus' a little. You know I'll pay you back."

Polly nodded, defeated. *This time tomorrow I'll be out of here,* she told herself. *If I can find Fred the Chinaman.*

"So where's Fred now then?" she asked.

"You don't half go on, Poll Parker," said Bill with a touch of exasperation. "I don't know. Somewhere in the gaol, that's where, and he can stay there as long as he likes, if you ask me." He put his arm around Sally Cox and nuzzled up to her neck, while she giggled.

She slipped out of his grasp and flounced out of the kitchen, leaving the others alone.

Polly started thinking. *If he was lifted at the docks,* she supposed, *then he can't have got far. There's magistrates at Shoreditch, so they'd put him away somewhere close. And where's closest to Shoreditch and the Docks?*

She nodded. She knew where he was, all right.

A commotion broke out in the house from one of the upstairs rooms – shouting, boots on the floor stamping, doors opening, slamming shut.

Polly got up from the chair by the table and moved to the kitchen door.

Bill Hickey came up behind her, put his hand on her waist.

She gave him a look of resignation then glanced up at the top of the stairs.

"Leave me alone!"

A rough Irish voice, a girl's, came roaring down the stairwell.

Polly watched as two men dragged the owner downstairs, wriggling and yelling. "I haven't done nuttin'!"

The bulkier of the two men growled at her to shut up, but she only yelled louder and aimed a kick at him. At a signal from him the smaller man pinioned her arms and lifted her bodily off the ground.

She screeched and thrashed her head back, trying to hit him with her bonnet.

"Get out, you thieving Irish whore!"

The call came from one of the rooms upstairs and silenced the commotion momentarily, the household frozen. Then the girl screeched again, a banshee wail like fingernails down glass.

"Thief! I ain't no thief you filthy feckin Jewish pig!"

The burly man told her to shut up again, although to everyone in the house it was obvious that she had no intention of doing anything of the kind, and slapped her at this point, hard across the face.

"Hey!" Polly moved out of the kitchen doorway trailing the hapless Bill Hickey behind her. "There ain't no need for that."

The burly man turned towards her, but she'd moved onto the girl now.

"You, keep the noise down. There ain't no need for all this hollerin' neither."

The Irish girl tossed her head and stopped wriggling long enough for the small man to force her towards the door. "You can't do this to me!" she cried out. "You got no feckin right! I paid! Ask the bastard Jew – I feckin paid!"

The small man took no notice as she continued in this vein all the way along the hall to the front door, where the burly man held open until she was ejected.

Polly turned to the burly man, noting with no interest the fact that Bill Hickey had crept back into the kitchen and was watching through the open doorway, but was in no way supporting her or taking part in the confrontation. "What's all this about, Liskey?"

"None of your business, Poll Parker. You keep your nose out of it."

Polly took a breath, aware she was shaking, and she could feel the emotions weeping off the big man like fumes. "There was no need to hit her, Liskey."

There was a kick at the front door and a stream of invective, more fluent and imaginative than most, cursing the owner for being the son of a whore and in the pay of the Jews.

The burly man snorted. "I don't mind who stays here, Poll, just as long as they don't go robbin' my other guests. You know the rule."

"Still, like I says, you didn't have to hit her."

The small man brushed past the pair of them on his way back up the stairs. "You don't like that, do you, Poll? Don't like being pushed around."

Polly said nothing. It was true. She hated it, hated seeing it. She hadn't been brought up to it, grew up in a warm family where arguments were few and dealt with in accordance with the teachings of Jesus. Once she was married she'd found out to her cost that not all men were so gentle.

"She got any stuff, Joe?" Polly asked the small man. "A bag or anything?"

The small man sneered. "Nah. Come in off the boat this morning if you ask me. Or out the poorhouse."

Hammering fists pounded the door a sharp tattoo, and yet another bark of insults.

Polly felt her ire rising and knew she'd have to get rid of it somehow.

Annie appeared in the hallway, bleary-eyed and questioning, her arms wrapped tightly around her body as if to keep in the warmth she'd harvested from the kitchen.

Bill Hickey had wandered back to the kitchen table and Polly knew he'd scoffed the rest of the cup of rum.

She needed a drink, in a bad way. She walked to the door and drew the bolt, threw the door open and strode out into the street to where the Irish girl was staggering.

The girl threw her head back and stared uncertainly at Polly, a certain pride near-suffocated by drunkenness. There was a bruise on her cheek and she was developing a puffy eye from where Liskey had slapped her.

Polly felt sorry for her, aware too painfully that she couldn't rescue every girl the age her daughter should be. "Come on," said Polly, "We're going for a drink."

The Irish girl regarded her with suspicion but drew herself up to her full height. She was shorter than Polly by a good six inches, and Polly herself was barely five foot three.

Polly crossed the street towards the Tower Arms and heard the Irish girl fall into line behind her. Annie's shuffling footsteps weren't far behind and the door to the guesthouse slammed shut, the crack echoing down the alleyway at the side of the public house and bouncing off the courtyard beyond.

At the pub door, Polly glanced over her shoulder. "What's your name?"

The Irish girl spoke quieter now, as if she didn't want anyone else to hear. "Mary Kelly," she said, her accent softly burring round the 'r'.

Polly smiled. "Not your street name, love. I meant your real name."

"My real name IS Mary Kelly," said the Irish girl, that haughty anger returning to her face and her voice hardening.

Polly turned away, her smile replaced with a look of surprise, and pushed open the door into the snug.

Mary Kelly, as it turned out, had a pocket full of coins and an appetite for rum.

Polly Parker sat in the snug of the Tower Arms with her and Annie, sipping a beer, listening to the girl's life story. It was much the same as the rest of the women she knew – widowed early, or on the run from a violent man.

Polly listened to the Irish girl's story with a lack of interest that was not dispassionate. She watched the girl's dainty hands clasp the beer glass, saw them clench into tiny grimy fists at the points of her tale where it was required, then relax, showing stubby nails bitten to the quick.

Her eyebrows were black and thick, her mouth small, unpromising. A smear of rouge on her cheeks seemed unnecessary, fading underneath the freckles as her complexion grew rosy while she sipped at the rum in the glass before her.

"I was in France," she said, "For a while. Working, like. I was in a big fancy house with carpets and maids, but by God they treated me sorely." She took a deep draught of the rum. "Jesus, that numbs the pain, but I tell you it don't hide the bruises." Her hands tightened into fists again. When the girl pushed her sleeves up and adopted a pugilist's pose to illustrate some further point of the conversation, the dark hair on her arms lit up with a coppery glint in the sunlight that streamed through the stained glass window at the far end of the bar.

"So how did you end up in Whitechapel?" Polly asked.

"Ah, I ran away, so I did," Mary said with a half-bashful smile. "There were a couple of sailor lads – nice lads, you know?"

Polly nodded, but she disagreed. She stretched out her legs in front of their table, enjoying the warmth of the sun even though it travelled across the entire length of the pub to reach them. In contrast, the coal fire on the other side of their partition barely raised the temperature by one degree. She glanced at the barman and was distressed to recognise him, and immediately she felt on edge. Turning her back on him, she faced the Irish girl again. "So what happened?"

"We came over last night and they got paid off, and after we'd had a few beers an' all, they paid for us all to go into a dosshouse – a proper one, an' all," said the Irish girl, stabbing the tabletop with her index finger to make the point. "Water in the washstand an' all. They was proper gents, for sure."

"An' where did they get to, then?"

"Dunno," said Mary. "I woke up this mornin' with a terrible thirst on me, so I came out the place to look for some more rum and by Christ if I couldn't find my way back again when I got to the end of the road!" She laughed, full and throaty, shaking her head. Her bonnet came undone and she removed it, letting her thick auburn hair uncoil across her shoulders, the hat-pin in her mouth as she rolled up her hair again, tucked it into an elaborate chignon and placed the bonnet on top.

"What ship did you come in on?" Polly asked.

The Irish girl shrugged. "Dunno," she mumbled, the hat-pin in her mouth. She removed it and pinned her bonnet on then patted her hair into place. "It wasn't a big 'un. It was one of them with the chimney. Don't care, 'm not going back there."

"D'you know where you'll go?"

Mary shrugged again, more defiance in the gesture this time.

Polly knew that the girl was faking bravado. Her eyes had the sort of false strength that Polly felt ebbing away from her – or maybe just the younger woman was more full of the fight. When the light went out, the promise of a kind strong husband and healthy kids – when that sunlight went out, and all that was left was this bleak day best seen through a glass; that's how Polly felt. She swallowed the rest of her beer at a gulp.

Mary pushed a penny across the table towards Polly. "I'll come with *you*," she said in a flat voice. "Get us all another drink, before we go."

Polly took the penny, went to the bar, came back with two more glasses – rum for Mary Kelly, beer for herself. Annie still clutched the half-empty one like it was a talisman or a holy relic. Mary was singing a hymn, softly, and she swayed to the rhythm of the song like a reed in a breeze. The sound was loud in the quiet pub and her voice was sweet and tuneful.

Polly sat beside the others and blessed the God who created drink, and coal fires, and pubs. Annie laid her head back on the window-ledge and closed her eyes; within minutes, she began to snore.

The door opened, swung shut; a stranger's voice at the bar, a dog's claws on the floor tiles, then hubbub again, clinking glasses, laughter.

When Mary Kelly finished the hymn, she picked up the glass of rum and sniffed at it in appreciation with a wry smile on her lips. "That's a fine tot, there," she said, almost to herself, and toasted Polly's good health.

Polly nodded in return, a grim smile forced onto her lips.

Annie stretched out across the bench and laid her head in Mary's lap.

The Irish woman stroked her hair like a mother would fuss over a child. "What's with her?" Mary whispered, nodding in Annie's direction.

Annie's eyes were glazed, but she was not asleep. Polly caught her gaze and saw her bottom lip tremble.

"She's not well," said Polly in a quiet voice. "She swore me to secrecy, on the grave of her poor boys, that I wouldn't tell. So I won't."

"Have you ladies been friends for long, like?"

Polly shook her head. She wasn't sure if she was denying the duration of their friendship, or the depth. "Couple of years, maybe?" she said. "We met up in the Spitalfields Workhouse. Stuck together when we got out. It's safer if we stick together."

And Annie does things for money that I won't, Polly added mentally, *so I need her more than I feel sorry for her.* "I look after her when she's poorly," she went on. "There's no reason to abandon good Christian charity just because we're down on our luck."

"Aye, it's a life of trouble all right," Mary said, and drained the rum glass.

Polly put her half-empty beer glass down on the table and Annie sat up, drank half of it, and spilled the rest onto Mary's skirt.

"That was nice, Poll," slurred Annie, a happy little smile on her lips. Mary's pale freckled hand stroked Annie's hair gently and she began to hum a song under her breath. Polly recognised the tune. It was 'Rose of Tralee'.

The afternoon's pale sunlight crawled along the bar top, washing the women golden and coppery through the stained glass windows, the square tiles on the floor warming in its rays, rose and gold and yellow, Polly's cigarettes layering smoke in whorls that eddied round the women. The noise from the street seemed distant, the other voices in the bar a rumbling murmur. Polly held her glass of beer within a firm hand, her mind on other things.

The shadows lengthened in the pub as the day wore on and the money ran out. Mary's last farthing went on another tot of rum and a song, out of tune and loud by now. Annie snored gently, out of reach of the raucous noise.

The barman yelled over for her to calm down.

Mary Kelly yelled back.

"Look, girl, pipe down," Polly hissed with a wary glance towards the barman. "That's Ted Anstruther at the bar, he's got a vicious streak a mile wide when it comes to women and I've been on the end of his temper more times than I like to remember."

He was watching them, his face edged with grim glee.

Polly turned away from him, the sunlight fading behind him and leaving her part of the pub in shadow. She wished she'd got more to drink, wished she didn't have to face the evening or the rest of the night, not this sober, wished she could spend the rest of Eternity in the warmth of the snug with a glass of beer in her hand.

Mary tossed the last of the rum down her throat and the barman was over at the table, urging them out.

"Is it time yet, Poll?" Annie asked, staring up from where she lay, her eyes wide with the question.

Polly shook her head.

"Time for what?" asked Mary. A guarded look came into her eyes.

"Time to make enough pennies to pay for tonight's bed," Polly replied in a low defeated tone. *Dear Jesus,* she prayed, *how much longer do I have to live this life?*

"Get out into the street where you belong," the barman snarled as he snatched away the Irish girl's glass.

"Here!" shouted Mary, "I weren't done with that!"

The barman tipped the glass up to show it was empty. A drip fell, caught Annie in the eye. She cried out.

Mary leapt to her feet, hands balled into tiny fists to protect her new friend, Annie's head thudding onto the leather banquette behind her.

It gave the barman the excuse he was looking for and he grabbed the Irish girl. His massive hands gripped her shoulders, crushing her so that there was little force in the blows she pummelled into his chest. He heaved her over the table.

Her feet caught under the edge as she rose, tipping the table over with a crash that sent the contents of the ashtray spilling across the floor tiles.

Polly sighed and decided enough was enough. She shouldered the trembling Annie with a comforting word and followed Ted Anstruther, still holding the wriggling girl, to the street.

The barman dragged the shrieking Irish woman to the pub door without her feet touching the ground, his head turned to one side to avoid her scrabbling hands reaching for his eyes.

She kicked at him with no obvious effect, screaming obscenities in his face.

He threw her to the gutter in full view of the entire street, and roared after her: "Get out of my bar, you worthless bitch!"

Mary Kelly landed like a tailor's mannequin on the cobbles and lay winded, glaring up at the pub door with a red face puffing for breath.

"Nice one, Ted," said Polly in a flat sarcastic tone as she pushed past him, protecting Annie with one arm. "I got to quiet her down now. Thanks."

"Pick better friends in future, Poll Parker," he sneered and made a show of dusting his hands of them all. With a glare that took in all three he stamped back into the pub.

Polly didn't smile at him, just took the Irish girl by the arm and helped her up.

Anger blazed in the redhead's eyes and she yelled obscenities over Polly's shoulder even as Polly heard the pub door snick shut behind her.

Polly shook her with one hand, stared her down. "Now you listen here," she hissed, "You shut your yap or the Bill will be onto us. Got it?"

Mary Kelly spat at the pub door but stopped wriggling. "He's a bastard, I'll feckin' kill him, I will." She kept on but her voice dropped in volume while she muttered her curses and rubbed at her shoulder where the barman had held her with such force. "I reckon he's bruised me, Poll. The bastard."

"Poll?" Annie curled herself into the hollow of Polly's shoulder, her arms tight around Polly's waist.

Polly let go of the Irish girl to tend to Annie, pulled her face away from the darkness, saw she was crying. "Here, none of that," she began, rubbing Annie's shoulders to comfort her – then she had to turn away and grab Mary Kelly's upraised arm before the Irish girl could throw the loose cobblestone she'd picked up.

Polly and Mary struggled, Annie forgotten and crying off to one side, until Polly's height got the better of the redhead and she dropped the cobble. Polly hated herself for the next thing even before she did it, but with her free hand she slapped Mary hard across the face, loosening the girl's bonnet and making it flop over her eyes.

Mary gasped and looked up at Polly with a vicious glare, rubbed her cheek. "Cow," she said under her breath.

"Don't," said Polly, breathless. "Just don't, okay? Let it go." She returned Mary Kelly's glare with one of her own. "We got to go to work now, girl. It don't do to start fights with the punters. You better learn it."

Mary sagged, turned away from Polly, and began adjusting her bonnet. She was muttering under her breath again, her challenging stare thrust at each passer-by.

Polly puffed out her breath. She turned back to Annie, whose crying had stopped as she watched wide-eyed, but the wetness of the tears still shone on her ruddy cheeks. She was rubbing her hands together, washing them over and over, her mouth hanging slack and her breath misting in the pale afternoon sun.

Polly held her arms open and Annie stumbled into them, eyes still wide, her expression one of guarded fear. "Shh," Polly said, kissing Annie on the forehead and rocking her back and forward like a baby. "It's all done now."

After a moment Annie let her head drop onto Polly's shoulder again, and when she spoke it was a whisper. "Is it, Poll?"

Polly shook her head. *Not yet*, she thought.

She gazed out over the street, past Mary Kelly stabbing a hatpin through her bonnet and the coiled loops of her long auburn hair.

Bill Hickey, Polly's erstwhile admirer, stood in the doorway of the guesthouse with Sally Cox in his arms, the pair of them laughing at some private joke. Carts passed by on the road. On a wall someone had posted a flyer for the Salvation Army with a big picture of the Reverend Booth and some quote from the Scriptures in a typeface too small for Polly to read.

Annie clung to her like a frightened child.

"I'm sorry, Annie," Polly whispered.

Annie's shoulders relaxed, then her fists unclenched and she drew away, nodding. "M'okay, Poll," she sniffled, rummaging in her skirts. She withdrew a spotted handkerchief and unfolded it, blew her nose on it and returned it to the pocket it came from.

Polly realised that Annie hadn't looked at Mary Kelly since they'd left the pub. *What's on your mind, girl?* She thought. *There's something wrong there, but I know you – you won't tell me, except in your own sweet time.* She knew Annie well enough not to ask. The answer would surface when Annie had found time to put it into words, like something risen from the bottom of a pond.

"Here, girl," said Polly, and took her own handkerchief out. She made Annie wet it with saliva, then dabbed away the tear streaks on Annie's cheeks as if she were a child. They shared a laugh about it.

Mary stood looking at them, hat securely pinned, hands on hips, a challenge in her fiery eyes. "Where to now, Poll?" she said in a brusque voice, her Irish accent strong.

Polly took a deep breath. Her mouth felt dry, her temper brittle, an unsettling flutter in her stomach as ever at this point of the evening. She swallowed bile. Pushed her breath out hard and said, "Burr Street." Her lips were set in a thin hard line.

The three women made their way slowly along Glass House Street to St Katherine's Dock, wary, on the lookout for custom. Or at least two of them were. Annie Cook was there in body, but not in spirit. More than once on the walk from Whitechapel she'd tumbled over to the side of the road to be sick, Polly rubbing her back, eyes darting round them with a challenge for the gawpers.

"Oh, dear God, Poll," Annie whimpered, "He don't half punish me for my sins." And then she began to cry, real tears, sobs that shook her like jolts of electricity.

She'll let up when her throat gets raw, thought Polly with a lack of that Christian charity of which she was so fond, and it rankled her.

Mary Kelly had obtained a bunch of purple grapes from somewhere. "Want some?"

Polly realised she hadn't seen from where they came, and thought they may be stolen, but the Irish girl offered them and Polly took some all the same. She was afraid for Annie now, and too tired, this afternoon, for much patience.

Her spat with Mary Kelly outside the pub had spent her irritation like a wasted bet and the walk down to the docks had given her time to numb herself against the night's promise.

She knew some of the women enjoyed the work, in a way, each fumble part of a game of chance, a bit of a laugh in spite of the dangers. Polly was not one of them. Apparently Annie had been, once. But not Polly, no, she hated it with the pious reserve of a good Christian wife, hated it even as she lifted her skirts in an alleyway and avoided their mouths seeking hers.

At one point, while she waited for the froth to cease foaming from Annie's mouth, Polly was sure she saw the coach she'd seen that morning at the river. She knew it was pointless trying to get any sense out of Annie so she turned to Mary Kelly, who was eyeing up the delivery boys loafing outside the warehouses on the opposite side of the road.

"See that coach?" Polly asked.

"Which one?" Mary said between grapes.

"The cream one with the bay pair," said Polly, and turned back to pat Annie on the back in comfort. "Come on, girl, let it all up. That's good."

Mary Kelly grunted an acknowledgement then spat her grape pips into the road. "Bastard," she sneered, then paused, peering at the coach. "Maybe."

Polly peered at her. "You know it?"

The Irish girl grunted again. "Could be one of the bastards that ran me in France. There was a coach like that: same livery. Same pair, likely."

"Who is it?" said Polly. "I thought he only – well, this morning I saw him try to pick up a boy."

Mary Kelly shook her head. "Not if it's the same one. Likes women, but doesn't like 'em. Bastard! Runs opium too," she added, and tossed another grape into her mouth. Polly watched the coach make its way down Houndsditch through the traffic. Shortly afterwards, at a snail's pace, they followed.

The coach was ahead of them at the corner of Upper East Smithfield and when the three women reached the gates to North Quay on Nightingale Street, it was halted with the window partly down and one of the dockers was talking to whoever was inside.

Polly squinted, trying to make out the man's face. She was sure she knew him.

The man's breath misted in front of him, mingled with smoke that came in thin gusts from the carriage's open window. He doffed his cap to whoever was inside, and the coach moved off.

Polly hissed under her breath as the dockhand strolled off in the opposite direction, his gait as familiar as his blocky shoulders. "Fred the Chinaman," she sneered. "I might have guessed."

The late afternoon sun lay flat along the surface of the water, crimson and glistening, a pale mist already rising from the surface.

Polly shivered.

She felt Annie shiver too, one last rhythm of the shakes that sent her into a coughing fit. The afternoon's alcohol was wearing off and the night was drawing in, and neither of them had money to survive it.

Polly's train of thought went like this: turn a trick for money; exchange money for drink; drink enough to turn another trick; continue until too tired or too disgusted with herself and find a lodging-house to take her stinking body, God save her soul.

She shivered again and set off in pursuit of the disappearing dockhand with her two companions in tow.

CHAPTER 14 – The Raven Master And The Crucible

Louis took Benton with him when he entered the Tower of London. "It will do you good," he said as they disembarked from the cab. *And it will provide you with some inkling of what we are up against, in this game.*

The Tower of London squats on the edge of the City's Square Mile, on the river's northern bank between the Bank of England and the sprawl of the docks. In times past it served many functions – prison, fortress, treasure vault – and as Louis led Benton past the curve of The Tower Gardens, where the castle's moat had been grassed over, he gazed up over the battlements to the Tudor rooftops, leaden grey under a bright sky. The flags on each were fluttering in a light breeze, a little to the northward, and beneath the eaves their slender windows were blank.

They crossed the underground access point that led from Traitor's Gate – a water-level entrance most famously used to bring Queen Elizabeth to gaol while her Catholic sister ruled a split nation – and as Louis had anticipated, the waterway beneath him turned his legs to jelly.

"Benton," he gasped, and gripped the young man's arm for aid.

"Are you all right?" Benton asked, his face showing concern beyond the norm. He fumbled with the glass-topped coin case tucked under his spare arm, but Louis shook his head.

"I'm – all right," he gasped. "The tide is – just – on the turn." Louis winced. *No wonder I'm breathless,* he realised with a smile that brought tears to his eyes. *I'm still linked to the Lady.*

With a rush of joy, of love returned, as hopeless as a devoted husband, he staggered over to lean against a stretch of the wall until the stitch was gone and he regained control of his trembling legs.

This close to the water, he felt the gentle lull of the tide as the vast estuary of the Thames sat at bay like a predatory beast, awaiting the point where the waters would move again. He could tell that moment was close. As Consort, it maddened him as much as it delighted him. Soon, he knew, he'd lose the ability to concentrate if he stayed here. And he wondered how it would affect the youth who drowsed in his parlour.

He turned to Benton who still clutched the coin case, a worried expression on his young face. "We don't have much time," said Louis, and beckoned the numismatist to follow him through the castle gates into its entrance yard.

The Raven Master was expecting them.

"Cummins rang me to say you were on your way over," he explained as he led them through the draughty lanes between the castle buildings. "To tell you the truth, I would have expected someone from the Club sooner or later."

"Really?" Louis asked, his interest prickling at his palms. He was aware of Benton's nervousness, and introduced the two men.

The Raven Master seemed unsettled too, his usual formality somewhat strained.

"It's the birds, sir." The Raven Master shook his head. "They're behaving strangely. I've never seen them like this." He unlocked an iron gate between two low stone buildings and gestured for the visitors to pass through. "I can't get them to settle. The ladies are all hunched up in a corner, and the chaps are strutting like peacocks."

Louis suppressed a shudder. His heart leapt with delight at the news, and he followed the Raven Master round to the mews with a spring in his step which had been dampened by his crossing of Traitor's Channel.

"Which are your oldest birds?" he asked, when they reached the courtyard where the birds were kept.

"Magnus," said the Raven Master, pointing to a large specimen perched on a low stone wall, its head in the air and its clipped wings outstretched to catch the breeze. "And Lady Jane." He indicated a female which huddled in the centre of a crowded group of birds, black rags in a bundle under the lee of the northernmost wall of the enclosure.

"I need to ask you a favour, Sergeant," Louis said in a low voice. "It's Club business, of course."

The Raven Master nodded and with great care he waded into the flock and picked up the female he'd identified as Lady Jane. She sat in his arms with a confused appearance, almost dazed, tucked up tight to keep her wings from batting his face. He dug a titbit from his trouser pocket to entice her but she turned away. "Anything you ask, sir," said the sergeant. "Just don't harm the birds, please?"

Louis felt as if the female was watching him. He chided himself for being fanciful. "How old is this bird, Master?"

"Lady Jane? Thirty-eight."

"So she hatched in – " Louis began to calculate back, but Benton beat him to it.

"Eighteen-fifty," said the young man.

Louis nodded his thanks. "And the other – the male? How old is he?"

"Hatched in eighteen-fifty-one," the Raven Master confirmed. "Am I correct in thinking you need birds that were born before Crown Prinz Wilhelm?"

Louis scratched his neck. "Correct. I don't need to take them away," he said cautiously. "I just need you – someone – to keep an eye on them. And report to the Club if they start to behave more oddly. In particular," he added, "I want to know if any of them takes flight."

"They won't do that, sir," said the Raven Master with a grin. "They all have their wings clipped."

"I know," said Louis. "Nonetheless, will you let Cummins know? At the Club? Immediately?"

"Certainly, Mr Beauregard," said the Raven Master, a puzzled expression on his face. He bent to nuzzle the bird in his arms, his eyes dangerously close to her great grey beak, but she merely sat, frozen in pose, her focus still fixed on the visitors. "Will there be anything else?"

Louis nodded, then shrugged. "I don't know," he said. "Perhaps an unusually high spring tide on the river. A mist, or fog, accompanied by the scent of pine resin. And maybe more of those birds than you normally have."

The Raven Master stared at him with a wary eye. "Does the Constable know?"

"Yes," said Louis. "He's been informed. I understand there are procedures to follow on occasions such as this – such as this might turn out to be." He turned to Benton. "Don't be concerned, lad."

"I'm not, sir," said Benton, his gaze fixed firmly on the raven in the sergeant's arms. "I've just never seen such a creature at such close quarters."

"Would you like to hold her?" asked the Raven Master.

Benton shook his head in a very definite refusal.

Louis was silent all the way from the Tower to the police station in Limehouse, his thoughts troubled.

Benton walked next to him clutching the coin case with both hands, equally moribund.

Louis struggled to fix his thoughts on one subject, his mind fluttering from one point to another like the Raven Master's nervous birds, and while on more than one occasion he breathed deep and prepared to speak, words failed him, and he merely sighed.

The pair met up with the secretary to the Assistant Chief Constable, a thin man named Reed who looked as though he barely shaved and sprouted brushy eyebrows in a pale shade that matched his hair. With the briefest of greetings he escorted the two men into the strong room, where the station's duty officer brandished a sheaf of paperwork.

"Is this really in the best interest?" asked the duty officer. "It's highly irregular."

"Have you ever had a set of gold coins in your safekeeping before?" asked Reed, his voice steeped in officialdom and authority.

The duty officer shook his head. Cowed, he spun the dial on the safe while Louis signed the forms in triplicate, and brought out a small cardboard box.

When Benton saw the coins inside, he caught his breath so audibly it sounded as though he'd choked.

"Were you expecting this?" asked Mr Reed.

Louis nodded. "Pretty much," he said in a laconic tone which he hoped would not betray the excitement he felt in his throat. He turned to the numismatist, hunched over the box and peering closely at the contents. "What's your opinion?"

Benton coughed and straightened up. "I've never seen markings like this before," he admitted. "I'll need to examine them back at the museum."

Louis patted his shoulder and gave the sheaf of paperwork back to the duty officer with a smile. *If things go to plan*, he thought, *I'll never be held accountable for those signatures.* The notion pleased him with a certain degree of freedom.

"You heard the man," said Reed to the duty officer. "Hand 'em over."

Benton removed a pair of white cotton gloves from his pocket and slipped them onto his hands. With exquisite care he lifted each little coin from the cardboard box and placed it in a slot on the velvet bed of the coin case. He worked quickly and the case was not full when he finally locked it and returned the empty box to the policeman.

"Thank you, gentlemen," said Louis in his most flattering tones, and without further ado he and Benton left the station by cab.

"I can't understand why you needed me there," said Benton, clutching the coin-case even more firmly now and glancing down at the lock as if to check it was secure. "You could have done that yourself."

"Ah," said Louis with a faint smile, "I'm afraid i wasn't exactly honest with you, Mr Benton." He turned to face the young man in the cramped confines of the cab. "We aren't taking them to the museum. Hold tight to that case, now."

Benton stared at him in incomprehension and continued to do so, wordlessly, while the cab rolled away from the docks. They passed the Royal Mint and turned up The Minories, then onto Houndsditch and a dog-leg into London Wall; dodged through back streets between the Smithfield Markets and Charterhouse, at last drawing to a halt in a little courtyard off Saffron Hill. Benton stared even harder at the workshops around the courtyard, an expression of horror spreading across his face.

I'm sorry, Benton, thought Louis. *If I'd told you this was what I planned to do, you'd never have gone along with it. And I need you to be strong. Sometimes we have to make hard decisions.*

"Come on," said Louis with grim determination, and forced himself out of the cab. He almost dragged Benton with him. "We have work to do. And I'm not keen on this either."

Louis gripped Benton by the arm with some force and propelled the numismatist into the vestibule of Ogilvy's, the goldsmiths.

"It's Club business, is it?" said Mr Ogilvy Senior as he interviewed Louis and Benton in his office.

Louis nodded. The three men sat around a leather-topped desk close to the door, crowded out by a large safe at the far end of the room and, at its side, a jeweller's bench very much like the ones in the workshop below, except this one was utterly bare, and the half-moon cut out of its surface was filled with a wooden board.

Mr Ogilvy wore a leather apron over the bones of his business suit and peered at his visitors through half-moon spectacles. He rose from his chair and pointed to the wall above the bench, aiming his finger at one particular framed certificate amongst the charters which crowded out the more prosaic charts of alloys and hallmarks. "Otherwise, you understand, it isn't a commission I would undertake."

"The Lady is in grave danger," said Louis. He acknowledged the charter that Ogilvy indicated, noted the arms of the City of London's Guildhall at its head, understood the man's reluctance to barter his membership of the Worshipful Company of Goldmsiths. But that did not deter him one jot. "I'm not going to mince my words here – the Russians are after her. Nearly caught her last night."

"She was in London last night?" The elderly goldsmith raised his eyebrows in surprise. "Was there a letter in the Times?"

Louis nodded. "First, second and City editions. I was surprised you weren't at the Club at lunch."

Mr Ogilvy Senior sucked at his teeth and shook his head. "We're short of staff at the moment," he said with a shrug of apology. "There are a lot of Jewish workers in the city now, come over from the Continent. Poles, too."

Louis gave him a stern look. "Your company's reputation was founded by a Pole, Ogilvy. I shouldn't have to remind you of that."

Ogilvy nodded in agreement. "I know, and I'm sorry for it. I've had a devil of a job keeping on the journeymen. Plenty of apprentices, enough old hands to train them. Trouble is," he said, peering out of his office window over the heads of his goldsmiths, "They're too old, some of them. Eyesight goes, or the steady hand."

"Pawel Czerczy still works here, though?" Louis's tone was hopeful, because he hadn't seen the man on his way to the director's office.

Ogilvy nodded, and smiled. "We've given him a workshop of his own," he said. "It's on the other side of the yard."

"Ogilvy," Louis said, and drew the man to one side, "Do you think he'll do it?"

Ogilvy glanced towards Benton before he replied. "He'll do it, all right. But will your assistant allow it?"

Louis dropped his gaze to the floor and took a deep breath. He heard Benton shuffle his feet, the floorboards scuffing under the leather soles of his shoes, and turned to look at the numismatist with as much kindliness as he could muster. "Benton?"

"Mr Beauregard?" Benton's eyes were wide and his arms were strapped tight around the coin-case.

"Will you please show Mr Ogilvy the coins?"

Benton hesitated, then relaxed his grip on the case.

Ogilvy moved to the empty bench at the far end of the room, drew up a stool from under the bench and flicked on an electric light over the worktop. He beckoned Benton over, laid the case flat, nodded and tutted when he saw the hoard. "May I?" he said to Benton, indicating the lock on the case.

Benton fumbled the key out of his pocket and unlocked the case, then stood back with one hand over his mouth.

Ogilvy flipped the lid up with customary ease and took a jeweller's eyeglass from his pocket, screwed the loupe into one eye socket, then peered at the coins on the velvet lining. He hummed to himself, tunelessly, a little staccato rhythm, and straightened up. "Nice," was all he said.

He brought a small wooden case from one of the bench drawers and opened it to display what looked like a chemical-testing kit. Ogilvy took one of the coins and shaved a sliver of metal off the edge with a sharp steel gouge, ignoring Benton's gasp of alarm, then picked up the shard with tweezers and placed it in a ceramic dish in the wooden case. He withdrew a dark bottle from a lower drawer, its sides ridged like a poison container, and added a single drop from its pipette to the dish with the metal.

After a few moments he nodded. "It's pure," he said with an air of nonchalance gained from a lifetime of working with precious metals. "Thought it might be, really."

Louis patted Benton on the shoulder in a friendly, paternal way. "It's all right, Benton," he said, trying to comfort the young man. "You'll understand later."

"You're going to melt them down, aren't you?" said the numismatist, unable to disguise the bitter distaste in his voice.

"Yes."

"Where did you get them?" asked Ogilvy as he returned to the chair behind his desk. "I'd like to know, before I ask Pawel to destroy them." He regarded Louis with keen eyes which seemed stronger over the top of his glasses.

Louis was reminded of the eye of the raven at the Tower, and told him. There was no need to hide any of his motives any more.

Pawel Czerczy was older even than Louis and he still worked the trade he'd inherited from his father. Louis greeted him as an old friend, but one whose first language was not English and never would be, the elderly goldsmith's Polish interspersed with a smattering of Yiddish and French.

"Mr Beauregard has a commission," explained Ogilvy in French.

The elderly man's eyes lit up. "For the Club?" he asked, again in French.

Louis nodded. *I understood that, at least.*

Czerczy beckoned with twisted fingers. "Tell me," he said in English. He cleared a space on his workbench and brought out a paper notepad which he flipped to a new clean page, and laid a short pencil on top of it.

Louis made a few brief sketches. In his youth he'd learned to draft like a map-maker, whilst in Egypt, and the skill helped to disguise his natural hamfisted artistry. He was still glad it wasn't a complicated idea.

The Pole nodded and stuck his tongue between his lips with concentration while he listened. "Gold?" he asked in English. "Or silver?"

"Gold," said Louis, and beckoned Benton over with the case of coins. "This gold."

Czerczy sucked in a whistling breath over his teeth, but he never stopped nodding. He said something which Louis failed to translate and assumed it to be Yiddish, or some specialist terms amongst goldsmiths.

Louis glanced at Ogilvy, who shook his head.

"Yes, yes," said Czerczy, and placed the case on his workbench on top of a box of needle files. He flipped the coins out like a man accustomed to handling items of rarity, his scarred thumbs rubbing the ridges of pattern on each. He glanced once at Ogilvy and asked, in French, if the metal was good.

Ogilvy nodded.

"When?" asked Czerczy.

"Now, if you can manage it," said Louis with a smile of apology.

Czerczy raised his gaze to the ceiling with a dramatic sigh, but he was grinning by the time he turned to Louis again. "Your blood?" he asked.

"What?" asked Benton.

Louis turned to the numismatist and was dismayed to see how pale the young man had become. "My blood, Benton," he said. "If you're unwell, you can wait in the yard. Or, I suppose, Mr Ogilvy's office." He raised his eyebrows towards Ogilvy, who nodded his acquiescence.

"What is going on?" Benton asked, shaking his head at the offer. "I'm – I'm not used to such things."

"None of us are," said Ogilvy behind him. He fetched a wooden chair from beside the door of the little workshop and steered Benton towards it. "Except perhaps Mr Beauregard, and Pawel." With a gentle shove he deposited Benton in the chair and slipped out of the workshop, crossed the yard and went back into his office with the air of a man who intended to return.

Czerczy tipped the gold coins into a tiny crucible no bigger than an egg-cup and added a generous spoonful of borax paste. He set the crucible in a furnace at the end of his workbench and pumped its air-bellows until the charcoal glowed hot, turning away for only a few seconds at a time in order to withdraw a small ingot-mould from a workbench drawer. His leather apron slapped against his legs as he moved, back and forth, puffing the bellows and shaking the crucible in the heat.

Louis removed his jacket and handed it to Benton for safekeeping, then removed the cufflink at his left wrist and slipped it into his pocket. He rolled his sleeve up beyond the elbow, folding it over the stiff cuff to keep it in place. "You're not scared of the sight of blood, are you?"

Benton shook his head. "What do you intend to do?" he asked. Some of the colour had returned to his cheeks and he seemed to have lost his uneasy concern. "I mean, once you've melted them down?"

Louis sighed. "I want to make a chain for the Lady," he said. "Not to imprison her, but to protect her."

Ogilvy returned carrying a small glass jar and a length of mdeical bandage fabric. He handed both to Benton, who stared at them in dismay, then turned to Louis. "All set?"

Louis nodded.

Ogilvy removed a small blade from his pocket. He held Louis's thumb over the glass jar in Benton's hand, nudged the numismatist to hold it steady, and cut a wide slice into the thick part of Louis's thumb-pad. Blood spurted out in a pulsing stream and Ogilvy held the thumb steady, pressing when the wound began to tighten up, his face intent and beads of sweat forming above his eyebrows.

After the first wave of pain, Louis turned away from the injury and watched Czerczy instead. *Another of us old men*, he thought, and for once he was delighted that he wasn't the oldest man in the world.

The goldsmith coaxed the gold in the crucible until it formed a molten pool, grinning occasionally at Louis through wrinkles that narrowed his eyes.

"You look like your father," Louis said at one point.

Czerczy chuckled and tapped his breastbone. "Old man," he said. He stretched one arm across the distance between them and tapped Louis in the same place. "Old man," he repeated. He turned back to the crucible and lifted it in one smooth movement from the furnace to the firebrick where the ingot-mould lay prepared. With a twist of his wrist he poured the molten metal into the mould and turned his head away to avoid the rush of heat that flowered above the ingot as the hot crucible made ridges of the air.

After he replaced the crucible by the furnace to cool, he lifted a chip of charcoal in the grips of a set of long-handled tongs and withdrew a clay pipe from his apron pocket, lit it with the glowing chip, and perched on a stool by the bench while he waited for the metal to cool. With his crinkled face he watched Louis being bled.

Louis, in turn, watched the surface of the gold as it wrinkled and cooled, drawing away from the sides of the mould as it darkened to the colour of his hair. When he glanced back at the draining of his thumb, he winked at Benton.

Czerczy put the pipe back in his apron and slid off the stool. He removed the gold – now in the form of a rough rectangular ingot – from the mould and thrust it back into the charcoals of the furnace until it glowed.

Louis watched as the goldsmith heated the ingot and let it cool, then hammered the metal into a longer form; heated it again, hammered, heated – he repeated the process five times.

After the last heating the Pole slipped a ceramic cover over the coals and allowed the metal to cool, again puffing on his clay pipe for a few moments.

"Will that be enough?" asked Ogilvy.

Louis turned and saw that the glass jar was half full. He realised that Ogilvy was addressing Czerczy, not him, and turned back to the elderly goldsmith.

Czerczy nodded. "Help me?" he said, and beckoned Benton over to the workbench, where the numismatist stood staring at the tools in front of him with as much discomfort as if he'd been asked to assist a dental surgeon.

Louis sat down in the chair and held the glass jar in his good hand while Ogilvy bandaged his other thumb. The liquid in the jar was thin and thick at the same time, fluid yet clinging to the sides of the jar where it had swirled up, unbalanced. *I hope this works*, he thought.

Czerczy indicated a huge set of tongs and pushed the sharp nose of the metal bar through the largest hole in an iron plate, then gestured for the numismatist to grip it with the tongs, and pull.

Benton shook his head.

Czerczy shrugged and set to work himself.

"Mr Benton?" Louis asked, rolling his sleeve down and refastening the cuff, "Do you know who Pawel Czerczy is?"

Benton held out Louis's jacket. "No."

Louis put his jacket on again and sat watching Czerczy draw the wire down through increasingly smaller holes in the metal plate, the gold stretching out in length as it became thinner. "Mr Czerczy's father founded the Cuckoo Club."

"Really?"

"He was an elderly man when I – when I first met him," said Louis, his natural caution bringing a smile to one half of his face. "I was younger than you are."

"And you did – this?" Benton found a spot behind the door which was out of the way of Czerczy and his increasingly-unwieldy length of wire, and propped himself against the doorframe.

Louis shook his head. "No; there was no need, then. The world has changed so very much."

In the silence that followed, Ogilvy cleared his throat.

Louis turned, raising his eyebrows in a query.

"Is there anything else I can help with?" asked Ogilvy. "Only I'd rather be back in the office. I have a business to run."

"Actually, there is," said Louis. "Have you ever seen a bullet made of amber, with a silver casing?"

Czerczy sucked an indrawn breath through his teeth. He caught Louis's glance and shook his head with mutterings in a mixture of languages. He made the sign of the evil eye – uncommon for someone with his ancestry – and crossed himself as if for good measure.

That tells me all I need to know, thought Louis.

"He said a number of words for 'wicked', i think," said Ogilvy. "Under the circumstances, I agree."

"Thank you, Mr Ogilvy," said Louis with a nod of his head in acknowledgment. "I think we'll be fine."

Ogilvy gave them a curt nod, and left.

Czerczy looped the wire into a coil around a cylindrical rod the width of a pencil and began snipping the gold into rings. When he was done, he swept the rings into a small dish and placed it on his workbench, just under a slim nozzle of brass tubing that rose from the bench surface in a swan-neck curve. He turned on a tap at the foot of the tubing and when a rush of escaping gas hissed out Czerczy sparked up a flame at the tip of the tube.

He adjusted the tap and the nozzle to trim the flame to his requirements and while Benton and Louis watched, the Polish goldsmith turned the rings into solid links, the links into a solid, slender chain.

"An amber bullet?" asked Benton. "What for?"

"To mark a man."

"Who?" asked Benton. "You?"

Louis shook his head. "Not me. The next Consort. A young man who is currently lying insensible on my parlour settee, sedated and injured."

Benton gave a sharp twitch of his head as if in surprise, or disbelief. "Why would anyone kill the next Consort? Doesn't the current Consort have to die first?"

"Correct."

"Or the current Consort kills his rival."

Louis nodded slowly. "You've been talking to the other Club members, haven't you?"

Benton nodded. His face was still a mask of confused dismay.

"I can only speculate," Louis sighed, "But I suspect the amber bullet wasn't meant to kill the young man. There is a rival – faction, shall we say? – who also wish to control the Lady." He sighed again. "At *least* one. Say, for a moment, that one of them learned about the contact our boy had with the Lady."

"The incident on the bridge?"

News does *travel fast*, Louis thought, nodding. "Now, does the rival faction know her habits well? The Lady has her favourites, just like the heroines in mediaeval legend." He felt a tingle at the base of his scalp. The memory of the time he'd spent with her still heated a fire in his blood. He chose his words carefully as he continued, unwilling to stir up his emotions with an open wound on his left hand. "When she chooses a Consort, it's like she's falling in love – or lust. She's a primeval creature." He paused, cautious and surprised at his own prudishness. He wasn't prepared to share those secrets, not even now.

"And the Lady's fallen for this other man?"

"Seems so," Louis said with a grim smile. "Anyway," he went on, "Our rival knows – or thinks he knows – how She will behave. He's studied Her history, followed Her trail like a hunter. He knows how She will react if Her chosen Consort is in danger."

"Do you think that's why he was shot?"

"She will know he's been injured and will react to protect him."

"Unaware that it's a trap."

"Exactly." Louis glanced up at the younger man with a smile in renewed appreciation of his sharp mind. "She chose me, many years ago, and I have to do all I can to protect her. This" – he indicated the entire workshop and the busy goldsmith with a wave of his bandaged hand – "is part of that." *And who knows whether it will work?*

Some time later Czerczy turned off the gas flame, stepped away from the workbench and beckoned Louis over to the furnace while he removed the ceramic cover to reveal the coals, still aglow. The goldsmith took the glass jar from Louis's hand and arranged it on a wooden tree-stump studded with tiny anvils.

"Now," said Czerczy, and he thrust the finished chain into the charcoals of the furnace. He kept it moving amongst the coals until the links glowed, deep and lustrous. With a final glance towards Louis he removed the chain and dropped it into the jar of blood.

It hissed, it spat, it frothed and burnt and filled the air with a stink so foul the three men escaped into the yard for fresh air. Louis clutched his bandaged hand but in his heart was a dark despair. He'd hoped to feel the effect of the gold in his blood. There was nothing.

Nothing, that is, until the men re-entered the workshop, and found the air filled with the scent of pine pollen.

CHAPTER 15 — What The Butler Saw

Alf awoke from sedation as Louis's butler was lighting the lamps in the parlour. The delicate hiss of gaslights had been replaced in this household by the gentle hum of incandescent bulbs and the silent butler padding across the room from lamp to lamp seemed unreal. As Alf slowly came to consciousness, as if he was rising through deep water to the surface far from where he had been plunged, he experienced more than a few moments of panic as he tried to remember where he was.

For a while he lay still and watched the butler as the man stoked the fire and drew the curtains against a darkening sky. The room was warm, its décor comforting, and Alf wondered how he had come to be there. He seemed to be alone with the butler. Whoever his host was, watching over his guest didn't seem to be a priority.

He felt a genuine nausea, light-headed and trembling, and as he shifted on the sofa he felt a burning pain in his shoulder. He raised a hand to touch the pain and found bandages, a naked chest and arms under a thin blanket. Then he panicked. He drew breath against the pain as he sat up. The butler turned at the sound and moved in one swift motion across the room to aid him.

"How are you, sir?" the butler asked, his voice neither cold nor harsh. "My name is Dodman. I have been told to accommodate you in whatever means you wish."

"What place is this?" Alf asked, almost by instinct.

"A safe house," said Dodman.

"How did I come here?" Alf mumbled. "I remember a cab ride with two gentlemen. Is that right?"

"Yes, sir. His Lordship, Robert, Lord Camden, and the Viscount Smedley of Tuam," Dodman replied. "You are in the house of Mr Louis Beauregard. Brought here for your own safety, sir, after the unfortunate incident on the bridge, I believe."

Alf shook his head, trying to clear it. He couldn't remember much about the bridge except sudden shock, his plans for the remains of the day overturned and an anger at what had happened. *But what* did *happen?*

"There was a crowd," Alf said slowly, picturing them. A man in a check suit. A woman, with a small child sucking a lollipop. Others too, beige- and brown- and black-clad strangers and a cluster of boots. Cold flagstones against his legs and that unbelievable pain in his shoulder all down his side where he must have been leaning against a spiky pillar. Shortness of breath. The shrilling of police whistles.

"It appears that you were shot, sir," Dodman informed him.

"Shot?"

Alf pictured the moment afresh. He was gazing out over the Thames, playing over and over in his mind the girl diving into the water, trying to follow the flow of the river with his eyes, trying to find the spot she'd waved from. Failing. The pattern of masts and funnels had changed since the morning and the tide was wrong. He realised he'd almost felt its ebb.

He'd heard a coach, one amongst many on the bridge behind him, and ignored it as part of the general traffic. But now in the silence of this comfortable parlour with no distractions he heard the coach slow down, heard the thunk of the window sliding open, heard a voice – not his own – raised in surprise.

– Then a force like an iron spike punched him in the shoulder, spun him around and threw him to the ground with such velocity he lost focus. One moment he was staring out across the river and the next, he was trying to drag himself upright from the stone flags of the bridge, dust beneath his fingers and his left arm not responding, a spray of blood on the parapet in front of him, cries of concern in clamour and hands around him, dragging – the PAIN!

"Shot?" he repeated. His stomach turned over. He felt the blood drain from his face.

The butler poured him a glass of water from a pitcher on the side table and held it out towards him with a look of concern on his face.

Alf took the glass with both hands and gulped at it deeply.

"The anaesthetic will have that effect, sir, so I'm told," said Dodman, and took the empty glass from him.

"Why would someone shoot me?" Alf asked, almost to himself in bemusement.

Dodman remained silent.

"I don't have any enemies," Alf began, trying to think who he could have insulted, finding no-one. He thought of Sylvester de Winter, the only other person who'd come into his life recently, but the man was an ally, surely? Alf shook his head without thinking, and another wave of nausea abruptly stopped him. "I can't sit around here all day," he gasped. He sat up and began looking for his clothes.

His eyes fell on the occasional table where the contents of his pockets were laid out on a small silver tray. He was relieved and delighted to see the gold coin amongst them, and also a little dismayed. Whatever had happened was made real by the presence of the coin. He couldn't have come by it any other way. He saw dark shadows at the edge of his vision and realised they foretold another fainting spell. He slumped back onto the cushions of the sofa with a groan.

"The orders of the doctor who tended you were that you should rest," said Dodman.

"I have to meet your master," Alf said. He reached out for his shirt and began to struggle into it. He tried a number of times, but the butler came to his aid when it became clear that Alf was unable to move his left shoulder much without causing pain.

"Mr Beauregard?" said Dodman. "Certainly, sir."

"I need to ask him a few questions – and thank him for all this." Alf waved his free hand at the room and the sickbed on the sofa. With a confusion of shame and embarrassment he realised there was blood all over the cushions. "I – I'm sorry," he said, and glanced up at the butler as if for rescue.

"You can telephone from here, sir, and talk to Mr Beauregard at his club."

Alf shook his head, taking more care with the movement this time. "No," he said, "This is something I should do face to face." He was starting to feel irritated. *Who are these men?* he thought. They seemed to be using him for some higher purpose and not telling him what that was. *Face to face*, he thought, *Like I did with Sylvester de Winter.* "I want to see the man's expression. I want his full attention."

He was angry now and he stubbornly punched his way into his waistcoat, ignoring the pain that shot through his shoulder. "Where should I find this Louis Beauregard?"

Dodman gave Alf the address of the Cuckoo Club. "Shall I call you a cab, sir?"

Alf scooped up the items on the side table and began to fit them back into his pockets. The dwindling number of coins in his possession were a reminder that his funds were limited, and his credit to his rescuer was probably much overdrawn. "No," he said, "Tell me how to get there on foot from here."

Dodman gave a barely audible sigh and outlined simple directions that would take Alf all the way to Piccadilly.

Alf stood up while he listened and a whiff of antiseptic rose into the air with the movement. Although part of him wanted to enjoy the hospitality of Mr Beauregard for a long time there was a gnawing unease that nagged at him. He felt as if he should be elsewhere – not just back at school, but somewhere else entirely, even a sense of being out of place in time. Something tugged at him like a strain on a wound that was knitting together out of shape. He couldn't put a name to it but it dragged at him and he felt he must be away from here, back to the river.

"I can call a cab and charge it to Mr Beauregard's account at the Cuckoo Club," suggested the butler as he helped Alf into his jacket.

"No, thank you," Alf refused. He shrugged his shoulders carefully, settling the garment round his wounded side. "I'm already in debt to the man. I don't want to make it financial as well."

He wasn't even sure he'd go to the man's club. If he took a cab he couldn't stop on the way – he was under the control of the others again. On foot, once he was back in a part of town he recognised he would be at leisure in the city.

He felt a slight give where his wound was and ignored it; it was worse when he breathed too deep. Heaven knew how agonising it would be were he to cough or retch. He tried not to think of it. His head was spinning and he gasped for breath again, found little air to his liking in the now-overheated parlour.

"Are you sure you'll be all right, sir?" Dodman asked, concern at last showing in his voice.

Alf nodded with a degree of vigour that was intended to impress the other man. The action made him realise for the first time how many muscles were connected to the human shoulder. "Need fresh air," he puffed.

He moved out to the hallway, found it cooler and fresher, his breathing easier. When the butler opened the front door for him, a gust of cold air swept into the hall, chill with the odours of coal smoke and birch pollen. Across the street from the house was a little park in a square with high iron railings, and the trees there were just springing into bloom. Their shadows were dark beyond the faint early glow of the municipal streetlights.

"What time is it?" Alf asked, puzzled.

"A little after four," replied Dodman, his face showing a degree of concern which exceeded professional standards.

Breathing deeply enervated Alf. He thought of smacking his hands together, grimaced instead. *Can't let the man see how much this hurts,* he thought. *He'll have me back inside in a flash*. He nodded an acknowledgement and stepped down the steps of the house with his hand on the railing.

Already there was a thin film of mist above the grass of the park, settled in the hollows like dew on a cobweb.

A carriage clattered by and pulled up ahead, the door on the pavement side springing open to spill a bevy of small girls onto the pavement with a governess and a bundle of hatboxes in tow. The small girls and the governess tumbled up a set of stairs into another of the houses further along the terrace, the children giggling and playfully tugging the woman's sleeves while she wrestled the hatboxes through the house's front door. The carriage pulled away from the kerb and clattered off down the street, turning the corner beyond the park into a side street where it disappeared from view.

Alf took the first steps along the pavement and heard the butler closing the door behind him. After he passed the house where the governess and the children had been, he realised he'd forgotten to make a note of which house he'd come out of. He turned and looked back for some clue but found none. A wave of mild panic hit him and he crushed it down. *Don't be silly,* he chided himself. *You have a set of directions. You are going to meet this Louis fellow and find a few answers.*

Another voice in his head said, *And then what?*

As he set off towards Mayfair, he pondered his response to that question. His options were greater in number than they had been earlier in the day. His life had changed so much since he'd stepped off the train that morning. The thought of returning to school dismayed him.

With this wound? he thought. *How will I explain it?*

He realised that while it might bring him some reputation amongst the more robust of his fellows, he would be subjected to lengthy questioning from the school nurse, and probably from his housemaster. The thought made him nervous.

Sylvester de Winter? he thought. *If the man's hospitality is still open.* He debated with himself over the matter, and came to no conclusion.

Above him the night sky drew down upon the city and he turned off Piccadilly as if drawn by an unseen force underground, lost in his thoughts. When he finally noticed his surroundings he was surprised to find himself halfway along Queens Walk in Green Park, under dark trees, the streetlights of The Mall ahead beyond black iron railings.

Without thinking, he was headed back to the river again.

CHAPTER 16 — The Pipe

The cabby's rebuke ringing in his ears after he paid a tuppence fare with a sixpence and refused the change, Alf staggered along the Strand under the influence of whatever anaesthetic he'd been fuelled with. He felt invincible, couldn't believe that anyone would try to stop him doing whatever took his fancy.

Anything is possible, he thought, staring at his feet while he placed them on the paving-stones with care, stepping between the gaps as deliberately as a monk on a pilgrimage.

Walking on air? He raised his head and gazed at the last sunlit clouds ribbed high over the city. *Definitely*. He nodded, and smiled at a well-dressed gentleman who avoided him with a quizzical glance.

Walking on water?

He drew a sharp breath. *What about the girl?*

At the thought of his river maiden, he was overwhelmed with remorse at his forgetfulness. He sat down on the kerb and put his hand in his pocket, fumbling for the little gold coin she'd given him – *yes, she gave it to me*, he told himself – and resolved to see her again, to try his utmost to remove the sad look he remembered on her face. He had begun to think of her as alive, like the Russian had told him, in spite of his best intentions.

He pushed himself to his feet and zig-zagged across the street to the riverward side, his footsteps nimble as a dancer's under the side-effects of the drug as he dodged through the traffic. His agility almost rendered him unsplattered by the muck on the road too, although a passing landau caught him with its rear lantern, tearing the sleeve of his tweed jacket.

He swung around with the impact of the collision but did not lose his balance, merely swayed as he stepped onto the crowded pavement, fondled the tattered rent in the sleeve and smiled, amused at his own lack of anger at the carelessness of the carriage driver.

Matron will hate me for this! he giggled, imagining the rebuke awaiting him back at school when he presented the garment for mending. Under the streetlights the pattern of his jacket fascinated him, the colours washed out by the glare of the lamps.

The thought of his school, and of his arrival in London that morning, sobered him somewhat, but it was a timeless confusion which did not distress him. His thoughts drifted, unfocused, and he barely noticed his progress past Somerset House to the streets beyond.

He was unaware of exactly how long he meandered along Aldwych before Sylvester de Winter's carriage pulled up beside him at the kerb. The driver slowed the horses so that the carriage kept pace with Alf as he swayed along the pavement. The door swung open in a thin billow of Turkish tobacco smoke, the warmth of the amber interior a dark hollow in the gloom of dusk, signalling welcome.

Alf clung to the open door like a shield as he plodded close to the carriage, driving other pedestrians out of his way, his grip on the door handle increasingly firm as the strength in his tired legs ran out. He grew fascinated by the satin buttocks of the carriage horses as the huge muscles flexed, their iron-shod feet stumbling on the cobbles as the driver fought to keep them to a slow walking pace. A tap-tapping sound came from inside the carriage.

Alf saw, too, through the pane of the carriage window, the orange glow of a brazier where a street-vendor had set up a stall. Closing one eye and squinting, he tried to gauge the shrinking distance between the carriage and the brazier, found it impossible and opened both eyes again.

The vendor glanced up, spotted the carriage approaching, opened his mouth in an 'O' of surprise that shaped itself into an "Oi!" of indignant warning.

The carriage stopped.

Alf didn't. He bumped his forehead against the top of the door, grazed his knuckle against the tight-gripped handle, stumbled onto one knee with a jolt that made him gasp. He felt a rush of warm air against the back of his ears, then a leather-gloved hand grasped his collar and hoisted him to his feet with apparent ease.

Sylvester de Winter growled in his ear, breath chill and sour. "Get in, boy."

With the Russian's grip on his collar Alf found it impossible to demur. He half-climbed into the carriage, was half-dragged with a lack of delicacy and sank onto the rear-facing seat in an awkward pose, aware of a burning sensation in his weight-bearing shoulder. He shut his eyes to try to locate the source of his pain as the carriage door slammed shut.

The bolt slithered into place with a steel whisper and he heard the window slide closed, the blind pulled down, blocking out the streetlights to make his closed eyes darker.

He sat upright as the carriage jerked into movement, opened his eyes as the hoofbeats increased in tempo to a pace comfortable for the horses. Glimpsed Sylvester de Winter settling back into the seat opposite.

Alf winced, shut his eyes again and took a deep painful breath as the carriage shook him to one side. He heard the scratch of a Vesta safety match and smelled the fumes as Sylvester de Winter lit up. He glanced over and saw the man's chiselled features lit in the flame like some demon stoking his own private hell. Another jolt, another rush of pain, this time with a rolling wave of nausea that lived on with dread.

"Where are you taking me?" he gasped.

The match showed Sylvester de Winter's black eyes peering at him until the rosebud mouth extinguished it with a puff. "The streets are not safe, dear boy," the Russian replied in an insouciant tone. "Have you learned nothing today?"

Alf's every breath ripped at him and he took care with each one. *Can he see me in this gloom?* he thought. *I hope not.*

The only light came from the lit end of de Winter's cigarette which glowed dull, then flared as the Russian inhaled, then dulled again.

Alf saw the faint outline of de Winter's fingers, saw his cheekbones and nose, watched the cigarette dance like a firefly in the man's hand.

Nausea rolled over him in waves now, pulsing out from the pain in his shoulder in a rhythm of its own. His eyes made circles in the darkness, spiralling inwards, then out, changing each time he blinked. His breathing became hoarse, dragging at the perfumed air in the carriage.

The tap-tapping sound he'd heard earlier returned. The gentle sound was rhythmic but irregular and Alf found himself becoming disorientated as he listened to it.

"Someone shot you," de Winter said flatly.

Alf nodded, wheezed, gasped out a reply. "Yes." He discovered that when he moved his head, shooting pains jabbed up his neck and along his collarbone.

"Do you know who it was?"

"No," Alf replied through gritted teeth.

"Have you any suspicions?"

"No."

Sylvester de Winter raised the blind, opened the carriage window and flicked his cigarette end through the sliver of light. Layers of tobacco-smoke swirled in the carriage like ribbons in the breeze that sliced through the gap, and the fresher air hit Alf in the face.

He gulped at it, eager to breathe a clearer head for himself and a steadier stomach. The air brought the scent of coal smoke and through the gap squeezed the screech of metal scraping against metal, then the tell-tale huff of a locomotive.

Light and shadow played across the tiny slit of the open window as the carriage passed under a railway bridge and Alf's stomach twisted with a nausea unlike any other he'd known. Ignoring the agony that wrenched at his shoulder, he leapt for the window and slammed it open. He forced his head up to the gap and out into the cool night air, his mouth hanging slack and drooling thin spit down the paintwork.

The carriage swept past the crowded pavement outside an amusement-hall of some kind, Alf barely aware of the people on the street; a group of youths jeered and a woman laughed, holding a barking dog on a long metal chain while it snapped its jaws mere inches from his face. Alf felt as if he was being pulled sideways, as though a magnet in the pit of his stomach was attracted to the metal rails high above on the bridge, or some other huge force tugging at the fibres of his muscles. He gulped his breaths and found his thoughts clearing. Each tiny jiggle of the coach yanked at his shoulder and the pain was growing unavoidable.

He drew his head back into the carriage and found Sylvester de Winter observing him with a rapacious interest. Alf sank to his knees on the carriage floor, his left hand tucked into his waistcoat to cradle it from further movement, right hand gripped tight round the window frame.

"What's happening to me?" he whimpered. In the now-cold air of the carriage his breath misted and melted into the remaining wisps of smoke.

Sylvester de Winter smiled, and when he spoke his voice was a murmur almost too faint for Alf to hear. "So you *are* affected." The Russian leaned forward until his face was almost level with Alf's eyes. He rapped on the carriage roof with the knob of his cane and the horses slowed to a halt. Sylvester de Winter placed his gloved hand on the window next to Alf's and leaned out to speak to the driver. "Turn back towards Blackfriars," he ordered. "After we turn under the railway bridge, follow my original instructions."

The Russian withdrew into the amber interior and threw himself against the plush seat as the carriage picked up speed and turned a corner down a quieter side street. He said nothing for a few minutes, during which Alf sat feeling the pain in his shoulder grow intense.

"Where are you taking me?" he asked, but received no reply.

Sylvester de Winter stared through the carriage window into the streets outside, paying no attention to his passenger.

Alf felt a chill spasm ripple through the muscles of his arms, draining through him like a hangover as his body cleansed itself of the remnants of the anaesthetic. It cursed him all the way down to his ankles and he began to shiver. He felt his blood leaking out from under the dressing – just a trickle, but constant, and warm, every time he moved. The wound felt on fire – and colder than ice.

He let go of the carriage window, sank against the door and fished out his pocket handkerchief to wipe his face. He noticed, for the first time, that his clothes were damp and mud-stained. All the time he watched Sylvester de Winter who in turn watched him the way a rat would watch a piece of food floating down the sewer towards it.

"We just crossed Counter's Creek, dear boy." Sylvester de Winter slid the carriage window up with a firm movement and sat back in his seat. "I do believe you felt it as we did so. You have become aware of the tidal river system, haven't you?"

"I don't know what you're on about," Alf said. The darkness around him was filled with the rattle and creak of the carriage and then the tapping noise began again. It came from Sylvester de Winter's direction and Alf realised the man was tapping the band of his signet ring against the brass knob at the head of his cane.

Alf tried to guess when the next tap, or series of taps, would come in the silence, tried to make some kind of sense of the rhythm. *Is it a drumbeat?* he thought, *Or a signal – some form of semaphore or code he wants me to decipher?*

Just when he thought he had caught the rhythm, the tempo or the volume changed and he lost it in the confused rattle of the carriage. "What do you want?" he asked of the darkness inside the coach, tired of waiting.

His reward was a rustling in the darkness as of fabric on some harder substance, then the flare of another match in a pause between ring-taps; the sight of Sylvester de Winter lighting not another cigarette but a long-stemmed pipe, his dark lips sipping at the mouthpiece, smoke curling around his nostrils as it escaped from his mouth. The Russian did not inhale this smoke as he did a cigarette.

"What is that?" Alf asked before the match died. He knew – of course he did – but he'd never seen it before, nor smelled the chicory-bitterness that whispered of release.

De Winter's voice was seductive. "It will ease your pain, dear boy."

Another match flared in the coach and Alf saw the thin china-clay pipestem pointing in his direction, Sylvester de Winter's grip finger-dainty round the bowl where a grain of opium glowed.

"Take it!"

Alf plucked the pipe from the Russian's hand like a child grasping a rare orchid. He put the stem to his lips and they curled away from it as his tears welled up, twisting his face at the edges, and the match died. Alf sucked hard, breathed the smoke deep into his lungs, coughed and felt tears run down the side of his nose as he suckled the opium pipe and waited for the pain to ease.

Sylvester de Winter lit another cigarette.

Alf shut his eyes, ignored the tap of the ring on the cane, and let the tears come. He continued to suck at the mouthpiece of the pipe long after the fire in the bowl had gone out. The rocking of the coach became soothing instead of disturbing and he settled back into the seat. He let himself nod off in the warm darkness and was half-asleep when the coach came to a dead stop. He heard the voice of the coachman as he calmed the horses, felt the clunk of the brake handle as it slammed back against the coach body, heard the door lock flick and the door itself swing open.

Sylvester de Winter stepped out of the carriage. "Stay here, boy," he said. "I won't be long."

He closed the door behind him and Alf heard a key being turned in a lock he had not noticed before. He slid forward to the door opposite and tugged at it with his good hand, but it was locked. The window slid down into the body of the door and seemed to open onto nothing.

The coach was parked on an empty quayside close to the water's edge. Beneath Alf's window was an iron bollard set on the cobbles of some dock. The sky overhead was a lacework of crimson against blue, high clouds underlit by the last reflections of sunset with the promise of a cold night ahead. A thin mist was gathering on the empty waters out in the middle of the dock and Alf's breath clouded in front of his eyes.

Out across the expanse of the dock Alf saw a couple of little boats pushing through the mist. The water was calm. On the far side of the water, lights burned in the grid of the dock building windows, lamps on the boats and ships moored along the piers. Smells of cooking thickened the air. Laughter and conversation in a dozen languages bantered back and forth amongst the hulks.

Alf felt the water pulling at him, a seductive summoning, a lullaby to gentle slumber. In his current state he was powerless to give in.

The carriage rocked and he heard a thumping noise from the rear. The door behind him was unlocked and Sylvester de Winter threw a bulky parcel onto the carriage floor, glanced at Alf then locked the door again. Alf heard low conversation from the other side of the coach. Sylvester de Winter appeared again at Alf's back and resumed his seat.

"Get your nose in, boy," Sylvester de Winter ordered.

Alf obeyed, slowly, his eyes on the world outside the carriage where warmth and companionship and food beckoned. He felt nauseous again, this time a plain sensation with none of the strange undercurrent of danger.

Sylvester de Winter slid the window up with a firm movement. "I mean it."

Alf sat in the bench and rearranged his feet around Sylvester de Winter's parcel on the floor. The coach rocked and Alf heard the coachman hunch up on his seat, release the brake and chuck the horses. With a gentle lurch they were off again. After a few moments Sylvester de Winter lit a lamp on the inside of the carriage and began observing Alf with his black eyes. Alf let him.

"Do you feel it?" Sylvester de Winter asked.

Alf glanced up. The swirling patterns in the amber panels that lined the carriage were as hypnotic as the Russian's cigarette smoke. "What?"

"The river," Sylvester de Winter went on. "Can you feel it, at all?"

Alf shook his head, unsure still of the Baron's intent.

"Who shot you?"

"I don't know."

"Who bandaged you up?"

Alf debated with himself before he responded. *Should I tell him about Beauregard? What should I tell him? How much can I trust this man?* He shook his head, trying to clear his thoughts. *How much do I trust Beauregard?* With his good hand he rubbed his face. With a shock he realised his cheek was rough with stubble, like a man's, the reality of his maturity only months in experience.

"I should be back at college," he mumbled, a feeling of dread creeping over him as he considered the consequences of the day's events. *Who knows what trouble I'm in?* His rail ticket ran out at midnight. He had to get the last train home. But how would he explain his injuries to the doctor at college?

"Is that all?" Sylvester de Winter snapped.

"None of this makes any sense, sir," Alf said with another miserable shake of his head. And then he knew what he wanted. A surge of emotion rolled through him as he saw again in his mind's eye the girl on the bridge and the frightened look on her face. He stared at the floor, ashamed. His voice, when he spoke, was husky and emotional. "I just want to save her."

Sylvester de Winter, not without guile, said nothing for a long while. Then he said in a soft voice, "So do I."

Alf felt as if the blood had drained from his head. "Who is she really?" he whispered.

Sylvester de Winter did not reply to the question, but he looked away as if it were a matter of decency. "We just crossed the Walbrook," he said, and lit yet another cigarette from the flame of the lamp.

"Where are we going?"

"Spitalfields," said the Russian. "To the hospital." He tapped the parcel with his cane. "To deliver this."

"What is it?"

Sylvester de Winter smiled but did not reply, his eyes hard as iron.

CHAPTER 17 – Nepenthe

Louis returned to the Cuckoo Club from Hatton Garden exhausted, and collapsed into a chair in the hallway within feet of the door, leaning on the walls for strength. The Porter brought the telephone apparatus to him, trailing brown cloth-wrapped cord across the parquet of the entrance hall, his heels clicking on the polished surface.

Louis listened and barely spoke as his butler informed him of Alf's departure. His mind was on other things. When the brief call was over he handed the earpiece back to the Porter with a brief nod of thanks. "Stick close to that contraption, Parsons," he warned. "I expect it will be busy tonight."

The Porter nodded and retreated back to the desk, reeling the telephone cable in behind him as he went.

Louis put his head in his hands and cursed. *Just what we don't need,* he thought. *That fool boy haring off around town, dragging the Lady towards him like a magnet on a heap of iron filings. How the hell do we find him again? Do I have to have him arrested to keep him in one place?*

He hauled himself to his feet and waved away the Porter's offer of assistance. As he turned to the stairs – *might as well have a nap in the office,* he thought – he glanced at the painting on the wall behind him. One of Turner's seascapes, the Tudor points of the Tower of London breaking through a thick mid-century smog. Louis sighed. *No wonder the Lady deserted London then,* he thought, staring at the artist's muddy river stuck like toffee on the canvas.

Louis turned away from the Porter's Desk and entered the Members' Lounge. At this hour on a normal evening the room would be quiet, the members not yet in attendance for pre-dinner drinks. Tonight was different.

Members sat around in groups and there was a low murmur of conversation, broken by an occasional cough or the click-crack of a billiards game in progress. Louis felt glances towards him as he strode through the room. A burst of laughter exploded from one corner, the noise out of place with his mood.

He glanced around, saw the tension drawn on the face of each man in the room, knew his face must be tense too – his jaw hurt, and when he rubbed it with his hand he felt the first rasp of stubble on his skin. He straightened his back and glided out of the Members' Lounge as if on castors, steps brisk and even, and made his way upstairs.

"Louis?"

The voice called out as Louis passed the open door of the Chairman's Office.

Louis waved with a lazy hand and returned the greeting.

The Chairman beckoned him in. The room was cramped by an ornate desk piled with crates of wine sent on approval from one of a half-dozen of London's wine merchants. Books and documents spilled from the bookcases lining one wall, glass display cases containing Club curios not yet assigned a place in the Club's Museum Room slotted into gaps between the papers.

"We're in for a long night," Louis said with a sigh as he sank into the spare chair opposite the Chairman. "The damn boy's gone walkabout."

"I thought you said you'd keep him safe."

Louis nodded and let a wry smile play around his lips. "I did say that, yes. Apparently he had other ideas. You know how impetuous these young men are. Anyway," he went on, "The matter rests. He has gone missing, and I'm waiting to see if we can find out where the cab took him. He can't – won't – have gone far."

"I wish I shared your optimism. London's not as small as it used to be, Louis."

"No," he said, making his words mirror his thoughts. "But I understand the situation. Our boy won't stray far from the river."

The Chairman man glared at him, unable or unwilling to mask the contempt on his face. "Of course. Your experiences tell you all you need to know. This is going to strain the Club funds. I hope you know what you're doing."

Louis felt tension streaming out of the other man and found his own temper growing short. He pushed himself to his feet and leaned over the desk towards the Chairman. "You *need* me," he said in a tired voice that nonetheless showed his ire. "Of course, you have telegrams and railway locomotives and repeating rifles; but the Lady knows NOTHING of these, and they mean nothing to her. She cannot understand them. It is as if they are of no consequence. But She will seek out the boy, wherever he is and in whatever company, and She cannot understand what danger she is in."

The Chairman went red and spluttered something Louis didn't catch.

He glared at the Chairman, fought the urge to slap him, saw beads of sweat on the other's grey scalp at the edge of his receding hairline, noted the intense lines round the man's lashless eyes. *We're all tense,* thought Louis. He sighed. "She'll come back tonight."

"How can you be sure?"

Louis shook his head. "I need a rest," he said, and apologised to the younger man. Without another word he crept into his office, laid his head on his desk, and slept.

CHAPTER 18 — The Bite That Splits

"Who's your pretty friend, then, Annie?"

The man approached them shortly after their arrival in Lower East Smithfield. The evening was just beginning but Polly felt a chill in the air that predicted frost by morning. He hailed them from across the street, then stepped into the roadway from the shadows of a warehouse building.

"Who is he?" Polly whispered as he slipped between the traffic towards the three women.

"Dick Granger," said Annie. Her tone was bewildered.

"He work round here?"

Annie nodded. "Think so."

"I'm Mary Kelly," said the Irish girl when he'd reached their side of the road. Her hair gleamed dark in the lamplight, her chin tilted up with pouting lips and that air of challenge she seemed to carry with her always.

Polly smelled the gin on her, and beer off the man.

He sauntered up, slid his arm around Annie's waist and nuzzled into her neck, murmuring something into her ear that had made her chuckle. But Polly noticed he never took his eyes off Mary Kelly all the time, even as he handled Annie's behind. He ignored Polly completely.

It made her uncomfortable, but she didn't feel like making a fuss.

"Well, then, Mary," said Dick Granger, disengaged himself from Annie and moved onto the Irish girl. He made the same move on her that he'd made on Annie, the same approach, same dip of the head to the woman's ear and the murmured proposal.

"Eeh, you dirty beggar!" Mary Kelly screeched, laughing and wriggling in his grip – but not escaping.

"Only, Annie here –" the man said with a nod in her direction, "– won't let me."

The pair giggled together, Mary Kelly and the stranger, but Polly watched closely and Mary Kelly's face was working all the time, eyes keen and calculating. Her bonnet barely reached the man's shoulder. Polly watched it bob and nod as Mary Kelly agreed to something else that Dick Granger murmured in her ear.

"Wait for me, Poll?" the Irish girl asked over her shoulder as she led the man away towards the corner by Irongate Wharf.

Polly nodded. Turned her back on the couple and walked over to the warehouse doorway for shelter. Annie followed. The look on her face was hard to fathom but Polly guessed it was hurt.

When Annie spoke again, it was a whisper. "Need my medicine, Poll," she ghosted. "Need a drink." Then she snuggled into Polly's arms like a kid and she was warm and Polly didn't mind the heat.

Me too, thought Polly bitterly. She was thinking, much too hard, about Mary Kelly and Annie.

"She's gone, hasn't she?" Annie mumbled.

"No, love," Polly replied, patting Annie's shoulders for comfort. "She's only gone round the corner with 'im."

"She's took him with her, hasn't she?"

"Yes."

"What about us, Poll?"

Polly was torn in two. Annie was the only friend she had. But Annie seemed to have lost her touch. What had just happened was a threat to Polly and Annie's livelihood together, especially Polly's ability to avoid encounters like the one that the Irish girl was away enduring.

Mary Kelly was still an unknown quantity – but she was young, pretty, and Polly wasn't daft. There was an opportunity there.

"Don't leave me, Poll, won't you?"

Polly glanced down at Annie's head in the lamplight and fought the urge to shiver. "No, love," she said, and prayed that Jesus would understand it wasn't a lie. She held Annie close to her, partly for warmth and partly to keep the other woman quiet. She didn't want to be disturbed while they waited for the Irish girl to return.

As the pair of them stood in the shadows, a cream-coloured coach entered the docks from the direction Burr Street. It passed them by and stopped at an empty wharf not 20 yards in front of Ivory House. A dapper man got out, locked the carriage door, disappeared into one of the warehouses in the undercroft of the dock building.

"What's up, Poll?" Annie whispered.

"That coach we were looking for this morning," Polly said in a low voice. "The one on the bridge, remember?"

"No, Poll."

"You don't half stretch my Christian charity, Annie, love," said Polly under her breath. In a louder voice she continued: "That coach that Fred the Chinaman was looking for. It's over on the other side of the dock gate. He can shove his shilling."

"I'm not well, Poll," Annie whimpered. She clung to Polly's arms with her tiny hands gripping like the claws of a hawk. Polly recognised the signs. Annie was ill, and the medicine she took to ease the symptoms produced symptoms of its own, and when the medicine ran out and there was no money for more, Annie suffered.

And now Annie's charms are fading, thought Polly. She dreaded the reality that she'd have to work more to keep them both alive. The thought turned her stomach. *I need another drink, sweet Jesus love me.*

The dapper man came out of the warehouse, followed by another man carrying a package. Dapper Gent opened the coach door, put the package inside, closed the door.

Polly heard footsteps from the alleyway to her left, the sound of hobnail boots on cobbles, heard a man hockle and spit. Annie's friend appeared in the shadows, all beer and animal smells. He chuckled to himself as he stared Polly in the eye for the first time.

"Poor old Annie, eh?" he laughed under his voice. He pressed his body up against both of them.

"Ain't you done yet?" Polly snapped.

He pushed his face close up to hers. His hand found her breast behind the corset and squeezed it hard. "Slut," he spat like a slap in the face.

The carriage interrupted her vision. It must have turned half circle and was heading past the little group. Through the open window Polly thought she spotted the youth from that morning. Her bile rose.

"You filthy bastard," she muttered under her breath as the coach headed off in the direction of Nightingale Lane.

The man laughed and leered, stepped back from her, took Annie's face in one hand and turned it up to meet his.

He stuck his tongue in her mouth just briefly, and when he withdrew it a long strand of saliva linked the pair a moment longer. When it broke it fell on Annie's jacket where her buttonhole held a grubby handkerchief.

Polly, up close to both of them, smelled musk on the man's hand. She jerked her head back to stop him trying the same manoeuvre with her. "Get out of here!"

Another laugh from the man, who followed her gaze towards the disappearing carriage. He shook his head with a loose throaty chuckle. "Leave it alone, bird," he said. "Them's too good for the likes of you."

Polly said nothing, just let go of Annie and wrenched herself away from the man.

Annie clung to Polly's arm and looked up at her, eyes wide and full of a sudden, startling clarity.

"Who is he?" Polly asked, indicating the space where the coach had turned the corner and disappeared.

The man shrugged. "Dunno. Some Russian toff, comes down here for a shipment now and again. Opium, I reckon. Or hashish."

"Poll," Annie whispered, tugging at her sleeve.

Polly glanced down into frightened eyes and patted Annie's hand. "Yeah, Annie, I know."

"Poll, I need it," Annie begged.

Dick Granger laughed, sneered, patted Annie's cheek roughly and rolled away from them. "Tell your Irish friend to look me up sometime," he called over his shoulder with a sour beery belch.

Polly glared at him, at the back of his head. *Curse you*, she thought, *I got nothing for my troubles and you got Annie all worked up.*

Annie was pleading with her again. "Poll, I need my medicine," she whimpered. "Poll?"

Polly was lost deep in thought, more sober now than she'd been all day. She hated it.

There was a coughing and retching noise from the alleyway behind them, then Mary Kelly's voice rang out. "Right, then, me sisters, who's for a drink?"

Polly heard false bonhomie in the Irish girl's voice, the shake and tremor betraying an underlying fear, but Polly's overwhelming need was for a drink. She turned, ignoring Annie again, and cried out at the sight of the Irish girl under the streetlights. "Saints, girl, what happened to you?"

A stream of blood, black in the faint lamplight, was trickling across Mary Kelly's thin white collarbone.

"What?" The Irish girl's voice rose as she spoke, narrowed eyes searching Polly's face. "What're you on about?"

Polly pointed, reached out her hand, realised that Mary was too drunk to have noticed.

She noticed the blood though, and screeched, shaking her head as if she was trying to see her own neck.

"Shh," Polly said firmly, "That'll only make it worse. Here –"

The Irish girl struggled as Polly fought to hold her head steady, to one side.

"Turn towards the light so I can see you better." Polly fished a handkerchief from one of her skirt pockets and dabbed at the blood. "Annie?" she said over her shoulder, "Keep lookout, will you?"

She turned back to Mary Kelly and wiped her neck clean, searching for a wound with her fingers, up under the girl's hair. Mary flinched and raised her hands in protest.

"What happened, girl?"

Mary shrugged, frowning. "The usual," she said. "He was quick. Got in right close to me too." She wrinkled her nose as if she were disgusted.

Polly found the source of the blood and wiped it with the handkerchief.

Mary Kelly yelped and jerked her head back in surprise, her indrawn breath a sharp gasp.

"It ain't deep," Polly snapped. She peered closer. "Looks like teeth marks."

"Yeah?" Mary Kelly's voice began to rise until she was screeching again. "He bit me! The bastard! I'll have his filthy eyes out, I will!"

"Hey!" Polly cried. She hushed the Irish girl with her arms, held her tightly to stop her shadow boxing with anyone and herself, calmed her down with the soothing noises a mother might make to a fractious child. "Lose it," Polly said into Mary's good ear, the brim of the girl's bonnet jabbing into her eyebrow. "He paid, didn't he?"

Mary Kelly nodded.

"Then shut your yap and let's go spend it before someone nicks it off us."

Mary Kelly wriggled free from Polly, stood off with a guarded look in her eyes. "I earnt it," she said haughtily, free hand touching the bite mark. "Me, myself, all on my own." Her eyes darted from Polly to Annie and back again. "What did you do to get it?" she spat. "It's mine, and I'm going to spend it."

Polly didn't have an answer. "I reckon you got a point, there," she conceded.

The Irish girl swung around on one heel and set off down the wharf towards the tavern on her own, unsteady on her feet, bonnet bobbing as she swayed.

"Poll," said Annie in a weak voice.

Polly turned back again at the sound of her name. Over Annie's head she saw a police constable start his patrol along the wharf.

Annie was pawing her now, begging, and Polly knew with a sinking feeling what that meant.

"Come on, then," said Polly, offering her arm to Annie.

The shorter woman took it in silence and Polly led her away down to the end of the wharf, away from the police constable, keeping alert for trouble. A sick hunger was rising in her. She needed a drink, but Annie needed medicine. Both items needed money, of which they had precisely none.

Annie, in this state, was too weak to earn any. So Polly knew her only option was to earn it herself. She fought to deaden the feelings of fear and disgust that were companions as faithful as Annie, and just as reliable.

Polly cursed in her head and prayed under her breath in equal measure as she and Annie left Irongate Wharf. They ducked under the shadow of Tower Bridge and turned north along Little Tower Hill, edging around the City of London through the East End, towards Whitechapel Road, heading for the asylum at Spitalfields and a source of solace for them both.

CHAPTER 19 — An Irishman, In Shadows

The coach rattled on through the streets as early evening drew down over the rooftops of the city. Alf found his concentration waning. More than once he fell asleep, just for a moment, then jerked awake with a sudden movement, not knowing where he was or how long he'd slept. The journey seemed to take all night, stopping, starting, Sylvester de Winter smoking or not. Alf became bewildered but somehow unconcerned.

The pain had gone. He was numb all over like those times when, as a child, he'd been out in the snow and the feeling had gone from his fingers and toes. He wanted to ask if this was normal, because it certainly didn't feel so, but Sylvester de Winter's gaze was dark and stern when it flitted over him, like the eye of some steely beast; like a vulture watching a thirsty man die his way across the desert.

The coach halted. Alf heard the coachman scrape the brake handle into place with a solid thudding sound that reverberated through the amber-lined carriage.

Sylvester de Winter slid open the window beside him a slit, glanced out, pulled on his leather gloves. Glanced towards Alf, and met his gaze.

"You might benefit from joining me now," said Sylvester de Winter in a tone that suggested he was not overly concerned one way or the other.

"Where are we?" Alf asked. It was the first of many questions in his mind and somehow it got out first.

Sylvester de Winter snorted. "Limehouse," he replied. "At the house of – an associate of mine."

The Russian unlocked the carriage door and slid from the seat onto the pavement outside. He looked around him and beckoned to Alf with his free hand, holding the door open with the other. "You'll see. Come."

Alf slid along the bench seat to the door, holding on wherever he found something to grip. He wasn't sure if his legs would hold him. They didn't quite respond as normal. He tapped his feet on the kerbstones before he lifted his body out of the cab, like a man testing thin ice on the surface of a pond.

The air of the street had begun to take on the chill of the night air and Alf noticed his breath misting in the light that dropped from the windows of the tall building beside the carriage, its high casements filled with opaque glass and tar-paper. He breathed deep, caught scents familiar and unfamiliar – horses; tobacco; wet linen, boiling; aniseed and jasmine and cabbage.

Voices raised in the street on the other side of the cab spoke something not English, long on vowels through the nose, the consonants clipped and choppy. Chalked on the wall beside the doorway in front of him he saw a tangle of straw-stick pictograms. He looked up, his eye drawn by empty washing lines criss-crossing the narrow street like the sheets of a sailing ship, up to the dim lights of the rookery showing three, four storeys high. Somewhere up there a window was open, the sounds of laughter and music escaping.

The carriage door closed behind him with a sharp sound like a stick breaking underfoot. Keys jangled in Sylvester de Winter's hand as he locked the door, then his free hand gripped Alf on the upper arm and Alf was led over to the door of the building nearby.

A tiny man no more than four feet tall greeted Sylvester de Winter with a bow and led them deeper into the building. The air was thick with the reek and smoke of incense.

Alf's breath still misted in the cold corridors. The small man rattled on in a language Alf assumed was Chinese. Sylvester de Winter seemed to be ignoring him except for the occasional grunt in place of a civil reply.

Once, on their way along a long corridor with a musty smell, they passed an open door where a corpse lay on a table surrounded by candles and a group of Chinese clad in white, still as statues, stood around the coffin like guardian spirits. None of them paid any attention to the trio passing by.

At the end of one corridor the man knocked on a door with an iron grille set into it at a level with Alf's chest, but which the tiny Chinese could barely reach. Behind this a small flap slid open.

The man exchanged words with someone out of sight and with an elaborate flourish of unlocking the door swung open to let Alf and Sylvester de Winter inside.

The suite behind seemed bright after the gloom of the corridor but each chamber, except for one, was lit by only one lamp. In the brightest and largest room sat an imposing man in an ornate chair surrounded by three other men,

Chinese in appearance, dressed in simple black pyjama-style clothes with their long hair drawn back into pigtails.

The man in the chair was dressed in the manner of the East, but he was European, with red hair and pale freckled skin.

De Winter bowed to this man who rose from his chair and bowed in return. He spoke some kind of greeting which The Russian returned. With one hand Sylvester de Winter indicated Alf, off to one side, and then he was dismissed almost as if he were of no consequence.

The freckled man waved a hand over towards a pair of couches flanking the fireside and de Winter joined him.

Lacking any other direction, Alf followed.

They sat in silence for what seemed like ages. Alf grew increasingly uncomfortable with the situation, the three Chinese men staring at him intently but the Europeans ignoring him, as if he were invisible, and also curiously ignoring one another.

Then an elderly Chinese woman entered the room with a tray laden with tea things. She laid it on the table by the fire and prepared to serve the men.

Only when the tea was poured and the first cup sank did the other man speak. His accent was Irish, his voice soft. "Since you mangle my Cantonese so roughly, let us treat in a language neither of us respects."

Sylvester de Winter grinned. "As ever, Kavanagh, your wisdom in these matters exceeds mine."

"Have you a shipment for me?"

Sylvester de Winter nodded and withdrew a slim package from the breast pocket of his jacket. It was about the size of a volume of poetry, wrapped in oilskin or some sort of lacquered linen. He laid it on the table with a flourish and pushed it towards Kavanagh.

"Its quality?"

"The very highest," said Sylvester de Winter. "Afghan."

Kavanagh nodded. "You understand, however, that I must test this for myself?"

In reply Sylvester de Winter dipped his head to his teacup and took a delicate sip.

Alf saw swirls of steam rise from the surface of the pale fluid, watched Sylvester de Winter's thin red lips nip at the rim of the china, his fingers gently round the tiny handle, nails trimmed and scrupulously clean. There were fine hairs on the man's fingers, dark between the ridges of his knuckles, but he was not as hirsute as the Irishman.

The scent of the tea – jasmine and oolong – was as delicate as blossom and Alf felt his mouth pucker. Kavanagh had not offered him any.

From her belt the elderly servant brought out a porcelain tube decorated in blue and white glaze. At first glance it resembled a flute or some other musical instrument but then Alf saw the large perforation at one end, the metal gauze lining therein, and he licked his lips in recognition.

Kavanagh and Sylvester de Winter sat sipping tea, neither glancing at each other nor the woman.

Alf was fascinated.

The elderly woman took Sylvester de Winter's package from the tray and moved it to the end of the marble table in front of her. She laid the pipe on the marble, setting it at an angle so it would not roll off. Her stained fingers unsheathed a small pocket-knife and with a nimble movement she flicked at the wrappings around the package until one corner lay open.

Inside, the drug lay brown and as the woman poked it with the tip of the knife, small fragments crumbled off. The smell of it was earthy, the packaging smelled musty, and Alf felt himself grow hungry as she scooped up a tiny flake no bigger than his pinkie nail and laid it onto the gauze in the pipe.

She turned her back on Kavanagh with a bow of apology and Alf felt like he'd stepped into a Rembrandt, the planes of her face shaped by the firelight as she bent to light a spill from the coals. The spill flared up, filling the room with the scent of burning paper, and the woman put the pipe to her lips and lit it.

Alf's mouth watered and the pit of his stomach fluttered in excitement and envy. Already he wanted this, his one taste not enough to start a craving or a habit but an excitement, the hunger in him for experience and forbidden knowledge. He felt a bitter memory resurface of his previous vows of abstinence, and forced it back where it came.

The Chinese woman let the smoke sit heavily in the bowl of the pipe for a second, then sucked on the mouthpiece with a sharp gulp, taking the smoke into her open mouth and holding it there a moment before she seemed to swallow it. Closed her mouth, then her eyes, seemed to rest motionless kneeling on her heels for an age, then the smoke billowed out of her nostrils and was swept up the chimney by the fire's updraught.

Alf watched with bitter envy as the woman emptied the remainder of the opium from the pipe into the fire, tapping the gauze with the penknife to remove the last of the sticky crumbs. *I would have had that,* he thought.

Kavanagh broke the silence with a phrase of Cantonese directed at the woman.

She did not turn back to face him, merely rocked on her heels and murmured her one-word reply. "Ah."

Kavanagh put down his cup and saucer with delicate grace and waited while Sylvester de Winter did similar before he spoke again. "It is agreed," he said. "The quality is – good enough."

Sylvester de Winter gave a thin smile. "You bargain like a coolie, Kavanagh. I know the purity of this shipment. I know every step of its route here, from the soil in which the poppies grow to the pilot who brought the ship upriver into London. Nonetheless," he paused for a second to bring out his cigarettes, "I believe we can come to some agreement."

Kavanagh nodded. "Of course." He smiled. "Any Yunnan peasant can buy and sell cheap opium to the lower classes. But my clients expect better from me."

The Irishman watched Sylvester de Winter light his cigarette, and if he was displeased none of it showed in his expression. Then the pair began to talk business, money and poundage and delivery, and Alf's eyelids drooped as he became bored by the details.

He sat and watched the package at the far end of the table, his mouth watering and sour, unable to concentrate on anything else.

He examined the elderly woman too, her eyes closed and puffed in the red-orange glow of the fire. The bags under her eyes and her high black eyebrows made her face seem permanently surprised. Her hair was cropped short, salt and pepper in colour, half hidden under a peakless grey cap. But she had a smile on her lips, a gentle smile that deepened the creases round her mouth, twisted at the furrows of her whiskered upper lip. Alf was starting to find her disgusting when his concentration was broken.

Kavanagh clapped his hands.

The Chinese woman's eyes shot open and she turned to the Irishman with a low kowtow and again, that single word, "Ah."

Kavanagh waved her in the direction of the tea-things with one hand and away with the other.

She tidied the things onto the tray in another silence then asked something in the language Alf assumed was Cantonese.

Alf glanced at her and realised she must have been watching him while he was looking at her, because she regarded him now with what looked like amusement. He became aware how intensely he'd been staring at the opium still on the table.

"Well, why not?" said Kavanagh with a jovial smile. He then addressed Sylvester de Winter. "Would your boy like some of our consignment?"

Sylvester de Winter glanced at Alf with a sleek movement of his head and nodded as a smile broadened his lips. "I'm sure he would." He turned to Alf. "Wouldn't you, dear boy?"

Alf didn't speak, just nodded in reply. *Yes,* he thought while he fought with his conscience until he ceased to care. *Just let me have some more. Just this once.*

The elderly woman packed the pipe away in her clothes, wrapped the opium back into its packaging and removed the tea things on the tray. Alf watched her go in dismay. She returned empty handed and beckoned to him.

Without a backwards glance he let her lead him out of the sumptuous room into the corridor outside. He followed her deep into the warren of the rookery, not caring where they were going, paying no heed to the people they passed on the way, white men, Chinese women, as if they were all wraiths under the spell of some goblin king.

The corridors were cold, the plasterwork slick with condensation. Stripes of grime stood out against the peeling paint where passers-by had rested nonchalant boots, greased hair, grimy shoulders. Some of the doors were screened with velvet curtains, stained and moth-eaten.

The Chinese woman moved quickly but Alf's longer stride kept pace with her without exertion. She brushed the other inhabitants out of their way with a chatter of her own language. If they stared at Alf when he passed, he barely noticed.

She drew to a halt outside a plain-looking door painted green. The woman rapped on it and yelled something staccato and the door swung open. She ushered him inside before her with a word, maybe two, of Cantonese.

Alf had been expecting an opium den like something out of Thomas de Quincey, but he was pleasantly disappointed. While the room was not as plush as the one holding Kavanagh and Sylvester de Winter, it was spacious, well-furnished, and at least as clean and warm as his room at school.

The room's other occupant was a stubby Chinese girl – probably no older than he – who held out her empty hand and beckoned him over.

He glanced at the elderly guide as she backed out of the room and saw a grin spread across her face. But then he turned his attention to the girl and the brass tube in her hand.

The package that Sylvester de Winter had given Kavanagh lay open, unwrapped, on the side table beside her and as Alf slid onto the chaise longue that she indicated, his eyes never left the crumbs she shook into the pipe-bowl and lit for him.

Some time later Alf lifted his head from the plump cushion behind him and watched Sylvester de Winter enter the room with Kavanagh. They spoke to one another, possibly about him. He cared not.

The Chinese girl, at a slight signal from Kavanagh, left Alf's side and moved to the two men. She bowed to the Irishman, then to Sylvester de Winter.

The Russian walked around her like a man examining a beast at market while she stood with her head bowed. Then he nodded and the girl dipped her head again. She led Sylvester de Winter out of the room leaving Alf befuddled and alone with Kavanagh.

Alf closed his eyes again and when he opened them the room was empty.

Still, he cared not. The drug had performed its intoxicating effect and he felt enveloped in warm numbness. Time passed. The fire in the grate died down. Sylvester de Winter and Kavanagh did not return.

The elderly Chinese woman reappeared and lifted him from the chaise, led him back down the corridor that now seemed endless, pushed him into a room where Sylvester de Winter and two Chinese girls sat drinking.

The room smelled animal, gamy, like high meat. The three of them watched as Alf swayed, steadied himself, then slumped into an armchair.

They giggled.

He saw Sylvester de Winter's coat and hat laid across another chair, saw the man had his collar and tie off, observed that his braces hung down loose from the waistband of his trousers. Noticed that under their delicate gowns the Chinese girls were naked. Saw more than that when one of them laid back across the sofa she lay upon, the folds of her dress parting to reveal her thighs, her thighs parting to reveal the glistening folds of her flesh.

Alf stared in shock, his temperature rising like a blush across his cheeks. He leapt to his unsteady feet and left the room.

The chill stinking air of the corridor woke him. Took away none of the numbness, though, and did not erase the picture in his mind.

Emotions tumbled through him. Disgust and fascination. Curiosity and revulsion. Disbelief. His heart was pounding hard and he felt a flutter in his stomach. *Had she really meant me to see that? What was I meant to do?* His lame body began to answer for him in a display of animal reactions that horrified him further.

There were people out in the corridors alongside him, strangers he did not recognise, most of them Chinese, some of them women. He crouched down on the floor, avoiding the puddles of piss, in an attempt to hide his erection. The folds of his trousers cut into him, rubbed painfully, maddening, enticing. *Why now?* he thought in shame.

He crouched there for what seemed like ages, the chill creeping through the soles of his shoes into the bones of his feet, until the door opened. The giggling Chinese girls slipped out, crept past him with sly glances, arms around each other. Their clog-like shoes clacked on the solid floor.

Alf crouched further, fighting back tears, wishing he could go home. He needed to find a lavatory, wanted somewhere of his own where he might find solitude from all these crowded strangers, wanted a cold bath to cool his passion and wake him up. He began to feel that the day had somehow gone sour.

He felt a warm glow at his side and realised his wound was leaking. A lump formed in his throat and he swallowed hard to clear it. *I really ought to go back to that other man,* he thought, *the one who so kindly bandaged me up.* He told himself he really ought to go to a hospital, for that matter, and get himself back to school.

And leave Sylvester de Winter? he reflected. The Russian had done little to help him tonight, just fed him opium and dragged him to this sordid pit to endure depravity and humiliation. Alf knew he was lost.

"What time is it, please?" he asked into the crowded corridor. His voice barely rose above the hubbub of conversation, and one of the Chinese nearby glanced down at him as though he were a dog, chained there by its master and making a nuisance of itself. No-one replied.

It's probably dark outside now, he thought, *and I have no idea where I am, or to get back to the city.* He didn't even know how to get out of the building. And the coachman was waiting.

The door at his side opened again and Sylvester de Winter appeared, fully dressed, his cane tapping the floor with an impatient rhythm, a cigarette dangling from his gloved hand. He tapped Alf with the cane. A small droplet of some fluid from the floor flew off the brass ferrule on the end and spotted Alf's sleeve.

"Come along, lad," said the Russian in a bright voice. "Not your cup of tea, eh?" He laughed at his own joke.

Alf scrambled to his feet and stumbled along the corridor after Sylvester de Winter, trying to keep his shameful privates covered with the crusty flap of his jacket. "Where are we going now, sir?"

The Baron swivelled, his coat flaring out around him, cigarette hand raised. "The night is young," he said in a cheerful voice that rang from the slick walls. "I have much to do. I need your help. But first," he raised a gloved finger off the silver cane top, "Some fun. We are going to Whitechapel, to pick up a girl for you. One more suited to your tastes, eh?"

Sylvester de Winter's teeth grinned in the dim lamplight. "And I need a drink."

CHAPTER 20 – Under Cannon Street Bridge

The man's hands were soft and he used them with delicacy. His nails were short and smoothed, and Polly felt his fingers explore under her skirt, parting the soft folds of her body, at the same time as she tried not to feel anything. He poked a finger into her and she switched her mind off, eyes on the wall opposite with its poster from last August advertising a circus on the Common. The paper was peeling off.

The soft fingers probed a bit more.

"Get on with it," she snapped.

The man's face was buried in her collar. He'd tried to kiss her but she never had any truck with that. "Sure," he muttered and stepped back from her to undo his trousers.

Polly smelled him then, pungent and strong, and then his cock nosed into her.

In spite of his fingering she was dry and his insistent thrusts chafed at her. "God, you're tight," he growled.

Polly said nothing, thought nothing, just stood there with her back against the brick wall and stared at the poster opposite. Her bonnet banged against the brickwork, tugging one hatpin against her hair. She began to get cramp in one leg.

He muttered something else.

Dear God, Polly thought, *Not a talker.* She gave a noncommittal grunt and he quickened his pace. *Animal,* she thought in disgust.

His soft hands sought for her breasts. To Polly he could have been handling kidneys down Smithfield Market, dead meat still warm. He finished and stood against her, pinning her body against the wall.

Polly got fed up waiting for him to pull out. "Get off me," she said sullenly and twisted her hips. She felt his cock slither along the strong tendon of her thigh, twitched her skirt hem away too late to avoid it being soiled. Slime drooled down her leg. Polly's disgust took over.

She left him in the alley without another word and crossed the lane into a courtyard. She turned her disgust against herself and the coins in her pocket that jangled as she took out a handkerchief to wipe down her privates.

The courtyard's water pump didn't work so Polly rubbed herself dry with the handkerchief and tied it into a tight knot. Her hands were sticky with residue as she thrust the hankie deep into a pocket. She sniffed her fingers and still smelled his semen on her, slut that she was.

Annie was still waiting for her at the far end of the alleyway. She greeted Polly with a smile that spoke of hopelessness,and her voice was weak when she spoke. "Got some, Poll?"

"Money? Yeah," Polly snorted, emerging out into the gaslit street with darting eyes. "Come on," she said, and rubbed her hands together. "I need to get to a courtyard with a working pump. That one there's busted."

"The next one's all right," said Annie. "I saw some kids using it earlier."

Polly strode off down the street without a word, Annie following like a little dog.

"Poll?" said Annie quietly.

Polly ignored her. Right now she needed a wash, and a drink, in that order, because no-one would serve her a drink with mess on her hands. She imagined the shame of handing money over a bar with hands that smelled like hers did now, knowing the barman and the whole pub would be able to see the mark on her. She felt the shame of a good Christian woman, not the shame of a brazen whore. She always felt this way about the work.

"Poll?" asked Annie again, still quiet.

Polly glanced behind at the shorter woman. "What?"

Annie sniffed. "I been thinking, Poll," she said steadily, timid, but peaceful.

Polly grunted. When Annie was less than forthcoming with further words, Polly said, "What, then?"

"I don't want this any more, Poll." Her voice was tiny, weak, delicate, like a child's.

Polly stopped in her tracks and turned to look at Annie. The shorter woman's eyes seemed tiny in the lamplight, her irises expanded to fill the space between the lids. To Poll it was like looking into two dark pools. "What you on about?" Polly snapped. "You're acting funny, Annie, and I wish to God you'd snap out of it. You're giving me the shivers."

Annie wouldn't meet her eyes, stood with her hands clutched together like she was praying, staring at the ground. Her voice, when she spoke again, was a high whisper. "It's not a good life, Poll."

Polly felt a stone sink slowly into the pit of her stomach. She found no answer or comment. There was none, really. *Annie's right*, she thought, *It ain't a good life*, and Polly smelled it on her hands, felt it growing sticky on her thighs, condemning her like a running sore. Her thoughts were of unease, of nausea, of filth washing over her like self-loathing.

Annie broke the silence. "I been thinking, Poll," she said again in her small voice, cracking. "And I want out."

"How?" Polly regrasped the situation. She began walking again, expecting that Annie would follow as usual. After a few steps it was obvious, from the lack of footsteps, that Annie had not. Polly stopped and turned, retreated a few steps.

Annie's face was deathly pale, more sickly than anything Polly had ever seen, and her clasped hands didn't stop the tremors that shook her. But Annie's eyes were clear and her mouth was set in a tight line.

Polly could feel the terror streaming out of her and it set Polly's own bells ringing. "Annie," she said softly, "Don't talk that way. Things'll get better." Even as she said so she knew how much of a lie it was, and so did Annie.

Annie shook her head softly. "No, Poll, it won't."

"Just –"

"No," Annie said again. "It's never going to get better. I want out of it, I want to end it. I'm going to end it now, tonight, while I still have strength." She glanced at Polly for the first time. "Help me, Poll?"

Polly glared at her. "It's against God's teaching," she snapped. "What you're talking about, it's a living sin." She turned and strode off towards the alleyway, better to deal with the feelings through anger.

Annie's familiar footsteps pattered after behind her as usual, tiny steps, careful as a mouse.

Polly worked the pump in the courtyard until a good flow was going and soaked a rag from one of her pockets. She cleaned up her privates and the tops of her thighs, rinsed the rag, wrung it out and stowed it back in her pocket. All the time, Annie never spoke, and Polly's anger kept her from saying a word. As she washed, the coins in her other pocket rattled like the fee of Judas. She finished cleaning her hands and turned to Annie. "Drink?"

Annie shook her head with a beatific peaceful smile that terrified Polly even more. "Not now, Poll," she said in a gentle voice.

"Come on, Annie," Polly pleaded. "You'll feel better after a glass."

The look on Annie's face was almost one of pity. "No, Poll, I made my mind up now, haven't I?" She smiled without showing her teeth. "I want to go and be with my little boys, Poll."

Polly's fear coagulated then. She knew that feeling, that pit of despair, knew the way into it and the only way out of it through the neck of a bottle. "Just one, Annie. Just one."

But Annie shook her head, resolute and steadfast. "Help me, Poll. You're my only friend. Do this one thing for me?"

"It's against God's will!" Poll repeated. But even as she said it she felt the shakes coming on her and her grasping mind moved beyond Annie to her own needs. And one of them, now she was cleaned up, was a drink. With ruthless self-hatred she turned inwards on herself. "Okay, I'll help you." *And God help me drown my sorrows after on my own*, she thought angrily. "What's the plan?"

Annie moved swiftly now, for her; took Polly by the arm and began to steer her along the street. "Down by the river," she said dreamily, "That's what I reckon."

"The docks?"

Annie shook her head. "Off the bridge, Poll, so help me God."

"Dear sweet Jesus, darlin'," said Polly through gritted teeth.

"You asked, Poll, and I told yer," said Annie plainly. "And you said you'd help."

Polly said nothing, just strode on with her head held high as the pair continued in silence. She felt sick, sick with fear and disgust and self loathing, and she didn't like any feelings at all. Her teeth were clenched together to stop her trembling. *How can you be so calm, Annie? Knowing what you're about to do?* It was a mortal sin. Polly knew that. She knew it was a mortal sin to help her too, being tantamount to murder.

The women turned off Whitechapel High Street and began to make their way south, towards the river, still in silence. They passed other people out on the street this night but spoke to no-one. Polly was screaming in her own head. She glanced at Annie from time to time, who still had that peaceful childish smile on her face. Her eyes were half closed like a simpleton. Polly's stomach had turned from nauseous to an ice-cold iron lump. She couldn't breathe properly, her mouth dry.

Every pub they walked past seemed alien to her, an unknown sanctuary of warmth and light and common sense. The stale beer smell, the tobacco smoke, the coke-fire fug assumed almost hellish proportions in their torture. She stared indoors wherever she found open windows and caught sight of her own haggard face, eyes wide and disquieting.

They took a wrong turning down a small cut-through at the narrow end of Mansell Street and ended up blocked, trestles across the width of the road and a lamp burning red in the middle of it. Cobblestones lay strewn loose on the road surface, the bare sand underlay a warm coral-pink in the lamplight.

Annie slipped her hand out of Polly's arm and stooped to pick up a cobble. She fumbled among her skirts, then pushed the stone into a pocket. She stooped to pick up another.

Polly felt like running away, could have just then, thought about it. But then Annie looked at her and she couldn't. Too guilty.

"Promise me," said Annie, a little short of breath, "You won't go back on the drink, Poll?"

Polly almost laughed at the madness of it. *You want me to help you die*, she thought, *By your own hand, against God's law, and you expect me not to drink myself senseless doing it?*

She shook her head.

"Poll, you got to get out of this life," Annie said, reaching for a third stone. "I got my way all sorted, all thought out. You ain't."

"I'll take God's Judgement when he gives it me," Polly snapped.

Annie looked at her with an almost-sly expression. "But you ain't been to church for ages." She slipped the stone into another pocket and began to unbutton her jacket.

Damn you, thought Polly. Annie was right, it had been years. She stopped going when the drink helped numb her more than the promise of a sweet hereafter. But she wasn't sure that drink could help her any more, so she nodded softly in the dim light and said, "Sure. I'll go in the morning."

Annie said nothing, then, "And give up the drink?"

"Sure."

And when she said it, Polly told herself she believed it. She'd seen the Sally Army posters, hadn't she? Felt a twinge of guilt each time she read the words of the Reverend Booth, calling her a "sinner" as if it were a finger of guilt pointing her out in her scarlet shame. Shrugged it off with the first mouthful of the day's – or night's – beer or gin. *That's where I'll go*, she told herself. *Salvation indeed. Let the Reverend Booth sort me out.*

Annie handed her a couple of cobbles.

Polly looked at the squared-off stones, then at the shorter woman, puzzled. "What're you giving me these for?"

"I can't carry much more of 'em," said Annie. Her voice had become more polite, her accent slightly refined. "Would you mind? Just until we reach the bridge."

"Which one?" Polly stuffed the heavy stones into an awkward pocket.

"What's closest?"

Polly thought about this for a moment. They were on the edge of Whitechapel now, close to the City of London. "Tower Bridge is nearest." If she strained her eyes she thought she could make out the faint outline of its turrets against the night sky.

Annie shuddered and shook her head. "Not Tower," she said. "Too busy, too crowded. An' it's too near the wharves. And the current's not strong enough."

Polly's thoughts reeled away at this point, unwilling to grasp how thoroughly Annie had thought this through. She blew on her hands to warm her fingertips chilled by handling the damp cobbles, but no warmth came. It was as if her breath had turned to ice. *Tonight's going to be a cold one*, she thought instead. *And not just because I'll be on my own come sunup.*

"Southwark's better," said Annie, interrupting Polly's thoughts. "Or Blackfriars. Somewhere that's quiet at this time of night."

"They're all always busy," Polly snapped. "And they all got lights on 'em."

Annie's face seemed to sag at this point, like she hadn't thought of this. "I don't want folks to see, Poll," she said quietly. "It's not right."

And they might try to stop you, Polly thought bitterly. Then she realised that she wasn't one of them and her anger returned and she aimed it outwards at her only friend. *I need a drink, Annie, badly now, so let's get this done!* She nodded and touched Annie on the cheek, softly reassuring.

When she spoke again, it was the old Poll, in charge, capable, strong, that she'd dredged up from somewhere. "We can get up onto Cannon Street railway bridge," she said. "It's dark at this hour, and we just got to keep out of the way of the trains till we're out over the water."

Annie nodded and hitched up the waistband of her skirt. Polly saw then the lines of pain etched into the face of the other woman and realised that Annie was younger than she. It frightened her so she said nothing, kept the strong Poll showing.

"How far is it?" Annie asked.

"Half a mile, I reckon," Polly said through chattering teeth. *It's the cold*, she told herself; *You didn't dry off properly underneath and your body's trying to make up for it.*

"Best get moving then," said Annie.

The two women set off again and stopped only once, in the shadow of a church on East Cheap, while Annie had a smoke. "Poll, before I forget," she said with sudden brightness, "I got something I need to give you.". She rummaged around her waistband and pulled out a small drawstring purse that made no sound at all. She poked it open with a grubby fingernail and withdrew a clothbound package, a kingsman neck-kerchief folded into a tight bun. She unwrapped the cloth until the bright pattern covered her entire hand and hung down over it all like a stage magician's tablecloth. "I been keepin' these all these years," she said with a coy smile, and opened her fist.

Polly looked down and whistled. "Annie," she began, and couldn't finish the sentence. There were three silver threepenny bits at the heart of the fabric in Annie's palm.

"They was Christening favours," Annie whispered, "For my three dead boys." Her voice broke. "An' I kept them all these years, Poll."

You won't be needing them now, thought Polly and swatted the thought away like a dirty suitor.

"Do you reckon they'll pay for a proper burial?" Annie asked, her voice trembling now.

Polly nodded. "Yeah, I reckon." She was thinking of the coins they put over the eyes of a dead person to pay the ferryman across the Styx. And how much liquor she could buy for ninepence in the bar at the Crown & Feathers.

"Look after them for me, Poll," Annie asked. "When they find me, don't let them bury me in a pauper's grave. I – I done bad things in my life," she began, and stopped.

Too late to regret that now, love! she thought in an angry voice. She said, instead, in pious tones, "None of us is born a saint." She reached for the coins in Annie's hand. "The good Lord died to save us all."

Annie clasped her fist around the three little silver coins and wrapped them up again in the folds of the kingsman. She tucked the bundle back into the bag on her waistband and then untied it from her skirt. "Don't jingle, see?" she said, holding it up and shaking it in Polly's face. "The number of footpads I fooled with that." She chuckled.

Polly nodded and tied the purse to her own waistband, tucking it down inside her skirt for hidden. She felt a crushing weight in her chest, her stomach a bag of iron scrap. She knew she had no intention of doing anything with the coins – Annie's dead boys – except drinking them. Some friend *she* was. Some *Christian*.

But there's hope, she told herself desperately. *With threepence I can get a room and a bath, a proper hot one with soap and all*. And a bed for the night, all to herself, with fresh sheets and a water pitcher by the bed. She could set herself back on her feet for a bit.

Or she could spend it on Annie's eternal rest. Polly looked at Annie again, smoking in the dim lamplight with that little smug smile playing round her face.

Polly felt a huge surge of anger roll over her. *This is all your fault, Annie, all this, this whoring. I was a clean-living woman until I fell in with you and your drinking buddies in Spitalfields workhouse,* she thought, the bitter taint of bile on her tongue.

When they got out, Polly had no lodging and Annie's friend had promised the women a bit of work and a bit of money. Polly had been naïve about it, tried to maintain that naivety even through the first few customers and then through the haze of beer and spirits.

Now, of course, still raw from her last casual encounter, gasping for a drink, seeing Annie smug and determined, Polly's despair tore at her.

So she hated Annie, blamed the other woman for her own downfall even though she knew the reason she went on was not because she held out hope for the future, but because she was too scared to end it here and now. And she was deeply jealous that Annie had come to that point before her. Never one for pious display, she secretly offered a prayer to the nearest holy thing she could see – the statue of some saint or other above the doorway of the church at their back. Tears wouldn't come, she was too scared for that, terror holding her other emotions tight. Trembling, whether through fear or adrenaline or simple cold, Polly crossed her arms across her chest as the two women continued on their way.

They passed the deserted halls inland of Billingsgate Market and crossed over King William Street, heading towards St Paul's Cathedral, the side streets all parallel, north-to-south, away from the river – or towards it. The roadway outside Cannon Street railway station was thick with traffic. *And there's the Sally Army*, thought Polly, *Like a thorn in my side.*

The well-intentioned foot soldiers of the Salvation Army were pushing their pamphlets at illiterate, scared alcoholics outside one of the seedier music-halls along Cannon Street itself, men who'd more than likely use them as firelighters or to wipe their backsides with. A couple of the Sally Army were dressed in the scarlet frock-coat uniform that made them look like Chelsea Pensioners, but for the most part they were ordinary folk out on the streets, meaning well, with only an armband and a pocket full of leaflets. *And tomorrow night I could be one of them,* Polly thought. *But, sweet Jesus, not tonight!*

She jammed her chin into her bony breastbone and scurried past them to a safe distance, then had to wait for Annie to catch up. Polly watched as Annie's blasé drift seemed to repel any interest whatsoever. Her calmness was in direct proportion to Polly's unease.

"Hurry up, Annie," she hissed when Annie was within earshot. "I can feel my feet freezin' to the paving stones here."

Annie looked at her with that infuriating calm. "It *is* cold, isn't it, Poll? I don't seem to notice it any more." She paused, as if she was reconsidering what she was about to say and thought better of it. "Let's get on, Poll."

The two women took a left turn and headed down one of the side streets nearest the railway station and found themselves at All Hallows Pier. The traffic was still busy and there was a first faint hint of mist in the air that seemed thicker towards the river. Cannon Street Railway Bridge reared up ahead of them to straddle the river.

Polly's spirits rose when she saw there was no way the pair could gain access to the railway bridge without being seen by the workers down on the wharf.

"Look, Annie," she said, he spirits brighter now, "See how God works against your sin."

"Don't you give me that God stuff, Poll Parker," Annie said, suddenly sounding tired. "Not now, not here." Her face showed her disappointment but her eyes were searching around, still calm, and she spoke with quiet resolve. "There's got to be a way up onto that bridge."

She led on, determined, back along the wharf and up onto London Bridge.

Polly followed. She cursed and prayed in equal measure.

Once out over the river on the wide span of the bridge, Annie milled around in silence, once or twice leaning over the parapet while carriages and omnibuses rumbled past them. A train rolled out across the river on the railway bridge upstream to the west, sparks and smoke flying up into the night air from its chimney and the light of its firebox glowing in the open cab. The sound of the locomotive carried not so far in the misty air, dimmed and hacking like an old man's chesty cough. At last Annie pointed down, over the parapet, into the darkness, towards the south bank.

"What yer up to?" hissed Polly. "You'll have the law onto us with your antics." There didn't seem to be much point now and she was still itching for a drink.

"Look, Poll," Annie said, "There's a footpath there. And the tide's up."

Polly cursed under her breath. Her eyesight hadn't yet adjusted from staring at the bright lights of the railway station. Her thoughts were wavering between anger and sadness, each emotion tumbling over the other in a stew of fear. She followed Annie off the road bridge onto the south bank of the Thames, along Montagu Close and Clink Street towards Bankside.

As luck would have it, there was a small camp of men huddled round a fire at the near end of the brewery on Park Street and as the pair went by with a greeting, Polly's mouth watered at the sight of a bottle of spirits being shared around the group. She was sure her stomach rumbled too.

Annie seemed to pay them little heed, just gave a shy little wave and sailed on by. Beyond the fire there was darkness and the high brick walls of the brewery. Polly's eyes had to adjust between the light and shadow and while they did, focusing, one of the drunks wobbled over. Polly glared at him while he propositioned them.

"Maybe later," she cut him off in mid sentence. "All right? My friend here –" she indicated Annie with her elbow – "She doesn't feel too good right now."

The drunk stared at her for a while as this information sunk in, then he composed his face, nodded, went back to the group. Polly heard him belch as he slumped down onto a heap of sacking they were using to rest on. *Animal*, she thought, cursing. *And you could have shared some of that drink with me first, friend.*

"Poll?" Annie was whispering. "I want to go straight in, Poll. I don't want to just drift off." She pointed up to the massive sandstone piers of the railway bridge above them. "We can get through the fence here, and climb up. I think I can see a walkway."

Polly craned her neck upwards and stood there staring into the darkness. A passenger train rumbled over the bridge, the lights in the carriages flicking across the network of iron girders that spanned between each pier. Polly shaded her eyes from the streetlights on the far side of the river until she made out the faint stars pinpricking the sky, and dropped her gaze to the now-empty bridge. She saw some kind of platform almost slung under the tracks.

"I think you're right," she said, and the pit of iron scrap came back in her stomach.

They squeezed through a couple of loose fence posts, taking care with their footwork not to step on anything squalid. Judging by the smell, the place was used as a pissoir. The two women scrambled up the ash-strewn slope under the bridge.

The walkway was sturdy, built of rigid iron supports bolted to the girders of the bridge and shod with wooden planks that were fixed solid. The women made little sound as they shuffled out across the water.

Annie giggled in the darkness ahead of Polly.

Polly wasn't sure why, until she asked.

"Good job I can't see a thing, Poll," Annie said cheerily, "Or I'd never get up here. I got no head for heights, see?" And she giggled again while Polly gripped the handrails for dear life and cursed the God who'd brought her here without a drink in her.

They were out beyond the second pier of the bridge when Annie stopped.

Polly heard her footsteps halt and scuffle, then could hear their breathing clearly. Out here in the mist, it was surprisingly quiet. The sounds of the city were strangely muffled. Polly could hear the voices of the men around the fire but not make out any of their words except their laughter. The rushing water of the Thames rustled against the bridge piers thirty feet below, absorbing any faint noises from the sleeping wharves on the north bank.

On Southwark Bridge, upstream, the fuzzy streetlamps shone like playhouse limelights, the traffic some distant performance in a dark music-hall, the actors close but unreachable.

Polly shivered. The bridge smelled of engine oil and coal smoke, the river salty and foetid in equal measure, the fire outside the brewery an almost rural, rustic incense.

"Peaceful, innit?" said Annie, her voice low and gentle.

Polly agreed, fighting the urge to cry. It was unnerving, that such a cathedral of silence and calm should be found so close to the bustle at the heart of the city. But to Polly it was empty, there was no God there and no comfort either, and the chill rising from the water iced her bones. She fought to keep her teeth from chattering and folded her arms across her chest. For a moment she thought Annie had changed her mind.

"Annie isn't my real name," said Annie abruptly. Polly saw her face a faint moon reflecting the street lights.

"It's good enough," said Polly, *for the life you live*.

"But it's not my real name," Annie went on. "I ain't Annie Cook."

"You don't have to tell me," said Polly, wishing she wouldn't.

"I want to," said Annie. "I want to tell *someone*." Her breath must have caught in her throat because her next words came out hoarse. "I want to die with my real name, Poll. I want to leave Annie Cook behind me."

Polly shook her head.

Annie's voice strengthened in the silence Polly gave her. "I'm Anne Marchant," she said firmly. "Born in Romsey. Married to Fred Marchant at fifteen, widowed at twenty. Mother to John, Albert and Little Fred. – Oh dear God Poll, I don't half miss them all!"

Annie's warm hand gripped hers, then her little podgy body pressed against Polly's folded arms, a cool moist kiss landed on Polly's cheek and Annie was gone in a flurry of cloth ruffling over the handrail.

Polly never even heard her hit the water.

Her mouth went dry. She swallowed at nothing. After a few minutes, tears came. She let them roll away down her face, shaking with silent sobs, cold emptiness rinsing her ruthless.

CHAPTER 21 – The Committee Gathers For War

"Where the Hell is the boy?"

Louis found his patience growing thin. His network of informants across London was failing him and he felt the pull of the tide grow stronger with each passing moment.

James Frazer touched him gently on the elbow. "Stop fretting. Come and have something to eat – or at least take a drink." The Scotsman's accent rolled the R in 'drink', the only trace of his upbringing left in his voice.

Louis turned towards the man and sighed. "This uncertainty is unbearable."

"Think about it, Louis," the other man cajoled. "If he's been taken by another group they can't have moved him far – not tonight."

Louis nodded. "They'd be stupid if they did. With that wound –"

"If he turns up at any of the London hospitals, we'll know about it."

"What if he doesn't? What if he's just lost, out there on his own, wandering about like a Fool?"

Frazer stared at him with a look of concern in his eyes, then said in a quiet voice, "Louis, you did tell him how important this is, didn't you?"

Louis nodded slowly. "Frazer, I – I don't know. I can't remember." He shook his head. "I wasn't much use when he was brought to the house. Perhaps the others explained it after I left."

"Well, let's say they did. Is he likely to jeopardise that?"

Louis sniffed. "I don't *know*," he said painfully. "He might take a lot of persuading."

"*You* didn't."

"No – but I had more direct contact with her. His first encounter was different."

Frazer nodded, a keen expression on his face. Louis realised that the Scotsman was perhaps the only other man in the Cuckoo Club who understood the delicacy of the matter.

"She rescued me," Louis said. "But *he* encountered her when *She* was vulnerable. I don't know how that will affect their relationship – if it has any effect at all."

Frazer's brow furrowed and when he spoke, his words were hesitant. "The Old King is meant to be sacrificed for the New." Then he paused, as if he'd spoken ill of the dead.

Louis nodded with a grim smile. "I know." He took a deep breath. "I've waited all my life for this, Frazer. Every man I encounter, every stranger on the street, could be my replacement. There are men out there who have wished it were them, but lacked the conviction to assassinate – yes, I use that word with due respect – to assassinate me. There are others whose actions would merely harm me, and have no concept of the effects such harm might have on the powers of the Consort or his court. Every day – especially the last forty years or so –" Louis smiled with a look of charm which was only half-bravado – "Every day has been a vigil against the unknown."

"Ye gods, Louis," Frazer gasped, shaking his head. "I had no idea. How do you manage?"

Louis shrugged. "What the Fates have decreed, will be," he said in a voice of gentle wonder. "You of all people should understand that."

Frazer nodded. Whatever his thoughts were, he kept them to himself.

As the pair crossed the hallway, Louis heard the telephone ringing behind the Porter's desk. His stomach tightened and he slowed his pace, a feeling of foreboding washing over him.

A group of the less eminent Club members tumbled through the door on their way to the bar, greeting him as they passed and drowning out the words of the Porter into the mouthpiece. The Porter nodded and glanced up, saw Louis, beckoned him over.

Louis cleared his throat, his mouth dry. He wished he'd been a bit quicker into the bar, taken Frazer's offer of a drink.

The Porter mouthed the words, "Prussian Ambassador" as he held the receiver out.

Louis was barely aware of Frazer at his side as he took the apparatus from the Porter with a nodded thanks. He barked his name into the mouthpiece.

"Herr Beauregard," an exhausted voice echoed down the wires.

"Ambassador," said Louis, his breath controlled and measured.

"We have news from Potsdam."

"What?" Louis felt the muscles in his jaw tense.

"Bad news, I'm afraid. The Kaiser is dead."

"Frederick?" Louis asked as his mind reeled. Beside him, Frazer stiffened.

"No," said the Ambassador. "Kaiser Wilhelm."

"So?"

"So His Excellency Crown Prinz Frederick von Hohenzollern is now Kaiser."

"I know," said Louis with a sigh of relief. "And do you know where Crown Prinz Wilhelm is?"

There was a sharp bark of laughter from the telephone receiver. "Your guess is as good as mine," came the reply. "Or quite possibly better. Your agents are more numerous than ours. And London is your city, after all."

Louis let that one pass, unsure whether the man meant the agents of the Crown, or those of the Cuckoo Club. "If you find him, can you let me know?" he asked instead.

"Of course," said the Prussian Ambassador. "If you will extend the same courtesy to us." As Louis began to agree, the Ambassador cut him off by adding, "That includes news of your mystery boy."

Louis coughed to cover up his surprise. "Of course," he recovered. "How did you know?"

There was a chuckle from the other end of the line. "I have my informers too," the Ambassador said, and even over the crackling telephone line it was impossible to ignore the glee in his voice. "He was seen, not two hours ago, in the Strand, being picked up by a coach with cream livery drawn by a bay pair."

There was a pause. Louis mentally cursed but said nothing. His hands had begun to shake.

The Prussian Ambassador continued, "Not one of yours, I wager?"

"No," Louis admitted through gritted teeth. "Not one of ours." He wanted the conversation over. He wanted to notify his agents of this new information, but the niceties of protocol precluded a quick finish. *Goddammit, man,* he thought angrily, *I thought you were on our side!*

"Well," the Ambassador continued, "I'd best be off. Don't want to keep the new Kaiser waiting. Or his heir. That would never do."

"He's probably in a brothel somewhere in Chelsea being spanked by a fat-bottomed whore," Louis growled. *Get off the line!*

"Chelsea? Hmm," the Prussian Ambassador murmured. "I'd never have thought of looking there."

He rung off leaving Louis unsure as to whether the last comment was genuine or an example of the infamous Prussian sense of humour.

Louis turned to Frazer, waiting in the hallway and wringing his hands like an expectant father. "Call the Committee together," Louis commanded. "My office, five minutes."

Frazer nodded and hurried off towards the Dining Room.

Louis glanced at his pocket watch for the time. He stared at the hands going round, controlling his breathing to the movement of the second hand, aware he was clutching the fob too tight. His knuckles showed white and bony under the skin; pink, blueish veins traced across it like a map of the Niger delta. He headed for his office, up the stairs on the first floor.

The corridor upstairs was quiet but he heard the scrape of chairs from the room below as the Club Committee gathered. Louis took the heavy key from his waistcoat pocket and unlocked the dark oak door. The lamp on his desk had been lit and the wall sconces glowed with the gentle comforting hiss of mains gas.

Louis crossed to the window, looked out onto the street below. The night was dark, the streetlights blotting out the night sky, their glare wrung dry by the gentle mist that was settling on the city. He always thought this weather made the streetlamps look like they were submerged. At times it reminded him of being deep underwater, seeing the lights of a search party on the surface diffused by the depths.

On nights like this, he thought, *Astronomers sit waiting for hours, neither clear enough for observation nor too obscure to go home to the hearth and an early bed. Of course, it makes no difference to Her, whose days and nights pass like seconds in childhood.*

Louis again felt a wave of desolation wash over him, cold, clear, terrifying. He'd spent his entire adult life tainted by her appearance, tantalised by her reappearances, tortured by the memory of her and unable to taunt any other man far enough to relieve him of the burden.

He was interrupted by Frazer, whose footsteps were near-silent on the wooden floors. "What else can I do to help?"

Louis spoke without turning from the window. "Frazer, you know, I cannot abdicate." He heard the other man's footsteps come closer, saw his reflection in the glass as a silhouette against the lamplit doorway. He continued. "I tried, in middle age, to work some damage into my life. All it did was teach me the meaning of those late heroics of the

Ancients. Only Alexander the Great achieved it. One takes incalculable risks and gets away with it, not so much because one has Her special magical protection, but because one's fellow men expect it so."

He paused, watching the traffic in the street move at a timeless pace. "The expectation of success, which leads to success. Unholy confidence."

Frazer shook his head. "I don't understand."

"You want to, though, don't you?" Louis turned and faced the younger man with earnest urgency in his voice. "This new Consort needs all the friends he can get."

"I'm not sure any of us are ready for that yet."

"Frazer," Louis said, his voice softening now, "I killed the King before me. Like William Rufus, the event was reported as an accident."

"You mean the death in the New Forest? England's second Norman king?" Frazer, ever the historian, reeled off the dates of the king's birth and death without pausing to think, having learned them by rote like any schoolboy.

Louis nodded impatiently. "But everyone knew I'd done it. Especially me. I never lost the feeling that followed it," Louis reached out to the younger man and gripped his arm. "The years of my survival have allowed me to rationalise the shame."

"Louis, you're not the only one who's killed a man in a duel."

"I know. That's what Byron told me." Louis laughed and shook his head clear of the memory, then grew serious again. "I mean accepting that I have to be challenged – and, for a while, the shame of looking forward to that challenge. I came to *provoke* men to challenge me. I enjoyed the risk."

He glanced away again, finding the memory painful even now, and gestured for Frazer to remain silent. "I grew to accept the sort of monster that made me. Because I always won. I have been invincible for nearly sixty years."

"You have done so much good in that time, Louis," said Frazer. "The Club has been a haven for so many."

"Notwithstanding those I put in that position of dependency by my actions," said Louis, his voice guarded. "I have been a very fortunate Consort, Frazer. I've seen the man who must follow me. He is... so very different."

They were interrupted by the noise of footsteps and chatter in the corridor outside, followed by three members of the Committee. Louis turned away from the window to greet them as they settled round the long table in front of his desk.

The Club Secretary sidled in on his own, sat at the back like a child who was being punished, did not glance at the others.

On any other night Louis would have chided him to sit amongst the group, but not tonight. His patience was short. He had no time for such theatrics. When the long table was full and the room murmuring, he called them to attention with a glance.

"Gentlemen," he began, "No doubt you've heard the news."

Nods and susurration of agreement around the table. "What's to be done, Louis?" asked the Chairman.

Louis settled into the winged leather armchair behind the desk, leaned forward on his elbows and regarded the group. "I was rather hoping you'd all come to some conclusion yourselves," he said through a wry smile. "However, let me lay the situation before you." He leaned back, his shoulders tense as he began to count points off on his fingers.

"First," he began, "Kaiser Wilhelm is dead. Frederick is now Kaiser. This means that Crown Prinz Wilhelm is heir apparent."

"Frederick is dying, isn't he?" asked the Club Secretary.

Louis nodded and a number of the other committee members agreed.

"How long has he got?"

"While I appreciate the sentiment behind the question, that's rather blunt, isn't it?" interrupted Sir Henry Burke, the Club Treasurer and the genealogist scion of the man behind Burke's Peerage.

"Why not?" Louis interrupted the argument before the committee took further steps. "I'm an old man, some of you are almost as old and a few are older than Frederick. While none of us has his illness, we have no idea when that situation might change. I don't think it's a spurious question, especially under the circumstances. When Frederick dies, Crown Prinz Wilhelm will become Kaiser, and there is every indication that those who would seek to influence him also seek to make him Consort."

"Before or after he becomes Kaiser?"

"Both, probably," said Louis, his mouth a grim line.

"And none of Victoria's sons show promise in this regard?"

The committee members grumbled.

"No," said Burke. "None of them. The only prospect was Leopold, but of course he is haemophiliac."

"That precludes him?"

"He has – somehow – developed a marked tendency towards more gentle pastimes than we would expect of a future Consort. And he will never be King. He has three brothers above him."

"It's important that it's royalty, is it?" asked the Club Secretary.

"No. Not while we have the youth I encountered this afternoon," said Louis, bringing the conversation back to ground. "He has been chosen by the Lady. He will become Consort."

"You *are* certain of that, aren't you?"

Louis nodded. "If I can help it. With your assistance."

The Committee murmured assent.

"Now," Louis went on, "We all know the riskier elements of Wilhelm's personality. The volatility, the infantilism, the recklessness, impatience, arrogance of the man. What kind of ruler he becomes to Germany remains to be seen. We must hope that the experience of government will eliminate – or at least curb – some of his more rash pronouncements and actions."

"What if it doesn't?"

"Time will tell. However, right now, we don't have the luxury of worrying about that. The Prussian Ambassador doesn't know where Wilhelm is, except that he's somewhere in London. This brings me onto point number two." Louis paused, took a breath. "The boy."

George Buckle, the editor of the Times, caught Louis's attention. "May I offer a summary of the situation?"

Louis nodded and gestured in acquiescence.

"There is a youth who had contact with the Lady this morning. After their encounter, she escaped, and dived into the Thames from Westminster Bridge." Buckle paused at an indrawn breath from those committee members who had not already heard that news, then continued. "However, she left behind in his possession a small purse containing a number of gold coins, which the lad handed to the police this morning."

There were murmurings of approval around the room.

Buckle went on. "The coins were removed for safekeeping by one of our junior members, a numismatist at the British Museum, and taken to Ogilvy's in Hatton Garden. Mr Ogilvy Senior is, as you will recall, a Club Member of long-standing, and his chief goldsmith is none other than Pawel Czerczy's son."

"*The* Pawel Czerczy?" asked Sir Henry Burke.

Louis nodded. "His son is also named Pawel."

George Buckle waited for a moment, then continued with his report. "The coins have been manufactured into a talisman of a sort," he said, and shook his head at the remainder of his notes. "Louis, I can't see the sense in explaining the rest of this, can you?"

Louis agreed, and thanked him. "Gentlemen, it is my opinion that this youth is the Lady's new chosen companion, and that She will return to him if he is in danger."

"Is that likely?"

Louis nodded. "He was shot and wounded this afternoon, during a disturbance outside the Houses of Parliament. He was brought to my home for treatment by Smedley and Camden."

"Do we have him still?"

Louis shook his head and winced at the sharp intake of breath that came from around the table. "We had him earlier. He took off on his own."

"Where is he now?"

Louis shrugged into the silence. "We don't know. But he's wounded – the gunshot to the shoulder was an amber-lined bullet, which Mr Pearson succeeded in removing under anaesthetic. When the tide's right, She'll come for him."

"Was this your doing?"

"No. I *can't* kill him," Louis said with patient deliberation. "He must kill me to become the new Consort."

"Or someone else must," said the Club Secretary.

Louis nodded again. He saw alarm on the faces of the younger men around the table and when he next spoke it was with a gravitas he'd learned to borrow for such occasions, like that of an elder statesman, although he often didn't feel that way inside. "Such is the way of things," he admitted. "None of us – Her Consorts – is destined to die in our beds."

The assembled Cuckoo Club members were quiet.

"That is one of the minor points that I would have liked to cover later, however as it's come up now we may as well address it."

"How can you be so calm about this?"

Louis shrugged again. "Destiny, kismet, whatever you may care to call it – I've had decades of Her protection, which is more than most men enjoy." He glared at them, thinking of the rivals of his youth. "I've despatched a number of wholesome men whose vanity would not permit them to leave me alone, and men for whom the challenge was too great. I've spent too many nights tossing over this subject to be concerned by it now. The Divine Right of Kings is all very well, but there has to be some power in the arm that wields those rights."

The assembled committee members were silent, their attention focused on his next words.

"Gentlemen," he went on in a different vein, "I have seen this agency grown in stature from a small conspiracy between a handful of eccentrics to the important agency it is today. I guided that growth to enable such a moment as this. There are perils to be met that the century has proved new for us. There will be greater still, as progress takes us into the next century. We must prepare to meet those challenges – must start to prepare now."

The men around the table nodded in agreement.

"I am too old," Louis went on without a hint of sadness or self-pity. "I am this century's man. We must have another, younger man. And this is our current peril. There are those who seek to replace me – with Wilhelm."

"It's only a matter of time," said the Lord Chamberlain.

Louis nodded in acknowledgement. "We have no idea how much longer Friedrich will survive. However, he is now in a unique position, one which threatens us all."

"How so?"

Louis gestured for Frazer to explain.

The Scotsman stood up and addressed the group. "He is an uncrowned king. He has a wound which cannot heal. And," he paused to consider how best to phrase it, "He cannot speak – he is voiceless, mute, silent. According to the myths which preserve our code, he should be the Old King who must be killed in Spring, in order for the new king to succeed him. There's the matter of sacrifice, and suchlike." He stopped, as if embarrassed, and resumed his seat.

"But he isn't the Old King. Louis is."

Louis nodded in agreement, this time with a small smile.

"If Wilhelm is to succeed you, how is it to be organised?" interrupted the Club Secretary. "Can he just take you out like a common thug?"

"Doubtful, even with his temperament," said Lord Gainsborough with a hint of a sneer. "He's all bluff. Likes shooting deer, but I'll wager he's not up to committing a murder."

"Assassination," said Louis slowly, quietly.

"However you describe it," said Frazer, "If he is to succeed, he has to kill Louis."

"Or the man who kills me. Or the last in a chain of men, the first of whom kills me." Louis paused while this sank in round the table. "That is why it is important that we find this young man. We must control him – have him on our side. If Sylvester de Winter holds his allegiance, I have no doubt that once the boy becomes the sole Consort – by whatever means – he will be carefully positioned to be despatched in some kind of contrived accident, no doubt by Wilhelm or someone to whom he holds special allegiance. It is the way of these matters." He leaned back in his chair and steepled his fingers. *Don't ask me how I know.*

"Then we must act, and swiftly," said Lord Gainsborough.

"Correct." Louis sighed. "But there is no point in acting without direction. That is why I called you here."

The men sat patiently silent for a moment, then the Lord Chamberlain spoke. "What are we to do, Louis?"

"I will lay the floor open to the Club Armourer, gentlemen. Cummins?"

The Armourer laid out a plan of action for the committee members. Each one was assigned a small group of the ordinary or Common Members, one of which would be armed according to the list that Louis and Cummins had discussed earlier that day.

"Only one?" asked the Club Secretary.

"I don't want the entire city to be awash with armed men," said the Assistant Chief Constable. "It's bad enough with the Irish."

"I would still have thought –" the Club Secretary persisted.

"No, Martens," said Louis. "The others can arm themselves with whatever they feel adequate, but not firearms. It's too risky."

Cummins waited for Louis to provide a sign that he could continue, then said, "It's important that each group should have a good knowledge of whichever part of London their watch is to cover." He laid out a set of maps on the table in front of the committee. "I've divided the maps along parish lines. Each group will cover one parish. It doesn't sound like much, but on the ground, at night, in a crowded city, you'll find it's more than enough."

The Committee Members acknowledged the Armourer's experience with their silent agreement while he distributed the maps.

"What about the City?" asked the Lord Chamberlain.

"The Lord Mayor was kind enough to promise the assistance of those Guilds whose members have a particular interest in our cause," said Louis with an impish grin. "The City of London's Constables will be on full alert tonight, and the streets will be patrolled more regularly than even we can manage."

"And the Tower?"

"Confirmed," the Armourer nodded. "The Constable of The Tower, and the Warden Watchmen, have been alerted."

"We have observers stationed all the way along the river," said Louis. "From the Naval Academy at Greenwich all the way to Lambeth Palace on the south bank, and on the north bank from the Royal Chelsea Hospital to the Isle of Dogs."

"That's quite a territory," said Lord Gainsborough with a gesture of appreciation.

"No larger than your estate in Northamptonshire," Louis grinned. "It's based on what we know of the Lady's previous appearance. On the north bank, we will spread out to Spitalfields and round in an arc to lead back to the river no further west than the Grosvenor Canal, following the outskirts of the mediaeval city where possible."

"Certain locations are of particular strategic importance," Cummins continued, unfurling a larger map on Louis's desk at which he proceeded to point while he reeled off a list of locations. "London Bridge. Westminster. All along the streets of London Wall, Houndsditch and The Minories. Victoria Embankment, its entire length, paying particular attention to those stretches where it overlooks landing areas and jetties. The outflow of the Fleet under Blackfriars Bridge. And the heathlands, parks and open spaces of the city where in olden times there would have been fairs."

"We'll be thinly spread," the Club Secretary pointed out.

"Yes," Cummins agreed, "But not without guidance. Each group of Club Members will carry a water-compass. It's near-impossible to fu– to foul up using one of them."

"What of the rookeries, the thieves' dens, the music halls and the like?" asked Lord Gainsborough.

Louis smiled and shook his head. "Not tonight, gentlemen. Unless you find news that Wilhelm is there –

which I am assured is unlikely. She will not be looking for entertainment. Not the way we do. Remember," he raised a finger to emphasise the point, "She isn't human. She may not even understand our language any more."

"Didn't you speak to her?" The questioner had a sheepish look, but earnest intent.

Louis nodded. "Yes. I spoke to Her, and She to me. But it wasn't modern English. It was more like Shakespeare – or Chaucer." He cast his eyes to the ceiling, trying to recall, then shook his head. "In fact," he said, lowering his eyes to the table with a gentle smile of remembrance, "What little we said was in a tongue more akin to Beowulf than anything else I can describe."

The assembled men looked at him aghast. "What hope have we of discourse with her, then?"

"Little," Louis admitted brusquely and dismissed the subject. "We have to find the boy. She will come for him, I'm sure."

It was time, he realised, to force the destiny he'd been in love with all these years. He knew the boy was the one, not Wilhelm. He shook his head at the thought of what disastrous consequences might follow, were it Wilhelm. *It doesn't bear thinking about. No, it's the boy. He even looks a bit like me when I was that age.* And while he'd kept himself vigorous, it was time for a change. He was just disappointed he wouldn't be around to see it.

Suddenly Louis felt a wave of pressure wash over him. Some thick force tightened his chest. His stomach turned and his mouth flooded. Like an unnameable terror the spasms twisted him over.

The Committee Members struggled to their feet as Louis clutched his chest. No agony, but otherwise just like a heart attack. He gasped for air like a man drowning, caught on nothing, unable to speak.

Cummins patted his back, to no effect.

Not now, thought Louis, and shook his head angrily. He sank back into his chair, gripped the armrests until his knuckles shone white through the skin, seized breath though his gritted teeth until the seizure passed. There was a rushing in his ears like falling water and it drowned out all other sounds. He shut his eyes. Tears forced out with pain trickled along the furrows of his face.

Slowly, he released his left hand from the armrest of the chair to wave the members back to their seats. He watched them reluctantly leave him. Each face now had a look of concern, of growing genuine seriousness. Louis gasped for air and spoke in short bursts, carefully phrasing each statement to make best use of his breath.

"Gentlemen," he began, "I'm not dead yet."

A few half-smiles glimmered around the table.

"It's just a warning." Louis nodded, let his gaze drop to the map on the table and then up again to the Committee. "It is serious, though." He let his glance fall on each man in turn as he spoke. "Now is the time for action."

His breath was coming easier in spite of the tremors he felt in his limbs. "Arm yourselves and summon the carriages. We'll meet in Parliament Square. Let's go hunting."

The Cuckoo Club Committee Members sat as if dumbfounded, watching him, glancing at each other. Louis seized another breath from the future and hauled himself to his feet. "Come on," he whispered, low and rough, his voice more effective at this subtle range than if he'd roared across a battlefield. He strode from the room as if all was well; and the Committee followed him.

CHAPTER 22 – Whitechapel Woman

Just inside a seedy pub on the fringes of Whitechapel High Street, Alf took his time over a drink while Sylvester de Winter looked for a woman. Alf stood by the door, his concentration poor, the first mouthful of neat gin fiddling with his head, nervous to be among so many people, and afraid of Sylvester de Winter.

Almost as if he could smell it, the Russian knew that Alf still had one of the tiny gold coins and reminded him that, as long as it was in his possession, he was a thief. De Winter also convinced him that his gunshot wound was a matter for the police, and they would ask unpleasant questions about the events that led up to it. "You don't want that, now, do you?" he asked as he tipped a measure of gin into his mouth.

Alf shook his head. He gripped his own glass with both hands and stared at the floor while the Russian spoke to him. The wound in his shoulder tugged at him as the blood began to knit it together. Each episode of these last few hours repulsed him. He was confused, convinced that he was part of Sylvester de Winter's cruel world, implicated in the man's crimes. Smuggling, drug dealing, Chinese gangs – and heavens knew what else. *What else can I do?* he thought.

"Ah, there's a prize for you," said Sylvester de Winter just as he raised the glass to his lips, and he turned away without warning. He left Alf at the bar and sidled through the crowd towards a group of women who stood beside the fire, chatting and laughing while they held out their bare hands to the warmth.

The Russian greeted them in a casual manner that was not quite so smooth as his actions in the Irishman's company, but one of the women seemed to pay attention as he spoke, and as Alf watched, Sylvester de Winter caught her gaze and offered her his half-finished drink.

A sly smile twitched her cheek and her eyes sparkled as she took the glass from Sylvester de Winter's gloved hand. She laughed at him over the first sip of gin, but the coyness she feigned was false, brazen, apparent to all.

She's done this before, thought Alf, and his inexperience nettled him as much as her casual submission.

Sylvester de Winter leaned in towards her, his free hand waving in a vague direction towards the outside door as his head dipped towards her neck, to her ear, to mutter something lost in the cackle of the pub.

Her expression changed to excitement, and Alf was too naïve to acknowledge the slight edge of mistrust in the glance she threw at her companions as she left them.

Sylvester de Winter turned with his keen eyes glittering and his teeth bared.

Alf drained his glass then to avoid looking at the man.

The night air was cold when the trio stepped out into the street and Sylvester de Winter immediately lit one of his Turkish cigarettes.

With a backward glance the girl set off to an alleyway beside the pub, then she turned and came back and pushed between the two men, taking each by the arm, steering them towards the darkness.

The woman was young, younger than Alf even, with a high forehead and wide brown eyes. She was tiny of frame, her hands like those of a child, and her freckled cheeks were flushed with a glow that heightened the pink of her lips. Her breath smelled of juniper and violets, a mixture of gin and cachous. Alf found the warmth of her body arousing, the sweetness of her breath and the hesitant Essex drawl of her chitchat enchanting.

"Right now, gents, who's first?" she asked briskly as she turned to face them. The light from the pub's upper windows gave a poor illumination on the scene, but it fell on her face and her bonnet and made shadows in the dimples of her cheeks.

Sylvester de Winter made a stiff-backed bow and indicated Alf with a flash of his teeth in the dim light.

At that point Alf froze. In spite of his state of arousal he found the situation repugnant, not to mention apprehensive. He'd never been with a woman before, had no idea where to begin in spite of the insistence of his groin. The thought of sexual congress in this stinking alleyway mere yards from the street, in front of Sylvester de Winter, was disgusting. And yet his erection was there.

"Come on, now, sir," said the girl as she advanced on him. She reached out and grabbed his privates in a move that was practised and horribly enticing.

Shocked, Alf gritted his teeth and put his hands on her upper arms with the half-confused thought of pushing her away.

She smiled and tilted her head to one side. Her hand was warm and its caresses made his thighs quiver. She raised her foot so she stood on one leg and with her other hand she hitched up her skirt, then put his hand on her thigh. "There you go, love," she said, her voice gentle.

Alf felt her soft leg tremble under his hand and when she pressed closer to him he realised her whole body was shaking and her eyes had lost the bravado she'd had in the pub. The look in her eyes, he realised, was greed.

There were too many distractions. Sylvester de Winter's cigarette end glowed in the dark. People and carts passed in the street not thirty feet from where they stood. Alf smelled the girl's sweat mingled with the scraps in the bins behind the pub, stale beer, boiled ham, night-soil, Turkish tobacco smoke.

"No," he said, removing his hand from her leg, trying to remove her hand from his crotch.

She giggled and fought him until he was holding her by the wrists, pushing her away from his face, and she was wriggling her torso against him.

Sylvester de Winter coughed and grunted. He tossed his cigarette to the side and came up behind her to stare Alf in the face above her bonnet.

"Don't you want her, boy?" he rasped. He pushed against her and the girl cried out and began to turn towards the Russian, still held tight by the wrists by Alf.

"Oi!" she cried, panic edging her voice. "Wot's your game?"

"Shut up," Sylvester de Winter hissed, close enough to her ear for Alf to feel the man's cold breath in his eyes. "You've been paid, haven't you?"

She began to protest again and kicked Alf just above the ankle. "This wasn't what we said! Liar!" She tried to twist away but Alf still held her wrists. Her hands bent into claws and reached for his eyes.

Sylvester de Winter clasped his gloved hand over her mouth. He hitched up her skirts at the back with a ruffling of fabric, his weight trapping Alf between her and the wall.

Her terrified eyes cursed Alf with panic, then blinked shut as Sylvester de Winter thrust at them both.

Alf let go of her wrists with a cry of alarm and tried to push her off him.

She clutched at his shoulders like a drowning woman. Tears rolled out of her eyes, furious and fearful and sore, her lids screwed shut tight. Mucous ran from her nose across the stitching of the Russian's leather gloves, fingers clamped across her mouth, forcing her head back. And the girl's body was rubbing against Alf's hot crotch, driving him mad.

Sylvester de Winter's grunting face was inches away. The Russian grimaced and tried to catch his eye.

Horror rose up in him like heartburn. He pushed, hard, with all the strength in his legs, against her and Sylvester de Winter.

The man was using such force against the girl that Alf had little success until he grabbed the girl by the arms and shoved her backwards when the Russian's rhythm relented.

He pushed again, and succeeded in moving her away just far enough for him to slip sideways, out of her grasp.

Her hands reached out but he took her wrists and forced her arms away from him.

He gasped with pain as the wound in his shoulder tore apart.

The girl wriggled and opened her eyes.

Sylvester de Winter cursed but he didn't let go of her mouth.

Her gaze followed Alf as he shuffled out of the space between her and the wall.

She whimpered, helpless, as Sylvester de Winter wrestled with her and pinioned her to the brickwork.

Alf paused to catch his breath and considered helping her – and then he noticed that, in spite of his exertions in the chill night air, there came no puffs of breath from Sylvester de Winter's nostrils or his gaping mouth. The man was breathing all right – Alf could hear his grunts and gasps – but it was as if his breath came not from a living, warm body. Alf was struck with a cold terror then that drove him back a few steps, away from the sordid scene, his thoughts still half concerned with helping the girl.

The Russian gave a long low groan clearly audible above the other sounds of his actions, jerked his body against the girl and turned his face towards Alf.

Alf's bile rose and he fled.

He ran to the lamp-lit street and did not pause, not heading for the pub where he knew no-one. He ran into the sparse traffic, feet clattering on the cobbles as he dodged between carts and delivery bicycles. There were no thoughts in his head except to escape, to put as much space between him and Sylvester de Winter as possible.

He ran along the centre of Whitechapel Road, not knowing which direction he was headed, until he heard a hue and cry erupt some few hundred yards behind him. Glancing back as he paused for breath, he realised he stood out a mile, running along the main street. He set off again and dived down a side street to lose himself further.

He lost track of the turns he took, paid no heed to street signs or direction, ran into dead-end yards and back out again. His shoes splashed through puddles, splashing his trouser cuffs. He fell, skinned his hands, tore a hole in one knee that bled into the ripped tweed of his trousers, but he rose up again and ran again, wiping his hands on his jacket as he did so.

His lungs hurt. His shoulder hurt. He got a stitch in his side and ran through it, breathing in huge whooping gasps until it was run out of him. His shoelaces worked themselves loose, flapping around his ankles until his shoes became too loose to run in. He bent quickly to tie them up, not caring that the ends were smeared in muck.

At last he fell to a heap, exhausted. He was in a dark yard, only one light in the surrounding houses, and the noise he made gasping for breath was abominable. He held onto his diaphragm with both hands as he sunk down onto his haunches against the house, then collapsed into the corner against the wall of the privy. When his breathing recovered to normal levels, the tears came.

He was lost in Whitechapel. He was terribly afraid. He refused to think about Sylvester de Winter and the girl, but he couldn't help it. Like probing a rotten tooth the sights and sounds and smells came back to him again and again.

Why didn't the man breathe? Alf's own breath whistled out of his lungs in a cloud of steam into the night air of London. *What kind of man is Sylvester de Winter, that he can control his own body temperature like that?*

Alf sat crying, unable to think of what to do now. The wound in his shoulder had begun to bleed again and the afternoon's drugs, whatever they had been, were wearing off, leaving him with a sick headache and trembling nerves.

He was hungry too. And, of course, implicated in all of Sylvester de Winter's terrible actions.

Why didn't I save that poor girl? he thought in despair. *Why didn't I stop him?*

Then he remembered the physical force Sylvester de Winter had brought to bear on the girl when he – when he desecrated her – from behind.

Alf realised he'd been no match for the shorter, older man.

His stomach clenched on nothing. Tears streaked his dirty face, his handkerchief balled into a grubby fist. In the darkness, in pain, shivering with fear and exhaustion, Alf realised his only hope was to find the man who'd bandaged him up that afternoon.

CHAPTER 23 – The Betrayal of Annie's Dead Boys

Polly stood on the walkway under the bridge for a long time after Annie disappeared. Her mind raced over many thoughts, none of them comforting, none of them holding her attention for long. Her attention skipped from one to the next like a stone skipping over the surface of a flat pond.

She cried silently into the darkness, hiding her sobs, not drawing attention to her grief. She cried as one who expects no comfort from another, hiding the shameful tears in the stiff wind that forced its way upriver from the sea. Down on the bank where the vagrants had their camp, the fire dwindled, and went out.

At one point she prayed to God for aid, expecting the usual reticence. And sure enough, no solace, no reply came. *Who would comfort a ruined old woman like me?* she thought in her misery. *Not even compassionate Jesus*, she cried as her shoulders shook with self-pity. *I am being justly punished for my sins on Earth.* She stood on the narrow walkway over the dark rushing water, her hands on the railing gripped tight. The bridge rumbled and vibrated with each passing train as it clanked overhead, the engine coughing sparks that eddied down around her like fireflies dying.

She left the bridge ice-cold and made her way as if sleepwalking to the Three Bells, where she broke into the first of Annie's threepennies for the swift release of gin and a beer chaser. After three of those she left the Bells and moved on to the Black Boy, then the Crown & Feathers. Each drink made her betrayal less painful, made it easier to promise herself that she'd make it up to Annie when she had to.

But under her thirst, under her hunger, was a gnawing terror that sickened her and turned all her drink to ash. She was afraid for herself. With no Annie, she'd have to work alone. That meant more danger, more discomfort.

Maybe she could hook up with that Irish girl who still swore her name was Mary Kelly.

Maybe she'd go to the Salvation Army, get herself clean, get back on her feet again. Viewed through the bottom of a glass, anything was possible.

Polly was well soused when she tipped out of the Crown & Feathers. She still felt cold, felt the chill air rising from the river, the breeze blowing upriver from the coast of the North Sea. There was a smell of sleet in the air, common enough this early in March.

She made her way towards the rooming houses of Flower & Dean Street and was searching for the door to the privy in some darkened yard when she realised she was not alone. With a practised swiftness she locked herself in the privy and braced the door with her body while she bent double and vomited into the cesspit. In the darkness she wasn't sure she'd aimed in the right place. With one hand she found a handkerchief in her pocket and wiped her mouth, then stood as silent as she could, listening for sounds in the yard outside.

The houses round the yard were always full. She knew this instinctively, without needing to know the address. This part of town was crowded. In the darkness she could hear voices from the buildings, laughter now and then, a lone voice singing, footsteps in the alleyways moving on. She held her breath. Someone was sobbing, outside.

Polly worked her mouth and swallowed, trying to clean her palate of the acid she'd brought up. Her heart was hammering. Her head hurt. But she knew she wouldn't be able to stay in the privy for long. One or more of the residents would demand its use, sooner or later. With a deep breath she wrenched the door open and stepped out into the yard.

Above the familiar smells of a slum courtyard Polly noticed another odour, one which pricked the senses into panic: raw blood. Her eyes were adjusted to darkness now and she stood waiting for the sounds to come again. When another stifled sob broke the silence, she knew where to find its source.

She found the young man in a corner of the yard, away from the lit windows and out of sight of the alley that led to the street. She wobbled over to where he crouched, whimpering. *Leave well alone*, whispered the voice in her head, but the youth was crying like a small child, and she was too recently guilty to ignore him.

"What's up?" she asked. Her voice was hoarse and throaty. She tasted her own acid on her breath.

He glanced up at her and his face was utter misery, his words a weak mumble. "Don't let him find me."

"What?" She leaned in closer to him and noticed for the first time that his shirt was soaked with what looked like blood. In the gloom of the yard she barely made out his form, but a nagging sense of recognition tugged at her. *I've seen you before, young man.*

"Please, ma'am," he said, his eyes wide in his grubby face, "Please don't let him find me."

"Who?" Polly asked with a frown. *Move on, move away, let it lie,* the voice of her common sense whispered.

Guilt kept her by him. She peered more closely at his face and his clothes, and underneath the alcohol her memory floated his likeness up from some deep well of recognition. She remembered the scene from that morning on the bridge and her common sense was smothered by a mixture of motherhood and fiscal greed.

"You want a bed for the night and to get that –" she nodded towards his bloodstain – "Seen to."

He nodded and sniffed. "I want to go home," he whispered in a hoarse voice.

"I can't manage that," Polly said, "But I can get you seen to, by a proper sawbones. Nick the Saw from Colchester, he runs the medical house in Fashion Street." *And in the meantime,* she thought, *I'll have an ally.* She held out her hand to help him up. "Come on."

His suit had been a good one this morning. Now it was much the worse for wear – as was he. She saw the mud on his shoes, the rent in his sleeve, and a sudden thought crushed her compassion.

"Got any money?"

"A – a bit," he said. "Will you help me?"

"Let's see," she said, and helped him to his feet. "How about a drink?"

"No!" he cried, jerking away from her. His jacket fell open with the sudden movement and his face crumpled up in pain. He began to shake violently, trembling, and backed away from her.

"Why, love?" Polly coaxed. She'd seen how much the bloodstain marked his shirt. "What's up?"

He shook his head, very faintly, the light from a first-floor window glinting on his hair. "Don't let him find me," he said again, his voice a whisper.

"Who?" she asked. "What sort of trouble are you in?"

But he wouldn't answer that one.

Her initial plan to head back to the pub – any pub – for a few more numbing drinks, was out of the question. No matter how she cajoled, the boy was having none of it. In the end Polly shrugged. Irritated, her inner conflict an ongoing debate between whether to help him find some sort of medical treatment, or ditch him to fend for herself, she found no answer. She was desperately afraid of being alone. And Annie's dead boys in her pocket kept jingling against her conscience. *Save this one,* they seemed to chorus at her. She bitterly acceded.

"What's your name, son?" she asked.

He stared at her and made no answer.

"Come on, love, I've got to call you something if we're to make a go of it," she coaxed. "I'll make one up for you if you like." She bit down hard on the first name that came to mind. *Too many memories,* she thought, shaken.

"Alf," said the youth.

"That wasn't too hard, now, was it?"

Alf leant on her arm and she led him out of the courtyard towards the rooms at Fashion Street. He was hers to protect, and it made her feel safe. But he didn't make her task any easier.

Now and then he glanced around and she realised he was startled by the sound of any coach & horses, but when she asked, he wouldn't say more than, "Don't let him find me", accompanied by a fierce painful grip on her arm. So they stuck to the back streets, taking a round-about route through the poorly-lit alleys between courtyards, Polly all the while itching for another drink and keen to find out how much money the ragged boy was toting.

He leaned on her, not heavily, as they crept around in the dark, and he never asked where they were headed. His utter dependence on her was part comforting, and part annoying.

"What's the matter with you?" she asked at one point when his wheezing breath grew painful to hear and they stopped while he recovered.

"I lost a – a girl, this morning," he said with a gulp. "She went into the river, and I couldn't stop her."

"Really?" said Polly, her stomach muscles constricting with fear. "I – I lost a friend to the river," she said, and felt her heart thud behind her ribs.

He stayed silent, seizing the air with great rasping breaths that eased as time passed.

"You been in a fight?" she asked.

He shook his head. "Gunshot," he said, and didn't explain. They set off shortly afterwards, silent as mice.

Polly's initial thoughts had been to take them beyond Fashion Street, where she realised she'd have to answer too many questions from people she knew, and head out to Spitalfields Workhouse. Then she reminded herself that, this late at night, the chances of a bed there were slim, and the thought of just abandoning the boy on the doorstep tugged at her like a destitute child.

She sobered up when she realised that the workhouse would separate them. The beadle would demand to know of the boy how he came by his wound, and the lad was so honest that she guessed he'd tell them straight up it was a gunshot, like he'd told her, without guile or pretence. So then the authorities would call her in, just as she was getting settled, and start asking questions. They'd move onto Annie, and the fact of her absence, knowing the two women stuck together.

And they'd want to know how Polly came into the coins in her pocket.

Polly cursed herself and began to retrace their steps through the alleys, away from the workhouse, back towards the rooming house in Flower & Dean Street. They might still have a room available, one of them, even at this time of night, and she had money to pay for it now, and one of the other women would help her clean up the boy – maybe even get him some laudanum for his pain, or some clean clothes.

He was shivering, he stank, the cuffs of his trousers were soaked and filthy, his jacket was torn and his shirt blood-soaked. His face was gaunt and grey with pain in the washed-out lights that chinked into the alleys when they passed one of the major streets. She found it hard to believe this unshaven wreck was the same boy as that morning's golden youth on the bridge.

She tried asking him about himself but got few answers – and most of them nonsense. He seemed dog-tired, delirious almost, his vowels choked.

A bit of a toff, thought Polly to herself, unable to understand much of his speech. *Or maybe just foreign. Plenty of them in the East End, all right.*

He didn't look right either. There was something in his eyes beyond the terror that suggested he was unhinged.

Perhaps it's the pain, she thought, but she wasn't convinced.

After what seemed like an hour of this creeping and halting, she couldn't stand it any more. She propped the boy up in an alleyway with the promise that she'd return quickly, and she ducked into the Four Feathers. The warmth of the smoky air wrapped around her with a stale welcome that was nonetheless comforting. She wriggled to the bar through a crowd of stokers.

"Gin, Harry," she greeted the barman, slapping a farthing on the counter-top.

He grinned at her in disgust. "Who you been with, then, Poll?" he leered as he set down a pale glass half empty on the copper sheeting.

"None of your business," Polly rasped, and sunk the gin in one smooth gulp.

"Where's Annie, then?" he asked with a sly glance as he picked up the empty glass like it was alive.

Polly felt the stinging warmth of the gin hit her like heartburn. "Never you mind," she gasped, and pushed herself away from the bar, burning heat spreading from her gullet and the fumes making her nose itch. She jostled her way back to the street door without looking back or replying to any more questions.

The night air was chill and set her nose running. She fished in her pockets for a handkerchief, setting Annie's dead boys jingling in another pocket, and the footpad came on her from behind. Her arms were pinioned to her body in a grip that held without crushing, as if the assailant were afraid of getting dirty.

"I smell coin of the realm, cow," growled his voice in her ear, "An' it's comin' from your direction." The hands moved then so one clasped her mouth and the other lifted her off her feet, dragged her down the lane beside the pub, squeezed her torso so tight she found it hard to breathe.

Polly writhed and kicked, to no end.

The man set her on her feet against a rough brick wall and clenched his fist around her face. "Gimme them pennies, now."

You can't have them! she thought, *I need 'em!*

But the hand round her mouth was cutting off her air and she couldn't breathe through her streaming nose, so she struggled as best she could while the free hand searched her pockets, guided by the jingling until she weakened and he found the knotted handkerchief with Annie's threepennies – her dead boys – for the other woman's funeral expenses.

"Now," came the voice again, silken hoarse, "'Ave you anything else worth 'aving in that skirt of yours?" And the free hand groped its way under her petticoat as she blanked out her body, separated her mind from the sensations that followed, the rough hand scratching up her thigh until two sharp fingers tore into her. He gave a couple of thrusts, poked her anus with his thumb, then withdrew and wiped his hand on her skin before removing it from under her skirt.

"I thought not," he sneered, close enough that she felt his breath cold on her cheek. Then he switched hands and she smelled her body on his fingers. There was a jigging motion which she realised was him forcing the handkerchief, coins and all, into the pocket of his trousers. He threw her away from him.

She hit the ground hard, gasping for breath as his footsteps retreated into the night. There was dirt on her face, mucus and waste and snot, and the smell of it all made her vomit so hard some spurted out of her nose, stinging the delicate tissue with gin and bile.

Coughing and sniffling and sore, she minced to the nearest courtyard where she clung to the communal sink and worked its squealing pump until the water splashed into the deep basin. She cupped one hand and splashed her face until it was rinsed, then switched hands to clean the lot.

She was seething with rage, the only way she knew how to fend off despair. The funds for her night in the rooming-house were gone. She felt like ash. She'd let everyone down – Annie, this boy Alf, Annie's dead boys. *And you still ain't had your fill of drink, Poll,* she argued with herself. *You can't count the ones you sicked up.*

She summoned her dignity and waddled over the road to where she'd stashed Alf.

He was crouched against the wall of a one-room house, not far from where she'd left him. He was shivering violently, nursing his wounded shoulder, and in the dim light of the alleyway she wasn't sure if he'd been crying again. At the sound of her approaching footsteps he glanced up and a moment of panic flashed across his face.

She smiled, held out her scrubbed hands like a mother, beckoned him to her, dragged him into her arms, hugged him for comfort. Whispered in his ear.

"Where's that money, precious?"

CHAPTER 24 – Last Orders

Louis and James Frazer took a cab to London Bridge, some distance downstream from Westminster and just within sight of the Tower. When the cab driver attempted to take them via the south bank, across at Waterloo, Louis had Frazer stop the cab and insist they stay on the north side of the Thames. After a short discussion about the difficulties of traversing the volume of traffic at that time of the evening and the subsequent offer of an additional tip, the journey continued.

"I can't cross the river," Louis admitted to Frazer when the cab set off again. "I'm trapped, as it were, on the north bank."

Frazer nodded his understanding. "I take it this is normal?" he asked.

Louis nodded. "The effect isn't this fierce, on an ordinary day. I expect it to grow stronger around the high tides, and at other crossing-points of time and motion. It's a trial by fire –" he laughed, self-aware – "or rather, trial by water."

"The solstices and equinoxes?" Frazer asked. "What about at dusk, at dawn, and the phases of the moon? I ask on a purely professional basis, you understand."

Louis smiled and patted the other man on the arm. "Your work is of such great value to the Club," he said like an indulgent uncle. "We need more men like you."

Frazer said nothing. Louis could see he was thinking, and shortly the Scotsman asked, "Who else will follow the Consort who follows you?"

With a purse of his lips Louis turned away to stare out of the cab window. "Let's get tonight over and done with first, shall we?"

In silence they passed over the Fleet and the Walbrook, flowing fast in their underground channels through London's new sewerage network, and Louis shivered when they crossed. The chain in his pocket was ice-cold. He kept his hands on the box nonetheless, unable to keep himself from touching it, as if it were a lifeline. His thoughts, on that cab ride, were only of the Lady.

He thought of her loneliness during the Ice Ages: how she had wandered alone through centuries of nothingness, awaiting the return of her peers. And he imagined her horror when they did emerge, millennia later, through glaciers that ground the landscape flat underneath. Oh God, he felt for them all! But her – unscathed, still earthly – she hadn't shared the experience the others had endured, was unable to understand the transformation they had undergone, became an outcast amongst her own kind. He found his eyes brimming at the thought of it.

"Frazer?" Louis asked.

The younger man snapped alert. "Yes?"

"This chain," Louis began, fumbling in his pocket for the case. "What if the Consort is killed while She's wearing it? Will it lose what protective power it has?" He paused but did not wait for an answer. "Will it harm Her?"

Frazer pursed his lips and spent a moment in thought before he replied. "Nothing like this, to my knowledge, has been tried before – at least not since the time of the Prose Eddas." His brow knitted. "Who can say what parts of those are fact and what are fancy?"

"You aren't being much comfort, Frazer," said Louis with a grin that only touched the corners of his mouth.

Frazer nodded and apologised. "The chain is a magical talisman," he said. "I'm not a magician. I only study the documents that others have compiled, to gather that knowledge as a scholar, and make no practical attempts of my own."

"But you know what I'm trying to do, don't you?"

"I think so. You think that perhaps it will protect the Lady while She's on land – away from the river."

Louis turned to face the Scotsman. "I thought it had to be worth trying." He fell silent, his mouth dry at the thoughts he had next. "Of course, the problem will be to get it around Her."

Frazer said nothing. His brow was wrinkled with concern and he was obviously thinking of a response.

"I won't let this Russian take Her," Louis said, his voice hoarse with tension. His blood was thumping in his chest. "She'll die by my hands before I let him do that."

Frazer gave him a look of utter shock.

Louis drew back at the younger man's reaction and shook his head. "I'm sorry, Frazer," he apologised. He realised he was unsure how prepared he was to carry out that threat, and his emotions were growing wild. He gripped the case in his pocket with chill fingers and felt the corners dig into his palm. "I'm weak," he admitted. "It's the blood loss, I think." His palpitations grew stronger and he leaned forward to peer out of the cab window. "Where are we?"

"King William Street, I think."

Louis took a deep breath. *Here I go,* he thought, and braced himself against the door as the cab swung out onto the roadway that led up onto London Bridge.

Alone on the Bridge, silhouetted against the streetlamps, Louis knew he was taking a tremendous risk.

The cab behind him waited, Frazer inside, ready to provide rescue should any be required.

Louis knew that he was an easy target for a marksman on the southern shore. The youth in his parlour had been shot in broad daylight on a crowded thoroughfare in full view of Parliament's police constables. Here the bridge was crowded with vehicles, not pedestrians, and each of the passing carts had somewhere to go, an urgent destination for their cargo that sped them on with haste and no time for strangers. The rumble of their wheels upon the cobbles, the clatter of the hoofbeats, rose and fell in an irregular pulse. A man with a Lee-Enfield rifle on the riverbank would be able to effect an assassination with little risk of discovery.

The world had changed significantly since the Ice Age ended. A man no longer had to lay hands on another man to kill him. Louis had often considered – to no satisfactory conclusion – what would be the consequences of an unconnected killing.

And would he be the first Consort to die by the bullet? It took less courage to shoot a man with a gun than it did to kill him in the old-fashioned way, his breath hot on your skin, his blood slippery on your weapon, the final thwarted look on his face when you won.

Louis shook his head to clear his memories. He'd seen more of those faces than he cared to remember. The emotions of disappointment varied from man to man, the base nature of their challenge revealed by in the truth of their defeat: lust, greed, anger, envy, pride. Each one a valid motive, none the less deadly for its urging. Some he regretted; few, in truth. For the most part he dealt with the consequences in his own way. The man who would be Consort had to prove himself worthy to be the successor.

Until last night, Louis had never felt he needed any connection with the hero who would come forward to claim his crown, and now he was faced with nervous confusion. The impatience he'd felt for the last decade or so – waiting for a contender, while none appeared – now seemed too brief, the transition not quite ripe. He wanted more time to prepare the lad for his future.

It wasn't just the role of Consort. The Cuckoo Club was the tool of the Consort in the modern world and it was shaped to his character. Under Louis's predecessor it had been louche, decadent as the man himself, a den of libertines and gamblers.

Louis had more philanthropy in his nature. By his hand the Cuckoo Club had grown to be powerful, yet discreet, a force for just stewardship within an increasingly belligerent Empire. The Club's coffers had swollen – modestly – to credit, without excess.

It was Louis who set up the financial mechanisms that paid for the care of the Club's servants when they retired from its service; made benevolent grants available to school the sons of his despatched rivals and support their widows as needed; sponsored boys from the lesser London boroughs as apprentices in trades the Club found useful. The Club's current Armourer was the first of these.

All this was maintained by Louis's ruthless dispatch of his rivals, with or without an eye on posterity. The only rival Louis regretted was a man who had to be provoked into his challenge – one who sniped from the sidelines, undermined others, pushed them into a position he feared.

Louis, when he found out, spent a long time considering his options, debating whether he wanted to become the kind of man he would have to become in order to deal with this rival.

In the end it was Louis's own impatience that got the upper hand. The man was provoked into challenge, and Louis killed him. It was this situation that drove Louis to commit to good works – an atonement, of sorts, for a long lifetime and the steely arrogance of a younger man. The man's widow never forgave him.

I have to be killed, he thought with a deep indrawn breath.

The Club records mentioned one or two old Consorts who had killed themselves, one who died of an illness – and each had left a Club which dissolved into chaos and disarray until the new Consort – chosen by the Lady – was discovered, often decades later, like a Tibetan lama. There was even a century of dissolution when the kings existed, unrecognised, in an East Anglian village famous for its family feuds – boatmen all, commoners from the hamlets around the Mersea.

Louis knew he had to be killed, even if he had to force his assassin to do it.

The bridge beneath Louis's bare hands shook, with a thick heavy heartbeat, without moving a fraction. He smelled a sharp tang on the air as the North Sea spray reached him on the breeze. His mouth watered, nervously, apprehensive, sick with hope and the courage he'd lived with all his adult life. He took his hands off the parapet and felt his full age for the first time in years, his heart thumping and his knees weak. This far out above the river, he felt every tug of the current, every ton of the tide, and it made his head spin.

He withdrew the little box with the gold chain from his pocket. It was warm from his body heat, and inside, the chain links were smooth and dull. He laid it out full length along the slight curve of the stone parapet and he felt sure the air shivered. He placed his hands over the chain so he touched both the gold and the stone – and his nostrils flooded with the scents of pollen and pine trees in Spring.

His body reacted like he'd been hit by a bolt of lightning. He couldn't move his hands – it felt as though they were rooted to the bridge – and his knees sagged as he felt a great current surge through him, down the stone piers of the bridge and into the river, a thousand torrents sweeping him out to the estuary faster than gravity, far out into the North Sea, his consciousness dissolving in the mass of water until it reached the Lady and he was drained, kneeling on the bridge with his face clammy and his hands stuck to the parapet above his head.

Then the energy surge turned like the tide and it rushed back to him like a tidal bore, rapid and ruthless and primeval, forcing him to his feet, pushing him up until the thick white hair on his head stood up at the roots and he stifled a cry like sexual union. Energised, he snatched the chain from the stone and slipped it back into his pocket. The wind rippled his hair as it fell back into place and he turned to the cab, Frazer's keen face pinned to the window.

He leapt into the cab with the energy of a much younger man and barely glanced at Frazer who stared as if Louis were some kind of supernatural being. "She's at Sheerness," Louis snapped, "And moving fast!"

Louis bounded out of the cab before the horses had halted. He strode into the hallway of the Cuckoo Club and danced down the stairway to the Water Chamber. The Armourer scurried to keep pace.

The Water Compass, suspended from a beam above the centre of the room, hummed with energy.

Barely six hours earlier, Louis had taken its measurement, an insignificant change from the day before. Now it hung eastwards, hovering over the point of the compass marked on the floor slabs beneath it. Louis's stomach fluttered in nervous excitement as, while he watched, the great bronze dish began to move. It swung slowly away from direct east as he watched.

There was only one explanation, and it confirmed his experience on the bridge. The Lady was moving towards London on the rising spring tide, that very night.

Louis snatched up a handful of small versions of the bowl, very much like the censers used by priests in the Catholic Church, and half-filled them with water from the cauldron. They stuck out from his hand as if the chains were solid rods.

Dowsing rods, he thought, *to find a god. Or lightning bolts to bring one to mortality.*

He left the Water Chamber and while the Armourer locked the door behind him, Louis mounted the stairs to the hallway.

"Parsons? Get me the Prussian Ambassador on the telephone, please. I'll be in the Shooting-Gallery."

The Porter nodded, staring at the bowls in Louis's hand, and lifted the receiver.

Louis headed off back downstairs to the Shooting-Gallery, the bowls tugging towards the river like a pack of otter-hounds on the scent. He couldn't remember the last time he'd felt like this.

He met the Armourer on the stairs and together they entered the Shooting-Gallery.

"I've got the Cromwell maps," said Cummins. He lifted one document from a sheaf of papers stacked neatly on his workbench. "Want a look?"

Louis nodded. Between them they unfolded the map and laid it out across the surface of the workbench, uneven and creased. "Can you make a note of each sighting since dusk last night?" he asked. "On a Master Copy, if possible. I don't think the Members need one, but it might be useful for the briefing session."

The Armourer nodded. "There are confirmed sightings and possible sightings. D'you want both?"

Louis thought for a moment, then nodded. "Yes. Put the location of the interested parties as well, please. Consort in Mayfair, Wilhelm in Chelsea, Victoria's sons in Pall Mall or wherever they were – George Buckle can fill you in with the details."

"And a path of the Lady's preferred routes?"

Louis nodded in agreement. At that point there was a knock on the door and he was summoned to the front desk of the Club to take the telephone call he'd requested. He climbed the stairs with more vigour than a sportsman.

"Ambassador?" he asked down the mouthpiece of the telephone apparatus.

"Yes, Mr Beauregard," said the Prussian Ambassador. "I understand you would wish my assistance."

"I certainly do," said Louis. "The future of your next Kaiser may well be in the balance."

"The *next* Kaiser?"

"You heard me. Keep a close eye on Crown Prinz Wilhelm tonight, please." Louis began to pace the hallway, turning from the desk to face the Turner seascape on the opposite wall, back to the desk, then towards the painting.

"You know that's easier said than done," said the Ambassador with what sounded like a smile.

Louis nodded into the mouthpiece, then he snapped his fingers. "I've got it," he said, and he didn't bother to hide his own pleasure at the fitting solution. He walked up close to the Turner, so close he was inches away from the ridges of paint on the canvas. "Take him to the Tower of London." He grinned at his own ingenuity.

"Why?"

"I will arrange for him to have a private viewing of the Crown Jewels," said Louis, and thought *even if I have to mortgage the Club to do so*.

The Prussian Ambassador made an indistinct noise on the other end of the telephone line. "It might be more effective if you offer him a private tour of the Armoury. You know what he's like."

"Brilliant," said Louis, resisting the urge to touch the Turner, still absorbing the Ambassador's agreement while he thought of a way to make the arrangements. "I'll let you have the details in a little while. Shall I send a carriage?"

The Ambassador snorted down the telephone line. "You take liberties, my friend. We will provide Wilhelm's transport, and a discreet guard as well. I don't know what you're planning – but I want my Royal charge to be safe."

Louis acknowledged the other man's concerns and hung up.

"Parsons?" he asked the Porter. "Ask the Armourer to call in his debt with the Constable of the Tower."

In Parliament Square the carriages huddled under the shadow of Westminster Abbey. Louis's men had formed into groups of six or seven each by the time he arrived with the Club Armourer in his carriage.

The Armourer handed out firearms according to the list that he'd agreed with Louis that day. To one of the men in each group – not the man with the firearm – Louis gave one of the miniature water-compass bowls.

Without knowing where the youth was, the best action available to the Club was to track the Lady's movements and attempt to protect Her. It was an impossible task. Arranged in a cordon from Limehouse to Westminster Bridge, each man with instructions how to track her using the miniature water-compass and a parish map drawn up two hundred years earlier. Louis wondered if any of them felt as helpless as he did.

He still felt a rushing in his veins, and knew it wasn't just adrenaline. Somewhere, off to the east, the tide was rising and the Thames responded.

Louis walked over to the Houses of Parliament and was greeted by the Black Rod as he stepped over the threshold of the Entrance Hall.

"What news, Mr Beauregard?"

Louis almost heard himself crackle as he nodded in greeting. "Brigadier Doyle," he replied, grasping the other man's handshake. "The Lady's returning," he said in a low voice, his words whispering through the high chamber. "Is the Commons Shooting Club prepared?"

Black Rod smiled and nodded. "I took the liberty of despatching them to their stations earlier this evening."

"Good man!" Louis slapped him on the shoulder.

"Shall we discuss this somewhere more comfortable?" asked Black Rod, and indicated a small room just inside the main entrance to the building. "I have information you may find useful."

Louis nodded. He felt salt in his blood, and the chain in his pocket was heavier than it ought to be. He took a seat in the oak-panelled office and tried to relax.

"We have taken telephone reports from various places tonight," said the Brigadier as he fished amongst a sheaf of papers on his desk. They rustled, crisp, as he leafed through them. "The Tower, the Russian Occidental, a couple of West End theatres, the Prussian Embassy." He read out a series of reports filed by police stations and Cuckoo Club members and parliamentary clerks on their journey home, each one dated to a minute's tolerance and the location clearly noted.

Louis raised his chin and his eyebrows in an encouraging gesture. He stopped the Brigadier at a report of increased crime in the East End, by Spitalfields and Whitechapel, which piqued his interest, and had the man repeat the message. *That's him,* he thought, and something in him snapped like a steel thread. *It won't be Wilhelm,* he thought with relish, *Not tonight. He's too far from the River.*

"Has anyone reported a cream-coloured coach with Russian livery?" he asked briskly.

The Black Rod ruffled his papers and nodded. "Ten o'clock, approaching Parliament from the direction of St Thomas's Hospital on the South Bank. Seen prowling the Strand before midnight, then slowly weaving through the City until –" he checked his papers again – "Half an hour ago, at Houndsditch."

Louis nodded. "And the report from the Tower," he said, "I'll wager that came in about half an hour ago too."

The Lord Lieutenant checked and nodded. "The Raven Master reports some agitation amongst the birds – uncommon, apparently, at this hour."

"That's our man," Louis said, nodding to himself. *I'll wager it was more than just uncommon disturbance too.* He thanked the Brigadier and returned to the crowded coach-yard outside. It was noticeably colder and his breath formed phantoms in the air.

The Cuckoo Club members were watching him, their faces a mixture of fear and apprehension, and the tension was palpable.

"Gentlemen," said Louis, "We have our man." He took a deep breath to steady his voice. "The Lady is on the rising tide." His voice was steely as he continued. "By daybreak, She must have a new Consort."

A couple of the Club members raised cries of protest.

Louis waved them to be silent and his voice was pure iron when he spoke next. "It is our duty to ensure the right man becomes Consort tonight. There is more than the future of the Club at stake. We face a new century: it must be a new man, a man of the times, who is Consort. The shape of the future is at stake. Do *not* fail me."

He looked around at the ashen faces of the Club members in the gathering.

"Gentlemen," he reminded them gently, "Remember the oath you swore when you were admitted to this Club."

A few dropped their gaze in shame. A handful of the others swallowed great gulps, some regarding him with a clear-eyed fascination. One or two – Louis was pleased to note Benton, the young numismatist, was amongst them – stared straight ahead, not shrinking from what he had to say.

"Tonight I summon you to your duty – not your privilege." He took another deep breath. "I have reason to believe our quarry is in the East End, right now, and as you know he may be in some peril. I, and he, need your aid. In fact, the future of the Club may be at stake, at least in the form you know so well." He paused for emphasis. "Bring the Lady's chosen Consort to the safety of the river, on the north bank, by sunrise. As close to the Tower as you can," he added.

"For Queen and Country!" cried the Chairman suddenly, and the square echoed with the roar of their response. Then, with quiet steps and murmured agreements, each group mounted their coach and departed for their station, paying their respects to Louis as they passed him by on the way out of Parliament Square.

When they were gone Louis glanced up into the eyes of the coachman, who tipped his hat. Louis climbed into the coach, alone, and when he'd secured the door he rapped on the ceiling and the vehicle trundled on its way.

In his pocket the gold chain quenched in his blood lay chill in its wooden box. Louis loosened his collar and removed his cufflinks, discarded his weapons, removed his socks and shoes and placed his personal belongings in a small trunk under the seat. It felt remarkably liberating. The ring on his left hand, a gold band set with a sea-creature seal from Ancient Sumer, he kept, but his watch and watch-chain he put away.

Destiny kept time never so small as human hours.

CHAPTER 25 – A Rough Trade

"Where's that money, precious?" Polly asked in a whisper, and withdrew from embracing him, still crouched in the corner of the courtyard.

The boy called Alf said nothing, didn't move a muscle except for his eyes, focused on the street beyond her, twitching as he watched the traffic moving past the narrow entrance to the alley.

Polly hunched down in front of him with her hands tucked under her skirt behind her knees and repeated the question.

He looked at her with a sad apology. "I've only a couple of shillings."

The unclouded part of Polly's mind pushed aside the dry-mouthed monster that clamoured a hoarse hurrah. *'Only'*, the calm voice said, *'Only' a couple – of SHILLINGS*. Polly looked at his rags and filth and reminded herself of his previous appearance.

Yes, she thought, *He's a toff all right*. She saw with new discernment how well the cut of his clothes fitted him, saw the weight of the cotton of his shirt – *That's got to be good stuff to soak up that much blood*. His shoes, too, though filthy, had a fine look about them of the sort she hadn't seen for years.

"Where d'you live?" she asked in as kind a voice as she could manage. She was still bruised by despair at losing Annie and not yet inspired by the joy of finding Alf. *'Shillings'*, the voice in her head whispered, over and over.

"With my aunt. In Epsom."

Polly sucked her teeth and with a push of her hands on her knees she stood up. "Wot about the rest of yer family?" she asked, brain still tick-ticking away with the recent information. *Maybe he's a runaway*, she thought. *Maybe there's a reward*. She rested her hands on her hips and watched him as his gaze fell.

"My father's in India," he began, then paused, as if reconsidering.

"Is that the geezer in the coach?"

"No!" Alf's eyes shot wide open and he struggled to his feet, his face fierce and terror in his eyes. "Where is he?" he asked, his voice betraying a hint of panic. "You mustn't let him find me." He reached out to her as if to grasp her shoulders or upper arms, then let one hand fall to his side as he slid the other one under his muddy jacket. The lapel flapped as his hand floundered around underneath, and he grimaced with a wince. "Can you help me?"

"Sure," said Polly, her teeth close to chattering. The night air was growing colder and she still hadn't fully warmed up from her adventure under the bridge. All the time her mind was tick-tock, tick-tock, working out odds, tactics, strategies, advantages, solutions.

They might – again – get lodgings together. She could help fix him up – and hide him from the gent in the coach. Send someone out for a bottle, some fried fish, a hot pie. Her mouth watered as her stomach rumbled. And the rational part of her said she had so much more to gain by looking after him. Not once did she consider trying to find the gent in the coach to surrender Alf up to him. There was no obvious reward there.

"Can you get me to Mayfair?" Alf asked.

Polly blinked. This wasn't in her plans. "Mayfair?" she echoed. And her mind was off again, plush dinner parties, imagined finery, a big house with maids and a butler. Drinks on a silver tray. They might even let her sit by the fire in the kitchen to warm up before she left him. And then reality stepped back in, and she made sure to ask up-front. "What's in it for me?"

He heaved a sigh. "There's a club," he began, and changed tack. "I know a man. Or he knows me." He pulled his hand out from under his jacket and at the sight of his fingers smeared with blood, he gulped and began to fight back tears. As if without thinking, he wiped his hand on the thigh of his trousers.

"Can I –" Polly began to ask if she might get a drink at this place in Mayfair, then thought better of it. *Get one on the way*, she told herself. *And this time, take the lad*. She set off with him leaning on her arm, both trusting her sense of direction in unfamiliar streets.

Polly insisted they have a drink when they passed the Guildhall, ducking down Milk Street towards Cheapside. Her nerves were shot and she wasn't sure she had strength enough without a half-hour's break in the warm.

Alf murmured and didn't argue with her. There was pain masking his eyes when he nodded.

The pub they found was an unfamiliar one for Polly and she hid Alf in a booth by the fire before taking some of his money to buy them both a beer. At the bar she kept herself to herself, placing her order without glancing around like she would on a normal night, her voice low and her gaze avoiding any social approaches. The back of the bar was lined with a pitted mirror and its reflection showed her no-one she recognised. She asked for two beers and a single shot of gin which she gulped down in one as she waited for her change.

On his return the barman gave her a disdainful look while he picked up the empty glass as if it might bite him. Without a word he managed to convey the implication that she and her sort were not welcome in this particular establishment.

She picked up the beers and pressed her way back to the snug.

Alf was warming his filthy hands at the fire. She noticed a graze on his knuckle under the grime. His face was ashen pale, streaked with miasma. The look on his face was grateful when she put the beer in front of him, but more than anything she was struck by his fragile beauty, the blue of his irises shown into sharp contrast by the redness of his eyes. They sipped at the beer, reluctant to hurry the moments of quiet warmth. Neither spoke.

Polly began to warm up, began to relax, letting go of her aches and pains as the gin's effects spread from her heartburn to loosen her tense muscles. She let her mind relax a little too, but not too much.

She thought of Annie, slipping herself into the river like that, with no regard for those she left behind. Polly found herself grinding her teeth. *How dare she!* she thought bitterly. *An' then leaving me with all that money, for nothing.*

And now Polly was supposed to go find Annie's body, rescue it from a pauper's grave with money they might have used to good effect themselves on frozen nights when the tricks were few and nasty. To think that Annie'd had them then, had them all the time – was prepared to go to extremes in order not to spend them on a little comfort. Polly's disdain surmounted. Annie, the dirty little slut, must have enjoyed the joyless encounters.

Polly's mouth set in a thin hard line. She vowed not to cry for Annie any more. *Save your tears for yourself, Poll Parker. Life dealt you a bad hand.* It wasn't fair, and it wasn't Christian, but she'd been a bit lax with her duty to God recently so perhaps this was his way of punishing her. And the young man at her side was a short salvation. She glanced sidelong at him nodding by the fire, his blond hair matted.

Maybe in the morning, she told herself, *when we get to this place in Mayfair, maybe they'll let me have a wash there.* Then she would be able to go to the Sally Army and say, *Look, I've had a bad turn of luck but I want Jesus to save me,* and maybe they'd take her in and she could set herself up again, right enough. Even though they frowned on drinking. Sat there in the warmth with a beer in her hand it seemed possible.

They left the pub after almost an hour and set off westwards once again. She was in an unfamiliar part of the city now, high stone buildings and empty pavements. Their progress was slow.

Alf dived for cover every time a coach approached and had to be coaxed out with smooth words.

Polly lost her bearings at one point and they had to ask a passer-by for directions. She was dismayed to find out they were little further west than Covent Garden. The people here were strangers, outside her normal circle, more prosperous, and she felt as if they were looking straight through her to the blackest sin she carried within. She was scared they'd ask about Alf, too, and while she had him for companionship she'd never felt so alone.

They were crossing St Martin's Lane when a cream-coloured carriage pulled up beside them.

Alf stumbled and fell to his knees as the carriage rolled to a halt. A gentleman stepped out of the coach in a sable fur coat, all smiles and sparkling eyes and thin moustache pulled back to show his teeth in his little red lips. His hand was out to raise Alf up and the other hand, with the silver-topped cane, was raised as if to administer a blow.

Polly cried out in surprise and had little time to prepare herself before the coachman leapt from his seat up front to help the newcomer bundle Alf into the coach. The thought of leaving her meal ticket made her bold and she pummelled the man in the sable coat on the back with her raw cold fists, her breath steaming as she yelped at him.

Alf disappeared into the coach, subdued by the coachman. The gentleman in the sable coat whirled round and caught her wrists in his hands, the cane clattering to the cobbles.

"Madam!" he hissed, his breath cold in her face, eyes dark as jet.

Polly struggled, kicking at him, but he seemed not to notice the impact of her boots.

His face contorted in a sneer that stretched his cheek muscles, little tufts of stubble showing on his cheekbones. His nostrils flared, his chest and stomach heaving with the effort of breathing. "Get in the coach, madam!" he growled, his grip intensifying on Polly's wrists to the point where her hands went limp.

She stopped struggling. She thought about spitting in this man's face, but an intuition stopped her. The cold weight in her stomach turned over and her mouth went dry. She was not angry at this man, not angry enough. The emotion he stirred in her was fear.

She had no doubt that the strenuous grip on her wrists could be transferred to her throat with an equal, if not greater, pressure. When she spoke her voice came out as a croak.

"Don't hurt me, mister."

He laughed in her face, a soft chuckle of achievement, and whisked her round until her back was to the open coach door. The empty street behind him was gaslit and silent. Then someone grasped her around the waist and dragged her backwards into the coach with such force that her heels banged the door sill. Numbing pain shot up her legs.

Outside, the gentleman scooped up his cane from the gutter and his furred bulk blotted out the doorway and the coach rocked on its springs as he climbed on board.

Polly put out her hands to steady herself in the darkness as the hands around her waist let go. Her right hand found wetness and warmth, and she realised it was Alf's tweed jacket soaked with his blood.

The coach rocked again as the coachman climbed out of the door at her back, then it slammed shut with a gust of air that tickled the stray hairs around her face. She heard bolts being shot in place behind her.

The man in the sable coat settled into the far corner of the coach, opposite Alf, and pulled his door shut with a firm click of the lock.

Polly kneeled on the coach floor gasping for breath, one hand on the leather seat and the other in Alf's weak grip. She heard him breathing, hard and laboured, and it took her a while to realise he was weeping. Lots of questions clamoured in her mind. She didn't have the gall to ask any of them. She'd been scared before – when she was working, out on the streets at night – but never like this. And after Annie's disappearance, who now would miss her? A bottomless pit yawned open in her stomach, leaden all the way down to her boots.

The coach moved off. The gentleman lit a cigarette.

Polly watched him, wary, saw the light of the Vesta match reflect off the coach interior as if it was made of lacquer. Beside her, Alf groaned and moved his legs in a struggle to sit upright. Polly's heart thumped. Her mouth was still dry and her knees were weak, but she still had strength to ask a question.

"What d'you want, sir?"

The stranger flicked his cigarette ash into a small container in the side of the cab and his eyes glittered as he peered at her. His lips drew back from his teeth again when he replied.

"I only want the best for him," he said. "I want to save him too."

Although his voice was gentle it sent shivers up Polly's spine. His accent was almost familiar. She frowned. "Save him from wot?"

The man waved a dismissive gesture like a wisp of smoke as if the question were irrelevant. He gazed out of the coach window for a moment, then said, "*For* what, is closer to the truth." His voice was so quiet it was almost as though he was talking to himself.

"Who is he, then?" Polly asked, more sharpness in her voice than she intended. "Is he important?"

"Oh, yes," the other man breathed, leaning towards her. "Yes, he's *very* important." He sat back again and with a shrug, said, "*Who* he is, his name and background, is really of no matter." Then he fixed her with a sidelong look. "Is it?"

"Might be, to someone," Polly said without thinking. She felt sick at the thought she'd been taken for a ride. She was confused by this man. "So there's no reward, then?"

The man laughed out loud, throwing his head back against the collar of his sable coat. Then he nodded. "Oh, there's a reward, all right," he said, again almost to himself. He peered at her, his manner brisk. "But I think you are not interested in that. What do you want? Money? Drink? Opium?"

"Yes," said Alf. The word was clipped, curt, uttered between gasps. His hand was probing under his jacket again, the other loose in Polly's spare hand. "Yes, for the love of God."

Polly stared at him and her words came out like those of a stern mother. "You're not going to touch that filth, are you?"

The voice of the other man came from behind her. "I don't think he has much choice. Do you?"

"Please," Alf choked.

The man extinguished his cigarette and withdrew a pipe from somewhere in the darkness. He began to fill it and as he did so, he spoke with a soft insistence that chilled Polly's bones.

"My name is Sylvester de Winter," he said. "I encountered this young man this morning, in some distress, and shared my hospitality." He paused. "Where were you headed, tonight?"

"Mayfair," Polly said, bewildered. "He asked me to."

"And what were your intentions there?"

"Dunno." Polly shrugged.

Alf muttered something faint and broken.

"Speak up, boy!" Sylvester de Winter snapped. "Go on – *tell* me."

Alf sobbed with a huge indrawn breath.

Polly stared in the darkness at him, afraid he'd died or something.

When Alf spoke it was twisted by tears. "I wanted to find the man who helped me."

"Foolish boy," tutted Sylvester de Winter. "I helped you, did I not?"

"When I was shot," gasped Alf.

"Again, I helped you when you were shot. What can this other man provide that I cannot?"

"Answers," gasped Alf.

"Answers?" Sylvester de Winter laughed. "To your foolish questions, no doubt – which are entirely wrong, believe me." He snorted. "What are your plans for the future, boy?"

Alf let out a stifled sob.

Polly felt a surge of anger rise up in her, trapped between these two who seemed to have forgotten her, and it overruled her fear. "Mister," she pleaded, "Let me out now. You got the boy, you can keep 'im."

Sylvester de Winter knocked on the coach roof three times and the carriage rocked to a halt. He snicked open his door and let it fall open.

"After you, madam," he sneered. The pavement outside was empty and desolate.

"No!" Alf grabbed her arm with a quick lunge and gripped her tight. "Don't leave me alone with him!"

She recognised his tone of voice. It was the same one Annie had used, the voice that pleaded for rescue, the one that told her she had strength enough to carry on and save them both. Polly, as ever, was powerless to resist.

She shook her head. The door clicked shut, the coach moved on. She crawled to the other seat and watched in distaste as Sylvester de Winter passed the opium pipe across the coach.

Alf reached his trembling hand to take it.

Sylvester de Winter tossed a box of Vestas onto the seat.

Polly struck one and held it over the pipe-bowl while Alf inhaled. The stink of the sulphurous match made her cough. She was appalled at how Alf's face appeared drawn and aged in the eerie light. She looked hatred at Sylvester de Winter, but he was gazing out the window again, drumming his fingers on his silver cane.

Alf's desperate puffing on the pipe reminded Polly of a hungry baby at the nipple and a worm crawled into her heart and died there.

"So, madam," Sylvester de Winter began, and she heard the smirk in his voice, "You seem to be stuck with him." He leaned forward on his cane, pushing his face towards hers. "Let me make you an offer."

Polly waited, saying nothing, her mind a blur. She huddled on the floor of the coach in an awkward jumble, the door handle at her back banging into her shoulder-blade with every lurch. Her gnawing urge for a drink had begun to return.

"There appears to be some kind of manhunt in London tonight," Sylvester de Winter said, his manner light and arrogant. "I have a ship berthed in the East India docks, which is due to sail with the tide, tomorrow morning, before dawn. I recommend you both embark – soonest – as my companions."

"No," Alf groaned.

"Where to?" said Polly, cautious with suspicion.

"Ah, excellent, madam," Sylvester de Winter said, and tapped his hand against the metal top of his cane in a type of applause. "You see the peril you are in, and the best – easiest – solution. In the first instance, the ship will stop at Hamburg. It will then continue along the North Sea coast of Jutland, headed for points further north. That is of no matter to us. I intend to disembark at Hamburg and continue my journey by rail – and I expect you to join me." He chortled. "I expect you to have no choice."

Alf shifted position in his seat.

Sylvester de Winter reached out to pluck the pipe from Alf's drooping hand before the glowing embers spilled onto the coach cushion.

Polly squinted at him.

"I *ain't* got no choice, have I?" she said in a sharp little voice, turning to Sylvester de Winter.

He was tapping the ash from the opium pipe into the ashtray at his side, not looking at her. "Not really, my dear."

Polly turned back to Alf, moved his knee to one side so it no longer pushed into her shoulder, and realised he was insensible. "He needs a doctor," she said. "He's bleeding."

"Yes, and yes," said Sylvester de Winter. He patted the coach seat beside him, nodded towards it, then offered a hand to her as she struggled to rise from the floor.

She ignored it, even though her legs had gone numb in the cramped position, pins-and-needles in her calves and feet making them weak and difficult to control. The thought of cramming onto the coach seat next to Sylvester de Winter abhorred her. She pushed Alf's loose limbs to one side and squeezed in beside him, facing the man in the sable coat, who regarded her with an amused smirk.

"As you wish, madam," he said, and lit another of his infernal cigarettes.

CHAPTER 26 – The Wild Hunt

Louis, barefoot, directed his carriage to the Tower of London, wincing with recognition when they passed over each of the city's subterranean rivers. He rested his head on the window-frame and stared out into the streets during the journey. He didn't expect to see anyone he recognised. He began to feel every one of his eighty-three years.

In his pocket he held the chain he'd made from the Lady's coins. Its links, smooth except where the goldsmith had fused the cut ends together for strength, slipped through his fingers as easily as a set of prayer beads.

At the Tower the carriage parked up in a corner and sat in darkness while Crown Prinz Wilhelm von Hohenzollern arrived for his tour of the Royal Armouries. The Prussian Ambassador alighted from the coach first and stood waiting, listless, like a lovesick man at a wedding. As the Crown Prince alighted from his coach – in the full dress uniform of a British Field Marshal – he held his right arm close to his side, a disability that chilled Louis to breathlessness.

You were right, Ambassador, Louis said to himself. The old familiar band of pain crushed his chest again, but he did not dare to move or open a window for fresh air, afraid to draw attention to himself. *Who knows what hangs on that dead arm?*

The Crown Prinz strutted about the courtyard inspecting the company of Warden Watchmen lined up to present themselves for guard duty. He laughed and joked, his voice a brazen tone that carried far and betrayed the Prussian accent and bounced off the castle walls like copper sheets.

Louis shut his eyes. He pictured the youth he'd left bleeding on his parlour settee that afternoon, comparing him with the prince. He prayed that Alf was safe under some benevolent protection somewhere; but he feared the lad was in danger. He knew what strategy he'd use, were he in the place of his enemies. He hoped his men were better placed to swing the result for London.

Some time after the visitors entered the Tudor Gate as guests of the Constable of the Tower, Louis spotted the Raven Master crossing the courtyard towards him. The man ran low and craven as if he did not want to be seen. He darted his eyes from side to side, checking for trouble.

"What is it?" asked Louis when he opened the carriage door.

The Raven Master puffed and climbed into the carriage, his breath pale in the chill air. "No news of the young lad yet, Lord Camden says to tell you." He paused to inhale. "And I've lost Magnus," he said with a shake of his head.

"Lost him?" Louis asked. He felt his heart hop.

The Raven Master nodded.

"When was this?"

"About fifteen minutes ago," said the Raven Master. "I don't know how it happened. I'm glad –" he drew a deep breath – "I'm glad you warned me."

Louis nodded in the direction of the Prussian carriage across the yard. "I take it you have to be on duty for the visitors tonight," he said.

The Raven Master nodded.

"Do you know what Wilhelm's plans are for the evening?"

"After he leaves here? Not a clue."

"That's all right," said Louis, "I understand. Thank you for the news. Do you think this bird will go far?"

"No," the Raven Master shook his head. "His wings were clipped just last week. Lady Jane and the other girls are distraught. I have to go back to them."

Louis thanked him as he slipped out of the carriage and sprinted across the yard back to whence he came. Even in the inner courtyard of the Tower, Louis was unable to feel safe. He tapped the roof of the carriage and when the driver appeared over the edge of the window-sill, Louis shook his head and apologised. *I'll just have to bear it*, he thought. *Live for the present. Think nothing of the future – or the past.*

His nerves were frayed but not through worry. He longed to get out and stretch his legs. To feel the ground beneath his bare feet, to breathe fresh air, to see another sunrise – he wondered whether Sir Walter Raleigh had felt the same, incarcerated here, awaiting his fate.

About midnight Louis awoke to the sound of Crown Prinz Wilhelm and his party departing. He hoped the prince would retire to Clarence House and play cards with his grandmother, but he also realised how slim was the chance of this occurring. He did not realise he was tense until the Prussian coach left the courtyard and his hands relaxed.

Lights were brought out and Robert Napier, the Constable of the Tower, summoned Louis over to the Tudor Gate.

"What news?" Louis asked when the man climbed into the carriage.

"Louis," Napier exclaimed, "It's perishing in here. You'll catch your death!" The phrase was uttered without any apparent irony, and the man rubbed his hands together as if to warm them. "You ought to have some heating in here. Why don't you come into my office?"

Louis smiled and shook his head. "I'm fine," he said. It was true. "If I come across your threshold, now, I'll never leave again. I barely made it through the portcullis gate, and that was an hour ago. The tide's almost high."

Napier shook his head. "I'm sorry, Louis," he said, "I forgot the tunnel." Underneath the Tower's gateway was a channel that led under the castle from Traitors' Gate to a subterranean jetty. "I can get one of my men to bring you a blanket, if you wish?"

"No, thank you," said Louis. "What news is there? Any progress?"

"Yes, sir," said the Constable. He described a handful of false sightings, a cream-coloured coach involved in each one, across Chelsea and Belgravia and St James.

Louis shook his head. "It doesn't sound like that's a success, then." He sighed.

Napier went on. "Runners arrived at the Club at eleven, apparently, telling of a riot in the Tower Hamlets."

"Really?" Louis perked up.

"News came in that a young girl was violated behind a pub in Whitechapel, a couple of gents involved," said the Constable, and gave Louis a condensed account.

Within an hour a vigilante committee had formed, its members sweeping through the back streets and alleys with clubs and cudgels, challenging any stranger they found on their turf. Police and community groups appealed for calm. Parallel dragnets swarmed east along Cable Street and the

Commercial Road, pushing an invisible wave of petty crime from Aldgate out to Spitalfields.

"Meanwhile," Louis interrupted, "The Club is searching for a missing youth. The parishes of the Cromwell maps are more complex now than when they were drawn up. It's impossible." He shook his head in despair.

"Louis?"

Louis considered asking Napier about Wilhelm's visit, the Crown Prinz's demeanour, what items of the Armoury were of particular interest. He realised he was looking for coincidence, for synchronicity, for a clue as to the events of the evening. He also realised he was tense. "What time is it?"

"Half past twelve, or thereabouts."

"Would you contact the Club, please?" Louis asked. "I'd like to have James Frazer here. Tell him I'll be waiting by the entrance to the Thames Subway."

"By Tower Stairs?" asked the Constable.

Louis nodded. *I need to make a move,* he thought. *And I need Frazer's knowledge to guide me.*

James Frazer departed the Cuckoo Club on foot and made his way to the rendezvous along Upper Thames Street. The night air was chill on his cheeks and he stepped briskly. As he passed Cannon Street station he sidetracked north up Walbrook Street to avoid a commotion in the roadway around the entrance to the railway terminus, and was hailed by the contingent of Club Members patrolling the parish of St Paul's.

"What news?" asked the Club Treasurer. He was armed with a water-compass which stuck out in his hand towards the east, hovering like a stage-magician's trick. He indicated the device with his free hand. "What d'you make of this?"

Frazer smiled and shook his head. "Great stuff," he puffed, the walk from Mayfair faster than he would have liked. "No reports of anything at the Club, I'm afraid."

The Treasurer nodded. "I feared as much. I reckon it will be a wasted night."

Frazer took a deep breath before he replied. "I hope so," he said, and turned to leave.

At that moment a cry went up from one of the other Club members at the opposite end of St Paul's Churchyard and the clamour was taken up by the rest of the parish contingent. "It's a coach!"

"A coach!" cried the Treasurer and sprinted off in that direction without a further word.

"What?" asked Frazer. He was already out of breath with his walk and the cries of the Club members were growing fainter. A carriage – one of the Club coaches – clattered past him at speed and he yelped as its tail lamp clipped his sleeve. For a brief moment he thought of following the coach and the other Club members in the hunt. Then he remembered his rendezvous with Louis Beauregard.

He stared around the street and was surprised to find himself almost alone. Even at this hour, in London, he expected at least a handful of poor companions. There were none. The streetlights were faint and the commercial buildings around him were unlit, the looming bulk of St Paul's wreathed in stars and high-altitude clouds. Frazer shivered and set off towards the Tower.

As he passed the fountain by the cathedral, a shadow as dark as some huge bird settled on the railings of the churchyard and hopped down onto the grass. Frazer glanced towards it and felt a strange lurch in his stomach. It seemed to be watching him. He turned away and sprinted down Watling Street, his shoulders heaving with the effort.

When Frazer arrived at the waterside he found Louis's carriage facing the water. The horses were restless and cold. The coachman tipped his hat in greeting and Frazer rapped on the window.

"What?" snapped Louis through the glass, then smiled in recognition.

Frazer leaned on the side of the coach and breathed in great painful gasps that misted up the window pane. He tried to speak and found the chilly air constricting his voice. Sweat ran into his eyes and stung his flaming cheeks, his hands and legs trembling.

The window of the coach slid open. "Are you all right?" asked Louis.

Frazer nodded. He made another attempt to speak and gave up again, waving away any attention with one hand while he tried to calm down.

"What news?" asked Louis, and the note in his voice was concern.

Frazer shook his head. "Not sure," he gasped. "Seen – something."

"The coach?"

"No. Yes."

"What?"

"Maybe. A bird. Maybe a bird." Frazer stepped away from the coach and started coughing.

"A bird?" asked Louis, and the carriage door opened.

Frazer shook his head. "There was a carriage," he said. "By St Paul's. It went – north, I think."

"And are the Club Members in pursuit?"

"Yes," said Frazer. "I was talking to Burke when it happened. And he hared off without a word. I was on my way here. So I didn't join in."

Louis pulled the coach door shut again and took refuge behind it. "North of St Paul's," he repeated. His brow wrinkled. "That leads – where?" He brandished an unfolded map through the open window.

Frazer took it and held it out in both arms as if it were a broadsheet newspaper. In the dim streetlights he found it hard to make out what should have been familiar landmarks and street patterns. "Is this the Cromwell Master?" he asked in frustration.

Louis nodded.

"The city's changed a bit, hasn't it?" Frazer's mild irritation dissipated as he found the river and traced its curves to the blot where the Tower squatted, then followed the streets with his eyes. "Cheapside, Gutter Lane, Paternoster Row – honestly, Louis," he sighed, "It could be anywhere."

Louis shook his head. "I don't think so. Gutter Lane isn't so far from Walbrook Street, and the Walbrook has been diverted under the streets in Mr Bazalgette's new drainage system. I think our man is toying with the youth, and with the Lady."

"How so?"

"Drawing the lad over the subterranean rivers, as I am drawing myself. The Thames is too strong – even leaving the Tower brought on a fit that I thought would kill me –

but the little rivers, the tributaries, are lively enough with the tide to act as a beacon."

Frazer squinted at Louis. "Do you think so?"

"Do you know better?"

Frazer sighed. "No. Unless you're talking about something akin to the Anglo-Saxon trial by water."

Louis indicated with a shrug of his eyebrows that the Scotsman should continue. "I was hoping you might be able to advise me."

"Trial by water," said Frazer, his hands on his hips now as he strolled around the coach, thinking aloud. "The ducking-stool, to catch a witch – or a river goddess masquerading as a mortal woman. Submerging the suspect to see if she drowns or thrives." He shuddered and barely stopped himself in time from speaking what he thought next: *And having her put to death by fire if she should survive.*

The moment was interrupted by a small boy running at full pelt towards them along the Tower Wharf. His hobnailed boots clicked on the cobbles, his pace steady and measured as if he were accustomed to running all day. "Mr Bo'gard!" the child cried. "Is this Mr Bo'gard's coach?" He stopped and stared at Frazer with dark eyes.

Louis leaned out of the window. "What is it, lad?"

"Mr Bo'gard is to come to the Tower," the boy gasped, leaning for breath with his hands on his knees. "Are you Mr Bo'gard?"

"I am." Louis swung the carriage door open and beckoned Frazer to join him, the urchin too.

Frazer scooped the child up in his arms and deposited him on the floor of the coach, climbed in beside Louis and barely had time to pull the door shut before the driver set off.

"Is something amiss?" Louis quizzed the child.

"There's a coach," said the boy. "Down by the site at Tower Bridge."

"A cream-coloured coach?"

The boy shrugged. "It's in amongst them woodworks."

"Do you mean the construction site?" Frazer asked.

The boy nodded.

Louis spoke with a cautious appreciation. "How very smart."

"What?" said Frazer.

Louis dipped his head in query. "Think it through, man."

Frazer paused. Then he pursed his lips and nodded in agreement. "On the riverside, near an unfinished bridge, by St Katherine's Basin – almost surrounded by water. Very smart indeed."

The foundations of the new Tower Bridge had been laid along Irongate Wharf the previous summer and the scaffolding stretched into the sky to a height that matched the surrounding dock buildings, the poles and ropes like the masts of a sailing-ship to steer the river towards dawn. Eerie light fell from the lanterns that hung at street level, warning of timbers and other obstacles jutting out into the roadway, and when Louis arrived the scene had a glow that painted everyone unhealthy.

Two coaches waited by the scaffolding at the water's edge. Cuckoo Club Members stood in a crowd, and when Louis arrived they turned to him for guidance.

"Where is he?" asked Louis, leaning out of the carriage window. In amongst the scaffolding he saw no coach. "Has he got away?"

The Club Treasurer shrugged. "I don't know. There was a coach which we followed –" he nodded to his companions standing by their coach – "but it turned away east. It left the parish to which we were assigned. I understood that we were not to leave the boundaries of the parish for which we had the map." His eyebrows were raised above the level of his horn-rimmed glasses as if he were nervous of some misdemeanour.

"That's right," said Louis. He leaned back into his carriage and opened the door to let the messenger-boy out, but when Frazer went to leave Louis stayed him with his hand. Louis leaned out of the window again. "East, you say?"

The Treasurer nodded. "I'm afraid he could be anywhere," he said with a worried shrug.

Louis shook his head. "Not tonight, I don't think," he said in a manner he hoped might reassure the assembled Cuckoo Club Members. "There's a riot in Parliament Square and a vigilante committee all over the Tower Hamlets. He'd be foolish to take the youth beyond the mediaeval city, so close to the tide turning." *What would I do?* he thought. "Frazer?"

"Yes?"

"What time is it?"

"Half past two."

Louis drew breath. *It's late*, he thought. *The Lady was at Sheerness not four hours ago. I know how fast She can move when She wants to.*

"Louis?" Frazer broke his concentration.

Louis shook his head. "Why isn't She here?" he asked aloud. He was dismayed, and tired, and he tried hard not to let it show in his voice, but failed. "What's She waiting for?"

"Maybe the Russian's hidden him," said Frazer after a moment's thought. "Got him shielded, perhaps? You said yourself, if there's a fragment of that amber bullet in the youth, she might not recognise him."

Louis nodded. "You're right," he said, but he found it hard to be enthusiastic. The night's exertions had drained him and he felt that he'd lost touch with reality somehow, his plans awry and the night drawing closer to an end. He put his hand in his pocket where the gold chain lay and felt its links, smooth and dull, catch on his fingerprints as if it were silk.

"Is there any way you can influence matters?" asked Frazer. "Bring things to a head, perhaps?

Louis sagged back into the bench of the carriage seat. *I don't want to*, he thought. *I'm an old man, and I'm ready to die – I think*. He glared at Frazer with irritation. "I thought you might have had some ideas yourself," he said, and regretted the spite immediately. "I'm sorry, Frazer," he apologised. "It's been a long night."

Frazer began to nod and then he rushed to the carriage window. Before Louis could stop him, the Scotsman was out of the door and halfway across the road to the wharf's edge.

"What is it?" cried Louis after him. He snatched up the water-compass from the floor of the carriage and despite containing only a tiny droplet of water, it stuck straight out towards the east and tugged at his hand. He felt his heart jump to a lively rhythm he'd felt before.

"Lights!" cried Frazer.

The Cuckoo Club Members assembled on the wharf turned to where the Scotsman pointed with his arm raised.

Louis craned out of the window and saw nothing. He crossed to the other door and saw a set of carriage lights, growing stronger with each passing second, along Little Tower Hill towards him. The water-compass in Louis's hand thrummed against its chain now, a force stronger than gravity, and he yelled out of the coach, "It's him! It's him!"

The thunder of hoofbeats and wheels echoed down the cobbled road between the Tower and the high warehouses of St Katherine's Dock. Behind the coach, a second carriage followed and, pell-mell, a crowd of people surged around the corner from the streets around the Royal Mint. Voices howled outrage, the words lost in anger.

The Club's coaches rolled into the road and parked across the entrance to Tower Wharf, blocking the exit away from the docks. Some of the Club Members withdrew scaffolding poles from the building site and made to create a barricade across Lower East Smithfield, but they left it too late. In seconds the cream-coloured coach was upon them and the horses bore down like cataphracts.

The Cuckoo Club Members stood their ground.

There was nowhere for the driver to go except the wharf, and thence into the river. He swerved the coach around, trying to avoid the Club Members and their half-made barricade, turning at too sharp an angle. The coach began to tip over, one set of wheels raised and spinning on air. The driver leapt clear and rolled across the ground.

The coach skidded along the roadway on its side, the woodwork of its decorative trim squealing against the cobbles and throwing splinters into the air. It slammed into the pillar of a streetlamp and came to a halt with its roof staved in and a shower of amber fragments from its broken windows strewn across the pavement.

With no driver, the reins flew loose and snarled up with the harnesses. The horses, confused and alarmed, began to panic and bucked at the tangle around their legs. When the limping coachman approached to calm them he was rewarded with a blow to the head from a flying hoof that knocked him senseless.

Louis watched from the safety of his carriage as the Club Members, pistols drawn and other weapons at the ready, stepped towards the upturned coach. Behind them the crowd that had come from Whitechapel slowed to a walking pace and approached the scene with a mixture of hate and uncertainty on their faces. Louis glanced from them to the ruined coach and the Club Members, and back again. "Not like this," he whispered, shaking his head. "Please, not like this."

He pushed open the carriage door and stepped out, barefoot, the chain in his hand.

A woman's head appeared through the coach window, followed by the rest of her skinny frame as she wriggled and kicked her way out onto the side of the doorframe. She yelped as a man's hand reached up from the coach and grabbed at her. She scrabbled and reached for a handhold on the carriage roof, shrieking in a voice of anguish as she slid over the edge and landed with a solid thump on the ground.

Her eyes were terrified as she glanced around at the Cuckoo Club Members, armed with guns and sticks and the water-compasses wavering towards the water, and she yelled out towards the crowd which had followed from Whitechapel. "Sweet Jesus save us!"

"You all right, Poll?" A man in workman's clothes stepped forward from the crowd, pushed by a small woman with dark hair and a pale, freckled face.

"Poll Parker!" the small woman yelled. Her voice was hoarse and had an Irish lilt that curved the vowels of the other woman's name. "Polly? Is dat you?"

The woman called Polly dragged herself to her feet and stood blinking into the distance as she ran her hands across her body as if to check that everything was in place. She whimpered and stepped between the still-spinning wheels of the coach, oblivious to the danger.

The man in the coach heaved himself out like a swimmer leaving a public baths, cursing loudly in Russian as he did so. He wiped at a cut on his cheekbone with his gloved hand and shook his head as if he were dazed, then vaulted off the top of the coach to land next to the woman. He grabbed her as she limped into reach. He held her round the neck, his arm like a noose, and a knife suddenly appeared from nowhere in his other hand.

"Who are you?" Louis called. "What kind of creature are you?"

The other man bared his teeth like a cornered mink. "I think you know me," he hissed.

Louis nodded in recognition, but refused to name the man. "Where's the boy?" he called out, his voice loud and flat in the pre-dawn mist. His body was trembling and he glanced at the sea-compass in his hand. It was stuck straight out, tugging at him like a sled dog. The stones beneath his feet were warm and he thought he found a faint tang in the air which rose above the salt of the river: pollen, pine forests, rich earth in sunshine.

"Smell that, men?" he asked, turning for a moment to the Cuckoo Club Members. "She's on her way."

The woman clung to Sylvester de Winter's arm like it was a lifebelt. Her face was pale and she had ceased to struggle, but at least she was still alive.

Louis was so close to the pair he could see she was holding him back from choking her. The pollen smell was growing stronger now, the dish in Louis's hand tugging harder, the chain humming.

Still Sylvester de Winter said nothing, but he glared hard at them all.

"Let the woman go," said Louis quietly. The horses – still trapped in the harness and tugging at the coach with each exertion – stamped and snorted, their eyes rolling white and foam at their jaws. From the south bank came the sound of a chained dog barking to raise the dead, rattling at its tether as it paced. Foghorns boomed up the river like strange birds. The Whitechapel mob murmured threats.

Sylvester de Winter threw the woman towards the Club Member to his right and mounted the coach single-handed. He cut the leather harness that tethered the horses and they raced off into the gloom along Tower Wharf dragging the traces behind them, metalwork ringing on the cobbles. With uncommon strength, the Russian prised open the carriage door and leaned in to haul out a very groggy Alf.

"Is this what you want?" he yelled, leering, shaking Alf by the collar until he groaned. "Or is he just the bait?" The Russian lifted Alf out of the coach and dragged him down to the ground, propped him up between the wheels and retrieved a silver-topped cane from the interior of the coach.

Louis had to stifle a gasp at his first sight of the boy – he was ragged and gaunt, a hundred years older than the youth who'd been shot barely twelve hours earlier. Louis let go of the water-compass, which shot away into the darkness over the Thames and splashed as it hit the river. He removed the gold chain from his pocket.

"Stay back, men," Louis signalled to the Club Members. "Hold your fire." He did not look to see whether they had obeyed him. He sidled round to the wharf's edge, bare feet on the paving-slabs, the pollen scent thick as honey.

Sylvester de Winter shook his cane apart to reveal a very prominent blade which he held out in front of him. In his other hand, the one still holding the knife, he gripped Alf's neck.

Louis realised that the Russian exercised a superhuman strength. He was close enough to see the man's eyes glitter in the pre-dawn light. The carriage wheels above their heads still spun slowly, the iron rims black and pitted. For ages the only sounds were breathing, the lap of waves against the wharf, boots scuffing on the cobbles as the Whitechapel mob began to disperse.

"She's close now, isn't she?" Sylvester de Winter called out in the clear morning.

Louis nodded. "Yes."

"I can't hear you," said Sylvester de Winter. "Come closer."

Louis stared into the man's eyes, his peripheral vision focused on that long steel blade that stretched out between them. He knew then that the Russian intended to have the youth kill him, like the proxy slaying of Balder by Hod in the old Norse tales. *Is it really my time?* he thought. *Is it still too late to change my mind?*

Louis stepped forwards toward the wharf, turning the chain between his fingers, the links cold as ice. He felt the presence of the Lady close by, and touching the chain set his blood tingling. *Can the boy feel it too?* Doubt settled on him like a winged shadow that would not be shaken.

Sylvester de Winter's eyes flicked to the chain then back to Louis's face. He pointed to the chain with his chin. "What's that, old man?" he sneered. "A love-trinket for the Lady? I think I have a better one here." He shook Alf by the collar. The action nicked Alf's neck with the knife and drew blood.

It was enough to let Louis surmise that the knife was very sharp indeed. He had no doubt that the sword-cane would be similarly honed.

Alf wriggled and slurred some irritated complaint, seemingly unaware of the blade at his throat.

The Club members tensed as a group and one or two took a step forward.

Sylvester de Winter chuckled. "Tell your men to drop their weapons," he said to Louis.

Louis waved his hand for them to desist. He noticed how his movements made currents in the air, and felt the hair stand up on his head. His nerve ends sparked on fire, worse than ever, and the chain in his hands was growing warmer. The air buzzed with an electric charge. It grew heavy and thick and scented with pine resin.

Poll Parker, crawling over the cobbles towards the Whitechapel mob, glanced behind her and began to wail. The crowd started to run now, their boots a staccato on the cobbles, voices silent in flight as they dispersed along Lower East Smithfield and back along Little Tower Hill.

Alf twisted round in Sylvester de Winter's grip and cried "Who's there?" He glanced wide awake over his shoulder, his throat pressed perilously close to the knife in the

Russian's hand, and turned towards the wharf, towards the river.

Towards the shimmering air surrounding a tiny woman in a dun tweed smock.

She stood at the water's edge, barefoot, her clothes dry but for a line of moisture at the hem. There seemed to be a stillness around her, the faint sound of bees out of place in the city but surrounding her like an aura.

Sylvester de Winter grinned.

Louis nodded. *Oh, my dear sweetheart*, he thought, his blood thudding in his chest as a rush of affection swept over him.

She was as he remembered Her: timeless, ageless, and utterly vulnerable, like the Arctic sun returning after winter.

He bowed to her and called a greeting in an ancient version of Anglo-Saxon, but saw no recognition or reward in her eyes. The chain in his hands had turned ice-cold.

Alf began to struggle.

Sylvester de Winter grabbed him with both hands and the sword-cane clattered to the cobbles.

Louis ducked under the carriage wheel to snatch it up. He levelled it at the Russian, the chain almost frozen to his palm, his attention flicking between Sylvester de Winter and the woman from the river.

She advanced towards them, little wet footprints on the paving-stones behind her, mist rising from the Thames and the foghorns booming. The sound of bees was growing stronger, the scent of honey and pine-resin sickening. She stepped on a shard of amber from the broken coach window – and howled.

Alf recoiled away from her, his face all shock and horror. He forced Sylvester de Winter backwards towards the carriage wheels.

The Russian overbalanced and fell, dragging Alf on top of him, still with the knife hand around his neck.

Alf fought, blood pouring from a fresh wound on his cheekbone. He tucked his left arm up against his injured shoulder, barring the hand that reached around to choke him, and pushed at the ground with the other.

Sylvester de Winter slashed again at Alf's throat.

Louis saw the knife glint in the Russian's hand and lunged to stop him, the sword-cane half-forgotten. He felt a deadbolt of ice shoot up his feet as he stepped on yet more of the amber fragments and slipped on the cobbles just as he reached the other men. Weakened, he put his hands out to stop himself from falling over, then in horror he realised he still had the sword-cane in his grip. He was unable to stop his forward momentum.

The sword punched through Alf's chest with Louis's full weight behind it.

The blade continued through the young man's flesh until it pierced its way out of his back, forced by Louis's falling weight, and continued into Sylvester de Winter's shoulder. When the point reached the cobbled street beneath the Russian's body, the hand-grip snapped off.

Louis stumbled and fell across the two men on the ground, one hand still holding the empty sword-pommel, the other with the gold chain clinging around his wrist.

And then the world became a maelstrom of whirling pain. Screaming wind tore at him. He felt himself lifted in the air and cast aside. The bees became a rage of noise and the air crushed out of his lungs like a whirlpool, ice-cold, eternal. He felt a thousand years of loneliness become hatred in an instant, heard words screamed in a language he had no right to understand, saw the world snowblind and lifeless.

He landed hard on the carriage wheel with a crushing pain across his ribs and wheezed himself upright to see the Lady drag Alf off down to the river without a backwards glance. The sword still pierced the youth's body. Its jutting edge flashed in the eerie lamplights that illuminated the construction yard of Tower Bridge as it snagged on the cobbles beneath him.

The Lady slipped over the edge of Tower Wharf with him without a sound, and into the river.

The air, thick with frost, shimmered and misted over the water and Louis felt the crackle of the pavement's puddles turn to ice beneath his hands.

Sylvester de Winter lay three feet away.

The Cuckoo Club Members stood transfixed in horror.

And Louis became aware of a low cunning chuckle from a walking corpse, the last sound he heard before he lost consciousness: Sylvester de Winter's sardonic mirth.

CHAPTER 27 – Nor Let Your Song Be Through

Louis was propped up in bed reading the first edition of the Times, his bedroom window open to the street and filled with the promise of a fine June morning, when his visitor was announced by his butler at the door.

"Mr James Frazer, sir," said Dodman, and made way for the familiar figure of the red-haired Scotsman who pushed into the room, his hand outstretched in greeting.

"Louis!" he said with a warmth that displayed his affection. "I asked if you were well, and Dr Ponsonby said you were up to taking a few visitors." He shook Louis by the hand, his eyes gleaming. "How's the injury?"

Louis grinned. "I'll live," he said with a droll wink. "Although if the good doctor doesn't let me out of this sickbed soon, I'll just as well die of boredom."

Frazer laughed, but it had an uneasy tone. "You're better, then?"

"Yes," said Louis. "It might have been worse. I've had a few falls, in my time," he added, still unable to disguise his pleasure at the sight of the younger man. "Taken a few hard injuries too, in my younger days."

Frazer pulled up a chair and sat by the side of the bed. "The Committee send their best wishes, as always," he began, glancing at the newspaper on Louis's lap. It had a lurid headline across three columns, and Frazer nodded towards it. "You've seen the news, then?"

Louis nodded and glanced at the paper himself. "Yes," he sighed. "Not before time, I suppose. Poor man. I outlasted him, at least."

Frazer said nothing, his face still smiling.

"Never mind, Frazer," Louis said. "Friedrich was always going to be nothing more than a stop-gap, and I think he knew as much. Now he's gone, the Club's problems really begin."

"Wilhelm." Frazer didn't ask. His voice was flat and his expression changed to concern.

Louis nodded and folded up the newspaper, replacing his hands on his lap. "Tell me, Frazer," he said in a gentle voice, "What happened after?"

"After?"

"After I fell on the ground," Louis coaxed. "After Alf – was taken. Nobody else will tell me. I trust you, Frazer, of all the Club Members, to tell me the truth. Has the boy reappeared?" He put his hand on the younger man's arm and stared into his eyes. "I know I failed," he said without self-pity. "I need to know what happened next. Summer's almost upon us." He smiled. "I want to know if I need to beware strangers at the Boat Race."

Frazer shook his head with a brief laugh. "You're amazing, sir," he said, his eyes shining.

"I'm still Consort," Louis reminded him with a wry grin.

Frazer nodded, his open expression full of light, and took a deep breath before he began. "It seems like an age," he said, his smile fading. "You were wounded and we were afraid you were dead. The Russian just lay there grinning like a devil, and the woman who'd been in the coach with him went mad, screaming some other woman's name and weeping terribly. She ran away before anyone was able to help her." He paused, as if for delicacy. "As you know, the Lady retreated to the river. There seemed little that we could do to stop her, and then that terrible frost spread across the ground."

Louis felt again the greasy wheel-rim against his face, heard the chuckle of Sylvester de Winter in his ears, saw the moisture between the cobbles rise up like blades of grass as it froze. He imagined the strength with which the Lady took Alf with her, back to the water, and through a cherished and time-worn memory he knew whence the pair would voyage. An involuntary shudder shook his frame. He sighed. "So She is safe from that Russian fiend," he said at last. "For now."

Frazer nodded, cautiously. "It would seem so. There have been no sightings since, as far as we can tell. No news from abroad either."

"What about the boy? Has he returned?"

Frazer shook his head with a sharp movement, his lips a grim line. "Not yet."

"It's been – how long?"

"Three months."

Louis sighed. "He could be anywhere," he said, but in his heart he knew it was unlikely.

"At least he's safe from the Russian," Frazer said with a kind of optimism. His eyes had a worried slant which betrayed his real thoughts, and he added, "For now."

"That man will try again, though," Louis warned. "His kind always does. Look out for him, Frazer, however long it takes." He began to cough, softly at first, a grating rasp within his lungs that radiated out until it shook his ribs and twisted up his fists upon the counterpane. He reached a shaky hand towards the bottle of linctus left by the doctor on the nightstand.

"If he recovers," said Frazer, pouring a spoonful of medicine as if he were a nursemaid. "Some of us gave him a pretty good kicking. Left him for dead."

"Fools," smiled Louis and took the proferred spoon. "It won't harm him – merely delay him. He's not as mortal as the rest of us." As if to prove the point he fell to coughing again.

"Is that why he had to use the boy – Alf – to kill you?"

Louis nodded. "Not being truly mortal, he can't become Consort. I don't think it's ever his aim, you know. I suspect he has a deeper secret, one that we might never understand, that drives him to challenge the Consort in the way he does."

Frazer watched Louis take his medicine, and took the spoon when Louis handed it back.

"What else?" Louis asked. He was struck by a sudden wave of fatigue as if a chill wind had blown in through the open window, but when he gazed out towards the little park in the distance the treetops were calm.

"He had an amber-lined carriage, the fiend."

Louis said nothing. He put his hand over his mouth and shut his eyes. "That –" he said, and his voice broke. He took a deep breath, and then another, fighting back his emotions. When he spoke again it was a hoarse whisper. "That would explain how we found it hard to locate the young man."

Frazer nodded, his expression serious now, his brow tied into knots. "We had to save you. You were coughing up blood. There was nothing we could do to help the boy, nothing more we wanted to do to Sylvester de Winter – and in addition to our personal regard for you, Club Rules state that Members must support and aid the Consort." Frazer smiled a brittle smile that did not express half the depth of affection in his eyes.

Louis smiled too, but it faded when he realised the outcome. "So," he said in a very quiet voice, "The office of Consort will go to Wilhelm after all."

Frazer looked guarded, as if he had discovered a state secret. "I – I thought it went to the man who kills the Consort."

"She chose the boy!" Louis whispered, his voice hoarse again and rising in pitch as he spoke, his fists curling in frustration. "He was next! He should have killed me – I should have let him – made him – do it sooner!" His legs itched and he longed to leave the sickbed and pace the floor. "She won't come back for ages – decades, possibly. Frazer – you know this. Her choice takes precedence." He fought back an overwhelming sense of bitterness. With moist eyes he was way too angry to hide from his friend, he said, "I have failed."

"No – Louis –"

"Yes. I have failed, " he went on, heart hammering. "I have failed the Club. I have failed myself – failed Her. I am a poor Consort."

"After all these years? All this?"

Louis nodded. "All the stewardship in the world is of naught if the outcome is not right. 'All's well that ends well'? – well, it has ended badly. However I die now –

suicide, assassination, accident, old age – Wilhelm becomes Consort." He sighed in bitterness. "Oh, it will be twenty, thirty years, so perhaps he will have mellowed by then – by the gods, I hope so!"

Both men fell silent for a while as they contemplated this. Then Louis cleared his throat, but it was Frazer who spoke first.

"The Club was attacked, too," he said with a glum shrug.

"Hm?" Louis seemed to rise from deep thoughts. "What?"

"We still don't know who was responsible," said Frazer. "The night we met the Lady, a party of ruffians broke into the Club and defiled the Water Chamber," said the Scotsman. "The police have no clue as to the culprits. They were so busy holding back the mob across the East End that they couldn't spare a man until the next morning."

Louis found his breath caught in his throat. "It's three stories underground."

Frazer nodded. "I know. Parsons was knocked to the ground and tied up."

"Parsons is all right, isn't he?" Louis asked.

Frazer nodded. "It was a group of foreigners, he said. Possibly Russian, judging by what he said of their accents."

"Okhrana," Louis nodded with a twist of his mouth. "Sounds reasonable. They are the Tsar's Secret Police, after all, and the Tsarina is Victoria's daughter." He passed his hand in front of his eyes. *So the Game goes on*, he thought, *and the players shake the dice once more.* He indicated for Frazer to continue, his mind concentrating on the Water Chamber that he had been forced to abandon since his confinement. "What of the instruments?"

"The Water-Compass chain was broken, the Nilometer smashed, some of the log-books desecrated," Frazer said. "Whoever did it sought to defile, not completely destroy. As though they were looking for something else and took revenge when they couldn't find it. Nothing else was missing, though – Cummins took a thorough inventory."

Louis stroked his chin, disturbed that such an action was possible against the Club he had worked so long to secure. Half-aware, thinking of the amount of work it would take to refurbish the room, he did not doubt that he would be able to find another set of instruments, or have the existing items mended, but the collection was damaged in his eyes.

He imagined his progress on a normal day around the chamber, trying to puzzle out what might have attracted such attention. One by one he pictured himself reading the instruments, making a note in the ledger, moving on to the next. It was only when he imagined handing the door key back to the Armourer that his fingers began to twitch.

He snapped his head up. "The chain! Remember?"

Frazer shook his head.

"The one we made. I had Ogilvy – Pawel Czerczy – make me a gold chain out of the coins the Lady left with the young man." He threw back the bedcovers and swung his feet out of bed, beckoning the Scotsman to help him up. His voice took on a keen edge. "It was hers," he said, "And it had my blood on it. Where is it now?"

Frazer shrugged. "I don't know," he said with concern.

"We have to find it," said Louis, agitation bringing on another coughing fit as he struggled into his dressing-gown. *Damn this!* he thought while he wheezed for breath. The crushing band across his ribs returned with fervour and he curled over with the pain. He beckoned to Frazer and leaned on the younger man's arm. "Help me downstairs," he said, and led the way when his breath returned. "Dodman!" he yelled at the top of the stairs. "Dodman!"

The manservant did not hide his disapproval when he saw Louis in the hallway. "Mr Beauregard," he said, halfway between a scold and his usual acknowledgement.

Louis ignored the sentiment. "When I came home," he said, "Was there anything in my pockets?"

"Yes, sir," said Dodman. "I put the items in a small box for safekeeping."

"Where are they now?" Louis asked, his heart loud in his ears.

"In your desk drawer, sir," said the manservant.

Louis pushed past him and dragged Frazer into the study. He collapsed into an armchair and gestured for the Scotsman to sit at the desk.

Frazer unlocked the drawer, withdrew a plain wooden box and passed it to Louis's outstretched fingers.

Louis pried the lid open and its contents tumbled into his lap. He put the box aside and lifted the chain, eyeing its perfect links as he counted them. He breathed a sigh of relief – they were all there –which descended into painful sobs that he let flow freely.

Frazer left the room, embarrassment plain on his face. Shortly after, the front door closed and Louis knew his friend had gone.

Louis didn't care. He no longer felt the movement of the tides; the gold neither burned nor chilled him. He cupped his hands around the chain and breathed deep, unable to detect the pine-resin pollen scent of the quenching, the bare metal smelling of iron and death. He'd lost her. His grief overtook him and he did not resist.

The sun was slanting in the windows low and orange when Frazer returned. He was carrying the evening copy of the Times and set it before Louis on the top of the desk in his study. "Wilhelm's Kaiser now," he said in a quiet voice. "The confirmation came from Potsdam at lunchtime. Just in time for the late papers."

Louis nodded, not in agreement but in acknowledgement. All he said was: "Extraordinary." He sat fingering the chain as if it were a set of worry beads while his butler brought a tea-tray for the two men. Once, for a brief moment, he glanced up at Frazer to make sure the younger man was still there with him.

The Scotsman was stoking the fire, his face turned away towards the grate with an earnest expression of concentration on the task at hand that made him seem scholarly and emphasised his youth.

Louis smiled to himself. "I've been thinking," he began once the pair were alone.

"Hm?" Frazer sat in an armchair by the fire and crossed one leg over the other, his attention elsewhere.

"I want to go away," said Louis.

"Go away?" asked Frazer. "You mean, for a convalescence?"

Louis shook his head. "I never had the courage to travel, not far from here, from Her – not after I came back from Egypt. Even then I had to be sedated on the Channel crossings." He smiled at the recollection. "I don't think I would have survived a long journey across ocean tides. Not without courting madness."

"What are you talking about, Louis?" Frazer said, his face growing worried.

"I don't think overseas travel will be a problem for me now," said Louis with a tinge of sadness.

Frazer stared at him in alarm. "You're not as young as you were," he began, "And you're still Consort." He paused. "Aren't you?"

Louis shrugged.

Frazer opened his mouth as if to say something, and took a deep breath instead. He let it out in a rush as if he were thinking hard over a sensitive matter, and when he spoke it was with an academic precision. "Do you intend to sacrifice yourself?"

"No," said Louis with a shake of his head. *I've thought about it, though*, he said to himself. "I think that soon, my years will tell on me. I've been Consort for a long time, Frazer, and I'm tired. I can't imagine how tired other men feel at my age."

"D'you think you've had protection from Her?"

Louis stared at the fire while he considered the hidden sensation that he'd come to recognise over the last few weeks, one which made him physically weak and did not fill him with confidence but which nonetheless nagged at his conscience like a ghost. The sensation that he was, after all, merely mortal. "Probably."

"Are you sure she's abandoned you?"

Louis paused before he replied as if he was thinking of an answer, but in truth, his soul told him otherwise. Cold; desolate; vast emptiness. His own personal Ice Age. "Yes. I'm certain."

"Why?" Frazer stared.

Louis noticed the academic inquiry behind the Scotsman's concern. He bent his head and then raised it, forcing himself to be honest. "I feel flayed alive, Frazer – but I've never felt *so* alive!"

Frazer shook his head. "I don't understand," he said. "I want to, for the sake of posterity. But I can't."

"No, I suspect no-one can," said Louis, smiling kindly at the younger man. *Only one other creature on this earth can understand me*, he thought, *and She will never speak to me again*. The notion filled him with a sadness that he realised was not his natural state. "Go back to Oxford, Frazer. Study this. Find out what you can, from the annals and folk tales, for the sake of the future Consort. For all of them."

"I will," said Frazer with an earnest, serious expression on his face. "I was thinking about it anyway, since the – since March. Will you help me?"

"I'm leaving," said Louis with a smile and a shake of his head, his voice growing bolder, his character stiffening into its old ways. "Whether or not anyone likes it, I am a decisive fellow. Lady or no Lady."

Frazer regarded him cautiously over the rim of his tea cup. "Where will you go?" he asked after a long silence.

Louis shrugged, and grinned. "Not decided yet."

He reached out to his globe and spun it, his fingers pushing against illustrated oceans and unmapped continents. The deserts of Western Australia looked promising; the high Andes, the Kalahari, Tibet. He noted the places his eye was drawn towards, areas where the beat of his heart grew faster as he looked, the other places where great rivers snaked across the surface of the map and made him shiver. He let his grin fade into a smile of self-awareness, and turned to Frazer with an air of purpose.

"Somewhere there isn't any water."

BONUS MATERIAL

A NOTE ON THE AUTHOR

Lee McAulay was born in Scotland and writes fiction in a variety of formats including short stories and novels. A complete list of published works can be found on her blog. As an artisan writer, Lee publishes her own work.

The Last Rhinemaiden is her first published novel, and the first novel in the "Cuckoo Club" series.

Contact Lee at: http://leemcaulay.wordpress.com. You'll also find links to Lee's other fiction, such as the short story, "All Roads Lead To The River", which tells of Louis Beauregard's time in Egypt as mentioned in this novel, an extract of which is included at the end of this section.

ACKNOWLEDGEMENTS

For editorial suggestions on the first draft, proofreading and copyediting, thanks to Tim Goodier and David Wake. For support and patience and the supply of inspiration, my endless gratitude to TDG, as ever. Thanks also to my friends and acquaintances who have lived with my enthusiasm for this project over the years and added their own ideas to the Cuckoo Club myths.

AUTHOR'S RESEARCH NOTES AND BRIEF BIBLIOGRAPHY

The Last Rhinemaiden is set in 1888 and relies heavily on the research done by others into the Jack The Ripper phenomenon. In fact, the first draft of the novel had closer links to the murders than appears in the final work. However, I am indebted to the authors of the books on the list below for their dedication and thoroughness, without which I would have made much more of a mess of the period and locations than I have done.

City of Dreadful Delight: Narratives of Sexual Danger in Late Victorian London, by Judith R. Walkowitz (University of Chicago Press 1992, ISBN-13: 978-0226871462)

Guns, Germs, and Steel: The Fates of Human Societies, by Jared Diamond (Paperback – 1999)

London's Lost Rivers, by Paul Talling (Random House Books 2011, ISBN-13: 978-1847945976)

Queen Victoria's Gene, by D.M. Potts & W.T.W. Potts (Sutton Publishing Ltd 1995, ISBN-13: 978-0750908689)

The Complete Jack The Ripper, by Donald Rumbelow & Colin Wilson (W H Allen 1987, ISBN-13: 978-0491034678)

The Golden Bough: A Study in Magic and Religion, by James Frazer (first published in 1922, many editions available)

And many others which have been influential and informative in equal measure, but not enough for me to remember all their names.

EXTRACT – ALL ROADS LEAD TO THE RIVER

The night before he first beheld the Nile, Louis Beauregard slept in the Libyan desert on the plateau above Giza, tense with anticipation, listening to dogs whining far off in the darkness under the crackling stars.

In the firelit encampment the Arab couriers broke their Ramadan fast and retired to their tents while the three Englishmen, Louis and Smyth and Petherick, sat by the fire talking over their plans for the following day, and beyond. When the other two left for their own tents Louis sat thinking long into the night, writing his journal, wondering if 1850 would be a more purposeful year for him.

So much of the previous decade had been spent travelling, since he'd left England, but all along he'd avoided Egypt. The opportunity had always been there, of course, for a man of his means, but other places had always drawn him aside, as if he were avoiding the country for some reason he couldn't quite articulate. Then Smyth and Petherick had crossed his path and invited him along on their expedition, and he accepted. He was growing tired of Europe and its petty revolutions, and he'd heard so much about Egypt by then that he could find no reason to defy his curiosity.

The journey through Libya had been odd. His fellow Englishmen observed how the desert seemed empty of life or sound but for the sanded wind. Not to Louis. At night it seemed great beasts swept overhead; in the daytime, their offspring swirled around the dusty tents like dust-devils until the travellers broke camp and set off, then they scampered around the camels' cloven footsteps on the sand. No mischief, he thought. Just curiosity, like a child seeking a new playmate. He understood that, felt a pang of recognition as the couriers exchanged snatches of talk in their own dialect, and Louis's solitary status began to vex him.

After his previous adventures on the Grand Tour – carousing around the Greek islands with playboys and poets, jousting with brigands in the hot Spanish plains, criss-crossing the Apennines with Garibaldi for the London newspapers – the time he'd spent in Africa thus far had been ascetic, as he followed Belzoni's footsteps across the desert in mufti. He'd come away from England after the duel which saw him kill a man; but everywhere he went, if he spent long enough in his own company, he felt the tug of duty calling him back. And something more.

…

Further information regarding the next Cuckoo Club novel, other work and short stories can be found online at http://leemcaulay.wordpress.com.

Printed in Poland
by Amazon Fulfillment
Poland Sp. z o.o., Wrocław